A *Regency*

Lady's Scandal

CAROLE MORTIMER

MILLS & BOON

Published in Great Britain 2016
by Mills & Boon, an imprint of Harlequin (UK) Limited,
Eton House, 18-24 Paradise Road, Richmond, Surrey, TW9 1SR

A REGENCY LADY'S SCANDAL © 2016 Harlequin Books S.A.

The Lady Gambles © 2011 Carole Mortimer
The Lady Forfeits © 2011 Carole Mortimer

ISBN: 978-0-263-91765-9

052-0116

Harlequin (UK) policy is to use papers that are natural, renewable and recyclable products and made from wood grown in sustainable forests. The logging and manufacturing processes conform to the legal environmental regulations of the country of origin.

Printed and bound
by CPI Group (UK) Ltd, Croydon, CR0 4YY

The Lady Gambles

CAROLE MORTIMER

Carole Mortimer was born and lives in the UK. She is married to Peter and they have six sons. She has been writing for Mills & Boon since 1978 and is the author of almost two hundred books. She writes for both the Mills & Boon® Historical and Modern™ lines. Carole is a *USA TODAY* bestselling author and in 2012 she was recognised by Queen Elizabeth II for her 'outstanding contribution to literature'. Visit Carole at www.carolemortimer. co.uk or on Facebook.

Prologue

April 1817—Palazzo Brizzi, Venice, Italy

'Have I mentioned to either of you gentlemen that I had thought of offering for one of Westbourne's daughters?'

Lord Dominic Vaughn, Earl of Blackstone, and one of the two gentlemen referred to by their host, Lord Gabriel Faulkner, found himself gaping inelegantly across the breakfast table at the other man in stunned disbelief. A glance at their friend Nathaniel Thorne, Earl of Osbourne, showed him to be no less surprised at the announcement as he sat with his tea cup arrested halfway between saucer and mouth.

Indeed, it was one of those momentous occasions when it seemed that time itself should cease. All movement. All sound. Indeed, when the very world itself should simply have stopped turning.

It had not, of course; the gondoliers could still be heard singing upon their crafts in the busy Grand Canal, the pedlars continued to call out as they moved along the canal selling their wares, and the birds still sang a merry tune. That frozen stillness, that ceasing of time, existed only between the three men seated upon the balcony of the Palazzo Brizzi, where they had been enjoying a late breakfast together prior to Blackstone and Osbourne's departure for England later today.

'Gentlemen?' their host prompted in that dry and amused drawl that was so typical of him, one dark brow raised mockingly over eyes of midnight blue as he placed the letter he had been reading down upon the table top.

Dominic Vaughn was the first to recover his senses. 'Surely you are not serious, Gabe?'

That mocking dark brow was joined by its twin. 'Am I not?'

'Well, of course not.' Osbourne finally rallied to the occasion. '*You* are Westbourne!'

'For the past six months, yes.' The new Earl of Westbourne acknowledged drily. 'It is one of the *previous* Earl's daughters for whom I have offered.'

'Copeland?'

Westbourne gave a haughty inclination of his dark head. 'Just so.'

'I—but why would you do such a thing?' Dominic made no effort to hide his disgust at the idea of one of their number willingly sacrificing himself to the parson's mousetrap.

The three men were all aged eight and twenty, and had been to school together before serving in Wellington's army for five years. They had fought together, drunk together, eaten together, wenched together, shared the same accommodations on many occasions— and one thing they had all agreed on long ago was the lack of a need to settle on one piece of succulent fruit when the whole of the basket was available for the tasting. Gabriel's announcement smacked of a betrayal of that tacit pact.

Westbourne shrugged his wide shoulders beneath the elegance of his dark-blue superfine. 'It seemed like the correct thing to do.'

The correct thing to do! When had Gabriel ever bothered himself with acting correctly? Banished to the Continent in disgrace by his own family and society eight years ago, Lord Gabriel Faulkner had lived his life since that time by his own rules, and to hell with what was correct!

Having inherited the extremely respected title of the Earl of Westbourne put a slightly different slant on things, of course, and meant that London society—the marriage-minded mamas especially—would no doubt welcome the scandalous Gabriel back into the *ton* with open arms. But even so…

'You *are* jesting, of course, Gabriel.' Osbourne felt no hesitation in voicing his own scepticism concerning their friend's announcement.

'I am afraid I am not,' Westbourne stated firmly. 'My unexpected inheritance of the title and estates has left the future of Copeland's three daughters to my own tender mercies.' His top lip curled back in self-derision. 'No doubt Copeland expected to see his three daughters safely married off before he met his Maker. Unfortunately, this was not the case, and as such, the three young women have become my wards.'

'Are you saying that you have been guardian to the three Copeland chits for the past six months and not said a word?' Osborne sounded as if he could barely believe it.

Westbourne gave a cool inclination of his arrogant head. 'A little like leaving the door open for the fox to enter the henhouse, is it not?'

It was indeed, Dominic mused wryly; Gabriel's reputation with the ladies was legendary. As was his ruthlessness when it came to bringing an end to those relationships when they became in the least irksome to him. 'Why have you never mentioned this before, Gabriel?'

The other man shrugged. 'I am mentioning it now.'

'Incredible!' Osborne was still at a loss for words.

Gabriel gave a hard, humourless grin. 'Almost as incredible as my having inherited the title at all, really.'

It was certainly the case that it would not have occurred if the years of battle against Napoleon's armies had not killed off Copeland's two nephews, the only other possible inheritors of the title. As it was, because Copeland only had daughters and no sons, the disgraced Lord Gabriel Faulkner had inherited the title of Earl of Westbourne from a man who was merely a second cousin or some such flimsy connection.

'Obviously, the fact that I am now the young ladies' guardian rendered the situation slightly unusual, and so I had my lawyer put forward an offer of marriage on my behalf,' Westbourne explained.

'To which daughter?' Dominic tried to recall whether or not he had ever seen or met any of the Copeland sisters during his occasional forays into society this past two Seasons, but drew a complete blank. He did not consider it a good omen that none of the young women appeared to be attractive enough to spark even a flicker of memory.

Westbourne's sculptured mouth twisted wryly. 'Never having met any of the young ladies, I did not feel it necessary to state a preference.'

'You did not!' Dominic stared at the other man in horror. 'Gabriel, you cannot mean to say that you have offered marriage to *any* one of the Copeland chits?'

Westbourne gave a cool smile. 'That is exactly what I have done.'

'I say, Gabe!' Osbourne looked as horrified as Dominic felt. 'Taking a bit of a risk, don't you think? What if they decide to give you the fat and ugly one? The one that no other man would want?'

'I do not see that as being a problem when Harriet Copeland was their mother.' Westbourne waved that objection aside.

All three men had been but nineteen when Lady Harriet Copeland, the Countess of Westbourne, having left her husband and daughters, had tragically met her death at the hands of her jealous lover only months later. The woman's beauty was legendary.

Dominic grimaced. 'They may decide to give you the one that takes after her father.' Copeland had been a short and rotund man in his sixties when he died, and with little charm to recommend him, either—was it any wonder that a woman as beautiful as Harriet Copeland had left him for a younger man?

'What if they do?' Westbourne relaxed back in his chair, his dark hair curling fashionably upon his nape and brow. 'In order to provide the necessary heir, the Earl of Westbourne must needs take a wife. Any wife. Any one of the Copeland sisters is capable of providing that heir regardless of her appearance, surely?' He shrugged those elegantly wide shoulders.

'But what about—I mean, if she is fat and ugly, surely you will never be able to rise to the occasion in order to provide this necessary heir?' Osbourne visibly winced at the unpleasantness of the image he had just portrayed.

'What do you say to that, Gabe?' Dominic chuckled.

'I say that it no longer matters whether or not I would be able to perform in my marriage bed.' Westbourne picked up the letter he had set aside earlier to peruse its contents once again with an apparent air of calm. 'It would appear that my reputation has preceded me, gentlemen.' His voice had become steely.

Dominic frowned. 'Explain, Gabriel.'

That sculptured mouth tightened. 'The letter I received from my lawyer this morning states that all three of the Copeland sisters—yes, even the fat and ugly one, Nate...' he gave a mocking little bow in Osbourne's direction '...have rejected any idea of marriage to the disreputable Lord Gabriel Faulkner.'

Dominic had known Gabriel long enough to realise that his calm attitude was a sham, and that the cold glitter in those midnight-blue eyes and the harsh set of his jaw were a clearer indication of his friend's current mood. Beneath that veneer of casual uninterest he was coldly, dangerously angry.

A fact born out by his next statement. 'In the circumstances, gentlemen, I have decided that I will shortly be following the two of you to England.'

'The ladies of Venice will all fall into a decline at your going,' Osbourne predicted drily.

'Perhaps,' Gabriel allowed dispassionately, 'but I have decided that it is time the new Earl of Westbourne took his place in London society.'

'Capital!' Osbourne felt no hesitation in voicing his approval of the plan.

Dominic was equally enthusiastic at the thought of having Gabriel back in London with them. 'Westbourne House in London has not been lived in for years, and must resemble a mausoleum, so perhaps you would care to stay with me at Blackstone House when you return, Gabriel? I would welcome your opinion, too, on the changes I instructed be made at Nick's during my absence.' He referred to the gambling club he had won a month ago in a game of cards with the previous owner, Nicholas Brown.

'I should have a care in any further dealings you might have with Brown, Dom.' Gabriel frowned.

An unnecessary warning as it happened; Dominic was well aware that Nicholas Brown, far from being a gentleman, was the bastard son of a peer and a prostitute, and that his connections in the seedy underworld of England's capital were numerous. 'Duly noted, Gabe.'

The other man nodded. 'In that case, I thank you for your invitation to stay at Blackstone House, but it is not my intention to remain in town. Instead, I will make my way immediately to Shoreley Park.'

An occurrence, Dominic felt sure, that did not bode well for the three Copeland sisters…

Chapter One

*Three days later—Nick's gambling club,
London, England*

Caro moved lightly across the stage on slippered feet
before arranging herself carefully upon the red-velvet
chaise, checking that the gold-and-jewelled mask covering her face from brow to lips was securely in place,
and arranging the long ebony curls of the theatrical wig
so that they cascaded over the fullness of her breasts
and down the length of her spine, before attending to
the draping of her gold-coloured gown so that she was
completely covered from her throat to her toes.

She could hear the buzz of excitement behind the
drawn curtains at the front of the small raised stage, and
knew that the male patrons of the gambling club were
anticipating the moment when those curtains would be
pulled back and her performance began.

Caro's heart began to pound, the blood thrum-
ming hotly in her veins as the introductory music

began to play, and the room behind the drawn curtains fell into an expectant silence.

Dominic hesitated at the entrance of Nick's, one of London's most fashionable gambling clubs, and one of his favourite haunts even before he had taken possession of it a month ago.

Newly arrived back from Venice that afternoon, he had decided to visit the club at the earliest opportunity, and as he handed his hat and cloak over to the waiting attendant, he could not help but notice that the burly young man who usually guarded the doorway against undesirables was not in his usual place. He also realised that the gambling rooms beyond the red-velvet curtains were unnaturally silent.

What on earth was going on?

Suddenly that silence was bewitchingly broken by the sultry, sensual sound of a woman singing. Except that Dominic had given strict instructions before his departure for Venice that in future there were to be no women working—in *any* capacity—in the club he now owned.

He was frowning heavily as he strolled into the main salon, seeing at once the reason for the doorman's desertion when he spotted Ben Jackson standing transfixed just inside a room crowded with equally mesmerised patrons, all of them apparently hearing only one thing. Seeing only one thing.

A woman, the obvious source of that sensually seductive voice, lay upon a red-velvet *chaise* on the stage, a tiny little thing with an abundance of ebony hair that cascaded in loose curls over her shoulders and down the length of her slender back. Most of her face was covered by a jewelled mask much like the ones worn in Venice during carnival, but her bared lips were full and sensuous, her throat a pearly white. She wore a gown of shimmering gold, the voluptuousness of her curves hinted at rather than blatantly displayed, and the more seductive because of it.

Even masked, she was without a doubt the most sensually seductive creature Dominic had ever beheld!

The fact that every other man in the room thought the same thing was evident from the avarice in their gazes and the flush to their cheeks, several visibly licking their lips as they stared at her. A fact that caused Dominic's scowl to deepen as his own gaze returned to that vision of seduction upon the stage.

Caro tried not to reveal her irritation with the man who stood at the back of the salon glowering at her, either by her expression or in her voice, as she brought her first performance of the evening to an end by slowly standing up to move gracefully to the edge of the stage as she sang the last huskily appealing notes.

It did not prevent her from being completely aware of that pale and disapproving gaze or of the man that gaze belonged to.

He was so extremely tall that even standing at the back of the salon he towered several inches over the other men in the room, his black superfine tailored to widely muscled shoulders, his white linen impeccable and edged with Brussels lace at his throat and wrist. His fashionably styled hair was the colour of a raven's wing, so black it almost seemed to have a blue sheen.

His eyes, those piercingly critical eyes, were the pale colour of a grey silky mist, and appeared almost silver in their intensity. He had a strong, aristocratic face: high cheekbones, a straight slash of a nose, firm sculptured lips, and a square and arrogantly determined jaw. It was a hard and uncompromising face, made more so by the scar that ran down its left side, from just beneath his eye to that stubbornly set jaw.

His pale grey eyes were currently staring at Caro with an intensity of dislike that she had never encountered before in all of her twenty years. So unnerved was she by his obvious disdain that she barely managed to maintain her smile as she took her bows to the thunderous round of applause. Applause she knew from experience would last for several minutes after she had returned to her dressing-room at the back of the club.

It was impossible not to take one last glance in the scowling man's direction before she disappeared from the stage, slightly alarmed as she saw that he was now in earnest conversation with the manager of the club, Drew Butler.

'What is the meaning of this, Drew?' Dominic asked icily under cover of the applause for the beauty still taking her bows upon the stage.

The grey-haired man looked unperturbed; as the manager of Nick's for the past twenty years, the cynicism in his tired blue eyes stated that he had already seen and done most things in his fifty years, and was no longer disturbed by any of them, least of all by the disapproving tone of the man who had become his employer only a month ago. 'The patrons love her.'

'The patrons have neither drunk nor gambled since that woman began to sing some quarter of an hour ago,' Dominic pointed out.

'Watch them now,' Drew said softly.

Dominic did watch, his brows rising as the champagne began to flow copiously and the patrons placed ridiculously high bets at the tables, the level of conversation rising exponentially as the attributes of the young woman were loudly discussed, along with more bets being placed as to the chances of any of them being privileged enough to see behind the jewelled mask.

'You see.' Drew gave an unconcerned shrug as he turned back to Dominic. 'She's really good for business.'

Dominic shook his head impatiently. 'Did I not make it clear when I was here last month that this is to be a gambling club only in future, and not a damned brothel?'

'You did.' Again Drew remained completely unruffled. 'And as per your instructions the bedchambers upstairs have remained locked and unavailable to all.'

A gentleman, an earl no less, owning a London gambling club of Nick's reputation was hardly acceptable to society. But it had been a matter of honour to Dominic, when Nicholas Brown had challenged him to a game of cards the previous month for ownership of Midnight Moon, the prize stallion kept at Dominic's stud at his estate in Kent. In return, Dominic had demanded that Nicholas put up Nick's as his own side of the wager and obviously Dominic had won.

Owning a gambling club was one thing, but the half-a-dozen bedchambers on the first floor, until recently available to any man who had wished for some privacy with…whomever, were totally unacceptable; Dominic drew the line at being considered a pimp! As such, he had ordered a ban on women—all women—inside the club, and the bedrooms upstairs to be immediately closed off. With the exception of the mysterious young woman, who had so recently held the club's patrons enthralled—and not just with her singing!—those instructions appeared to have been carried out.

Dominic's mouth compressed. 'I believe my instructions were to dispense with the services of all the… ladies working here?'

'Caro ain't—is not, a whore.' Drew visibly bristled, his shoulders stiffening defensively.

Dominic frowned darkly. 'Then what, pray, is she?'

'Exactly as you saw,' Drew said. 'Twice a night she simply lays on the *chaise* and sings. And the punters drink and gamble more than ever once she leaves the stage.'

'Does she bring a maid or companion with her?'

The older man looked amused. 'What do you think?'

'What do *I* think?' Dominic's eyes had narrowed to icy slits. 'I think she is a disaster in the making.' He scowled. 'Which gentleman has the privilege of escorting her home at the end of the evening?'

'I does.' The doorman, Ben Jackson, announced proudly as he passed them on his way back to his vigil at the entrance to the club, his round face looking no less cherubic for all that his nose had obviously been broken more than once. His ham-sized fists did not come amiss in a brawl, either.

Dominic raised sceptical brows. '*You* do?'

Ben beamed contentedly, showing several broken teeth for his trouble. 'Miss Caro insists on it.'

Oh, she did, did she?

Ben Jackson could make grown men quake in their boots just by looking at them, and Drew Butler was a cynic through and through, and yet *Miss Caro* appeared to have them both eating out of her delicate little hand!

'Perhaps we should continue this discussion in your office, Drew?' Dominic turned away, expecting rather than waiting to see if the older man followed him, his impatience barely held in check. Nevertheless, he still managed to greet and smile at several acquaintances as he moved purposefully towards the back of the smoke-filled club to where Drew's office was situated.

He barely noticed the opulence of that office as Drew followed him into the room before closing the door behind him and effectively shutting out the noise from the gaming rooms. Although Dominic did spot a decanter of what he knew to be a first-class brandy, and he swiftly poured himself a glass and took an appreciative sip before offering to pour one for the manager, too.

The older man shook his head. 'I never drink during working hours.'

Dominic made himself comfortable as he leant back against the front of the huge mahogany desk. 'Well, who is she, Drew? And where is she from?'

The manager shrugged. 'Do you want my take on her or what she told me when she came to the back door asking for work?'

Dominic's gaze narrowed. 'Both.' He took another sip of his brandy, giving every appearance of studying the toe of one highly polished boot as the other man began to relate the young woman's tale of woe.

Caro Morton claimed to be an orphan who had lived with a maiden aunt in the country until three weeks ago, the death of the elderly lady leaving her homeless. Consequently she had arrived in London two weeks earlier with very little money and no maid or companion, but with a determination to make her own way in the world. Her intention, apparently, had been to offer herself as companion or governess in a respectable household, but her lack of references had made that impossible, and so she had instead been driven to begin knocking on the back door of the theatres and clubs.

Dominic looked up sharply at this part of the story. 'How many had she visited before arriving here?'

'Half a dozen or so.' Drew grimaced. 'I understand she did receive several offers of…alternative employment along the way.'

Dominic gave a humourless smile as he easily guessed the nature of those offers. 'You did not feel tempted to do the same when she came knocking on the door here?' He had no doubt that Miss Caro Morton was a young woman most men, no matter what their age, would like to bed.

The older man shot him a frowning glance as he moved to sit behind the desk. 'My lord, I happen to have been happily married for the past twenty years, with a daughter not much younger than she is.'

'My apologies.' Dominic gave a slight bow. 'Very well.' His gaze sharpened. 'That would appear to be Miss Morton's version of her arrival in London; now tell me who or what *you* think she is.'

Drew looked thoughtful. 'There may have been a maiden aunt, but somehow I doubt it. My guess is she's in London because she's running away from something or someone. A brutish father, maybe. Or perhaps even a cruel husband. Either way she's far too refined to be your usual actress or whore.'

Dominic eyed him speculatively. 'Define refined?'

'Ladylike,' the older man supplied tersely.

Dominic looked intrigued; a woman of quality attempting to conceal her identity would certainly explain the wearing of that jewelled mask. 'And you do not think that actresses and whores are capable of giving the impression of being ladylike?'

'I know they are,' Drew answered. 'I just don't happen to think Caro Morton is one of them.' His expression became closed. 'Perhaps it would be best if you were to talk to her and decide for yourself?'

That the manager felt a fatherly protectiveness towards the 'refined' Miss Caro Morton was obvious. That the doorman, Ben Jackson, felt that same protectiveness was also apparent. If she really were a runaway wife or daughter, then Dominic felt no such softness of emotions. 'I fully intend doing so,' he assured the other man drily as he straightened. 'I merely wished to hear your views first.'

Drew looked concerned. 'Are you intending to dismiss her?'

Dominic gave the thought some consideration before answering. There was no doubting Drew Butler's claim that Caro Morton's nightly performances were a draw to the club, but even so she might just be more trouble than she was worth if she really were a runaway wife or daughter. 'That will depend upon Miss Morton.'

'In what way?'

He raised arrogant brows. 'I accept that you have been the manager of Nick's for several years, Drew. That you are, without a doubt, the best man for the job.' He smiled briefly to soften what he was about to say next. 'However, that ability does not give you the right to question any of my own actions or decisions.'

'No, my lord.'

'Where is Caro Morton now?'

'I usually ensure that she has a bite to eat in her dressing-room between performances.' Drew's expression challenged Dominic to question that decision of *his*.

Remembering the girl's slenderness, and the pallor of her translucent skin, Dominic felt no inclination to do so; from the look of her, that 'bite to eat' might be the only food Caro Morton had in a single day.

'I'd like to be informed if you decide to let her to go. She has wages owing to her,' Drew defended as Dominic looked surprised.

She also, Dominic decided ruefully as he agreed to the request before leaving the office, had the cynical club manager wrapped tightly about her tiny little finger, and no doubt the older man would offer her his assistance in finding other employment should Dominic decide to let her go.

Deciding for himself who or what Miss Caro Morton was promised to be an interesting experience. It was a surprising realisation for a man whose years in the army, and the two years since returning to England spent evading the clutches of every marriage-minded mama of the *ton*, had made him as cynical, if not more so, as the much older Drew Butler.

Caro gave a surprised start as a brief knock sounded on her dressing-room door. Well, not a dressing-room as such, she allowed ruefully, more a private room at the back of the gambling club that Mr Butler had put aside for her use in between her performances.

A room that he had assured her was completely off-limits to any and all of the men who frequented Nick's…

She stood up slowly, nervously making sure that her robe was securely tied about her waist before crossing the tiny room to stand beside the locked door. 'Who is it?' she asked warily.

'My name is Dominic Vaughn,' came the haughty reply.

Just like that, Caro *knew* that the man standing on the other side of the locked door was the same man who had looked at her earlier with those disdainful silver-coloured eyes. She was not sure why or how she knew that, she just did. There was an arrogance in the deep baritone voice, a confidence that spoke of years of issuing orders and having them instantly obeyed. And he was obviously now expecting her to obey him by unlocking the door and allowing him inside…

Her hands clenched in the pockets of her robe, the nails digging painfully into the palms. 'Gentlemen are not allowed to visit me in my dressing-room.'

A brief silence followed her statement, before the

man replied with hard impatience, 'I assure you that my being here has Drew Butler's full approval.'

The manager of Nick's had been very kind to Caro this past week, and, what's more, she knew that she could trust him implicitly. But having a man approach her dressing-room in this unexpected way and simply stating that Mr Butler approved of his being here and expecting her to believe his claim was not good enough. 'I am sorry, but the answer is still no.'

'I assure you, my business with you will only take a few moments of your time,' came the irritated response.

'I am in need of rest before my next performance,' Caro insisted.

Dominic's mouth firmed in frustration at this woman's stubborn refusal to so much as open the door. 'Miss Morton—'

'That is my final word on the subject,' she informed him haughtily.

Drew had claimed that Caro Morton was 'ladylike', Dominic recalled with a narrowing of his eyes. He could hear that quality himself now in the precise diction of her voice. A subtle, and yet unmistakable authority in her tone that spoke of education and refinement. 'You will either speak to me now, Miss Morton, or I assure you there will be no "next performance" for you at Nick's.' Dominic stood with his shoulder leaning against the wall in the darkened hallway, arms folded across the broad width of this chest.

There was a tiny gasp inside the room. 'Are you threatening me, Mr Vaughn?' There was a slight edge of uncertainty to her voice now.

'I feel no need to threaten, Miss Morton, when the truth will serve just as well.'

Caro was in something of a quandary. Having fled her home two weeks earlier, sure that she would find employment in the obscurity of London as a lady's companion or governess, instead she had found herself being turned away from those respectable households, time and time again, simply because she did not have the appropriate references.

Everything in London had been so much more expensive than Caro had imagined it would be, too. The small amount of money she had brought with her, saved over the months from her allowance, had diminished much more rapidly than she had imagined it would, leaving her with no choice, if she were not to return to an intolerable situation, but to try her luck at the back door of the theatres. She had always received compliments upon her singing when she'd entertained after dinner on the rare occasions her father had invited friends and neighbours to dine. Those visits to the theatres *had* resulted in her receiving several offers of employment—but all of them were shocking to a young woman brought up in protected seclusion in rural Hampshire!

She owed her present employment—and the money with which to pay for her modest lodgings—completely to Drew Butler's kindness. As such, she was not sure that she could turn Dominic Vaughn away from her dressing-room if for some reason the older man really had approved the visit.

Her fingers shook slightly as she took her hands from the pockets of her robe to slowly turn the key in the

lock, only to step back quickly as the door was immediately thrust open impatiently.

It *was* the silver-eyed devil from earlier! He looked
even more devilish now as the subdued candlelight illu-
minating the hallway threw that scar upon his cheek
into sharp relief and his black jacket and white linen
only added to the rawness of the power that seemed to
emanate from him.

Caro took another step backwards. 'What is it you
wished to speak to me about?'

Dominic deliberately schooled his expression to
reveal none of the shock he had felt as he looked at
Caro Morton for the first time without the benefit of that
concealing jewelled mask. Or the ebony-coloured wig,
which had apparently concealed her own long and gloriously golden curls. Those curls now framed sea-green,
almond-shaped eyes, set in a delicate, heart-shaped face
of such beauty it took his breath away.

An occurrence, if she were indeed a disobedient
daughter or—worse—a runaway wife, that did not
please him in the slightest. 'Invite me inside, Miss
Morton,' he demanded dictatorially.

Long-lashed lids blinked nervously before she
arrested the movement and her pointed chin rose
proudly. 'As I have already explained, sir, I am resting
until my next performance.'

Dominic's mouth hardened. 'Which I understand
from Drew does not take place for another hour.'

The slenderness of her throat moved convulsively,
drawing his attention to the bare expanse of creamy-
white skin revealed by the plunging neckline of her
robe. His hooded gaze moved lower still, to where the
silky material draped down over small, pointed breasts.

Her waist was so slender that he was sure his hands could easily span its circumference. He also privately acknowledged, with an unlooked for stirring of his arousal, that his hands could easily cup her tiny breasts before lowering to the smooth roundness of her bottom and lifting her against him for her to wrap those long, slender legs about his waist...

Caro found she did not much care for the way Dominic Vaughn was looking at her. Almost as if he could see beneath her robe to the naked flesh beneath. Her cheeks became flushed as she straightened her shoulders determinedly. 'I would prefer that you remain exactly where you are, sir.'

That silver gaze returned to her face. 'My lord.'

She blinked. 'I beg your pardon?'

He introduced himself. 'I am Lord Dominic Vaughn, Earl of Blackstone.'

Caro felt a tightness in her chest as she realised this man was a member of the *ton*, a man no doubt as arrogant as her recently acquired guardian. 'If that is meant to impress me—*my lord*—then I am afraid it has failed utterly.'

He raised dark brows as he ignored the sarcasm in her tone. 'I believe it is the usual custom at this point for the introduction to be reciprocated?'

Her cheeks burned at the intended rebuke. 'If, as you claim, you have spoken to Mr Butler, then you must already know that my name is Caro Morton.'

He looked at her shrewdly. 'Is it?'

Her gaze sharpened. 'I have just said as much, my lord.'

'Ah, if only the saying of something made it true,' he jeered.

That tightness in Caro's chest increased. 'Do you doubt my word, sir?'

'I am afraid I am of an age and experience, my dear Caro, when I doubt everything I am told until proven otherwise.'

There was no doubting that the cynicism and mockery of this man's expression gave him a world-weary appearance, and that scar upon his left cheek an air of danger, but even so she would not have placed him at more than eight or nine and twenty. Not so much older than her own twenty years.

Nor was she his 'dear' anything! 'How very sad for you.'

Not the response Dominic had expected. Or one he wanted, either; the wealthy and eligible Earl of Blackstone did not desire or need anyone's pity. Least of all that of a woman who hid her real appearance behind a jewelled mask and ebony wig.

Could Butler's assessment of her be the correct one? Had this young woman run away to London to hide from possibly an overbearing father, or a brutish and bullying husband? She was of such a tiny and delicate appearance that Dominic found the latter possibility too distasteful to contemplate.

Whatever the mystery surrounding this woman, he was of the opinion that neither he, nor his gambling club, was in need of the trouble she might bring banging upon the door. 'Are you even of an age to be in a gambling club, Caro?'

She looked startled. 'My lord?'

'I simply wondered as to your age.'

'A gentleman should never ask a lady her age,' she retorted primly.

Dominic slowly allowed his gaze to move from the top of that golden head, over the slenderness of her body, the delicacy of her tiny wrists and slender hands, to the bareness of her feet, before just as slowly returning to her now flushed and slightly resentful face. 'As far as I am aware, *ladies* are always accompanied by a maid or companion; nor do they cavort upon the stage of a gentlemen's gaming club.'

Her little pointed chin rose once more. 'I do not cavort, my lord, but simply lie upon a *chaise*,' she bit out tartly. 'I also fail to see what business it is of yours whether or not I have a maid or companion.'

Dominic glanced into the room behind her, noting the tray on the dressing table, with its bowl of some rich and still-steaming stew and a platter of bread beside it, a plump and tempting orange upon another plate, obviously intended as her dessert. No doubt that 'bite to eat' Butler had mentioned providing for her.

'I appear to have interrupted your supper,' he acknowledged smoothly. 'I suggest that we finish this conversation later tonight when I, and not Ben, act as your escort home.'

Her eyes widened in alarm before she gave a firm shake of her head. 'That will not be possible, I am afraid.'

'Oh?'

This was not a man used to receiving no for an answer, Caro realised ruefully as she took in the glittering arrogance in those silver eyes beneath one autocratically raised brow. And her lack of maid or companion was easily explained—if she had felt inclined to offer this man any explanation, which she did not! To have brought either maid or companion with her when she fled Hampshire two weeks ago would have placed them in the position of having abetted her in that flight, and she was in enough trouble already, without involving anyone else in her plight.

'No,' she reaffirmed evenly now. 'It would hurt Ben's feelings terribly if he were not allowed to walk me home. Besides,' she added as his lordship would have dismissed that excuse for exactly what it was, 'I do not allow gentlemen I do not know to escort me to my home.' A man she had no wish to know, either, Caro could have added.

Mocking humour glittered briefly in those pale grey eyes. 'Even if Drew Butler were to vouch for this gentleman?'

'I have yet to hear him do so. Now, if you will excuse me? I wish to eat my supper before it becomes too cool.' Caro's attempt to close the door in Dominic Vaughn's face was thwarted by the tactical placing of one of his booted feet against the door jam. Her eyes flashed a warning as she slowly reopened the door. 'Please do not force me to call upon Ben's help in having you removed from the premises.'

A threat that did not seem to bother the arrogant Dominic Vaughn in the slightest as he continued to smile down at her confidently. 'That would be an… interesting experience.'

Caro eyed him uncertainly. Ben was as tall as the earl, and obviously more heavily built, but there was an underlying air of danger lurking beneath this man's outward show of fashionable elegance. An aura of power that implied he could best any man against whom he chose to pit the strength of those wide shoulders and tall, lithely muscled body. Besides which, Caro very much doubted that the Earl of Blackstone had received that scar upon his face by sitting comfortably at home by his fireside!

She forced the tension from her shoulders as she smiled up at him. 'Perhaps we might defer discussing your offer to escort me home until after I have spoken to Mr Butler?'

And perhaps, Dominic guessed, this young lady would choose to absent herself without so much as bothering to talk to Drew Butler. 'I will be waiting outside for you when you have finished your next performance.'

The irritated darkening of those beautiful sea-green eyes told him that he had guessed correctly. 'You are very persistent, sir!'

'Just anxious to acquaint myself with one of my own employees.'

She gasped, those sea-green eyes wide with alarm. 'Your…? Did you say *your* employee?'

Dominic gave an affirmative nod, and took great pleasure in noting the way the colour drained from the delicacy of her cheeks, as she obviously realised he did indeed have the power to ensure she never performed at Nick's again. 'Until later then, Miss Morton.' He bowed elegantly before returning to the gaming rooms, a smile of satisfaction curving his lips.

Chapter Two

'I would prefer to walk, thank you.' It was a little over two hours later when Caro firmly dismissed even the idea of getting inside Dominic Vaughn's fashionable carriage as it stood waiting outside Nick's—a man Drew Butler had confirmed to Caro was not only the Earl of Blackstone, but also the man who had recently taken ownership of the gambling club at which they were both employed. That aside, she had no intention of placing herself in the vulnerable position of travelling alone in his carriage with him!

'As you wish.' He indicated for the driver of the carriage to follow them, his raven-black hair now covered by a fashionably tall hat, and a black silk cloak thrown about those widely muscled shoulders.

Caro shot him a sideways glance from beneath her unadorned brown bonnet, only a few of her golden curls now showing at her temples and nape. The brown gown she wore beneath her own serviceable black cloak was equally as modest in appearance, with its high neckline and long sleeves.

She had bought three such gowns when she'd arrived in London two weeks ago, this brown one, another in a dull green, and the third of dark cream, having very quickly realised that the few silk gowns she had brought to town with her stood out noticeably in the genteelly rundown area of London where she had managed to find clean and inexpensive lodgings. And being noticed—as herself, rather than as the masked lady singing at Nick's—was something she dearly wished to avoid.

To say that Dominic had been surprised—yet again!—by Caro Morton's appearance on joining him a few minutes ago would be an understatement. In fact, it had taken him several seconds to recognise her beneath that unbecoming brown bonnet that hid most of those glorious golden curls, and the equally unfashionable cloak that covered her from neck to ankle, so giving her every appearance of being a modest and unassuming young lady of meagre means.

That dark modesty of her clothing opened up a third possibility as to why Caro Morton was living alone in London and so obviously in need of work in order to support herself. Her slender hands were completely bare of rings, but that did not mean she was not one of those starry-eyed young ladies who, during the years of war against Napoleon, had abandoned all propriety by eloping with their unsuitable soldier beau before he marched off to battle, only to find themselves widowed within weeks, sometimes days, of that scandalous marriage having taken place.

No matter what the explanation, there was certainly

very little danger of any of the patrons of Nick's recognising this drably dressed young woman as the ebony-haired siren whose seductive performance had so easily bewitched and beguiled them all so completely twice this evening.

Himself included, he readily admitted.

'Perhaps you would care to enlighten me as to why an unprotected young woman should choose to work in one of London's fashionable gambling clubs?'

It was a question she seemed to have been expecting as her expression remained cool. 'For the money, perhaps?'

Dominic scowled. 'If you must work, then why did you not find more respectable employment? You have the refinement to be a lady's maid, or, failing that, to serve in a shop.'

'How kind of you to say so,' she returned oversweetly. 'But one needs references from previous employers to become either of those things. References I do not have,' she added pointedly.

'Perhaps because you have never worked as a lady's maid or served in a shop?' he pressed.

'Or perhaps I was just so inadequate at both those occupations that I was refused references?' she suggested tartly.

Dominic gave an appreciative smile at her spirited answer. 'So instead you have chosen to put yourself in a position where you are ogled by dozens of licentious men every night?'

Caro came to an abrupt halt, her own humour fading at the deliberate insult, both in his tone and expression, as he paused beside her in the flickering lamplight and allowed that silver gaze to rake over her critically from her head to her toes. 'It appears that I needed no references for that,' she informed him with chilling hauteur.

Dominic knew that it really was none of his concern if she chose to expose herself to the sort of ribald comments he had been forced to listen to following her second performance this evening, when the bets as to who would eventually become her lover and protector had increased to a level he had found most unpleasant. And yet... 'Do you have so little regard for your reputation?'

Her cheeks became flushed. 'The jewelled mask I wear ensures my reputation remains perfectly intact, thank you!'

'Perhaps.' Dominic's jaw tightened. 'I am surprised you did not consider a less...taxing means of employment.'

She looked puzzled. 'Less taxing?'

He shrugged. 'You are young. The comments of your numerous admirers this evening are testament to your desirability. Did you not consider acquiring a single male protector, rather than exposing yourself in this way to the attentions of dozens?'

Caro felt the flush that warmed her cheeks. 'A protector, my lord?'

'A man who would see you housed and suitably clothed in exchange for the pleasure of your...company,' he elaborated.

Caro's breath caught in her throat, that flush covering the whole of her body now as she realised that the earl was suggesting she should have taken a lover when she arrived in London rather than 'singing for her supper' at Nick's.

A lover!

When Caro's father had been so averse to any of his three daughters appearing in London society that he had not even allowed any of them to have so much as a Season, but instead had kept them all secluded at his estate in Hampshire. Had ensured his daughters were so overprotected that Caro had never even been alone with a young gentleman until now.

Although that description was hardly appropriate in regard to the arrogant Dominic Vaughn; that scar upon his otherwise handsome face, and the mockery that glittered now in those narrowed silver-coloured eyes, proclaimed him to be a gentleman in possession of a cynicism and experience that far exceeded his calendar years…

'I believe it would not be merely my *company* that would be of interest in such an arrangement, my lord.' She arched pert blonde brows.

Dominic was beginning to wish that he had never broached this particular subject. Indeed, he had no idea why he was taking such an interest in the fate of this particular young woman. Perhaps his sense of chivalry was not as dead as he had believed it to be? 'Surely the attentions of one man would be preferable to being undressed, mentally at least, by dozens of men, night after night?' he bit out harshly.

Her gasp was audible. 'You are attempting to shock me, sir!'

Yes, he was. Deliberately. 'I am attempting to stress,

madam, how foolishly you are behaving by repeatedly placing yourself in such a vulnerable position.'

Her eyes widened indignantly. 'I assure you, sir, I am perfectly capable of taking care of myself. I am in absolutely no danger—' Dominic put an end to this ridiculous claim by the simple act of pulling her effortlessly into his arms and taking masterful possession of the surprised parting of her lips.

He did it as a way of demonstrating the vulnerability of which he spoke. As a way of showing Caro how easily a man—any man—could take advantage of her delicacy. How the slenderness of her tiny body was no match for a man bent on stealing a kiss. Or worse!

He curved that willowy body against his much harder one as he took possession of the softness of those parted lips. With deliberate sensuality, his tongue swept moistly across her bottom lip before exploring farther, his hands moving in a light caress down the slenderness of her back before cupping her bottom and pulling her even more firmly against him as that marauding tongue took possession of the hot cavern of her mouth. Thrusting. Jousting. Demanding her response.

Nothing in Caro's previous life, not the twenty years spent in seclusion in Hampshire, or these past two weeks in London, had prepared her for the rush of sensations that now assaulted her and caused her to cling to Dominic Vaughn's wide and powerful shoulders rather than faint at his feet.

She was suffused with a heart-pounding heat, accompanied by a wild, tingling that began in her breasts, causing them to swell beneath her gown and the tips to harden so that they felt uncomfortable and sensitised as they chafed against her shift, that heat centring, pooling between her thighs, in a way she had never imagined before let alone experienced. She—

'What ho, lads!'

'Don't keep her all to yourself, old chap!'

'Give us all a go!'

Caro found those hard lips removed from her own with a suddenness that made her gasp, the earl's hands hard about her waist as those silver-coloured eyes glittered down at her briefly before he put her firmly away from him. He turned and bent the fierceness of that gaze upon the three young gentlemen walking slightly unsteadily towards them.

Caro staggered slightly once released, knowing herself badly shaken by the searing intensity of Dominic Vaughn's kiss—a punishing, demanding assault upon her lips and senses that in no way resembled any of her previous youthful imaginings of what a kiss should be. There had been none of the gentleness she had expected. None of the shy thrill of emotions. Only that heart-pounding heat and the wild tingling in her breasts and thighs.

Emotions not reflected in the hard intensity of his lordship's expression as he signalled to his coachman and groom that he was as in control of this present situation as he had obviously been whilst kissing her!

The young gentlemen had come to an abrupt and wary halt as they suddenly found themselves the focus of Dominic's glittering silver gaze, the three of them backing up slightly at the chilling anger they obviously recognised in his expression, that savage slash of scar running the length of his left cheek adding to the impression of impending danger.

'We meant no offence, old chap,' the obvious ringleader of the trio offered in mumbled apology.

'A little too much to drink, I expect,' the second one excused nervously.

'We'll just be on our way.' The third member of the group grabbed a friend by each arm before turning and staggering back in the direction they had just come.

Leaving a still-trembling Caro to the far from tender mercies of Dominic Vaughn!

That trembling increased as he turned the focus of his glowering attention back on to her. 'I believe you were assuring me that you are perfectly capable of taking care of yourself and that you believe yourself to be in absolutely no danger from any man's unwanted attentions?'

Caro felt a shiver run the length of her spine as she looked up into that harshly forbidding face; no wonder those three young gentlemen had decided that retreat was the best and safest course of action. She felt like retreating herself as she recalled how demanding and yet arousing that firmly sculptured mouth had felt against her own…

Her shoulders straightened determinedly. 'You kissed me deliberately, my lord, purely in an effort to demonstrate your superior strength over me.'

His nostrils flared as that silver gaze raked over her. 'In an effort to demonstrate how *any* man's strength would be superior to your own—even those three drunken young pups who just ran away with their tails between their legs.'

Caro raised a haughty brow. 'You exaggerate, sir—'

'On the contrary, Miss Morton,' he snapped coldly, 'I believe myself to be better acquainted than you with the lusts of my own sex.' His mouth twisted in distaste. 'And if I had not been here to protect you just now then I guarantee you would now find yourself in an alley somewhere with your skirts up about your waist whilst one of those young bucks rutted between your thighs and the other two awaited their turn!'

Caro felt herself pale and the nausea churn in her stomach at the vividness of the picture he painted. A vividness surely designed to shock and frighten her— and succeeding? Those three young gentlemen had obviously over-imbibed this evening, and were feeling more than a little playful, but surely they would not have behaved as shockingly as the earl suggested?

She looked at him in challenge. 'Then it is a pity that there was no one here to protect me from your own unwanted attentions, was it not?'

Dominic drew in a swift breath at the accusation. In the circumstances, it was a perfectly justified accusation, he allowed fairly. He had meant only to teach a lesson, to demonstrate her vulnerability by taking advantage of her himself. Instead he had found he enjoyed the honeyed taste of her as he explored the heat of her mouth, as well as the feel of her slender curves pressed against his much harder ones. To the extent that he had taken the kiss far beyond what he had originally intended.

He straightened, the expression in his eyes now hidden behind hooded lids. 'I meant only to demonstrate how exposing yourself on a stage night after night has left you open to physical as well as verbal abuse.'

'You are being ridiculous,' she dismissed briskly. 'Neither am I a complete ninny. It was for the very reason of protecting my reputation that I donned the mask and wig at Nick's. Indeed, I doubt that anyone would ever recognise the woman I am now as the masked and ebony-haired woman who sings in a gambling club each evening.'

There was some truth in that; Dominic had barely recognised Caro himself when she had joined him earlier. Even so... 'The fact that you are masked, and your own blonde curls hidden beneath those false ebony tresses, would, I am afraid, only protect your identity as far as the bedroom.'

Her throat moved convulsively as she continued to look up at him proudly. 'My...identity?'

Dominic gave an exasperated sigh. 'Your voice and manner proclaim you as being a lady—'

'Or a disgraced lady's maid,' she put in quickly.

'Perhaps,' Dominic allowed tersely. 'I have no idea what your reasons are for taking the action you have—and I doubt you are about to enlighten me, are you?'

Her mouth firmed. 'No.'

'As I thought.' He gave an abrupt nod. 'Of course, the simplest answer to this predicament would be for me to simply terminate your employment. At least then I would not feel honour bound to take responsibility for your welfare.'

She gave an inelegant snort. 'That would only solve the problem for *you*, my lord; *I* would still need to find the means with which to earn my own living.'

She was right, Dominic allowed sourly. But there was another alternative... He could offer to become her protector himself—his enjoyment of their kiss earlier proved that his senses, at least, were not averse to the idea. And no doubt, with a little coaching as to his physical preferences, Caro would be more than capable of satisfying his needs.

But in the ten years since Dominic had first appeared in town he had never once taken a permanent mistress, as many of his male acquaintances chose to do, preferring instead to take his pleasures whenever and with what women he pleased. He had no wish to change that arrangement by making the spirited and outspoken Caro Morton his mistress.

'Of course, if you were to decide to terminate my employment then you would leave me with no choice but to seek the same position elsewhere.' She shrugged those slender shoulders. 'Something that should not prove too difficult now that the masked lady has, as you say, gained something of a...male following,' she added.

It was a solution, of course. Except at Nick's, whether the chit was aware of it or not, Caro at least had the protection of the attentive Drew and Ben. And, apparently, now Dominic himself. 'If it is only question of money—'

'And if it were?' Caro had immediately bristled haughtily.

His mouth thinned. 'In those circumstances I might perhaps see my way clear to advancing you sufficient funds to take you back to wherever it is you originate from.'

'No!' Those sea-green eyes sparkled up at him rebelliously. 'I have no intention of leaving London yet.'

Dominic was unsure as to whether Caro's vehemence was due to his offer to advance her money, or his suggestion that she use that money to take herself home, so he decided to probe further. 'Is the situation at home so intolerable, then?'

She attempted to repress a shudder and failed. 'At present, yes.'

Dominic studied her through narrowed lids, noting the shadows that had appeared in those sea-green eyes, and the pallor of her cheeks. 'That remark would seem to imply that the situation may change some time in the future?'

'It is to be hoped so, yes,' she confirmed with feeling.

'But until it does, it is your intention to remain in London, whether or not I continue to employ you at Nick's?'

Her mouth set firmly. 'It is.'

'You are very stubborn, madam.'

'I am decisive, sir, which is completely different.'

Dominic sighed heavily, not wishing to send Caro back to a situation she obviously found so unpleasant, but also well able to imagine the scrapes this reckless young woman would get herself into, if she were once again let loose to roam the streets of London seeking employment. 'Then I believe, for the moment, we must leave things as they are.' He looked away. 'Shall we continue to walk to your lodgings?'

Caro shot him a triumphant glance. 'We have been standing outside them for some minutes, my lord!'

Dominic gave her an irritated scowl before glancing

at the house behind them. It was a three-storied building so typical of an area that had once been fashionable, but which was no longer so, and as such had fallen into genteel decay. Although the owner of this particular lodging had at least attempted to keep up a veneer of respectability, the outside being neat and cared for, and the curtains at the windows also appearing clean.

He turned back to Caro. 'In that case it remains only for me to bid you goodnight.'

She gave an abrupt curtsy. 'My lord.'

'Miss Morton.' He nodded curtly.

Caro gazed up at Dominic quizzically as he made no move to depart for his waiting carriage. 'There is no need for you to wait to leave until you are assured I have entered the house, my lord.'

He raised an eyebrow. 'In the same way you were in "absolutely no danger" earlier on?'

Her cheeks coloured prettily. 'I find your manner extremely vexing, my lord!'

'No more so than I do your own, I assure you, Miss Morton.'

Caro had never before met anyone remotely like Dominic Vaughn. Had never dreamed that men like him existed, so tall and fashionably handsome, so aristocratic. So arrogantly sure of themselves!

Admittedly her contact with male acquaintances had been severely limited before she came to London, usually only consisting of the few sons of the local gentry, and occasionally her father's lawyer when he came from London to discuss business matters.

Even so, Caro knew from Drew Butler's respectful attitude towards the earl earlier this evening, and the hasty departure of those three young gentlemen just minutes ago, that Dominic Vaughn was a man whose very presence demanded respect and obedience.

Except, after years of having no choice but to do as she was told, Caro no longer wished to obey any man. Not least of all the guardian she had so recently acquired…

She flashed the earl a bright meaningless smile before turning to walk to the front door of her lodgings, not even glancing back to see if he still watched as she quietly let herself inside with the key the landlady had provided for Caro's personal use when she had taken the rooms two weeks ago.

She waited several heartbeats before daring to look out through the lace-covered window beside the front door. Just in time to see the earl climbing inside his carriage before the groom closed the door behind him and hopped neatly on to the back of the vehicle as it was driven away.

But before it did so Caro saw the pale oval of Dominic Vaughn's grimly set face at the carriage window as he glanced towards where she stood hidden. She moved away quickly to lean back against the wall, her hands clutched against her rapidly beating heart.

No, being kissed by the Earl of Blackstone had been nothing at all as she imagined a kiss would be.

It had been far, far more exciting…

'So, where did you get to last night, Dom?' Nathaniel Thorne, Earl of Osbourne, prompted lazily the following evening, the two men lounging in opposite wing-chairs beside the fireplace in one of the larger rooms at White's.

'I was…unavoidably detained.' Dominic evaded answering his friend's query directly. The two men had arranged to meet late the previous evening, an appointment Dominic obviously had not kept as he had instead been occupied with seeing Caro Morton safely delivered back to her lodgings. For all the thanks he had received for his trouble!

Nathaniel raised a blond brow. 'I trust she was as insatiable as she was beautiful?'

'Beautiful—yes. Insatiable? I have no idea.' In truth, hours later, Dominic still had no idea what to make of Caro Morton, of who and what she was. He had taken the trouble, however, to send word to Drew Butler to continue feeding her, as well as arranging for Ben Jackson to escort her home at the end of each night's work; Caro might have no care for her own welfare, but whilst she continued working for Dominic, he had every intention of ensuring that no harm befell her.

'Yet,' Nathaniel drawled knowingly.

Both of Dominic's parents had died years ago, and he had no siblings, either, making Nathaniel Thorne and Gabriel Faulkner the closest thing he had to a family; the years they had all spent at school together, and then in the army, never knowing whether they would survive the next battle, had made them as close as brothers. Even so, Dominic could have wished at that moment that Nathaniel did not know him quite as well as he did.

Thankfully he had the perfect diversion from his lack of appearance the night before. 'I received a note from Gabriel today. He expects to arrive in England by the end of the week.' He lifted his glass of brandy and took an appreciative sip.

'I received one, too,' Nathaniel revealed. 'Can you imagine the looks on the faces of the *ton* when Gabe makes his entrance back into society?'

'He reaffirmed it was his intention to first go to Shoreley Park and confront the Copeland sisters,' Dominic reminded him.

Osbourne snorted. 'We both know that will only take two minutes of his time. By the time Gabriel returns to town, past scandal or not, I have no doubt that all three of the silly chits will be clamouring to marry him!' Nathaniel made a silent toast of appreciation to their absent friend.

It was a fact that Gabriel's years of banishment to the Continent and the army had in no way affected his conquests in the bedchamber; one look at that raven-black hair, those dark indigo eyes and his firmly muscled physique, and women of all ages simply dropped at Gabriel's feet. Or, more accurately, into his bed! No doubt the Copeland sisters would find themselves equally as smitten.

'What shall we do with the rest of the night?' After the dissatisfaction he had felt at the end of the previous evening, Dominic knew himself to be in the mood to drink too much before falling into bed with a woman who was as inventive as she was willing.

Nathaniel eyed him speculatively. 'I have heard that there is a mysterious beauty currently performing at Nick's...'

As close as the three men were, Dominic knew that some things were best kept to oneself—and his meeting with Caro Morton the previous night, his uncharacteristic, unfathomable sense of protectiveness where she was concerned, was certainly one of them! Although Dominic could not say that he was at all pleased that she was already so great a source of gossip at the gentlemen's clubs after only a week of appearing at his.

He grimaced. 'I believe the only reason she is considered such a mystery is because she wears a jewelled mask whilst performing.'

'Oh.' The other man's mouth turned down. 'No doubt to hide the fact that she's scarred from the pox.'

'Possibly,' Dominic dismissed in a bored voice, having no intention of saying anything that would increase his friend's curiosity where Caro was concerned.

Nate sighed. 'In which case, I believe I will leave the choice of tonight's entertainment to you.'

That choice involved visiting several gambling clubs before ending the evening at the brightly lit but nevertheless discreet house where several beautiful and accomplished ladies of the *demi-monde* made it only too obvious they would be pleased to offer amusement and companionship to two such handsome young gentlemen.

So it was all the more surprising when those same two gentlemen took their leave only an hour or so later, neither having taken advantage of that willingness. 'Perhaps we should have gone to view the mysterious beauty at Nick's, after all.' Osbourne repressed a bored yawn. 'Scarred from the pox or not, I doubt I could find her any less appealing than the ladies we have just wasted our time with!'

Dominic frowned, knowing that to demur a second time would definitely incur Nate's curiosity. 'Perhaps we are becoming too jaded in our tastes, Nate?' he murmured drily as he tapped on the roof of the carriage and gave his driver fresh instructions.

The other man raised a questioning brow. 'Do you ever miss the excitement of our five years in the army?'

Did Dominic miss the horror and the bloodshed of war? The never knowing whether he would survive the next battle or if it was his turn to meet death at the end of a French sword? The comradeship with his fellow officers that arose from experiencing that very danger? He missed it like the very devil!

'Not to the point of wanting to renew my commission, no. You?'

Osbourne shrugged. 'It is a fact that civilian life can be tedious as well as damned repetitious.'

Dominic felt relieved to know that he was not the only one to miss those years of feeling as if one walked constantly on the knife edge of danger. 'I am told that participating in a London Season often resembles a battlefield,' he mused.

'Do not even mention the Season to me,' the other man groaned. 'My Aunt Gertrude has taken it into her head that it is high time I took myself a wife,' he explained at Dominic's questioning look. 'As such she is insisting that I escort her to several balls and soirées during the next few weeks. No doubt with the expectation of finding a young woman she believes will make me a suitable Countess.'

'Ah.' Dominic began to understand his friend's restlessness this evening; Mrs Gertrude Wilson was Osbourne's closest relative, and one, moreover, of whom he was extremely fond. She reciprocated by taking a great interest in her nephew's life. To the point, it seemed, that she was now attempting to find him a wife. Reason enough for Dominic to be grateful for his own lack of female relations! 'I take it that you are not in agreement with her wishes?'

'In agreement with the idea of shackling myself for life to some mealy-mouthed chit who has no doubt been taught to lie back and think of king and country when we are in bed together? Certainly not!' Osbourne barely suppressed his shiver of revulsion. 'I cannot think what Gabriel is about even contemplating such a fate.'

It was a fact that all three gentlemen would one day have to take a wife and produce the necessary heir to their respective earldoms. Fortunately, it seemed that Osbourne, at least, was as averse to accepting that fate as Dominic was. Although there was no doubting that Mrs Gertrude Wilson was a force to be reckoned with!

Dominic's humour at his friend's situation faded, his mouth tightening in disapproval, as the two gentlemen stepped down from his carriage minutes later and he saw that Ben Jackson was once again absent from his position at the entrance to Nick's; obviously they had arrived in time for Nathaniel to witness Caro Morton's second performance of the evening.

However, the sound of shouting, breaking glass and the crashing of furniture coming from the direction of the main gaming room as they stepped into the spacious hallway of the club in no way resembled the awed

silence Dominic had experienced on his arrival the previous evening.

Especially when it was accompanied by the sound
of a woman's screams!

Chapter Three

Caro had never been as frightened in her life as she was at that moment. Even with Ben and two other men standing protectively in front of her, and keeping the worst of the fighting at bay, it was still possible for her to see men's fists flying, the blood freely flowing from noses and cut faces as chairs, tables and bottles were also brought into play.

In truth, she had no idea how the fighting had even begun. One moment she had been singing as usual, and the next a gentleman had tried to step on to the stage and grab hold of her. At first Caro had believed the second gentleman to step forwards was attempting to come to her aid, until he pushed the first man aside and also lunged towards where she had half-risen from the *chaise* in alarm.

After that all bedlam had broken loose, it seemed, with a dozen or more men fighting off the first two with fists and any item of furniture that came readily to hand.

And through it all, every terrifying moment of it, Caro had been humiliatingly aware of Lord Dominic Vaughn's dire warnings of the night before…

'Care to join in?' Osbourne invited with glee as the two men stood in the doorway of the gaming room still hatted and cloaked.

Dominic's narrowed gaze had taken stock of the situation at a glance. Thirty or so gentlemen fighting in earnest. Several of the brocade-covered chairs broken. Tables overturned, and shattered glasses and bottles crunching underfoot. Drew Butler was caught in the middle of it all as he tried to call a halt to the fighting. And on the raised stage, Ben Jackson stood immovable in front of where a head of ebony curls was just visible above and behind the *chaise*.

'Head towards the stage,' Dominic directed Osbourne grimly as he threw his hat aside. 'If we can get the girl out of here, I believe the fighting will come to an end.'

'I sincerely hope it does not!' Nathaniel grinned roguishly as he stepped purposefully into the mêlée.

Most of the gentlemen fighting seemed to be enjoying themselves as much as Osbourne, despite having bloody noses, the occasional lost tooth and several eyes that would no doubt be black come morning. It was the three or four gentlemen closest to Ben Jackson, and their dogged determination to lay hands on Caro as she crouched down behind the *chaise*, that concerned Dominic the most. Although to give Ben his due, he had so far managed to keep them all at arm's length, and even managed to shoot Dominic and Osbourne an appreciative grin as they stepped up beside him.

At which point Caro Morton emerged from behind the *chaise* and launched herself into his arms. 'Thank goodness you are come, Dominic!'

Osborne grinned knowingly at the spectacle. 'You take the girl, Dom; this is the most fun I've had in years!' He swung a fist and knocked one of the men from the stage with a telling crunch of flesh against teeth.

At that moment Dominic was so angry that he wanted nothing more than to break a few bones for himself. A satisfaction he knew he would have to forgo as Caro's arms tightened about his neck, a pair of widely terrified sea-green eyes visible through the slits in the jewelled mask as she looked up at him.

Dominic's gaze darkened as he saw that her gold gown was ripped in several places. 'Did I not warn you?' Dominic's voice was chilling as he pulled her arms from about his neck and swung off his cloak to cover her in it before bending down to place his arm at the back of her knees and toss her up on to his shoulder as he straightened.

'I— What— Put me down this instant!' Tiny fists pummelled against his back.

'I believe now would be as good a time as any for you to learn when it is wiser to remain silent,' Dominic rasped grimly as several male heads turned his way to watch jealously as he carried her from the stage and out to the private area at the back of the club.

The last thing that Caro had needed in the midst of that nightmare was for Lord Dominic Vaughn to tell her 'I told you so'. She had already been terrified enough for one evening without the added humiliation of being thrown over this man's shoulder as if she were no more than a sack of potatoes or a bail of straw on her father's estate!

Caro struggled to be released as soon as they reached the relative safety of the deserted hallway. 'You will put me down this instant!' she instructed furiously as her struggles resulted only in her becoming even more hot and bad-tempered.

'Gladly.' Dominic slid her unceremoniously down the hard length of his body before lowering her bare feet on to the cold stone floor.

'I do not believe I have ever met a man more ill mannered than you!' Caro looked up at him accusingly even as her flustered fingers tried to secure the engulfing cloak about her shoulders and hold the soft silk folds about her trembling body.

'After I have tried to save you from harm?' His voice was silky soft as those silver eyes glittered down at her in warning.

'After you have manhandled me, sir!' Caro was unrepentant as she tried to bring some semblance of order to the tangled ebony curls, all the time marvelling at how the jewelled mask and ebony wig had managed to stay in place at all. 'Your own anger a few minutes ago seemed to imply that you believe *I* am to blame for what just took place—'

'You *are* to blame.'

'Do not be ridiculous!' Caro gave him a scornful glance. 'Every woman knows that men—even so-called gentlemen—will find any excuse to fight.'

She might very well be in the right of it there, Dominic acknowledged as he remembered Osbourne's glee before he launched himself into the midst of the fighting. But that did not change the fact that this particular fight had broken out because Caro had refused to see the danger of flaunting herself night after night before a roomful of intoxicated men.

As it was, Dominic had no idea whether to beat her or kiss her senseless for her naïvety. 'I have a good mind to take out the cost of this evening's damages on your backside!' he grated instead.

Her eyes widened and her cheeks flushed a fiery red even as her chin rose in challenge. 'You would not dare!'

Dominic gave a disgusted snort. 'Do not tempt me, Caro.'

Caro gave up all attempt to bring order to those loosely flowing locks and instead removed the jewelled mask in order to glare at him. 'I believe you are just looking for an excuse to beat me.'

Dominic stilled, his gaze narrowing searchingly on her angrily defiant face. Just the thought of some nameless, faceless man ever laying hands on this delicately lovely woman in anger was enough to rouse Dominic's own fury. Yet at this particular moment in time, he totally understood the impulse; he badly wanted to tan Caro's backside so hard that she would not be able to sit down for a week! 'I assure you, where you are concerned, no excuse is necessary,' he growled.

'Oh!' she gasped her indignation. 'You, sir, are the most overbearing, arrogant, insulting man it has ever been my misfortune to meet!'

'And you, madam, are the most stubborn, wilfully stupid—'

'*Stupid?*' she echoed furiously.

'*Wilfully* stupid,' Dominic repeated unrepentantly as he glared back at her.

Caro had never been so incensed. Never felt so much like punching a man on his arrogant, aristocratic nose!

As if aware of the violence of her thoughts those sculptured lips turned up into a mocking smile. 'It would be most unwise, Caro.' His warning was silkily soft and all the more dangerous because of it.

Sea-green eyes clashed with silver for long, challenging moments. A challenge she was almost—almost!—feeling brave enough to accept when an amused voice broke into the tension. 'I came to tell you that Butler and his heavies have thrown out the last of the patrons and are now attempting to clean up the mess, but I can come back later if now is not a convenient time…?'

Dominic was standing directly in Caro's line of vision and she had to lean to one side to see around him to where a tall, elegantly dressed man leant casually against the wall of the hallway. His arms were folded across the width of his chest as he watched them with interest, only the ruffled disarray of his blond and fashionably long hair about the handsomeness of his face to show that he had only moments ago been caught up in the thick of the fighting.

'I believe our earlier assessment of the…situation to have been at fault, Blackstone.' The other man gave Dominic an appreciative smile before turning his dark gaze back to pointedly roam over the unblemished, obviously pox-free skin of Caro's beautiful face.

It was a remark she did not even begin to understand, let alone why he was looking at her so intently! 'To answer your earlier question, sir—I believe Lord Vaughn and I have finished our conversation.'

'Not by a long way.' One of Dominic's hands reached out, the fingers curling about Caro's wrist like a band of steel, as she would have brushed past him. 'I trust not too many heads were broken, Osbourne?'

The blond-haired man shrugged. 'None that did not deserve it.' He straightened away from the wall. 'Care to introduce me, Blackstone?' A merry brown gaze briefly met his friend's before he looked at Caro with open admiration.

'Caro Morton, Lord Nathaniel Thorne, Earl of Osbourne,' Dominic said coldly.

'Your servant, ma'am.' Lord Thorne gave an elegant bow.

'My lord.' Really, did every man she met in London have to be a lord and an earl? she wondered crossly as she pondered the ridiculousness of formally curtsying to a gentleman under such circumstances.

'If you were thinking of leaving too now all the excitement is over, Osbourne, then by all means do so,' Dominic said. 'I fear I will not be free to leave for some time yet.'

His gaze hardened as he glanced down pointedly at Caro Morton, his mouth thinning as those sea-green eyes once more stared back at him in silent rebellion.

She broke that gaze to turn and smile graciously at the other man. 'Perhaps, if you are leaving, I might prevail on you to take me with you, Lord Thorne?'

To all intents and purposes, Dominic recognised

impatiently, as if she were a lady making conversation in her drawing room! As if a fight had not just broken out over who was to share her bed tonight. As if Dominic's own property had not been destroyed in that mêlée.

As if she were not standing before two elegant gentlemen of the *ton* dressed only in a ripped gown, and with her ebony wig slightly askew!

Dominic gave a frustrated sigh. 'I think not.'

Those sea-green eyes flashed up at him with annoyance before Caro ignored him to turn once again to Nathaniel. 'I would very much appreciate it if you would agree to escort me home, Lord Thorne.' A siren could not have sounded or looked any more sweetly persuasive!

Dominic easily read the uncertainty in his friend's expression; a gentleman through and through, Osbourne never had been able to resist the appeal of a seeming damsel in distress. Seeming, in Dominic's estimation, being a correct assessment in regard to Caro Morton. The woman was an absolute menace and had become a veritable thorn in Dominic's side since the moment he'd set eyes upon her.

'I am afraid that is not possible,' Dominic answered smoothly on the other man's behalf.

Those delicate cheeks flushed red. 'I believe my request was made to Lord Thorne and not to *you*!'

Dominic allowed some of the tension to ease from his shoulders, aware that he had been in one state of tension or another since first meeting her. 'Lord Thorne is gentleman enough, however, to accept a prior claim, are you not, Osbourne?'

Osbourne's eyes widened. As well they might, damn

it; Dominic had as good as denied all knowledge of this woman earlier tonight, a denial that had been made a complete nonsense of the moment Caro had launched herself into his arms and, in her agitation, called him by his given name.

Hell and damnation!

'I believe you were quite correct in your assertion earlier, Blackstone,' Osbourne's drawled comment interrupted Dominic's displeasing thoughts. 'Personally I would say exquisite rather than beautiful!'

Dominic nodded irritably. 'Just so.'

'That being the case, Blackstone, I believe I will join Butler and Ben and enjoy a reviving brandy before I leave. My respects, Miss Morton.' Osbourne gave a lazy inclination of his head before leaving the two of them alone.

Caro blinked at the suddenness of Lord Thorne's departure. 'I do not understand.' Neither did she have any idea what tacit agreement had passed between the two men in the last few moments. But something most certainly had for the gentlemanly Lord Thorne to have just abandoned her like that.

Dominic released her wrist before stepping away from her. 'You should go to your room now and change. I will be waiting in Drew Butler's office when you are ready to leave.'

Caro frowned. 'But—'

'Could you, for once, just do as I ask without argument, Caro?' The scar on Dominic's cheek showed in stark relief against his clenched jaw.

She looked up into that ruthlessly hard face, repressing a shiver of apprehension as she saw the dangerous glitter in those pale silver eyes. Of course—this man had already told her that he held her responsible for the occurrence of the fight and the damages to his property, and he had also threatened to take out the cost of those damages on her backside!

Never, in all of her twenty years, had Caro been spoken to in the way the arrogant Dominic Vaughn spoke to her. So familiarly. So—so…intimately. A gentleman should not even refer to a lady's bottom, let alone threaten to inflict harm upon it!

Her chin rose haughtily. 'I am very tired, my lord, and would prefer to go straight home once I am dressed.'

'And I would prefer that you join me in Butler's office first so that we might continue our conversation.'

'I had thought it finished.'

'Caro, I have already been involved in a brawl not of my making, and my property has been extensively damaged. As such, I am really in no mood to tolerate any more of your stubbornness this evening.' His hands had clenched at his sides in an effort to control his exasperation.

'Really?' She arched innocent brows. 'My own patience with your impossible arrogance ended some minutes ago.'

Yes, Dominic acknowledged ruefully, this young woman was undoubtedly as feisty as she was beautiful. To his own annoyance, he had also spent far too much time today allowing his thoughts to dwell on how delicious Caro's mouth had tasted beneath his the night before.

'Would you be any more amenable to the suggestion if I were to say please?'

She eyed him warily, distrustfully. 'It would be a start, certainly.'

He regarded her for several seconds before nodding. 'Very well. I insist that you join me in Butler's office shortly so that we might continue this conversation. Please.'

A second request that was intended to be no more gracious than the first! 'Then I agree to join you in Mr Butler's office shortly, my lord. But only for a few minutes,' Caro added firmly as she saw the glitter of triumph that lit those pale silver eyes. 'It is late and I really am very tired.'

'Understandably.' He gave a mocking bow. 'I will only require a few more minutes of your time this evening.'

That last remark almost had the tone of a threat, Caro realised worriedly as she made her way slowly to her dressing-room to change. And for all that she had so defiantly told Dominic Vaughn the previous evening that she would simply seek employment elsewhere if he chose to dismiss her, after this evening's disaster she could not even bear the thought of remaining in London without the protection of Drew and Ben.

She had been completely truthful the evening before when she'd assured Dominic that she had every intention of returning home as soon as she felt it was safe for her to do so. Unfortunately, Caro did not believe that time had come quite yet...

Dominic made no attempt to hide his pained wince as he looked at the dull green gown Caro was wearing when she joined him in Drew's office some minutes later; it was neither that intriguing sea-green of her eyes, or of a style in the least complimentary to her graceful slenderness. Rather, that unbecoming colour dulled the brightness of her eyes to the same unattractive green, and gave the pale translucence of her skin an almost sallow look. The fact that the gown was also buttoned up to her throat, and her blonde curls pulled tightly back into a bun at her nape as she stood before the desk with her hands demurely folded together, gave her the all appearance and appeal of a nun.

Dominic stood up and stepped lithely around the desk before leaning back against it as he continued to regard her critically. 'You appear none the worse for your ordeal.'

Then her appearance was deceptive, Caro acknowledged with an inner tremor. Reaction to the horrors of this evening's fighting had begun in earnest once she had reached the safety and peace of her dressing-room, to the extent that she had not been able to stop herself trembling for some time. It had all happened so suddenly, so violently, and the earl's rescue effected so efficiently—if high-handedly—that at the time, Caro had not had opportunity to think beyond that.

She was still shaking slightly now, and it was the reason her hands were clasped so tightly together in front of her; she would not, for any reason, show the arrogant Dominic Vaughn any sign of weakness. 'I did not have opportunity to thank you earlier, my lord, for your timely intervention. I do so now.' She gave a stiff inclination of her head.

Dominic barely repressed his smile at this show of grudging gratitude. 'You are welcome, I am sure,' he replied. 'Obviously it is going to take several days, possibly a week, to effect the repairs to the main salon—'

'I have no money to spare to pay for those repairs, if that is to be your next suggestion,' she instantly protested.

Dominic looked at her from underneath lowered lids, seeing beyond that defiant and nunlike appearance to the young woman beneath. Those sea-green eyes were still slightly shadowed, her cheeks pale, her hands slightly trembling, all of those things evidence that Caro had been more disturbed by the violence she had witnessed earlier than she wished anyone—very likely most especially him—to be aware of.

He found that he admired that quality in her. Just as he admired her pride and the dignity she'd shown when faced with a situation so obviously beyond her previous experience.

Did that inexperience extend to the bedchamber? he could not help but wonder. After her initial surprise the previous evening, she had most definitely returned the passion of his kiss. But then afterwards she had appeared completely unaware of the danger those three young bucks had represented to her welfare.

Just as she had seemed innocent of the rising lusts of the men who returned night after night to watch her performance at Nick's. Perhaps an indication that she was inexperienced to the vagaries of men, at least?

Caro Morton was fast becoming a puzzle that Dominic found himself wishing to unravel. Almost as much, he realised with an inward wince, as he wished to peel her out of that unbecoming green gown before exploring every inch of her delectably naked body…

'It was not,' he answered. 'I was merely pointing out that Nick's will probably have to be closed for several days whilst repairs and other refurbishments are carried out. A closure that will obviously result in your being unable to perform here for the same amount of time.'

She looked at him blankly for several moments, and then her eyes widened as the full import of what he was saying became clear to her. She licked suddenly dry lips. 'But you believe it will only be for a few days?'

Dominic studied her closely. 'Possibly a week.'

'A week?' Her echo was distraught.

Alerting him to the fact that she was in all probability completely financially reliant upon the money she earned each night at the gambling club—her clothes certainly indicated as much! It also proved, along with her determination to remain in London 'for the present', that her situation at home must be dire indeed...

'There is no reason for you to look so concerned, Caro,' he assured her. 'Whether you wish it or not, for the moment, it would appear you are now under my protection.'

Her eyes went wide with indignation. 'I have absolutely *no* intention of becoming your mistress!'

Any more than it was Dominic's wish to take her—or any other woman—as his mistress...

His parents had both died when he was but twelve years old. Neither had there been any kindly aunt to take an interest in him as there had with Nathaniel. Instead Dominic's guardianship had been placed in the hands of his father's firm of lawyers until he came of age at twenty-one. During those intervening years, when he was not away at school, Dominic had lived alone at

Blackstone Park in Berkshire, cared for only by the impersonal kindness of servants.

It would have been all too easy once he reached his majority, and was at last allowed to manage his own affairs, to have been drawn into the false warmth of affection given by a paid mistress. Instead, he had been content with the friendship he'd received from and felt for both Gabriel and Nathaniel. He knew their affection for him, at least, to be without ulterior motive. The same could not be said of a mistress.

'I said protector, Caro, not lover. Although I am sure that most of the gentlemen here tonight now believe me to already have that dubious honour,' he pointed out.

She stiffened at the insult in his tone. 'How so?'

'Several of them witnessed you throwing yourself into my arms earlier—'

'I was in fear of my life!' Two indignant spots of colour had appeared in the pallor of her cheeks.

Dominic waved a dismissive hand. 'The why of it is not important. The facts are that a masked lady is employed at my gambling club, and tonight that lady threw herself into my arms with a familiarity that was only confirmed when she called out my name for all to hear.' He shrugged. 'Those things are enough for most men to have come to the conclusion that the lady has decided on her protector. That she is now, in all probability, the exclusive property of the Earl of Blackstone.'

If it were possible, Caro's cheeks became even paler!

Chapter Four

For possibly the first time in her life, Caro was rendered bereft of speech. Not only was it perfectly shocking that many of the male members of society believed her to be the exclusive property of Lord Dominic Vaughn, but her older sister, Diana, would be incensed if such a falsehood were ever related to her in connection with her runaway sister, Caroline!

Caro had left a note on her bed telling her sisters not to worry about her, of course, but other than that she had not confided her plan of going to London to either Diana or her younger sister, Elizabeth, before fleeing the family home in Hampshire two weeks ago, before their guardian could arrive to take control of all their lives. A man none of the Copeland sisters had met before, but who had nevertheless chosen to inform them, through his lawyer, that he believed himself to be in a position to insist that one of them become his wife!

What sort of man did that? Caro had questioned in outraged disbelief. How monstrous could Lord Gabriel

Faulkner, the new Earl of Westbourne, be that he sent his lawyer in his stead to offer marriage to whichever of the previous earl's daughters was willing to accept him? And if none chose willingly, to *insist* upon it!

Never having been allowed to mix with London society, none of the Copeland sisters had any previous knowledge of their father's heir and second cousin, Lord Gabriel Faulkner. But several of their close neighbours had, and they were only too happy to regale the sisters with the knowledge—if not the details—of his lordship's banishment to the Continent eight years previously following a tremendous scandal, with talk of his having settled in Venice some years later. Other than that, none of the sisters had ever heard or seen anything of the man before being informed that not only was he their father's heir, but also their guardian.

They had all known and accepted that a daughter could not inherit the title, of course, but it was only when their father's will was read out after his funeral that the three sisters learnt they were also completely without finances of their own, and as such their futures were completely dependent upon the whim and mercy of the new Earl of Westbourne.

But as the weeks, and then months, passed, with no sign of the new earl arriving to take possession of either the Shoreley Hall estate, or to establish any guardianship over the three sisters other than the allowance sent to them by the man's lawyer each month, they had begun to relax, to believe that their lives could continue without interference from their new guardian.

Until, that is, the earl's lawyer had arrived at Shoreley Hall three weeks ago to inform them that the new Earl of Westbourne was very generously prepared to offer marriage to one of the penniless sisters. An offer, the lawyer had informed them sternly, that as their guardian, the earl could insist—and indeed, would insist—that one of them accept.

Diana, the eldest at one and twenty, was half-promised to the son of the local squire and so was safest from the earl's attentions. Elizabeth, only nineteen and the youngest of the three, had nevertheless declared she would throw herself on the mercy of a convent before she would marry a man she did not love and who did not love her. Caro's plan to avoid marrying the earl had been even more daring.

Desperate to bring some adventure into her so far humdrum existence, Caro had decided she would go to London for a month, perhaps two, and seek obscurity as a lady's companion or governess. And when Lord Gabriel Faulkner arrived in England—as his lawyer had assured them he undoubtedly would once informed of their refusal of his offer—then Diana, incensed by the disappearance of one of her sisters, would reduce the man to a quivering pulp with the cutting edge of her legendary acerbic tongue, before sending him away with his cowed tail tucked between his legs.

A month spent in London, possibly two, should do it, Caro had decided as she excitedly packed her bag before creeping stealthily from the house to walk the half a mile or so to the crossroads where she could catch the evening coach to London.

None of Caro's plans had worked out at she had expected, of course. No respectable household would employ a young woman without references, nor the dress shops, either, and the small amount of money Caro had brought with her had been seriously depleted, as instead of being taken into the warmth and security of the respectable household of her imaginings, she was forced to pay a month in advance for her modest lodgings.

In fact, until Drew Butler had taken pity on her, allowing her to sing at Nick's, Caro had feared she would have to return home with her own tail between her legs, before the earl had even arrived in England, let alone been sent on his way by the indomitable Diana!

Dominic had been watching Caro's expressive face with interest as he wondered what her thoughts had been for the past few minutes. 'You know, you could simply put an end to all this nonsense by returning from whence you came,' he said persuasively.

A shutter came down over that previously candid sea-green gaze, once again alerting Dominic to Caro's definite aversion—maybe even fear?—of returning to her previous life. Once again he wondered what, or who, this beautiful young woman was running away from.

And what possible business was it of his? Dominic instantly rebuked himself. None whatsoever. And yet he could not quite bring himself to insist that Caro must go home and face whatever punishment she had coming to her for having run away in the first place.

What if it were that bullying father she was running away from? Or the brutish husband? Either of whom would completely crush the spirit in Caro that Dominic found so intriguing…

She shook her head. 'I am afraid that returning to my home is not an option at this point in time, my lord.'

He raised dark brows. 'So you have already informed me. And between times, is it your intention to continue turning my hair prematurely grey as I worry in what scrape you will next embroil yourself?'

'I do not see a single grey hair amongst the black as yet, my lord.' Amusement glittered in those sea-green eyes as she glanced at those dark locks.

'I fear it is only a matter of time.' Dominic pulled a rueful face, only to then find himself totally enchanted as she laughed huskily at this nonsense. He realised, somewhat to his dismay, that he was as seriously in danger of falling under this woman's spell as Butler and Ben—and possibly Osborne—so obviously were.

It was a spell Dominic had no intention of succumbing to. Bedding a woman was one thing; allowing his emotions to become engaged by one was something else entirely. It was about time he changed his tactics; if he couldn't persuade Caro to leave London by simply asking her, he would have to try a more direct approach…

Caro took an involuntary step back, her eyes widening warily, as Dominic rose slowly to his feet, his movements almost predatory as he moved around the desk to cross over to the door and slowly turn the key in the lock.

'So that we are not disturbed,' he murmured as he moved so that he now stood only inches away from her.

She moistened suddenly dry lips as she tilted her head back so that she might look up, fearlessly, she hoped, into that arrogantly handsome face. 'It is time I was leaving—'

'Not quite yet, Caro,' the earl murmured huskily as one of his hands moved up to cup the side of her face and the soft pad of his thumb moved across the pouting swell of her bottom lip.

'I— What are you doing, my lord?'

'You called me Dominic earlier,' he reminded her huskily.

Caro's throat moved convulsively as she swallowed. 'What are you doing, Dominic?' she repeated breathlessly.

He shrugged those broad shoulders. 'Endeavouring, I hope, to show you there could be certain…benefits to becoming my mistress.'

Caro's knees felt weak just at the thought of what method this man intended using to demonstrate those 'benefits'. She so easily recalled the feel of that hard and uncompromising mouth against her own the night before, the feel of his hands as they ran the length of her spine to cup her bottom and press the hardness of his body intimately into hers. 'This is most unwise, my lord.'

He made no answer as he moved to rest back against the edge of the desk, taking her with him, those strange, silver-coloured eyes fixed caressingly upon Caro's slightly parted lips, the warmth of his breath stirring the tendrils of hair at her temples.

Dominic was standing much too close to her. So close that she could feel the heat of his body. So close that she was aware of the way that he smelt; the delicate spice of his cologne, and a purely male smell, one that appeared to be a combination of a clean male body and musky heat, uniquely his own.

Caro made every effort to gather her scattered senses. 'Dominic, I have no intention of allowing you to—oh!' she gasped as he encircled her waist and pulled her in between his parted legs, her thighs now pressed against him, as her breasts were crushed against the firm muscles of his chest. She placed her hands upon his shoulders with the intention of pushing him away.

'I think not,' Dominic murmured as he realised her intention, his arms moving about her waist to hold her more tightly against him, quelling her struggles as he looked to where her hair was secured in that unbecoming nunlike bun. 'Remove the pins from your hair for me, Caro.'

She stilled abruptly. 'No!'

'Would you rather that I did it?' He quirked dark brows.

'I would rather my hair remain exactly—oh!' She gave another of those breathless gasps as Dominic reached up and removed the pins himself. It was a breathless gasp that he found he was becoming extremely fond of hearing.

'Better.' He nodded his approval as he reached up to uncoil her hair and allow it to cascade in a wealth of golden curls over her shoulders and down the length of her spine. 'Now for the buttons on this awful gown—'

'I cannot possibly allow you to unbutton the front of my gown!' Caro's fingers clamped down over his, even as she glared up at him.

Dominic found himself smiling in the face of this

display of female outrage. 'It has all the allure of a nun's habit,' he said drily.

'That is exactly what it is supposed to—' Caro broke off the protest as she saw the way those silver eyes had narrowed to shrewdness.

'Do...?' Dominic finished softly for her. 'As no doubt the wearing of that unbecoming bonnet was designed to hide every delicious golden curl upon your head?'

'Yes,' she admitted.

He shook his head as he resumed unfastening the buttons on the front of her gown. 'It is a sacrilege, Caro, and one I am not inclined to indulge.' He folded back the two sides of her gown to reveal the thrust of her breasts covered only by the thinness of her shift above her corset.

Caro had no more will to protest as she saw the way those silver eyes glittered with admiration as Dominic gazed his fill of her. Indeed, she found she could barely breathe as she watched him slowly raise one of his hands to pull aside that gauzy piece of material and bare her breast completely. Her cheeks suffused with colour as, even as she watched, the tiny rose-coloured nub on the crest of her breast began to rise and stiffen.

'You are so very beautiful here,' he said huskily, the warmth of his breath now a tortuous caress against that burgeoning flesh. He looked up at her enquiringly. 'I wish to taste you, Caro.'

She found herself mesmerised by the slow flick of Dominic's tongue across his lips. Mesmerised and aching, the tip of her breast deepened in colour as it became firmer still. In anticipation. In longing, she knew, to feel that hot tongue curling moistly over it.

Where had these thoughts come from? Caro wondered wildly. How was it that she even knew the touch of Dominic's lips and mouth against her breast would give her more pleasure than she had ever dreamt possible? Woman's intuition? A legacy of Eve? However Caro knew these things, she surely could not allow Dominic to—

All thought ceased, any hope of protest dying along with it, as he gave up waiting for her answer and instead lowered his head to gently draw the now pulsing tip of Caro's breast into the heat of his mouth. His hand curved beneath it at the same time as he laved that aching bud with the moist heat of his tongue, and sending rivulets of pleasure into her other breast and down the soft curve of her abdomen to pool between her thighs.

Caro was filled with the strangest sensations, her breasts feeling full and heavy under the intimacy of Dominic's ministrations, the muscles in her abdomen clenching, that heat between her thighs making her swell and moisten there. She discovered she wanted to both squeeze her thighs together and part them at the same time. To have Dominic touch her there and ease that ache, too.

Her back arched instinctively as his hand moved to capture her other breast, the soft pad of his thumb now flicking against that hardened tip in the same rhythm with which he drew on its twin.

Dominic's lovemaking had been intended as a way of showing Caro that she did not belong here in London, that she was no match for him or other experienced men of the *ton*. Instead he was the one forced to recognise that he had never tasted anything quite so delicious as her breast, the nipple as sweet as honey as he kissed her there greedily, the hardness of his erection pulsing in his pantaloons testifying to the strength of his own arousal.

He drew back slightly to look at that pouting, full nipple, stroking his tongue across it before moving slightly to capture its twin, drawing on it hungrily before looking up at her flushed face and feverishly bright eyes. 'Tell me how you wish me to touch you, Caro,' he murmured against her swollen flesh.

Her fingers dug into his shoulders. 'Dominic!' she groaned a throaty protest.

He took pity on her shyness. 'Do you like this?' He swept his thumb lightly over that pouting nipple.

'Yes!' she gasped, shuddering with pleasure.

'This?' He brought his mouth down to her breast once more, even as he allowed his hand to fall to her ankle and push her gown aside and began a slow caress to her knee.

'Oh, yes!'

'And this?' Dominic ran his tongue repeatedly over that swollen nipple even as his hand caressed higher still to weave a pattern of seduction along her inner thigh, the heat of her through her drawers, her dampness, telling him of her arousal.

Nothing in Caro's life had prepared her to be touched with such intimacy. How could it, when she had never realised that such intimacies existed? Such achingly pleasurable intimacies that she wished would never end.

'I would like you to touch me in the same way, Caro,' Dominic encouraged gruffly.

She swallowed hard. 'I—' She broke off her instinctive protest as someone rattled the door handle in an effort to open the locked door.

'My lord?' Drew Butler sounded both disapproving and concerned at this inability to enter his own office.

Dominic turned his head sharply towards the door. 'What is it?'

'I need to speak with you immediately, my lord.' The other man sounded just as irritated as Dominic.

He scowled his displeasure as Caro took advantage of his distraction to extricate herself from his arms before turning away to begin fastening the buttons of her gown with fingers that were shaking so badly it took her twice as long as it should have done. What had she been thinking? Worse, how much further would she have allowed these intimacies to go if not for Drew's timely intervention?

'Caro—'

'Mr Butler requires your attention, my lord, not I!' Caro protested, her cheeks aflame.

Dominic's gaze narrowed in concern on her flushed and disconcerted face, knowing, and regretting, being the obvious cause of her discomfort. He had not meant things to go so far as they had. As for demonstrating to Caro how ill equipped she was to withstand the advances of the gentlemen of the *ton*, Dominic knew full well that *he* had been the one seriously in danger of overstepping that line! 'Caro—'

'Mr Butler requires you, my lord,' she reminded him.

Dominic stood up impatiently to stride over to the door and unlock it, his expression darkening as the other man's gaze instantly slid past him to where Caro stood with her back towards the door. Dominic deliberately stepped into the other man's line of vision. 'Yes?'

Speculative blue eyes gazed back at him. 'There is… something in the main salon I believe you should see.'

Dominic frowned. 'Can it not wait?'

'No, my lord, it cannot,' Drew stated flatly.

'Very well.' He nodded before turning to speak to Caro. 'It appears that I have to leave you for a few minutes. If you will be so kind as to wait here for me—'

'No.'

Dominic's eyes widened. 'No?'

'No.' Caro rallied, still embarrassed by the intimacies she had allowed this man, but determined not to allow that embarrassment to render her helpless. She carefully lifted her cloak and bonnet from the chair she had placed them on earlier. 'Mr Butler, is Ben available to escort me home now?'

'Yes, he is.'

'I would prefer that you wait for me here, Caro,' Dominic insisted firmly.

She met his gaze unflinchingly. 'And I would prefer that Ben be the one to accompany me to my lodgings.'

A nerve pulsed beside that savage slash of a scar on Dominic's left cheek. 'Why?'

Caro looked away as she found she could not withstand the probing of that narrowed silver gaze. 'I would simply prefer his company at this time, my lord.'

'Drew, could you wait outside for a moment, please?' Dominic did not even wait for the man's compliance before stepping back into the room and firmly closing the door behind him.

'I have nothing more to say to you, my lord—'

'Dominic.'

Caro gasped. 'I beg your pardon?'

The earl gave a graceful shrug. 'You did not seem to have any difficulty calling me Dominic a few minutes ago,' he reminded her wickedly.

Caro's cheeks burned with mortification as she recalled the most recent circumstances under which she had called this man by his first name. 'I do not even wish to think about just now—'

'Do not be so melodramatic,' Dominic interjected. 'Or perhaps, on consideration, it is the hideousness of my scars you would rather not dwell upon?' His voice hardened even as he raised a hand to his scarred cheek.

'I trust I am not so lily-livered, my lord,' Caro protested indignantly. 'No doubt you obtained that scar during the wars against Napoleon?'

'Yes.'

She nodded. 'Then it would be most ungrateful of me—of any woman—to see your scar as anything less than the result of the act of bravery it undoubtedly was.'

Dominic was well aware that some women found the scar on his face unsightly, even frightening. He should have known that the feisty Caro was made of sterner stuff. 'I will endeavour to conclude my business with Butler as quickly as is possible, after which I will be free to escort you home. No, please do not argue with me any further tonight,' he advised wearily as he saw that familiar light of rebellion enter those sea-green eyes.

'You are altogether too fond of having your own way, sir.' She frowned her disapproval at him.

And his efforts to frighten this young woman into

leaving London had only succeeded in alarming himself, Dominic recognised frustratedly. 'And if I once again add the word please?'

'Well?' she prompted tartly as he added nothing further.

Dominic found himself openly smiling at her waspishness. '*Please*, Caro, will you wait here for me?' he said drily.

Her chin remained proudly high. 'I will consider the idea whilst you are talking to Mr Butler.'

Dominic shot her one last exasperated glance before striding purposefully from the room. He forgot everything else, however—kissing and touching Caro, her response to those kisses and caresses, his own lack of control over that situation—the moment he entered the main salon of the club and saw a bloodstained and obviously badly beaten Nathaniel Thorne lying recumbent upon one of the couches there...

Chapter Five

'Dominic, why—?'

'Not now, please, Caro,' he cut in as he sat broodingly across from her inside the lamp-lit coach.

Not that the lamp was really necessary, dawn having long broken, and the sun starting to appear above the rooftops and chimneys of London, by the time they had delivered Nathaniel safely to his home. The two of them had remained long enough to see him settled in his bedchamber and attended by several of his servants before taking their leave.

Caro had given a horrified gasp earlier when she'd ventured from Drew's office and entered the main salon of the club to see a group of men standing around Lord Thorne as he lay stretched out upon one of the couches, with blood covering much of his face and hands and dripping unchecked on to his elegant clothing.

Not that Dominic had spared any time on the pallor of her cheeks or her stricken expression as he'd turned and seen her standing there. 'Someone take her away from here!' he had ordered as Caro stood there, simply too shocked to move.

'Dom—'

'Stay calm, Nate.' His voice softened as he spoke soothingly to the injured man, some of that softness remaining in his face as he turned back to Caro. 'It really would be better for all concerned if you left, Caro.'

'I'll take her back to my office,' Drew offered before striding across the room to take a firm hold of her arm and practically drag her from the room.

She barely heard the older man's comforting words as he escorted her to his office before instructing Ben to remain on guard outside the door. Caro had paced the office for well over an hour whilst the two men obviously dealt with the bloody—and Caro sincerely hoped not too seriously injured—Nathaniel Thorne.

Dominic had grimly avoided answering any of her questions when he'd finally arrived to escort her home. Caro had gasped in surprise as he had thrown his cloak over her head just as she was about to step outside. 'What are you doing?'

He had easily arrested her struggles to free herself. 'Continue walking to the coach,' he had instructed.

Caro had thrown that cloak back impatiently as soon as she'd entered the carriage, any thought of further protest at Dominic's rough handling of her dying in her throat as she saw Lord Thorne reclining upon the bench seat opposite, the dressings wrapped about both his hands seeming to indicate that he had received the attentions of a doctor since she had seen him last. His face had been cleansed of the blood, revealing his many cuts and bruises, injuries that could surely only have been inflicted by fists and knives.

Caro felt herself quiver now as she remembered the full extent of those numerous gashes and bruises, and the imagined violence behind them. 'How—?'

'I am in no mood to discuss this further tonight,' Dominic rasped, the attack on Nathaniel having been a brutal awakening, a timely reminder that there was no place for a vulnerable woman like Caro in his world.

Sea-green eyes gazed back at him reproachfully. 'But why would someone do such a thing to Lord Thorne?'

'I should have realised that asking you for silence, even for a few minutes, was an impossibility.' Dominic sighed heavily. 'The simple answer to your question is that I do not know. Yet,' he added grimly. But he had every intention of discovering who was responsible for the attack on Nathaniel and why.

Caro flinched. 'He appeared to be badly injured...'

Dominic nodded curtly. 'He was beaten. Severely. Repeatedly. By four thugs wielding knives as well as their fists.' He knew more than most how strong a fighter Nathaniel was, but the odds of four against one, especially as they had possessed weapons, had not been in his friend's favour.

She gasped as her suspicions were confirmed, one of her hands rising to the slenderness of her throat . 'But *why*?' She appeared totally bewildered.

Nathaniel had remained conscious long enough to explain that he had been set upon the moment he'd stepped outside the club earlier, the wounds on his hands caused both from the blows he had managed to land upon his attackers, and defensively as he'd held those hands up in front of him to stop the worst of the knife cuts upon his face. Once he'd fallen to the ground, he had not stood a chance against the odds, as he was kicked repeatedly until one of those blows had caught him on the side of the head. After which he knew no more until he awoke to stagger back inside the club and ask for help.

Considering those odds of four against one, Dominic was sure that if murder had been the intention, then Nathaniel would now be dead. Also, his purse had still been in his pocket when he'd regained consciousness, the diamond pin also in place at his throat, so robbery was not the motive, either. From that Dominic could only surmise that the thugs had achieved what they had set out to do, and that the attack had been a warning of some kind.

But a warning to whom exactly...?

The words of caution Gabriel had given Dominic before he'd left Venice, in regard to Nicholas Brown, the previous owner of Nick's, had immediately come to mind. Dominic was well aware of the other man's violent reputation; while publicly Brown behaved the gentleman, privately he was known to be vicious and vindictive, his associates mostly of the shady under-world of London's slums. Also, the other man had been most seriously displeased to lose Nick's in that wager to Dominic.

No, the more thought he gave to the situation—when Caro allowed him the time to think about it, that was— the more convinced he became that Nicholas Brown was somehow involved. That tonight's attack might not been meant for Nathaniel at all...

Dominic had left for Venice only days after winning the wager that had cost Brown his gambling club, only returning back to London two days ago, a fact that would no doubt have reached the other man's ears as early as yesterday. As such, it would have been all too easy for the four thugs lying in wait outside the club to have assumed that the gentleman leaving alone, long after the last patron had left, with his face hidden by both the darkness and the hat upon his head, was Dominic himself.

He had discussed the possibilities briefly with Drew, the older man having agreed that his previous employer was more than capable of sending some of his paid thugs to attack Dominic. Except those thugs had not dealt the lethal blow to the man they had attacked. Drew had offered the possibility that it might not have been a case of mistaken identity at all; that Brown could well be deliberately hurting people known to be associated with Dominic, as both a threat and a warning, before later extracting his revenge from Dominic himself.

Dominic gave a grimace as he anticipated Caro's reaction to what was to be the subject of their next conversation. 'I have no idea as yet. But in view of the fact that the attack occurred outside Nick's, it has been decided that, for the next few days at least, all of us associated with the club should take the necessary precautions.'

Caro stared across at him blankly. 'But surely *I* am in no danger? No one except you, Lord Thorne, Drew Butler, and Ben Jackson has even seen the face of the masked lady singing at Nick's. That is the reason you threw your cloak over me when we were leaving the club earlier!' she realised suddenly, looking shocked.

He nodded grimly. 'It is not my intention to frighten you, Caro.' He frowned darkly as she obviously became so. 'But, until we know more, Drew and I are agreed that the masked lady must disappear completely, whilst at the same time every precaution taken to ensure the safety of Caro Morton.'

'Perhaps I might go to stay with Mr Butler and his family?'

'Drew and I dismissed that possibility,' Dominic explained. 'Unfortunately, Drew and his family share their modest home with both his wife's parents and his own so there is simply no room.'

'Oh.' Caro frowned. 'Then perhaps I might move to the obscurity of an inexpensive hotel—'

The earl gave a firm shake of his head. 'A hotel is too public.'

She sighed her frustration with this situation. 'Is there any real danger to me, or is this just another way for you to ensure that it is impossible for me to do anything other than return from "whence I came"?'

Dominic looked at her thoughtfully. 'Would you even consider it if I were to suggest it?'

'No, I would not,' she stated firmly.

'No,' Dominic conceded flatly. In truth, it was no longer an option; if Brown really were responsible for tonight's attack, there was also every possibility he was already aware of Caro's identity as the masked lady. He undoubtedly had informers and spies everywhere. As such, Caro returning to her home unprotected could put her in more danger than if she were to remain in

London. 'Drew and I have come up with another solution.'

Caro eyed him warily. 'Which is...?'

'That I now escort you to your lodgings, where you will pack up your belongings and return to Blackstone House with me.' Not an ideal solution, he allowed honestly, but one that more easily enabled him to ensure her safety. The fact that she would at the same time be all too available to the desire he was finding it more and more difficult to resist was something he had tried—and failed—not to think about.

No wonder Caro stared at him so incredulously!

He raised an eyebrow. 'If you choose to accompany me to Blackstone House, then I will do all in my power to ensure your stay there is a temporary one. If it appears that it is to be longer than two, or possibly three days, then I will endeavour to find alternative accommodations for you. In any event, my offer of protection is one of expediency only. A desire, if you will, not to find one, or more, of my employees dead in a doorway during the next few days.'

Caro felt her face grow pale. 'You truly do believe those thugs will attack again?' She was totally confused as to what she should do. She had managed her escape from Hampshire easily enough, but she knew her older sister well enough to realise that Diana would not allow that situation to continue for long. That, despite Caro's letter of reassurance, once Diana had ascertained she was nowhere to be found in Hampshire, then her sister would widen her search, in all probability as far as London.

Diana's wrath, if she should then discover Caro living

in the household of a single gentleman of the *ton* would, she had no doubt, be more than a match for this arrogant man!

She shook her head. 'Surely Mr Butler did not agree with this plan?'

'On reflection Drew agreed with me that at the moment your safety is of more importance than your… reputation.' Dominic's mouth twisted derisively.

She shook her head. 'I simply cannot—'

'Caro, I am grown weary of hearing what you can or cannot do.' He sat forwards on the seat so that their two faces were now only inches apart, his eyes a pale and glittering silver in the weak, early morning sunlight. 'I have told you of the choices available to you—'

'Neither of which is acceptable to me!'

He gave her a hard smile. 'Then it seems you must choose whichever you consider to be the lesser of those two evils.'

Caro understood that Dominic was overset concerning the injuries inflicted upon his friend this evening, and the damage also caused to his gambling club before the attack, that he was genuinely concerned there might be another attack on those working or associated with the gambling club. But having already suffered twenty years of having her movements curtailed out of love and respect for her father, she had no intention of being told what she could or could not do, either by her guardian, or a man she had only met for the first time yesterday. 'And if I should refuse to do either of those things—go home or accompany you?'

Dominic had admired this young woman's courage from the start. Appreciated that feistiness in her, her lack of awe, of either him or his title, as well as her willingness to disagree with him if she so chose. But at this moment he could only wish she was of an obedient and compliant nature! 'It is late, Caro—or early, depending upon one's perspective.' He sighed wearily. 'In any event, it has been a very long night, and as a consequence perhaps it would be best if we waited until later today to make any firm decision one way or the other?'

She nodded. 'Then we are in agreement that once you have returned me to my lodgings I will remain there until we are able to talk again?'

Caro had all the allure of a prim old maid in that unbecoming brown bonnet that once again hid most of her hair, Dominic decided dispassionately. In fact, she looked nothing at all like the delicious, half-naked woman he had made love to earlier. Which was perhaps as well, given the circumstances! Dominic had thought to teach her a lesson earlier, and instead he had been taught one—that at the very least, Caro Morton was a serious danger to his self-control.

'We are not agreed at all,' Dominic contradicted, making no effort to continue arguing with her, but instead tapping on the roof of the carriage and issuing instructions to his groom to drive directly to Blackstone House. 'I will send to your lodgings for your things later today,' he informed her.

'You—'

'Caro, I have already assured you that should my enquiries take longer than those two or three days, then I will make other arrangements for you; let that be an end to the matter,' he said as he relaxed back in his seat, one dark brow raised in challenge.

A challenge she returned. 'It is seriously your intention to introduce me—even temporarily—into your household?'

'Seriously,' Dominic said.

She gave a disgusted snort. 'As what, may I ask?'

'Should any ask for an explanation—' his tone clearly implied that there were few who would dare ask the Earl of Blackstone for an explanation concerning any of his actions! 'then I will suggest that you are my widowed and impoverished cousin—so many young women were left widowed after Waterloo. That you are newly arrived from the country on the morning coach, with the intention of staying with me at Blackstone House whilst I arrange a modest household for you in London.'

'Without clothes or a maid?' Caro scorned.

Dominic shrugged unconcernedly. 'An impoverished widow cannot afford to employ a maid until I arrange for one, and your trunk will be delivered later today.'

She eyed him impatiently. 'Does the Earl of Blackstone even have a widowed and impoverished cousin?'

'No.'

'Do you have *any* cousins?'

'No.'

She eyed him quizzically. 'Any family at *all*?'

'Not a single one.'

Caro could not even imagine a life without her two sisters in it. Admittedly she had put a distance between them now, but it had been done in the knowledge that she could return to them as soon as Gabriel Faulkner had been convinced by Diana that none of the Copeland sisters had any intention of ever marrying him.

'Do not waste any of your pity on me.' Dominic's tone was laden with warning as he obviously saw that emotion in her expression. 'Having witnessed the complications that so often attend having close family members, I have come to regard my own lack of them as being more of a blessing rather than a deprivation.'

Could that really be true? Caro wondered with a frown. Could Dominic really prefer a life derelict of all family ties? A solitary life that allowed for only a few close friends, such as Lord Thorne?

She was given no more time to dwell on that subject or any other as the coach came to a halt, a glance outside revealing a large town house in an obviously fashionable district of London. Mayfair, perhaps. Or St James's's? Whatever its location, Blackstone House was a much grander house than any she had ever seen before.

Shoreley Hall was a rambling red-bricked house that had been erected for the first Earl of Westbourne in the sixteenth century. It had been built upon haphazardly by succeeding earls until it now resembled nothing more than a rambling monstrosity surrounded by several thousand acres of rich farmland.

In contrast, Dominic Vaughn's home was of a mellow cream colour, four storeys high, with gardens all around covered in an abundance of brightly coloured spring flowers, the whole surrounded by a high black wrought-iron fence.

'Caro?'

She had been so intent on the beauty of Blackstone

House, so in awe of its grandeur, that she had not noticed that one of the grooms had opened the door and folded down the steps, and was now waiting for her to alight. 'Thank you.' She accepted the aid of the young man's hand as she stepped down on to the pavement, Dominic's obvious wealth making her more than ever aware of her own drab and unfashionable appearance.

Vanity, her sister Diana would have called it. And she would have been right. But that did not make Caro feel it any less!

Again, she was allowed no more time for protest as Dominic took a firm hold of her arm to pull her along beside him as he ascended the steps up to the front of the house. The door opened before they reached the top step—despite it being barely past dawn—by a footman in full livery. If he was in the least surprised to see his employer accompanied by a drably clothed young woman he introduced as his cousin, Mrs Morton, then the man did not show it.

The inside of Blackstone House was even grander than the outside, if that were possible—the floor of the entrance hall a beautiful mottled green-and-cream marble, with four alabaster pillars either side leading to the wide staircase and up to a gallery that surrounded the whole of the first floor. High above them, suspended from a domed and windowed ceiling, a beautiful crystal chandelier glittered and shone in the sunlight. Caro had every expectation that the rest of Dominic's home would be just as beautiful.

'Would you take Mrs Morton up to the Green Suite, Simpson?' Dominic ignored Caro's awestruck expression as he turned to address the butler who had now appeared in the entrance hall. 'And provide her with whatever refreshment she requires.' He turned away with the obvious intention of passing her into the care of the servants.

'My lord!'

He was frowning slightly as he turned. 'What is it now?'

She nervously ran the tip of her tongue across her lips before answering him. 'I—you recall my trunk will not be arriving until later today...'

Dominic's frown deepened at this further delay. 'I am sure that Simpson will be only too happy to provide you with anything that you require.' He nodded abruptly to the attending butler before turning on his heel and striding down the hallway to where his study was situated at the back of the house.

Dominic needed time in which to think. Time, now that both he and Caro were safely ensconced in Blackstone House, in which to try to make some sense of everything that had occurred during these past few hours.

And unfortunately, he recognised darkly, he was unable to think in the least bit clearly whilst in Caro Morton's company...

It was Caro's indignation at the abruptness of Dominic's departure that helped her through the next few minutes, as she was shown up to a suite of rooms on the first floor, that indignation not in the least mollified by the delightful private sitting room that adjoined the spacious bedchamber. Both rooms were decorated in a warm green and cream—the reason it was named the

Green Suite, no doubt!—with cream furniture in the sitting room and a matching four-poster in the bed-chamber, the latter surrounded by the same beautiful cream-brocade curtains that hung at the huge windows overlooking the front of the house and the square beyond.

Yes, it was all incredibly beautiful, she acknowledged once she had been left alone with warm water in which to wash, and a maid had delivered a pot of fresh tea to revive her flagging spirits. But the beauty of her surroundings did not change the fact that she should not be here.

Running away to London and posing as Caro Morton in order to avoid her guardian's marriage proposal was one thing, but chancing the possibility of ever being found out as Lady Caroline Copeland was something else entirely, and had certainly never entered into any of her hastily made plans.

It was not a part of her plans now, either. Just because Dominic had chosen to bring her here, supposedly for her own protection, did not mean that she had to remain. As such, she would escape at the first opportunity—

'I would seriously advise against it…'

Caro was so surprised to hear the softness of Dominic's voice behind her that she almost dropped the cup she had been nursing in her hands. As it was, some of the hot tea tipped and spilled over her fingers as she turned to find him lounging in the open doorway of the sitting room. 'Advise against what, may I ask?' she demanded crossly even as she placed the cup back in its saucer before inspecting her scalded fingers.

'What have you done now?' The concern could be

heard in the deep timbre of Dominic Vaughn's voice as he threw something down on a chair before striding across the bedchamber towards her.

She turned to glare at him at the same time as she clasped her hands tightly together behind her back. 'What have *I* done? *You* were the one who startled me into spilling my tea!'

'Let me see your hands.' Those silver eyes glowered down at her even as he reached behind her to easily pull her hands apart before bringing them both forward for his minute inspection.

Caro's protest died in her throat as she saw how pale and tiny her hands looked as he cradled them gently in his much larger ones. He was also standing far too close to her, she realised a little breathlessly, the light from the candelabra giving his hair that blue-black sheen as he bent over her so attentively, his strong and handsome face appearing all savagely etched hollows and sharp angles in the candlelight.

'Why are you here, Dominic?'

'Why?' He could no longer remember the reason why as he felt his response to the way she spoke his name so huskily; his chest felt suddenly tight, his arousal stirring, rising, inside his pantaloons. 'It was certainly not with the intention of hurting you,' he murmured ruefully as he lifted her hand to sweep the moistness of his tongue soothingly over that slightly reddened skin, even as he looked up and held her gaze captive.

'I—it was an accident.' Her lips were slightly parted as she breathed shallowly.

'One that would not have happened if I had not

startled you,' he apologised ruefully as he continued to stroke his tongue against her silky soft skin.

The slenderness of her throat moved convulsively. 'I—I believe my hand is feeling better now, my lord.' But she made no effort to release her fingers from either Dominic's hand or the attentions of his lips and tongue.

She tasted…delicious, he recognised achingly as he placed delicate kisses between each individual finger, a combination of lightly scented soap and the natural saltiness of her skin, the trembling of her hand as he held it gently in the palm of his an indication of the pleasure she felt from his caressing attentions.

Dominic's thighs ached now, throbbed, his arousal more engorged and swollen just from the eroticism of kissing Caro's fingers than he had ever known it to be under the ministrations of the most accomplished of courtesans.

She had removed her bonnet and cloak since he'd last seen her, several golden curls having escaped the confinement of the pins designed to keep them in place, those curls shining like the clearest gold in the mellow candlelight. Her eyes had grown dark and misty, her cheeks slightly flushed, the full swell of her lips slightly parted as if waiting to be kissed.

She snatched her hands from his now before stepping back, her eyes wide with alarm. 'I believe we are already agreed that I have no intention of ever becoming your mistress, my lord.'

Dominic drew in several deep and controlling breaths as he acknowledged he had once again fallen under the sensuous spell of this woman. A woman who refused to tell him anything about herself other than her name—and he suspected even that was a fabrication!

He gave a slight shake of his head as he straightened. 'It would appear, Caro, because Butler and Jackson make no effort to hide their admiration of you, that you are under the misapprehension that every man you meet must necessarily be as smitten as they are,' he drawled mockingly.

Caro's cheeks flushed a fiery red at the accusation. 'Of course I am not—'

'Perhaps that is as well.' He looked down the length of his arrogant nose at her with those pale and glittering eyes. 'I assure you, my own jaded tastes require a little more stimulation than the touch of a woman's fingers—moreover, a woman with an eye for fashion that would surely make even a nun weep!' That silver gaze raked over her critically.

Caro had no idea why, but she felt that he was being deliberately harsh with her. Not that this green gown was not as unbecoming as the brown one she had worn the night before, because she knew that it was. But that had been the purpose in buying them, had it not? Besides, Dominic had not seemed to find her gown so awful when he'd made love to her earlier! 'I chose my gowns to suit myself, my lord, and not you,' she said calmly.

'Your choices are deplorable.' His top lip curled. 'I will arrange for a dressmaker to visit you later today. Hopefully she will have some suitable day dresses already made that can easily be altered to fit you, but you will also need to choose some materials for an evening gown or two.' He scowled. 'If I must have you as a guest in my home for the next few days, then I can at least ensure you are a decorative one.'

'I am your unwilling guest, remember?'

Dominic shrugged. 'Your reasons for being here are not important—what is far more pressing is not having the delicacy of my senses constantly offended by your drab appearance, even for the short time you will reside here!' He was being deliberately cruel, he knew. Because he had not cared earlier, or even a few minutes ago, how unbecoming Caro's gown was, or even who she might be; he had only been interested in the alluring curves of the silken body he knew lay beneath that gown.

Those sea-green eyes sparkled up at him angrily now. 'You are offensive, sir!'

He looked completely unaffected by her annoyance. 'If you choose to find the truth offensive, then who am I to argue?' He turned to walk over to the door, coming to a halt halfway across the room as the garment he had thrown on the chair earlier drew his attention. 'In view of your earlier reticence, it occurred to me that you might feel uncomfortable asking Simpson to find you something suitable in which to sleep, and so I brought you this.' He indicated the white robe draped across the chair.

The thought was a kind one, Caro acknowledged— the offhand method of bestowing that kindness was not! Any more than she appreciated having Dominic Vaughn arrange for a dressmaker to call on her here later today. 'I cannot possibly—' She broke off abruptly as she recalled this man's scathing comment earlier when she'd stated what she could and could not allow.

'I am afraid, where my gowns are concerned, that your "delicate senses" will just have to continue to be offended, my lord!'

He eyed her incredulously. 'You are saying you do not care for pretty gowns?'

Of course she liked pretty gowns—did she not secretly long for all the beautiful gowns she had left behind at Shoreley Hall? If only so that she could wear one of them to show Dominic Vaughn how fashionable she really was!

But she did not long for those pretty confections of silk and lace enough to agree to have a dressmaker attend her here—almost as if she really were about to become Dominic's mistress! 'Not at the moment, no,' she said mendaciously, only realising the error of answering so unguardedly as she saw the earl's eyes narrow shrewdly.

'And why is that, Caro?' he prompted slowly. 'Could it be because you believe yourself to be less conspicuous in those shabby gowns?'

She instantly bridled at the description. 'I will have you know that these gowns cost me several crowns.'

'Then it was money obviously wasted,' he drawled, before adding softly, 'I should warn you, Caro, that every attempt you make to hide your true identity from me only makes me more curious to learn exactly what or who it is you are hiding from…'

A shiver of apprehension quivered down her spine. 'You are imagining things, sir!' Her scorn sounded flat—and patently untrue—even to her own ears.

'We shall see,' Dominic said as he continued his

stroll to the doorway before looking back at her briefly. 'I trust you will bear in mind what I said to you earlier?'

She gave a weary sigh, as tired now as he had claimed to be earlier. 'You have said so many things to me tonight—to which nugget of wisdom do you refer?'

'I also seem to recall we have said a great many things to each other—and most of them impolite.' The earl's mouth twitched ruefully. 'But the advice I am referring to now is not to attempt to leave here without my knowledge. As I have said, it is not my wish to alarm you,' he added more gently as she visibly tensed. 'But, until I know more about the events of this evening, I cannot stress strongly enough your need for caution.'

Her throat moved convulsively as she swallowed. 'Truly?'

'Truly,' he echoed grimly.

Caro could only stand numbed and silent as Dominic closed the door softly behind him as he left, the walls of the bedchamber instantly seeming to bear down on her, making her their captive.

No—making her Lord Dominic Vaughn's unwilling captive...

Chapter Six

Caro awoke refreshed, a smile curving her lips as she felt the sun shining upon her face while she lay snuggled beneath the warmth of the bedclothes. That smile swiftly faded as she remembered exactly where she was. Or, more exactly, who owned the bed she had been asleep in. That arrogant, silver-eyed devil Lord Dominic Vaughn, Earl of Blackstone!

Her eyes opened wide and she looked about her in alarm as she tried to gauge what time of day it was. The sun had not been shining in the bedchamber when she'd finally drifted off to sleep earlier, and now it completely lit up and warmed the room, meaning that she must have slept for several hours, at least.

Sleeping during the day had seemed decadent to her a week ago, but she had quickly learned that it was impossible for her to do anything else when the gambling club did not open until—

No, Nick's would now not be opening at all for several days, according to Dominic, which meant she could not work there in the evenings, either. She had enough money for the moment, courtesy of Drew Butler having paid her when she'd arrived for work the previous evening. But how was she supposed to fill her time now, incarcerated at Blackstone House for several days at least?

Caro had always disliked the usual pursuits expected of women of her class; her embroidery work was nondescript, and she had no talent for drawing or painting. She rode well, but doubted she would enjoy the sedateness of riding in the London parks. Perhaps Dominic had a decent library she might explore? She had always liked to read—

What was she doing? she wondered with disgust; as she had realised earlier this morning, she was not to be a guest here, but held virtually as a prisoner, albeit in a gilded cage, until Dominic Vaughn deemed it was safe for her to leave.

She threw the bedclothes back restlessly and swung her legs to the floor before standing up, only to become instantly aware of the garment the earl had provided for her to sleep in. White in colour, and reaching almost down to her knees, with buttons from the middle of her chest to throat and at the cuffs of the long sleeves, the garment could only be one of Dominic's own silk evening shirts.

A sensuously soft and totally decadent gentleman's white silk evening shirt. A garment that, once it had slid softly over Caro's nakedness, had evoked just as sensuous and decadent thoughts of the gentleman it belonged to...

Caro dropped down upon the side of the bed as she

recalled the wickedness of her thoughts before she had drifted off to sleep. Of how those memories, of Dominic's lips and tongue upon her bared breasts earlier, had once again made her breasts swell and the strawberry tips to become hard and engorged, evoking a warm rush of moisture between her thighs that had sent delightful rivulets of pleasure coursing through her when she'd clenched them tightly together. She—

'You're awake at last, madam.' A young maid had tilted her head around the slightly opened door, but she pushed that door completely open now before disappearing back into the hallway for several seconds.

Long enough, thankfully, for Caro to climb quickly back beneath the bedclothes and pull them up to her chin before the maid reappeared carrying a silver tray she dearly hoped had some tea and toast upon it; she had not eaten for some time and just the thought of food caused her stomach to give an unladylike growl. She grimaced self-consciously as the smiling maid bustled about opening up the small legs beneath the tray before placing the whole across Caro's thighs above the bedclothes.

Not only was there tea and toast, Caro realised greedily, but two perfectly poached eggs and several slices of sweet-smelling ham. 'This looks delicious.'

'I'm sure it will be, madam.' The young girl bobbed a curtsy. 'His lordship surely has the best cook in London.'

Unfortunately Caro's appetite had suddenly deserted her. The maid's continual use of the title 'madam' was a timely reminder that she was supposed to be Dominic Vaughn's poor and widowed cousin, a deception that did not please her at all. She didn't want to be connected to Dominic in any way, even in a falsehood!

'Eat up, madam,' the maid encouraged brightly as she hovered beside the bed. 'The dressmaker has been waiting downstairs for quite some time already.'

The dressmaker Caro had told the earl she did not require. She should have known that the arrogant man would completely disregard her instruction. Just as she fully intended to disregard his!

She smiled up at the maid. 'What is your name, dear?'

'Mabel, ma'am.'

Caro nodded. 'Then, Mabel, could you please go downstairs and inform the dressmaker that there has been a mistake—'

'No mistake has been made, Caro,' Dominic drawled as he strolled uninvited into the bedchamber, crossing the room on booted feet until he stood beside the bed looking down mockingly at a red-faced Caro. That silver gaze raked over her mercilessly before he turned to the blushing young maid. 'That will be all, thank you.'

'My lord. Madam.' The young girl bobbed a curtsy to them both before hurrying from the room.

Caro wished that she might escape with her, but instead she once again found herself the focus of those chilling silver eyes as the earl stood tall and dominating beside the bed. And looking far too handsome, she thought resentfully, in buff-coloured pantaloons above black Hessians, a severe black superfine stretching the width of those wide shoulders, with a grey waistcoat and snowy white shirt beneath.

No doubt a white silk shirt similar to the one that she now wore as a nightgown!

'Impoverished widowed cousin or not, I do not believe that entitles you to enter my bedchamber uninvited, my lord,' Caro hissed when she at last managed to regain her breath.

Dominic could not help but admire how beautiful Caro looked with her golden curls loose upon the pillows and the pertness of her breasts covered only by the white silk of one of his own dress shirts, the nipples standing firm and rosy beneath the sheer material.

His jaw clenched now as he once again resisted the urge to push that material aside and feast himself on those firm and tempting buds. 'Eat up, Caro; the dressmaker does not have all day to waste while you laze about in your bed.'

Her cheeks coloured with temper. 'I distinctly remember telling you that I did not require the services of a dressmaker.'

'And I distinctly recall telling you that I refuse to see you dressed in one of those drab gowns a moment longer.' Dominic bent calmly to pluck a slice of ham from the plate upon the laden tray after making this announcement.

Caro found her gaze suddenly riveted upon his finely sculptured lips and the white evenness of his teeth, as he took a bite of the delicious-smelling ham, unsure if the moisture that suddenly flooded her mouth was caused by that mouthwatering ham or the unexpected sensuality of watching Dominic eat...

Those lips and teeth had been upon her breasts only

hours ago, the tongue he now used to lick his lips having swirled a delicious pattern of pleasure on her flesh.

She wrenched her gaze away from the earl's dangerously handsome face as the contents of the tray placed across her thighs rattled in rhythm with her trembling awareness. 'I fear I am no longer hungry.' Her fingers curled about the handles of the tray as she attempted to remove it.

'Careful!' Dominic Vaughn took the tray from her shaking fingers to lift it and place it on the dressing-table before turning back to face her, the sunlight shining in through the window once again giving his hair the blue-black appearance of a raven's wing as that silver gaze narrowed on her critically. 'Speaking as a man who prefers a little more meat on the bones of the women he beds, I do believe you need to eat more,' he finally drawled.

Her chin rose challengingly. 'Speaking as a woman who has no interest in your preferences regarding "the women you bed", I prefer to remain exactly as I am, thank you very much!'

Dominic gave an appreciative grin; Caro had obviously lost none of her feistiness in the hours since he last saw her.

They had been busy hours for him, as he first set some of his associates from the army ranks, now civilians, the task of investigating Nicholas Brown's dealings over the past few days, before dispensing with his own household and estate business, and then returning to Nathaniel's home to see how his friend fared. Dominic's mouth tightened grimly as he thought of the other man's discomfort and obvious pain.

'Before you dismiss the dressmaker so arbitrarily, I believe you should be made aware that when your things were brought from your lodgings earlier, I instantly instructed one of the maids to consign all of the gowns inside into the incinerator,' he announced with satisfaction.

Caro gasped. '*All* of them?'

'All.'

Her startled gaze moved to the chair where she had placed her green gown earlier, only to find that chair now empty apart from her underclothes. And if the earl had indeed sent all her other gowns to be burned, then he must have included the three fashionable gowns Caro had brought to London with her two weeks ago. She turned back to him accusingly. 'You had no right to touch my things!'

'You were refusing to replace them.' Dominic gave an unapologetic shrug. 'It seemed easier to leave you with no choice in the matter rather than continue to argue the point.'

Her eyes sparkled indignantly. 'And I suppose I am now expected to go down to the seamstress dressed only in my shift?'

It was a pleasant thought, if an impractical one, Dominic accepted. 'She will come up here to you, of course. With, I might add, two gowns at least that you should be able to wear immediately.' He had personally instructed the dressmaker to bring a gown of sea-green and another of deep rose, the one reminding him of Caro's eyes, the other the tips of her breasts when they were aroused.

'Have you received word on how Lord Thorne fares?'

Dominic's thoughts of the anticipated changes to Caro's appearance completely dissipated at this reminder of the attack on one of his two closest friends. Not that he would ever forget that first moment of seeing Osbourne covered in blood in the early hours of this morning.

How could he, when it was such a stark reminder of the last memories Dominic had of his mother sixteen years ago?

He moved away from the bed to stand in front of one of the picture windows, his back to the room, his hands clasped tightly together behind his back as he fought back those memories. Memories that had returned all too vividly after Caro had questioned him concerning his family…

He breathed in deeply before answering. 'I have done better than that; I have been to see him.' He went on to explain that Nathaniel's aunt, Mrs Gertrude Wilson, having learnt that her nephew had suffered injuries and was confined to his bed, had wasted no time in having her own physician visit him, and fully intended removing Osbourne to her own home in St James's Square later this afternoon. An occurrence that aided Dominic's determination to ensure the future protection of his friend.

Dominic hoped to have some news later today concerning the enquiries into last night's attack, but if those enquiries should prove unhelpful, then he had plans of his own for later this evening that may give him some of the answers, if not all of them.

'And?' Caro prompted with concern as Dominic fell broodingly silent.

'And the physician has discovered he has two cracked ribs to go with his many cuts and bruises.'

Caro knew by the harshness of the Dominic's tone that he was far from happy at this news of his friend's condition. 'I am sure that he will recover fully, my lord.'

He did not look in the least comforted by her reassurances. 'Are you?'

'He is otherwise young and healthy,' Caro nodded. 'Now if—if you would not mind, I should like to get out of bed now.' She had not had time to deal with her morning ablutions before her bedchamber was invaded, first by the maid, and then Dominic Vaughn, and that need was becoming more pressing by the moment.

He raised dark brows. 'I was not aware I was preventing you from doing so?'

'You know very well that your very presence here is preventing me from getting out of bed.'

He gave a disbelieving laugh. 'You have flaunted yourself in a gambling club for this past week, in front of dozens of men, but now take exception to my seeing you clothed in one of my own shirts?'

Caro gave a pained frown. 'The gown I wore at those performances covered me from neck to toe.'

'And titillated and aroused the interest of your audience all the more because of it!'

Had it titillated and aroused this man's interest? she wondered breathlessly. Obviously something had, if his passion earlier this morning was any indication. A passion she had responded to in a way that still made her blush. 'Then it would seem the sooner I am clothed in one of my new gowns, the better it will be for everyone.'

His gorgeous mouth curved into a pleased smile.

'You are sufficiently recovered from your previous outrage to now accept the new gowns?'

Caro bristled. 'I believe it is more a case of having little choice in the matter when you have had all of my own gowns burned. I should become a prisoner of this bedchamber rather than just the house if I did not accept the new gowns, would I not?'

He winced. 'You are not to be a prisoner here, Caro, only to take the precaution of being accompanied if you should decide to go about.'

'I do not even know where "here" is!' she snapped caustically.

'Blackstone House is in Mayfair,' he elaborated. 'And as soon as you are dressed, and the seamstress has gone about her business, I will be only too happy to take you out for a drive in my carriage.'

'Accompanied by the maid I do not have?' she came back derisively.

'We are believed to be cousins, Caro,' he reminded her drily. 'Making such a fuss about the proprieties would be a nonsense.'

'In that case, if you would send the dressmaker up to me now I should very much like to go out for a drive.'

Her tone, Dominic noted ruefully, was almost as imperious as Osbourne's Aunt Gertrude's. Further evidence, if he should need it, that Caro Morton was a woman used to instructing her own servants and having those instructions obeyed. Because she was, in fact, a lady of quality?

He crossed the room to once again stand beside the bed. 'Have you considered the possibility, Caro, that I might be more…amenable, if you did not constantly challenge me?'

'I have considered it, my lord—and as quickly dismissed it.' Her expression was defiant as she glanced up at him. 'It goes completely against my nature, you see.'

Dominic could not prevent his throaty chuckle as he looked down at her admiringly. No, he never found himself bored in Caro's company, even when he was not making love to her! 'I will arrange for the carriage to be brought round in an hour's time.' He gave her a brief bow before taking his leave.

Caro did not move for several minutes after he had left the bedchamber, still slightly breathless from the transformation that had overcome his austere features when he laughed. Those silver eyes had glowed warmly, with laughter lines fanning out at their sides, the curve of those sculptured lips revealing the white evenness of his teeth. Even that savage scar upon his cheek had softened. The whole rendered him so devastatingly handsome that just looking at him had stolen her breath away…

'Relax, Caro,' Dominic drawled softly as she sat tensely beside him as he controlled the reins of his curricle, his two favourite greys stepping out lively in the sun-dappled park. 'By this time tomorrow, all of society will be agog to know who was the beautiful young lady riding in the park with Blackstone in his curricle.' And she looked every inch a lady of quality in her rose-coloured gown and matching bonnet, with several golden curls framing the delicate beauty of her face, and her hands covered in pale cream gloves.

'How disappointed they will be when they learn it is only your impoverished and widowed cousin up from the country,' she came back tartly. 'And the last thing I desire is to become the talk of London society,' she added with a delicate shudder.

It was rather late for that, when to Dominic's certain knowledge the male members of the *ton*, at least, had been avidly discussing the masked woman who had sung at Nick's for the past week! Not that any of those men would recognise the blonde woman sitting so demurely beside him in his curricle as the same masked and ebony-haired siren who had entertained them so prettily at Nick's; several of those gentlemen had already greeted Dominic as they passed in their own carriages, with no hint of recognition in their gazes as they'd glanced admiringly at the golden-haired beauty at his side.

'A beautiful woman, impoverished or otherwise, is always a source of gossip amongst the members of the *ton*,' he said.

Caro glanced at him beneath long golden lashes, noting how easily he kept the two feisty greys to a demure trot as he drove his elegant curricle through the park. She had also noted the admiring glances sent his way by all of the ladies in the passing carriages, before those covetous glances had shifted coldly on to Caro, no doubt due to the fact she was the one sitting beside the eligible Earl of Blackstone in his carriage.

Wearing a beautiful gown, and being driven through a London park in a fashionable carriage, with a wickedly handsome man at her side, had long been one of Caro's dreams. But in those girlish dreams the man had been totally besotted with her, something she knew Dominic would never be with regard to her.

Admittedly, the circumstances under which they had first met had been less than ideal, but if Lady Caroline Copeland and Lord Dominic Vaughn, Earl of Blackstone, had met in a fashionable London drawing room, he would certainly have behaved more circumspectly towards her.

Except she was not, at this moment, Lady Caroline Copeland, and the earl's casualness of manner towards her was reflective of that fact. 'I believe I would like to return to Blackstone House now, if you please,' she said stiffly.

Dominic glanced down at Caro, frowning slightly as he saw the way her lashes were uncharacteristically cast down. 'There is a blanket beside you if you are becoming chilled?'

'I am not in the least chilled; I would just prefer to leave now.' Her voice was huskily soft, but determined.

Dominic transferred both reins to his right hand before reaching down with his left to lift Caro's chin so that he might look into her face. Far from invigorating her, she seemed to have grown paler during the drive, and, unless he was mistaken, the glitter in her eyes was not due to her usual rebellion. 'Are you about to cry?' His voice sounded as incredulous as he felt.

'Certainly not!' She wrenched her chin out of his grasp and turned away. 'I merely wish to return home, that is all. To Blackstone House, I meant, of course,' she added awkwardly.

Dominic had known exactly what Caro meant. Strange, in all the years he had been the Earl of Blackstone, he had never particularly regarded any of his houses or estates as being his home—how could he, when all of them were a reminder of the parents who had both died when he was but twelve years old?

Or how, along with those memories, came the nightmare reminder of the part he had played in their deaths! Memories that were usually kept firmly at bay, but had haunted him this past few hours...

'Of course.' Dominic gave a curt nod before turning the greys in front of the curricle back towards Blackstone House. 'Perhaps you should go to your bedchamber and rest before dinner?'

'I am simply grown bored of driving in the park, Dominic; I am not decrepit!'

He gave an appreciative smile as Caro answered with some of her usual spirit, all trace of what he had thought were tears having disappeared as she glared up at him. 'I assure you, Caro, I would not have brought you out driving with me at all if I thought you decrepit.'

'Is that because only women you consider beautiful are allowed in your curricle?' she asked, regarding him with a scornful purse to her mouth.

Dominic dearly wished to kiss that expression from her lips. Damn it, he had wanted nothing more than to kiss her again since she had appeared downstairs earlier looking breathtakingly beautiful in the rose-coloured gown and bonnet!

'No woman, beautiful or otherwise, has ever been invited to accompany me to the park in my curricle before today,' he admitted after a moment of silence.

She eyed him curiously. 'Should I feel flattered?'

'Do you?' Dominic asked.

'Not in the least,' she said with a return of her usual waspishness. 'No doubt, as far as the gentlemen of the *ton* are concerned at least, it will only add to your considerable reputation if you are believed to have the ebony-haired masked lady from Nick's in your bed at night, and a golden-haired lady in your curricle by day.'

Dominic gave her a mocking glance. 'No doubt,' he agreed.

Caro's eyes flashed deeply green. 'You—Dominic, there is a dog about to run in front of the carriage!' She reached out to grasp his forearm, half-rising in her seat as the fluffy white creature ran directly in front of the hooves of the now-prancing greys, quickly followed by a young girl in a straw bonnet who seemed to have the same disregard for her own welfare as the dog as she narrowly avoided being trampled under the hoofs of the rearing horses before following the animal across the pathway, and on to the grass, and then running into the woodland in hot pursuit without so much as a glance at the occupants of the carriage.

It took Dominic several minutes to bring the startled greys back under his control, by which time the dog and the girl had both completely disappeared, leaving Caro with the startled impression that the young girl in the straw bonnet had looked remarkably like her younger sister, Elizabeth!

Chapter Seven

'Bring brandy into the library, would you, Simpson?'
Dominic instructed the butler as he kept a firm hold of
Caro's arm, unsure as to whether or not she might faint
away at his feet if he did not.

Admittedly, the near-miss in the park had been of
concern for several seconds, but even so he had been
surprised to see Caro so white and shaking after the
event. Damn it, she was *still* white and shaking!

His hand tightened on her arm. 'At once, if you
please,' he said to the butler briskly before taking Caro
into the library and closing the door against curious
eyes. He led her gently across the room and saw her
seated in the chair beside the fireplace.

Ordinarily, he would have been impatient with a
woman's display of nerves. But having already witnessed Caro's fortitude several times—when faced with
the ribaldry of three young bucks, in the midst of a
brawl, and then again when Osbourne had received a
beating by those four thugs—Dominic could only feel

concern that a minor incident, such as the one that had happened in the park just now, should have reduced her to this trembling state.

He moved down on to his haunches beside the chair in which she now sat, before placing one of his hands on top of her clasped and trembling ones. 'No harm was done, Caro. In fact,' he continued drily, 'I believe that young girl to be completely unaware of the near-accident that she caused.'

The young girl who had reminded Caro so much of her younger sister, Elizabeth…

For it could not really have been Elizabeth, could it? No, the young and ebony-haired girl in the blue gown and spring bonnet could not possibly have been Elizabeth, only someone who looked a little like her—because Elizabeth was safely ensconced at Shoreley Hall with their sister, Diana.

Caro had been reminding herself of that fact for the ten minutes or so that it had taken Dominic to drive the curricle back to Blackstone House—all the while shooting her frowning glances from those silver-coloured eyes, at what he obviously viewed to be her overreaction to the near-accident.

An assumption she dared not refute, for fear he would then demand an explanation as to what had really upset her.

She pulled both her hands from beneath his much larger, enveloping one. 'Do not fuss, Dominic. I assure you I am now perfectly recovered!'

Dominic straightened to step away and lean his arm casually upon the top of the mantel as he looked down at her; this caustic Caro was much more like the one he had come to know these past two days. 'I am glad to hear it.' He gave a mocking inclination of his head, giving away none, he hoped, of his own disturbed emotions with regard to the near-accident.

It was difficult, nearly impossible after all that had already happened this past twelve hours, for the incident not to have once again reminded Dominic of the carriage accident that had killed his mother sixteen years ago, and resulted in the death of his father, too, only days later. Especially when Caro had obviously been rendered so upset by it all.

'Ah, thank you, Simpson.' He turned to the butler as he entered to place the tray containing the brandy decanter and glasses down upon the table in the centre of the room.

'I trust Mrs Morton is feeling better, my lord?' The remark was addressed to Dominic, but the elderly man's gaze lingered in concern on Caro as she sat so white and still beside the fire.

She turned now to bestow a gracious smile upon the older man. 'I am quite well now, thank you, Simpson.' She continued to smile warmly as she removed her bonnet.

Dominic listened incredulously to the exchange— when, by all that was holy, had Caro managed to beguile his butler? An elderly man who was usually so stiffly correct he was in danger of cutting himself from the starch in his collar. 'That will be all, Simpson,' he dismissed the servant curtly.

Caro waited until the two of them were alone before speaking. 'I believe, Dominic, that you might find your servants were happier in their work if you were to treat them with a little more politeness.'

Brought to task by this little baggage, by damn! 'And what, pray, would *you* know about servants' happiness in their work?' Dominic decided to attack rather than defend, and was instantly rewarded with the flush that coloured her cheeks. 'Unless, of course, you were once a servant yourself?'

Her chin rose. 'And if I were?'

Then Dominic would be surprised. *Very* surprised! 'I will know the story of your past one day, Caro,' he warned softly as he moved to pour brandy into two glasses.

She eyed him coolly. 'I doubt you would find it at all interesting, my lord.'

He moved to hand her one of the bulbous glasses. 'Oh, I believe that I might…'

Rather than answer him, Caro took a sip of her brandy, her eyes widening as the fiery alcohol hit the back of her throat and completely took her breath away. 'My goodness…!' she gasped, her eyes watering as the liquid continued to burn a path down to her stomach.

Dominic eyed her with amusement. 'I take it that you have never drunk brandy before?'

She placed the glass carefully down upon the table beside her. 'It is dreadful stuff. Disgusting!'

'I believe it may be something of an acquired taste.' He took another appreciative sip.

Caro gave a delicate shudder, her stomach still feeling as if there were a fire lit inside it. 'It is not one I ever intend to acquire, I assure you.'

'I am glad to hear it,' he smiled. 'There is nothing so unattractive to a man as an inebriated woman.'

Caro wrinkled her nose delicately. 'Really? In what way?'

'Never mind. Would you care for some tea, instead?'

'That will not be necessary—oh. Do you play?' Caro had taken the time to glance about the comfortable library as the two of them talked, spotting the chess pieces set up on the table beside the window.

Dominic followed her line of vision. 'Do you?'

'A little,' she answered noncommittally.

His brows rose. 'Really?'

'You do not sound as if you believe me?' Her eyes sparkled with challenge.

He shrugged. 'In my experience, women do not usually play chess.'

'Then I must be an unusual woman, because I believe I play rather well.'

Dominic didn't doubt she was an unusual woman; she had been the source of one surprise after another since he had first met her.

'Would you care for a game before dinner?' she challenged lightly.

He grimaced. 'I think not. I was taught by a grand master,' he explained as Caro looked up at him enquiringly.

As the undisputed chess champion in her family and that included her father, she felt no hesitation in pitting her own considerable ability against Dominic Vaughn's or anyone else's. She was certainly a good enough player that she would not embarrass herself.

She stood up to cross over to the chess-table. The

pieces appeared to have been smoothly carved out of black-and-white marble, the table inlaid with a board of that same beautiful marble. She glanced back to where Dominic still stood beside the fireplace. 'Surely you cannot be refusing to play against me simply because I am a woman?'

'Not at all,' Dominic drawled. 'I simply prefer to play against an opponent I consider to be my equal in the game.'

Her eyes widened. 'How do you know I am not until we have played together?'

He quirked a brow. 'A game in the nursery with your nanny does not equip you to play a champion.'

Caro bristled. 'You are being presumptuous, sir!'

'Concerning your game or the nanny?'

'Both!' Caro was all too well aware how determined Dominic was to learn more of her past. 'But being a gentleman of the *ton*, perhaps you would find it more of a challenge if I were to propose a wager?'

He eyed her guardedly. 'What sort of wager?'

'Are you any further forwards in your enquiries concerning the attack upon Lord Thorne?'

Dominic's expression became even more cautious. 'I am hoping to receive news on the subject later today.'

'But you are not sure?' she pressed.

Dominic's mouth tightened. 'At this precise moment, no.'

Caro nodded briskly. 'In that case, if I win, I would like for you to find me other accommodation sooner rather than later.'

Those silver eyes narrowed. 'Why?'

'I do not have to state a reason, my lord, merely name a forfeit,' she pointed out primly. 'And if you win—'

'Should I not be allowed to choose your own forfeit for myself?' Dominic interjected softly, those silver eyes glittering in challenge.

She drew in a deep breath, not at all sure she had not ventured beyond her depth, after all; Dominic seemed utterly convinced that he would win any game of chess between them. But she could not back down now; she owed it to other females who played chess to defend their reputation against such obvious male bigotry! Besides which, she dearly wished to escape Blackstone House. And the disturbing Lord Dominic Vaughn... 'Name your forfeit, my lord.'

'Dominic.'

Her eyes widened. 'That is your forfeit?'

'That is only an aside request, Caro, and not the actual forfeit,' he said. 'I am sure you will not find it too difficult to do; you seem to have no trouble at all in calling me Dominic before launching yourself into my arms!' Those silver-coloured eyes openly laughed at her now beneath long dark lashes.

Caro's cheeks burned, not at all sure which occasion he was referring to—there had been so many, it seemed! 'Very well, name my forfeit...Dominic.'

He seemed to give the matter some thought. 'You will reveal something of your true self to me, perhaps?'

Caro looked at him warily. She knew of her own ability in playing the game of chess, but Dominic's self-confidence could not be overlooked, either; he was so obviously sure of his ability that he had not even attempted to dispute the forfeit she would demand of him if she were the victor. To agree to tell him something of her true self was not something she had ever intended doing, either now or in the future. But then, neither did she intend allowing him to win this game of chess… 'Very well, I agree.' She gave a haughty inclination of her head.

Dominic lounged back in his chair, his expression one of boredom as the game began, sure that he was wasting both his own time and hers by playing at all.

After only a few more moves in the game he knew that victory was not going to be so easily won. Caro's opening gambit had been an unusual one, and one Dominic had put down to her lack of experience in the game, but as he now studied the pieces on the board he saw that if the game continued on its current path, then she would have him in check for the first time in only three more moves.

'Very good,' he murmured appreciatively as he moved his king out of danger.

Caro could see that, instead of continuing to lounge back uninterestedly, she now had all of Dominic's attention. 'Perhaps we might play in earnest now?' Her heart did a strange leap as he looked up to smile across the table at her. A warm and genuine smile that owed nothing to his usual expression of mockery or disdain, and instead leant a boyish charm to the usual severe austerity of his face.

'I am looking forward to it, Caro,' he replied, his attention now fully on the chessboard.

The maid, Mabel, had come in and attended to the fire, and Simpson had arrived to light several candles whilst the game continued, but neither opponent had even been aware of their presence as they concentrated completely on the chessboard between them.

It had become more than a game of chess to Caro; it had come to represent the inequality of the relationship that currently existed between the two of them. An equality that would not have existed between Lord Dominic Vaughn and Lady Caroline Copeland, but which most definitely existed between Lord Dominic Vaughn and Caro Morton. As such, it had become more than a battle of wills to Caro, and she played like a fiend in her determination not to be beaten.

Something that Dominic was well aware of as he studied her flushed and determined face between narrowed lids. Her eyes were more green than blue in their intensity, and the flush added colour to her otherwise porcelain white cheeks and down across the full swell of her breasts. Those rosy tips were no doubt deeper in colour, too, and were perhaps swollen and begging for the feel of his—

'Check!' Caro announced with barely concealed excitement.

Dominic's attention was reluctant to return to the board rather than considering the taste of Caro's breasts. He moved his own piece out of danger.

Irritation creased Caro's brow before clearing again as she made another move. 'Check.'

Dominic studied the board intently for several seconds. 'I believe that we will only continue in this vein *ad nauseam*, and that this game, therefore, must be declared a draw.'

She eyed him mockingly. 'Unless you were to concede?'

'Or you were?'

She sat back in her chair. 'I think not.'

'Then we will call it a draw.' Dominic said. 'And hope that one of us will be the victor on the morrow.'

'We could play again now—'

'It is time for dinner, Caro,' he murmured after a glance at the clock on the mantel, surprised to learn that a full two hours had passed since they had began to play. Surprised, also, at how much he had enjoyed those two hours.

Caro did not talk as she played, but neither was the silence awkward or uncomfortable. More, despite the fact they were in opposition to one another, it had been a companionable and enjoyable silence. And he, Dominic, decided as the realisation caused him to rise abruptly to his feet, was not a man to be domesticated to his fireside by any woman. Least of all a woman who steadfastly refused to reveal anything of her true self to him!

'Does this mean that we both concede our forfeit or that neither of us does?' she asked.

Dominic's eyes narrowed as he glanced back to where Caro had now risen gracefully from the table. 'Stalemate would seem to imply that neither of us do,' he replied. 'As we are so late I suggest that neither of us bothers to change before dinner.'

'Oh, good.' She gracefully crossed the room on slippered feet as she confided, 'I am so ravenously hungry.'

Dominic found himself laughing despite his earlier uncomfortable thoughts concerning domesticity. 'Has no one ever told you that ladies are supposed to have the appetite and delicacy of a sparrow?' he drawled.

'If they did, then I have forgotten,' Caro retorted as

they strolled through the hallway and into the small candlelit dining room together, another fire alight in the hearth there to warm the room.

'I take it you are now, out of pure contrariness, about to show that you have the appetite and delicacy of an eagle.' Dominic pulled her chair back, lingering behind her a few seconds longer than was strictly necessary as he enjoyed the floral perfume of her hair.

Caro, in the act of draping her napkin across her knee, paused to give the matter some thought before answering. As far as she was aware, she had eaten nothing so far today. 'Perhaps a raven.' Not a good comparison, she realised with an inner wince, when the colour of Dominic's hair reminded her of a raven's wing...

Dominic was chuckling softly as he took his seat opposite hers at the small round table. Not so intimate that their knees actually touched beneath it, but certainly enough to create an atmosphere Caro could have wished did not exist.

She ignored Dominic to smile at Simpson as he entered the room with a soup tureen and began to serve their first course. It was a delicious watercress soup that Caro enjoyed so much that the butler served her a second helping.

'As I said, an eagle...' Dominic muttered so that only she could hear, wincing slightly, but not uttering a sound, as she kicked him on the shin beneath the table with one slipper-covered foot; no doubt it had hurt her more than it had hurt him!

He inwardly approved of the fact that she made no effort to hide her appetite; he had spent far too many evenings with women who picked at their food, and in doing so totally ruined his own appetite. In contrast to those other women, Caro ate just as heartily of the fish course, and her roast beef and vegetables, all followed by some chocolate confection that she ate with even more relish than the previous courses.

So much so that Dominic found himself watching her rather than attempting to eat his own dessert. 'Perhaps you would care to eat mine, too?' He pushed the untouched glass bowl towards her.

Her eyes lit up, before she gave a reluctant shake of her head. 'I really should not...'

'I believe it is a little late for a show of maidenly delicacy,' Dominic teased as he placed the bowl in front of her before standing up to pour himself a glass of the brandy Caro had so obviously disliked earlier. He sat down again to study her as he swirled the brandy round in the glass, easily noting the colour in her cheeks. 'I was commenting on the subject of food, of course...'

That colour deepened. 'If you are going to start being ungentlemanly again—'

'I was not aware that in your eyes I had ever stopped?' Dominic said, raising dark, mocking brows.

Perhaps not, Caro conceded, but there had been something of a ceasefire during and since their game of chess. In fact, she had believed she had even seen a grudging respect in those silver-coloured eyes when the game had ended in a draw. 'What shall we do with the rest of the evening?' She opted for a safer subject.

'I, my dear Caro, am going out—'

'Out?' She frowned after a glance at the gold clock on the mantel. 'But it is almost eleven o'clock.'

He gave an inclination of his head. 'And if Nick's

were open, you would still have a second performance of the evening to get through.'

True. But having spent most of the day sleeping, Caro was not ready to retire to her bedchamber just yet. 'Are you going to see Lord Thorne? If so, perhaps I might come with you?'

'No, on both counts, Caro,' Dominic said; engrossed as he had been in their game of chess, and much as he had enjoyed his dinner, he had nevertheless been continually aware of the fact that the news he had been waiting for concerning Nicholas Brown had not been delivered, leaving him no choice but to now instigate his own plans for the evening. 'I have already visited Osbourne once today, and doubt that a second visit this late in the day would be welcome.' Mrs Gertrude Wilson would most definitely frown upon it! 'And where I am going tonight you definitely cannot follow.'

'Oh.'

Dominic quirked one eyebrow as he saw how flushed Caro's cheeks had become. 'Oh?'

Caro frowned her irritation, with her own naïvety as much as with Dominic Vaughn. Just because he kissed her whenever the mood took him did not mean that he did not have a woman he occasionally spent the night with. That he was not going out in a few minutes to spend the rest of the night in bed with such a woman!

Strange how much even the idea of that should seem so distasteful to her…

She had, Caro realised in dismay, enjoyed Dominic's company this evening. The verbal exchanges. The challenge of trying to best him at chess. Even the teasing in regard to her appetite. She now found it more than unpleasant to be made aware of the possibility he might be spending the rest of the night in bed with some faceless woman.

Which was utterly ridiculous!

She stood up abruptly. 'In that case, with your permission, I believe I will go back into the library and choose a book to read.'

It wasn't too difficult for Dominic to guess what Caro's thoughts had been during these last few minutes of silence: that she imagined it was his intention to spend the night in some willing woman's bed. Much as the idea appealed—it had been some time since Dominic had bedded a woman; those few unsatisfactory forays with Caro did not count when they had left him feeling more physically frustrated than ever—it did not actually enter into his plans for the rest of the night.

No, Dominic's immediate destination had absolutely nothing to do with bedding a woman and more to do with personally paying a visit to Nicholas Brown... 'Do not bother to wait up for me, Caro. I expect to be very late,' he said after he emptied the last of the brandy before placing the glass down upon the table.

Her cheeks were flushed with temper. 'As if I have any interest in what time it will be when—or even if— you should return!'

Dominic chuckled softly as he strolled over to the door. 'Sweet dreams, Caro.'

'As long as they are not of you then I am sure they will be!' she snapped.

He paused in the doorway to glance back at her. 'I very much doubt that I shall ever have the dubious pleasure of featuring in any young girl's dreams,' he said drily before closing the door softly behind him.

Dominic could not be sure, but he thought he might have heard the tinkling sound of glass shattering on the other side of that closed door...

Chapter Eight

It was some hours later when Dominic finally returned to Blackstone House, and he could not help smiling slightly as the attentive Simpson opened the door for him as if it were three o'clock in the afternoon rather than the morning.

'Mrs Morton is in the library, my lord,' the butler advised softly.

Dominic came to an abrupt halt halfway across the marble entrance hall and turned back sharply. 'What the devil is she still doing in there?'

The butler turned from locking and bolting the front door. 'I believe she fell asleep whilst reading, my lord. She looked so peaceful, I did not like to wake her.'

Dominic felt no such qualms as he glanced in the direction of the library, his expression grim. 'Get yourself to bed, man. I will deal with Mrs Morton.'

'Very good, my lord.' The elderly man gave a stiff bow. 'I—I believe that Mrs Morton may have been upset earlier, my lord.' he added as Dominic walked in the direction of the library.

Dominic was slower to turn this time. 'Upset?'

'I believe she was crying, my lord.' Simpson looked pained.

What the hell! The last thing he felt like dealing with tonight was a woman's tears. Or, as was usually the case, having to guess the reason for those tears. Whatever could have happened to reduce the indomitable Caro to tears? Perhaps the danger he had warned her of had become all too real to her once she was left alone for the evening?

Whatever the reason it gave him a distinctly unpleasant sensation in the pit of his stomach to think of Caro alone and upset…

He could see the evidence of her tears on the pallor of her cheeks once he had entered the library and stood looking down at her as she lay curled up asleep in the wing-backed armchair beside the fire, the book she had been reading still lying open upon her knees.

He was also struck by how incredibly young and vulnerable she looked without the light of battle in her eyes and the flush of temper upon her cheeks. So young and vulnerable, in fact, that Dominic questioned how she could ever have survived her first week in London without falling victim to some disaster.

Not that he imagined for one moment that Caro would have succumbed quietly—she did not seem to do anything quietly!—but she wasn't physically strong enough to fight off a male predator, and her youth and lack of a protector would have made her easy prey for the seedy underworld of a city such as this one. As it was, he had no doubt that Caro had Drew Butler's visible protection to thank for her physical well being this past week, at least.

If Dominic had needed any reassurance that he had done the right thing in now placing Caro in his protection, then he had received it this evening when he'd visited Nicholas Brown at his home in Cheapside.

The bastard son of a titled gentleman and some long-forgotten prostitute, Brown, whilst now giving the appearance of wealth, had in fact grown up on the streets of London, and was as hardened and tough as any of the cut-throats that walked those darkened streets. A toughness he had taken advantage of by building himself a lucrative business empire that often catered to the less acceptable excesses of the *ton*; Nick's had been the more respectable of the three gambling clubs the man owned.

Within minutes of Dominic being admitted to Brown's house earlier, the other man had had the unmitigated gall to offer to allow the masked lady to sing at one of his other clubs, until such time as Nick's reopened. An offer Dominic had felt no hesitation in refusing on Caro's behalf!

Looking down at her now as she slept the sleep of the innocent, he could only shudder at the thought of her ever being exposed to the vicious and seedy underbelly of Nicholas Brown's world. At the same time Dominic feared that Brown, with his many spies in the London underworld, might already know that the young woman now staying with him and masquerading as his widowed cousin was that same masked lady...

Brown had not by word or deed revealed whether

or not this was the case, but the fact that the other man had denied hearing any gossip or rumours concerning the perpetrators of yesterday's attack on Nathaniel Thorne, when directly asked by Dominic, was suspicious in itself; Brown was a man privy to all the secrets of the London underworld.

Like the officer and soldier he had once been, Dominic had now only retreated in order to decide how best to deal with the villain.

But first he must see Caro safely delivered to her bed…

Dominic's expression softened as he picked the book up from her knee and placed it on the side table before bending down to scoop her up into his arms. She stirred only slightly before placing her arms about his neck and sighing contentedly as she lay her head down against his shoulder.

For all that she'd had such a hearty appetite earlier, she weighed almost nothing at all, and it was no effort for Dominic to carry her up the wide staircase to her bedchamber, to where the fire was alight, and candles were burning on the dressing table to light the room in readiness for when Caro retired for the night.

Dominic crossed the room to lay her down upon the bedcovers, having every intention of straightening and leaving her there, only to discover that he could not as her arms were still clasped tight about his neck. 'Release me, Caro,' he instructed softly. Her only answer was to tighten that stranglehold to the point that Dominic had to sit down on the side of the bed or risk causing her discomfort.

As he had absolutely no intention of having to remain

in this uncomfortable position for what was left of the night, he had no choice but to wake her. The Lord knew she was going to be indignant enough when she awoke and found he had carried her up to bed, without exacerbating the situation by giving into the temptation Dominic now felt to take off his boots, lie down beside her and then fall asleep with his head resting upon her breasts! 'Wake up, Caro,' he encouraged gruffly.

An irritated frown creased her brow and she wrinkled her nose endearingly before her lids were slowly raised and she looked up at him with sleepy sea-green eyes. 'Dominic?'

He raised mocking brows. 'Were you expecting someone else?'

Caro stilled, knowing by the candle lighting the room and the silence of the house that it must be very late. Which posed the question—what was Dominic doing in her bedchamber? More to the point, how did she come to be in her bedchamber? The last thing she remembered was sitting beside the fire in the library reading a book—

'You fell asleep and I carried you up the stairs to bed,' Dominic answered the puzzle for her.

Even if it did not provide the answer as to what he was still doing here! Or why her fingers were linked at his nape, and in doing so bringing his face down much too close to Caro's own?

She slowly unlinked those fingers, although her arms stayed about his shoulders. 'That was—very kind of you.'

He gave a hard smile. 'I am sure we are both aware that kindness is not a part of my nature.'

Caro could not agree. How could she, when he had saved her time and time again, from dangers she had not even been aware existed when she had left Hampshire to embark on what she had thought would be a wonderful adventure?

And in doing so, had left her two sisters, and everything in life that was familiar to her…

It was a fact that had been brought sharply home to Caro earlier today, when she had seen that young girl in the park who reminded her so much of Elizabeth. It did not matter that it had not actually been her sister; the familiarity, along with the game of chess she and Dominic had played earlier and which had so reminded her of the times she had played the board game with her father, had been enough to incite an aching homesickness once Caro was left alone, for both her home and family.

Dominic frowned as he saw the emotions flickering across her expressive face. 'Simpson seems to believe you have been…upset, whilst I was out this evening?'

That open expression immediately became a frown as she finally drew her arms from about his neck to push the curling tendrils of her hair back from her face. 'If I was, then I assure you, it had absolutely nothing to do with your own absence.'

This was more like the Caro he was used to dealing with! 'With what, then?'

She looked more cross than upset now. 'Does there have to be a reason?'

Where this particular woman was concerned? Yes. Most definitely. Dominic did not believe her to be the type of woman to give in to tears without good reason.

Just as her pride would not allow her to now reveal to him the reason for those tears. 'Perhaps you have found the events of the past few days more disturbing than you had first thought?'

'I believe they would have reduced any woman of sensitivity to tears,' she came back tartly.

And far too quickly for Dominic to be convinced that the excuse he had so conveniently given her was the true reason for Caro's upset. But he could see, by the stubbornness of her expression, that this was the only explanation she was about to give. 'I should leave you now and allow you to prepare for bed,' he rasped.

'You should.' Caro nodded agreement.

Still neither of them moved, Caro lying back against the pillows, Dominic sitting beside her on the bed looking so dark and handsome in the candlelight, the hard and handsome savagery of his face made to appear even more so with that jagged scar upon his cheek.

It was a ragged and uneven scar, as if the skin had been ripped apart. 'How did it happen?' Caro finally gave in to the longing she had felt to lightly touch that scar with her fingertips.

Dominic flinched but did not move away. 'Caro—'

'Tell me, please,' she encouraged huskily.

His mouth tightened. 'It was a French sabre.'

Caro's eyes widened before her gaze returned to the scar. 'It does not have the look of the clean stroke of a sword…'

Dominic gave a dismissive shrug, more than a little unnerved at the gentle touch of her fingertips against his ragged flesh. 'That is because I did not make a good job of it when I sewed the two sides together!'

Her eyes widened. 'You sewed the wound yourself?'

'It was a fierce battle, with many injured, and the physicians were too busy with my seriously wounded and dying men for me to trouble them over a little cut upon my face.'

'But—'

'Caro, it is late— What the—?' Dominic broke off, shocked to his very core, when she sat up to place her lips against the scar on his cheek. 'What on earth do you think you are doing?' He grasped hold of her arms to hold her firmly away from him as he glared down at her.

Caro ignored Dominic's anger and the firm grasp of his fingers upon her arms, too concerned—disturbed— by thoughts of the terrible wound he had suffered and then stitched himself. No doubt completely without the aid of the alcohol that would have numbed the pain but at the same time impaired his judgement. Just the thought of it was enough to make her shudder. 'War is barbaric!'

Dominic gave a ruefully bitter smile. 'So is tyranny.'

Reminding Caro that, although this man now gave every appearance of being a fashionable and dissolute man about town, he had admitted to being a soldier, an officer in charge of men, all of them fighting to keep England safe from the greedy hands of Napoleon.

Her gaze was once again drawn back to the scar upon his cheek. A daily reminder to him, no doubt, of the suffering and hardships of that long and bloody war. 'You were a hero.'

'Do not attempt to romanticise me, Caro!' Dominic stood up abruptly, a nerve pulsing in his tightly clenched jaw as he scowled down at her.

In doing so, he could not help but notice the way her breasts swelled over the top of her gown as she rested back on her elbows. Or how several enticing curls had come loose from their pins and now lay against the bareness of her shoulders. He acknowledged that at this moment his arousal was hard and throbbing, and that he wanted nothing more than to push her back against the pillows before ripping the clothes from her body and taking her with a fierceness that caused his engorged erection to ache and throb anew!

'I am not, nor will I ever be, any woman's hero,' he dismissed harshly.

Caro swallowed hard as she saw the fierce desire in those glittering silver eyes. She knew instinctively that Dominic was poised on the very edge of control; that one wrong word from her and he would in all probability lose it completely.

Caro, her emotions already so raw—from her fear during the brawl that had broken out at Nick's the previous night, the brutality of the attack against Lord Thorne that had followed, being whisked away by Dominic to the indulgent splendour of Blackstone House, and then that sighting earlier today of the young girl that had so reminded her of her younger sister—could not help but relish the very idea of Dominic losing the firm grip he was attempting to maintain upon his control.

She moistened her lips with the tip of her tongue. 'That scar upon your face says otherwise, Dominic.'

Dominic knew that women were more often than not repulsed by the ugly scar that ran the length of his face from eye to jaw; Caro had already assured him she felt no such repulsion. But then, Dominic already knew that she was unlike any other woman he had ever met…

He should leave. He needed to put distance between himself and Caro. Now!

And yet something in her expression held him back. The soft sea-green of her eyes, perhaps. The flush upon her cheeks. The pouting softness of her parted lips...

'You should tell me to go, Caro!' Even as he said the words Dominic was striding back to the bedside and pulling her roughly up on to her knees. He looked down at her fiercely. 'If it should transpire that you are a married woman—'

She gasped. 'I am not—'

It was all the encouragement Dominic needed as his mouth came down crushingly against hers and cut off further speech.

Caro felt on fire as his lips against hers gave no quarter, no gentleness, his arms like steel bands about her waist as he curved her body up into the uncompromising hardness of his, allowing her no time or chance for further thoughts as her fingers clung to the wide width of his shoulders.

Nothing else existed at that moment but Dominic. His lips hungry, his body hard and unyielding. His hands warm and restless as they caressed down the length of her spine before cupping her bottom and lifting her into him, a low growl sounding in his throat as he ground his thighs against her.

Caro seemed to melt from the inside out, as she felt the evidence of his desire pressing against her, so hard, so hot and pulsing, and inducing a reciprocal and aching heat inside her as her breasts swelled and between her thighs moistened. That heat increased, intensified as one of Dominic's hands cupped the full swell of one of her aching breasts before he pulled the material down and bared the fullness of that breast to his caress, capturing the hardened tip to roll it between fingers and thumb.

Caro groaned low in her throat as those caresses bordered on the very knife-edge between pleasure and pain, and rendering them all the more arousing because of it as she arched her breast into that caress even as Dominic's mouth continued to hungrily devour hers.

Her lips parted, invited, as Dominic ran his tongue moistly between them, gently at first, and then more forcefully as he thrust into the heat of her mouth in the same rhythm as he caressed the hard tip of her breast—

'No!' Dominic suddenly wrenched his mouth from hers, eyes glittering furiously as he straightened her gown before he put her away from him.

Caro felt dazed, disorientated, hurt by the suddenness of his rejection. 'Dominic—'

'I may be accused of many things, Caro,' he bit out harshly, hands clenched behind his back as though to resist more temptation. 'And I have no doubt that I am guilty of most of them.' His mouth twisted self-derisively. 'But, married or not, I do not intend to add seducing an unprotected female guest in my own home to that list, even when I am invited to do so!'

Could it be called seduction when Caro had been such a willing participant? When she still longed, ached, for the touch of Dominic's hands and mouth upon her? When just thinking of those things made her tremble in anticipation?

When his last comment showed that he was aware of all those things…

One glance at the savage fury on Dominic's hard and uncompromising face was enough to tell Caro that the moment of madness had passed. For him, at least... All that remained was for her to try to salvage at least some of her own pride. 'I did not invite you to seduce me, Dominic!'

His mouth thinned. 'You invite seduction with every glance and every word you speak.'

'That is unfair!' Caro gasped at the accusation. Yes, her body still ached with longing, but she had only to look at Dominic to see the evidence of his own hard arousal beneath his pantaloons.

'Is it?' Dominic's nostrils flared as his gaze raked over her mercilessly. This woman tempted him, seduced him, with just her presence. So much so that he did not believe he could be under the same roof with her for even one more night and retain his honour. 'Go to bed, Caro,' he instructed harshly. 'We will talk of this again in the morning.'

'I—what is there to talk about?' She looked confused.

Dominic's lids narrowed until his eyes were only visible as silver slithers. 'As I said, the morning will be soon enough—'

'I would rather we talked *now*!' Her eyes flashed in warning.

A warning that Dominic had no intention of heeding. Damn it, he had been a commissioned officer in the army for five years, had been responsible for the lives and discipline of the dozens of men under his command; the temper of one tiny woman did not concern or impress him. 'I have said the morning will be soon enough, Caro,' he repeated firmly.

Caro's cheeks flushed hotly. 'I am beginning to find your arrogance a little tiresome, Dominic.'

He gave a humourless smile. 'Then let us both hope that you do not have to suffer it for much longer.'

Caro sincerely hoped that meant his arrangements for her removal from Blackstone House were progressing as quickly as he had hoped they might; she really did not think she could bear to stay here with him for too much longer.

She sank back on the bed once Dominic had left her bedchamber and closed the door softly behind him; the tears that fell down her cheeks now were for a completely different reason than those she had shed earlier tonight.

What was it about Dominic Vaughn that made her behave so shamelessly? To the point that just now Caro had been practically begging for the return of his kisses, for his hands upon her breasts? Whatever the reason, she knew she was seriously in danger of succumbing to the temptation of those kisses and caresses if she remained at Blackstone house with him for much longer...

'Will Lord Vaughn be down soon, do you think, Simpson?' Caro enquired lightly of the butler at nine o'clock the next morning as she sat alone at the breakfast table, drinking tea and eating a slice of buttered toast.

What had remained of the night, once Dominic had left her bedchamber, had been long and restless for

Caro, as she'd tried to fall asleep but was unable to do so, her thoughts too disturbed after yet another incident of finding herself in the earl's seductive arms. All of those disturbing thoughts had come down to the simple fact that it was becoming nearly impossible for Caro to remain at Blackstone House, under Dominic Vaughn's protection.

'His lordship breakfasted and left the house some time ago, Mrs Morton,' the butler answered her question.

Caro's eyes widened. 'He did?'

'Yes, madam.'

Caro's heart sank. Much as she appreciated the grandeur of Blackstone House, and the attentiveness of the servants, the mere thought of having to idle away the morning here alone was unthinkable, reminding her as it did of the tediousness of the life she had been forced to lead at Shoreley Hall for the first twenty years of her life.

Strange, it had only been two weeks since she had come to London, and yet during that time—and despite some of the more *risqué* aspects of her behaviour!—Caro had come to enjoy having control over her own actions. So much so that she could no longer bear the thought of having her movements restricted in this way, least of all by a man whose emotions she could not even begin to understand...

She looked up to smile at the attentive Simpson as he stood ready to provide her with more tea or toast. 'Does his lordship have another carriage that I might use?' Caro held her breath as she waited to see if Dominic had acted with his usual efficiency and left instructions with the servants to restrict her comings and goings from Blackstone House.

The elderly man nodded. 'His lordship keeps four carriages for his use when in London, Mrs Morton.'

Caro's heart began to pound loudly in her chest. 'And do you suppose I might use one of these other carriages?'

The butler gave a courtly bow. 'If you wish, I am sure one can be readied for your use as soon as you have finished breakfast.'

Caro released her breath slowly, her features carefully schooled so as not to give away her inner feelings of elation; Dominic had not had the time—or, as was more likely, in his arrogance, he had decided he did not need to bother—to issue the instruction that Caro was never to leave Blackstone House unaccompanied.

Not that it was her intention to leave for good. She was not so foolish, and knew enough to believe Dominic when he'd warned of the danger that might be lurking outside these four walls—indeed, the attack on Lord Thorne was proof enough! But a drive in one of Dominic's own carriages, driven by his own servants, was surely safe enough?

'I do wish, Simpson,' she told the butler brightly. She stood up. 'In fact, I will go back upstairs this minute and collect my bonnet and gloves.' Caro hurried from the room to run lightly up the stairs, anxious to absent herself from Blackstone House before Dominic had the chance to return and prevent her from going.

Chapter Nine

Had Dominic ever been this angry in his life before?

He thought not; after all, until three days ago he had been in blissful ignorance of Caro Morton's very existence! Now, after years spent totally in control of his emotions, Dominic found himself the opposite; one minute aroused by her, the next enchanted, but more often than not, furiously angry. At this moment he was most definitely the latter as he had returned to Blackstone House at a little after ten o'clock, only to learn from Simpson that Caro had taken advantage of Dominic's absence and fled to heaven knew where. More insultingly, that she had made that escape in one of his own carriages!

Dominic paced the hallway as he waited for the return of that carriage so that he might learn where, exactly, the driver had taken her. And while he paced he listed all the ways in which he was going to punish Caro for her recklessness when he finally caught up with her. As he most assuredly would. He wanted an explanation as to exactly what she had thought she was doing by placing herself in danger in this way—

'I believe Mrs Morton has every intention of returning, my lord.' Simpson spoke diffidently, tentatively, behind him, having been made aware several minutes ago as to his employer's displeasure at finding Caro gone.

Dominic turned sharply, gaze narrowed. 'And what gives you that impression, Simpson?'

The other man gave a slight flinch at he obviously heard his employer's continued displeasure. 'I took the liberty, after our earlier conversation, of having one of the maids to go upstairs and check Mrs Morton's bedchamber.'

'And?' Dominic frowned darkly.

'All of Mrs Morton's things are just as she left them, my lord.' The man looked relieved at being able to make this pronouncement.

As far as Dominic was aware, all of her things now consisted of only the few belongings left to her after her other gowns had been consigned to the incinerator and he did not believe Caro felt strongly enough about any of them to return for them.

Just as Caro had felt no hesitation in leaving Blackstone House the moment Dominic's back was turned, despite his warnings. That, perhaps more than anything else, was what rankled, when Dominic's whole existence seemed to have been invaded by her in the three days since they had met. Not a pleasant realisation for a man who had long ago decided he would never allow any woman, even the wife needed to provide his heir, to dictate how he should live his life, let alone take charge of it in the way protecting Caro seemed to have done.

Nevertheless, the circumstances of the Nicholas Brown situation were such that Dominic could not—as he told himself he dearly wished to do—rid himself of that particular imposition just yet. The fact that Caro had not only attempted to leave Blackstone House unaccompanied this morning, but had succeeded, showed that one of them, at least, needed to have a care for her welfare.

Damn it.

Dominic gave a weary sigh as he answered his butler, 'I greatly admire your optimism, Simpson, but I am afraid in this instance I feel it is sadly misplaced. It would seem that Mrs Morton is dissatisfied with London society and has decided to return to her previous life.' He spoke with care, mindful of the fact that no matter what the household servants might think or say of this situation in private, publicly, at least, Dominic must continue to claim Caro as his widowed cousin.

The more Dominic considered her disappearance this morning, the less inclined he was to believe that she would have left without first saying her goodbyes to Drew Butler and Ben Jackson…and Dominic knew both those men were at Nick's this morning, overseeing the repairs.

'I believe I will go out again, Simpson.' Dominic collected up his hat and cane. 'If Mrs Morton should return in my absence…'

'I will advise her of your concern, my lord,' the older man assured as he held the door open attentively.

His concern? Dominic's feelings, as he climbed back

into his curricle, were inclined more towards wringing her pretty neck than showing her concern. A pleasure he continued to relish for the whole of the time it took to manoeuvre the greys through the busy London streets to Nick's.

He had been too hasty earlier, Dominic acknowledged as he entered the gambling club some half an hour later—now was the time he felt more angry than he ever had in his life before!

And, once again, Caro was the reason for that emotion.

As was usual at this time of day, the gambling club appeared closed and deserted from the outside, but almost as soon as Dominic had entered the premises by the back door he had been aware of the murmur of voices coming from the main salon. The deep rumble of Drew Butler and Ben Jackson's voices were easily recognisable, as was the lightness of Caro's laughter, but there was also a third male voice that Dominic found shockingly familiar.

The reason for that became obvious as Dominic stood in the doorway of the salon looking through narrowed lids at the four people seated around one of the tables: Drew Butler, Ben Jackson, Caro—and, of all people, the previous owner of the club, Nicholas Brown!

Admittedly, Drew and Ben were seated protectively on either side of Caro, with Brown sitting opposite. But that protection was completely nullified by the admiration gleaming in Brown's calculating brown gaze as he looked across the table at Caro beneath hooded lids.

The fact that the four of them appeared to be enjoying a bottle of best brandy, at only eleven o'clock in the morning, only increased his displeasure. 'I take it from your lack of activity, Drew, that all of the repairs have been completed?'

Caro gave a guilty start at the silky and yet nevertheless unmistakable sarcasm in Dominic's tone, and instantly saw that guilt reflected in the faces of at least two of the three men seated at the table with her. Drew Butler and Ben Jackson instantly rose to their feet and excused themselves before returning to the aforementioned repairs.

Only the relaxed and charming Nicholas Brown appeared unperturbed at the unexpected interruption as he turned to smile unconcernedly at the younger man. 'I am to blame for the distraction, I am afraid, Blackstone. After our conversation last night I felt I ought to come and see things here for myself. Finding the beautiful Mrs Morton here, too, has been an unexpected pleasure.' He turned to bestow a warm smile on her.

Caro blushed prettily at the compliment, although that colour faded just as quickly, and a shiver of apprehension ran the length of her spine, as she saw the dark scowl on Dominic's face as he looked across at her; his eyes were that steely grey that betokened banked fury, his cheekbones hard beneath the tautness of his skin, his mouth a thin and uncompromising line, and his jaw set challengingly. Although whether that displeasure was because of Nicholas Brown's admiration for her, or because Caro had so blatantly disobeyed his instruction earlier concerning leaving Blackstone House unaccompanied, she was as yet unsure.

Caro was inclined to think it might be the latter; after the way in which he had left her bedchamber so abruptly during the night after rejecting her, she could not think of any reason why he should be in the least upset by Nicholas Brown's attentions towards her. Although that man's comment, concerning the two men having spoken together last night, seemed to indicate that Dominic had been telling the truth when he'd claimed he was not going out with the intention of visiting a mistress.

'You must excuse my cousin, Brown. I am afraid she is fresh from the country, and unfamiliar with the dictates of London society that prevent her from venturing out without her maid,' Dominic bit out coldly as he strode across the room to stand beside the table where Caro and Brown now sat facing each other. Although a brief glance at the tabletop at least revealed that she had a half-drunk cup of tea in front of her rather than having joined the men in a glass of brandy. Dominic wondered with abstract amusement where in the gambling club Butler had managed to obtain the china cup, let alone the tea to put in it!

'I assure you, no apology is necessary, Blackstone,' Brown came back smoothly. 'Indeed, I find such independence of nature in a beautiful woman refreshing.'

Caro's cheeks had coloured at the rebuke in Dominic's tone. 'I had thought to offer my assistance to Mr Butler after you informed me of the damage that had occurred here.'

Dominic raised dark brows. 'And I had similarly expected you at Blackstone House when I returned.'

Caro raised her brows. 'You had already left the house when I came down for breakfast, and I did not relish the idea of spending the rest of the morning alone.'

'Perhaps I should withdraw and allow the two of you to continue this conversation in private?' Brown offered lightly.

Dominic's narrowed his gaze on the older man, not convinced for a moment by the innocence of the other man's expression. With his dark and fashionable clothes and politeness of manner, he gave every outward appearance of being the gentleman and yet he most certainly was not; it was well known that he would sell his mother to the highest bidder if it was found to be in his own best interests.

Nor was Dominic unaware of the significance of the older man's visit here so soon after their conversation about the attack on Nathaniel the evening before. It was only whether or not Brown knew of Caro's identity as the masked lady appearing at Nick's that was still in question…

Although Dominic could not attach blame to any young woman—including Caro—for being flattered by the older man's marked attention; at forty-two, with dark and fashionable styled hair, and a roguishly handsome face, no doubt the rakish Nicholas Brown was enough to set the heart of any young woman aflutter.

'Not at all, Brown,' Dominic dismissed with a casual tone he was far from feeling as he took the seat that Drew Butler had recently vacated. 'My rebuke was only made to indicate my disappointment at not finding my cousin at home when I returned earlier.'

Caro glared at him beneath lowered lashes, knowing very well that his emotion had not been 'disappointment' at not finding her exactly where he had left her—he had been, and obviously still was, furious. 'I am to come and go as I please, I hope, my lord,' she said airily, choosing to ignore the retribution promised in Dominic's pale silver eyes for this open challenge to his previous instructions concerning her movements to and from Blackstone House.

'Not without your maid—'

'Perhaps we should, after all, discuss this later?' Caro interrupted what she was sure was going to be yet another verbal reprimand concerning the inadvisability of her having ventured out alone on to the London streets. 'I am sure that neither of us wishes to bore Mr Brown any further with the triviality of what is merely a family disagreement.'

'On the contrary, Mrs Morton, I find I am highly diverted by it.' The older man eyed them both speculatively.

It was a speculation that Caro did not in the least care for. 'You must forgive poor Dominic, Mr Brown.' She reached out to lightly rest her gloved hand on the back of Dominic's as it lay on the tabletop. 'I am afraid my widowed state has made him feel he has been placed in a position where he has to act the role of my protector. Much like an older brother, or perhaps even a father.'

Dominic was not fooled for a moment by the coy flutterings of silky lashes over those blue-green eyes, knowing from experience that she did not have a coy bone in her gracefully beautiful body. Nicholas Brown was just as aware of her insincerity, if the appreciative humour sparkling in the darkness of his eyes as he looked at her was any indication…

Dominic turned his hand over and captured Caro's gloved fingers tightly within his grasp. 'I assure you, my dear cousin, my feelings towards you have never been in the least fraternal *or* paternal.' He lifted her hand, his gaze easily holding her widened one captive as he slowly, and very deliberately, placed a kiss within her gloved palm. He then had the satisfaction of watching as the indignant colour warmed her cheeks.

'I see the way of things now…' Nicholas Brown gave an appreciative laugh as he rose elegantly to his feet. 'I hope I did not cause offence by any of my earlier comments, Blackstone?' His movements were languid as he straightened his cuffs beneath his expertly tailored black superfine.

Dominic's fingers tightened even more firmly about Caro's, preventing her from snatching her hand away, as he looked up at the older man challengingly. 'Not in the least, Brown. I can see that in future I shall have to make sure I remain constantly at Caro's side in order to provide her with suitable amusement.' His voice had hardened in warning over that last statement, a warning he knew the other man was fully aware of as that calculating brown gaze met his in shrewd assessment.

Caro was very aware that Dominic had been manipulating the conversation these past few minutes. And in a way that she did not in the least care for; after the things he had both said and implied, she believed that the handsome and charming Mr Nicholas Brown could come to only one possible conclusion concerning the Earl of Blackstone's relationship with his 'cousin'!

'Perhaps, if you have time, Mr Brown, you would care to come for a turn about the park with me before taking your leave?'

Dominic had the grim satisfaction in seeing Caro's triumphant expression turn to a wince as his fingers tightened about hers. 'I do not think that advisable, Caro,' he grated harshly. 'For one thing, it has turned a little chill.' His tone implied that it was going to get a lot chillier! 'I am afraid Caro and I must also go to another appointment, Brown,' he informed the other man distantly.

Nicholas Brown turned to give Caro a courtly bow before handing her his card. 'You have only to contact me if you should ever again feel a need for company during another of your jaunts about London, Mrs Morton.'

Nicholas Brown would only ever be allowed to accompany Caro anywhere over Dominic's dead body! Which, he allowed grimly, was a distinct possibility if she continued to behave so recklessly...

'You little fool!' Dominic's teeth were tightly clenched together as he returned from dismissing the carriage Caro had arrived in earlier, a nerve now pulsing in the hard set of his jaw, the scar upon his cheek once again a livid slash as he lifted her up into his curricle as if she weighed no more than a feather.

She bristled indignantly. 'I do not think there is any need—'

'Believe me, Caro, you do not want to hear what my

particular needs are at this moment in time.' He gave her a silencing glare.

'You—' Caro's second protest was arrested in her throat as Dominic urged his highly strung greys on to what she considered to be a highly dangerous speed. Not that she did not have every confidence that he was in complete command of the sleek and powerful horses, but she did fear for the safety of the occupants of the other carriages who were driving at a more sedate pace along the busy cobbled streets.

Streets that did not look in the least familiar… 'This does not look like the way back to Blackstone House?'

If anything Dominic's jaw clenched even tighter. 'Possibly because it is not.'

'But—'

Dominic had turned and speared her with eyes that glittered a pale and dangerous silver. 'Unless you wish for me to stop the curricle this instant, and warm your bottom to the degree that you will not be able to sit down again for a week, then I urgently advise that you not say another word for the duration of our journey!'

Caution was not normally a part of Caro's nature, but she decided that in this instance it was perhaps the wisest course; Dominic was angry enough at this moment to actually carry out that scandalous threat!

That Dominic had been angry at finding her gone from Blackstone House in his absence was in no doubt. That he had been put to the trouble of seeking her out had obviously not improved his temper. That he had found her in the company of the charming Mr Nicholas Brown only seemed to have added to that displeasure.

Why any of those things should necessitate Dominic

now behaving with the savagery of a barbarian, Caro had no idea. Neither did she think it sensible at this moment—indeed, it might be highly detrimental to her health—to question him further.

She looked about her curiously as Dominic turned the curricle on to one of the city's quieter residential streets, the wide arc of cream-fronted town houses along this tree-lined avenue nowhere near as magnificent as Blackstone House, but of a style that was nevertheless elegant as well as quietly genteel. She turned to Dominic with a guarded frown. 'Are we to go visiting?'

His mouth twisted scathingly. 'Hardly.'

'Then why are we here?'

They were here because Dominic had realised, after almost making love to her last night, that for Caro's sake, as well as his own, he could not allow her to remain within his own household for a single night longer. That having her so freely available to him at Blackstone House was a temptation he was finding it increasingly hard to resist. The only solution to that dilemma, he'd felt, was to move Caro to other premises as quickly as was possible. With the added security of being able to staff that establishment with men and women Dominic could trust to ensure that she did not repeat this morning's recklessness.

In fact, the sooner she was made aware that the oh-so-charming Mr Nicholas Brown was, in fact, the danger Dominic was attempting to protect her from, the better for them all!

Dominic brought the curricle to a halt in front of the three-storeyed terraced house he'd had prepared for Caro's arrival only that morning, allowing an immediately attentive groom to take hold of the horses before he jumped lightly down to the pavement. He moved around to the other side of the carriage to raise his hand with a politeness he was far from feeling. 'Caro?' he prompted tersely as she remained seated.

Caro's earlier puzzlement had obviously turned to wariness as she stubbornly refused to take his hand and step down from the curricle. 'What are we doing here, Dominic?'

Dominic was not a man best known for his patience, and what little he possessed had already been pushed to its limit this morning by this infuriating young woman. Neither did he care to explain himself in the middle of the street. 'Will you step down voluntarily, or must I employ other, perhaps less dignified, measures?'

Her eyes flashed the same sea-green as her gown. 'You did not seem to have the slightest thought for my dignity earlier when you made a show of me in front of Mr Brown!'

'It is my dignity I referred to now, and not your own.' Dominic eyed her quellingly.

'Then let me assure you that I have absolutely no intention of going anywhere with you until you have explained— Dominic…!' The last came out as a surprised squeak as he wasted no further time on argument but took Caro by the hand to pull her forwards on the seat before throwing her over one of his shoulders. 'How dare you? Put me down this instant!'

No, Dominic acknowledged grimly as he began to walk down the path towards the house, dignity certainly had no part in these proceedings!

Chapter Ten

It was a little difficult for Caro to take in the unfamiliarity of her surroundings when she was hanging upside-down over one of Dominic Vaughn's broad shoulders. Even so, she did manage to take note of the quiet elegance of the hallway once they were inside the house, and several doors leading off it to what were probably salons and a dining room.

Several servants stood just inside the hallway as the Earl of Blackstone calmly handed one of them his hat before he began to ascend the staircase with Caro still thrown over his shoulder.

'Not a word!' he warned softly as he obviously guessed she was about to voice another protest.

Caro clamped her lips together, her cheeks red with mortification as the servants below continued to watch the two of them until Dominic had rounded a corner to enter a long hallway. 'You will be made to regret this indignity if it is the last thing I ever do!' she hissed furiously.

He gave a scathing snort. 'If I could be sure that was the outcome, I might allow you that privilege!'

'You are despicable! An overbearing, arrogant bully—' Her flow of insults came to an abrupt halt as Dominic entered one of the bedchambers and tilted her forwards over his shoulder before throwing her unceremoniously down on to a bed. Caro barely had time to glare her annoyance up at him before she suffered the further indignity of having her bonnet tilt forwards over her eyes as she bounced inelegantly upon the mattress.

Her eyes glittered up at him furiously as she pushed the bonnet back into place. 'How dare you treat me in this high-handed manner?'

'How dare you completely disobey my instructions this morning and leave Blackstone House unaccompanied?' Dominic thundered, appearing completely unaffected by her indignation as he glowered down at her.

Her eyes narrowed in warning. 'I do not consider myself in need of your permission concerning anything I may, or may not, choose to do!' She drew in an angry breath. 'Neither does anything I have done this morning compare to your outrageous behaviour of just now.'

'I beg to differ.' He eyed her coldly, dark hair rakishly ruffled, although the rest of his appearance was as elegantly fashionable as always: perfectly tied neckcloth against snowy white linen, a deep grey superfine over a paler grey waistcoat and black pantaloons above brown-and-black Hessians.

His sartorial elegance made Caro even more aware of her own dishevelled appearance. Her sea-green gown was in disarray, rumpled from where she had been thrown down on to the bed, her hair even more so as she sat up to untie and remove the matching bonnet completely.

She gave an unladylike snort as she threw the bonnet aside. 'I do not believe you have ever begged for anything in your life.'

'No,' he acknowledged unrepentantly. 'Nor am I about to start now.'

'What are we doing here, Dominic?' Caro still felt agitated by the fact that he appeared to have carried her into the home of someone she did not even know; there was no way she could know the owner of this house when she was unacquainted with anyone in London except Dominic himself. And Drew Butler and Ben Jackson, of course. And now Nicholas Brown.

Dominic watched coldly as Caro tried unsuccessfully to tidy the waywardness of her curls. 'I am more concerned at this moment with the fact that your recklessness in going to Nick's this morning may result in much more serious repercussions than what you view as the indignity of being carried against your will into this house.'

Caro ceased fussing with her hair to look up at him scornfully. 'You are being ridiculous. There was no danger involved in my choosing to visit Mr Butler and Ben—'

'And Nicholas Brown?' Dominic's nostrils flared angrily. 'Do you believe yourself to have been in absolutely no danger from him, too?'

Her chin rose. 'Mr Brown was charming, and behaved the perfect gentleman in my company.'

Dominic gave a fierce scowl. 'Ben Jackson is more of a gentleman than Nicholas Brown.'

She eyed him haughtily. 'After your most recent behaviour, I am inclined to believe Ben to be more of a gentleman than you, too!'

Dominic's eyes narrowed to icy cold slits, his jaw clenching as he once again fought the battle to retain his usual control over his emotions, rather than letting them control him. It was a battle he had been destined to lose from the moment he'd walked into Nick's earlier and saw Caro calmly sitting down and drinking tea with the man he believed responsible for the attack on Nathaniel Thorne. As for being a gentleman, Brown was a man whose rakish handsomeness often occasioned him being invited into the bedchambers of married ladies of the *ton*, but who would nevertheless never be invited into the drawing room of one.

Dominic's teeth clenched so tightly together he heard his jaw crack. 'You have absolutely no idea what you have done, do you?'

She looked unconcerned. 'I merely exerted my free will—'

'To sit down and drink tea with the previous owner of Nick's.'

'Oh.' Caro looked momentarily nonplussed by this information, before rallying once again. 'I am sure I do not understand why, when you now own the club, that you should choose to hold that against him.'

'It is an ownership Brown relinquished to me with great reluctance,' Dominic grated pointedly.

'No doubt. Even so—'

'Caro, I know you to be an intelligent woman.' Dominic spoke with controlled impatience. 'I wish that you would now stop arguing with me long enough to use that intelligence.'

She eyed him warily. 'With regard to…?'

'With regard to the fact that only minutes ago you sat down and drank tea with the man I have every reason to believe is the very same man I have these past two days been attempting to protect you from.' Dominic's hands were now clenched at his sides.

Caro looked startled. 'You are referring to Mr Brown?'

'I am indeed referring to the man *you* think is a perfect gentleman.' Dominic's tone implied he knew the man to be the exact opposite of her earlier description of him. 'I believe him to be behind the attack on Nathaniel.'

Caro swallowed. 'Are you sure?'

Dominic's expression was grim. 'After this morning, yes!'

Caro began to tremble slightly, as the full import of what she had done began to sweep over her. She had found Nicholas Brown affable and charming, had flirted with him lightly, as he had flirted with her. She had even invited him to go walking with her! Admittedly that had been in response to what she had considered to be Dominic Vaughn's overbearing attitude, but that did not change the fact that she had made the invitation. And all the time, the man was a complete villain!

'If you truly know this for certain, then I do not understand why you did not instantly challenge him with the despicable deed?' Caro, uncomfortably aware of the severity of her error, decided to attack rather than defend, only realising her mistake as she noted the anger smouldering in the depths of Dominic Vaughn's ice-grey eyes once more flare into a blaze.

'I was an officer in the King's army, Caro, and a soldier does not confront the enemy before he has his own troops firmly in place and, more importantly than that, the civilians removed from harm's way.'

She gave a dismissive snort. 'Apart from myself, there were but the two of you present this morning.'

'And Brown's cut-throats were no doubt waiting outside in the shadows, eager to assist him if the need should arise.' Dominic looked down at her coldly. 'One of my dearest friends has already suffered a beating on my behalf, I was not about to see the same happen to you this morning, or indeed Butler and Jackson.'

Her eyes widened. 'You believe the attack on Lord Thorne to have been meant for *you*?'

'Only indirectly. It would appear that, for the moment at least, Brown is enjoying playing a cat-and-mouse game of inflicting harm on my friends rather than a direct attack upon me.'

'Then that is even more reason, surely, for you to have confronted him this morning?'

'Caro, it sounds distinctly as if you are accusing me of lacking the personal courage to confront him.' Dominic's tone was now every bit as glacial as his eyes.

It would be very foolish indeed of her to accuse him of such cowardice, when three nights ago she had personally witnessed him challenging those three young bucks well into their cups. When he had not hesitated to come to her rescue in the middle of a brawl. When she knew him to have been a gallant officer as the mark of that gallantry was slashed for ever upon his face.

But foolish was exactly how Caro felt at learning how mistaken she had been concerning Nicholas Brown's nature. Foolish, and embarrassed, to have been flattered by the attentions of the man she now knew him to be.

Her chin rose proudly. 'I would have thought you might, at the very least, have allowed him to see that you are aware of his guilt.'

Dominic gave a hard smile. 'Oh I am sure he is well aware of that fact.'

'How could he be, when apart from making such a show of implying our relationship is that of more than cousins, you were politeness itself?' Caro asked.

'The fact that I implied our relationship to be that of more than cousins, as you so delicately put it, was done with the intention of warning Brown, should he even consider the idea, of the inadvisability of harming one golden hair upon your head.' A nerve pulsed in Dominic's tightly clenched jaw. 'Which is not to say that I now feel that same reluctance myself.' The very softness of his tone was indicative of the depth of his anger.

Caro's trembling deepened as she realised too late her mistake in questioning Dominic when he was already so displeased with her; the grey of his eyes had become so pale and glittery that they glowed a shimmering silver, the scar standing out harshly in the tautness of his cheek, and his mouth had thinned to a dangerous line.

If those things were not enough to tell Caro of her mistake, then the purposeful look in his eyes as he moved to kneel on the bed beside her before pulling her roughly up against him and lowering his mouth to capture hers certainly did!

There was no gentleness in him as he ground his lips against hers before his tongue became as lethal as an arrow as it speared between her lips to thrust deeply into the heat of her mouth, and one of his hands moved to cup and then squeeze the fullness of her breast in that same remorseless rhythm.

Caro knew she should have been at the least frightened, if not repulsed, by the force of Dominic's passion, but instead she found herself filled with an aching excitement; her cheeks felt hot, her breasts full and aroused, and between her thighs became damp and swollen.

Dominic roughly pulled the bodice of her gown and chemise down to her waist and pushed the two garments down about her knees, before his mouth once again captured hers. His hand cupped firmly about one of Caro's exposed breasts and his fingers began to tweak and tug on the hardened nipple.

She forgot everything else but Dominic. Her neck arched invitingly as he finally wrenched his mouth from hers to lay a trail of fire down the column of her throat, her arms moving up over his shoulders and her fingers becoming entangled in the dark thickness of hair at his nape, as his head moved lower still and he drew one of those hardened nipples deep into the heat of his mouth.

Caro gave a choked gasp as there seemed to be a direct line of pleasure from Dominic's rhythmic tugging at her breast to the dampness between the bareness of her thighs, her movements becoming restless as she pressed into his hardness in search of some sort of relief for that throbbing and hungry heat.

Dominic had meant only to punish Caro for her disobedience, for her questioning his courage, but as he kissed and caressed her he instead found himself more aroused than he had ever been in his life before. So much so that he had not hesitated to pull down her gown and chemise and expose the silky paleness of her naked body to his heated gaze. Her breasts were high and firm, her waist narrow and flat, with a tiny thatch of enticing golden curls in the vee of her thighs.

He continued to lay siege to both her breasts with his lips, tongue and teeth as one of his hands gently parted those thighs before cupping her silky mound with his palm and allowing his fingers to explore the heat beneath. Caro was so hot and wet as he parted those sensitive folds to caress a finger along the heat of her opening, slowly, gently, circling but not yet touching the swollen nub nestled amongst those curls, in no rush to hurry her release, but instead savouring every low aching groan she gave as he caressed ever closer to that sensitive spot.

He touched her there once, lightly, feeling the response of that hard and roused little nubbin as it pulsed against his finger, hearing but ignoring Caro's low moan as he resumed caressing the swollen opening below, fingers testing, dipping slightly inside, and feeling the way her muscles contracted greedily about his finger even as she pushed her hips forward in an effort to take him deeper still. An invitation Dominic resisted as he continued to tease and torment her.

'Dominic, please!'

He raised his head slightly in order to look into Caro's flushed and reproachful face. 'Please what?'

Her eyes flashed deeply green and her fingers clenched on his shoulders. 'Do not tease me, Dominic.'

'Tell me precisely what you want from me, Caro,' he encouraged gruffly. 'You have only to issue an instruction and I will obey.'

Could she do that? Caro wondered wildly. Could she really tell Dominic plainly, graphically, what it was she required from him in order to give her relief from the heat threatening to consume her?

'Do you want some part of me inside the sweetness of you, Caro?' Dominic prompted softly as he seemed to take some little pity on her desperate silence.

'Yes!' she groaned achingly.

'Which part, Caro?' he pressed. 'My fingers? My tongue? My shaft?'

Oh, help! Those satisfying fingers? The hot and probing moistness of his tongue? His swollen arousal that she could clearly see hard and throbbing beneath his pantaloons? From not knowing what she needed, Caro now knew she wanted to experience having all three of those things inside her.

'Perhaps we should experiment? See which it is you like the best?' Dominic looked down at her nakedness with eyes that had become both dark and hungry as he once again swirled his fingers into the silky curls between her thighs to unerringly find and gently stroke against that secret part of her.

Caro felt the instant return of that earlier pleasure, stronger now, more demanding, as she instinctively began to move into those caresses, knowing she was poised on the brink of—Caro had no idea what she was poised on the brink of, she only knew that she wanted, needed it, with a desperation she had never known before.

She moaned again in her throat as one long finger probed her before slipping inside her heat. Deeper. Then deeper still. At last giving her some relief for that aching need as she moved her hips in rhythm with that finger as it thrust slowly in and out of her.

'Lie back upon the bed, Caro,' Dominic instructed throatily even as he eased her back against the pillows, continuing that slow and penetrating thrust inside her as he discarded her gown and chemise completely before moving to kneel between her legs to lower his head between her parted thighs.

Caro's hips jerked up from the bed at the first hot sweep of his tongue against her sensitised flesh, her fingers contracting, clutching at the bedclothes beside her, at the second sweep. She cried out, her neck arching her head back into the pillows, as unimagined pleasure ripped through her, Dominic thrusting a second finger deep inside her at the same time as he administered a third sweep of his tongue against that pulsing nubbin.

Caro became pure liquid heat. She felt as if she were on fire as wave after wave of pleasure radiated from deep between her thighs, only to surge through the whole of her body, each caress of his tongue and fingers creating yet another, deeper, swell of that mind-shattering pleasure.

Dominic watched Caro's face even as he continued to lave her with his tongue and slowly thrust with his fingers, knowing the exact moment she became lost in the throes of her climax; her eyes were a wide and stormy blue-green, her cheeks flushed, lips slightly parted, her breasts thrusting, the nipples hard as pebbles, her thighs a parted invitation as the nubbin pulsed beneath his tongue and she convulsed greedily about his thrusting fingers.

As he looked at her Dominic knew he had never experienced anything more beautiful, more physically satisfying, than watching Caro lost in the pleasure she felt from the touch of his mouth and hands. He found it more satisfying even than attaining that climax for himself.

He had been so angry with her earlier, so absolutely furious, not least because by behaving in that reckless way she had exposed her whereabouts to Nicholas Brown. But he did not want to dwell on that here and now, when Caro still quivered and trembled from the ministration of his lips and hands. Not with her all but naked beneath him, her only clothing now a pair of white silk stockings.

Besides, he had no answer as yet to his earlier question: fingers, tongue, or shaft?

Caro lay back weak and satiated against the pillows as she watched Dominic quickly strip off his boots, jacket, waistcoat, neckcloth and shirt, to reveal a hard and muscled chest covered in a light dusting of dark hair that disappeared beneath the top of his pantaloons. Pantaloons he now unfastened and pushed down and off equally hard and muscled legs to reveal the surging power of his engorged arousal.

Caro had never seen a naked man in her life before, but even so she was sure that Dominic was a physically well-endowed man. Her gaze rose to look at his face, and she swallowed convulsively as she saw the flush to his cheeks and the slightly fevered glow in those silver eyes as he wrapped a hand around that impressive length before moving forwards to rub it slowly against the opening between her thighs.

Caro felt herself quiver with each stroke of that hardness against her sensitivity, breathing heavily as she felt the return of that heat between her thighs. Surely she could not feel that pleasure again so quickly?

She could, Caro discovered only seconds later as Dominic continued to stroke that silky hardness against her own reawakened nubbin, her breasts becoming firm, nipples thrusting achingly even as she felt herself moisten in anticipation.

'Fingers? Tongue? Or shaft?' Dominic prompted gruffly even as he moved his hips forwards into her opening, one inch, two, before pulling back and starting again. One inch. Two. Three this time, before he pulled out and started again.

Caro had never experienced pleasure like this in her life before. Never imagined anything so exquisite as looking down at Dominic as he knelt between her parted thighs and slowly breached her, inch by glorious inch.

Each time Dominic thrust inside Caro she felt full and satisfied. Each time he pulled out again she felt bereft and empty. And each time he thrust inside her a little deeper she was sure she had reached her limit, that she had inwardly stretched and accommodated him as far as she was able. Until Dominic pulled out before thrusting even deeper inside her the next time.

Caro had been convinced when she first saw the size of Dominic's arousal that she would never be able to accommodate anything so large—

'Oh, my God!' Caro tensed suddenly, eyes wide with shock as she felt herself start to rip apart inside the moment Dominic took his weight on his arms to thrust forwards urgently with his hips so that he surged into her completely. It felt as if she were being torn in two as she finally took his whole length inside her.

'What the—!' Dominic froze above her, his face suddenly pale, his eyes glittering like opaque silver as he stared down at her incredulously.

'It is all right, Dominic,' Caro assured breathlessly. And, incredibly, it was, that first searing pain having now faded, and so allowing her to once again become aware of the pleasure of having his fullness completely inside her.

His face was grim. 'It most certainly is *not* all right!'

'I assure you that it is,' she encouraged softly. Dominic's arousal had looked hard and fierce earlier, but now that he was completely inside her Caro realised that fierce hardness was encased in skin of seductive and silky velvet. She moved her hips up, and then down again, the better to feel that sleek and velvety smoothness as it moved against her sensitive flesh.

'Do not move like that again, Caro, or I cannot be responsible for the consequences.' Dominic's jaw was clenched, his expression pained, a fine sheen of moisture upon his brow.

But of course Caro must move! How could she not move, when every part of her, every sensitised inch of her, cried out for the relief of having that pleasure-giving hardness stroking inside her?

Dominic had been stunned into immobility the moment he discovered Caro's innocence. 'Why did you not tell me?' His gaze was fierce as he looked down at the flushed beauty of her face, angry with himself at the moment rather than Caro, knowing he should have put a stop to this long before it had come to the point of his breaching her virginity.

And he had every intention of putting a stop to it now!

Dominic moved up and carefully away from her as he slowly disengaged himself, frowning as he saw Caro's wince of discomfort as he slipped from her obviously sore entrance. That frown turned to a dark scowl as he looked down and saw the blood smeared between her thighs as well as on him.

'Do not move,' he instructed harshly as he stood up to cross the room to the jug and bowl on the washstand, pouring some of the water from the jug into the bowl before moistening a cloth and cleaning Caro's blood from his own body before returning it to the bowl to rinse it in preparation for her. The water was cold, of course, but would hopefully be all the more soothing because of it.

Caro had watched Dominic beneath her lashes as he stood up to cross the bedchamber, completely uncon-cerned by his own nakedness, his movements gracefully predatory, like the sleek movements of a large jungle cat. He stood with his back towards her now, his shoul-ders wide, his back long and muscled, his buttocks a smooth curve above heavily muscled thighs and legs. If a man could be described as beautiful, then Caro knew that he could be called such.

The colour warmed her cheeks, however, when he returned to sit on the side of the bed and began to bathe between her thighs with a cool and soothing washcloth, his face a study of unreadable hauteur. Caro attempted to push those attentive hands away. 'There really is no need—'

'There is every need.' Dominic barely glanced up at her before continuing that studied bathing between her sensitive thighs.

Caro felt embarrassed, both by the intimacy of his ministrations, and the fact that their lovemaking had come to so abrupt an end once he'd been made aware of her innocence.

Surely there should have been more to it than that? A completion? A reciprocal pleasure? Dominic had certainly not shown signs of experiencing anything like the pleasure that Caro had.

All whilst in the bedchamber of house she had never visited before!

Caro moistened her lips, instantly aware of how swollen and sensitive they still were from the force of his kisses.

'Exactly where are we, Dominic?'

He looked at her briefly before turning away to place the cloth back in the bowl. 'I hope you are a little more comfortable now.' He stood up abruptly, his arousal already noticeably depleted. 'Perhaps I should send for a physician and he might give you some sort of soothing balm to apply—'

'I have no intention of being attended by a physician!' Caro's cheeks were hot with embarrassment as she imagined having to explain this situation to a third party. 'Dominic, is it possible I might become with child from—from what just occurred between us?'

Dominic closed his eyes even as he gave a groan of self-disgust. An innocent. Damn it, he had just deflowered a complete innocent!

Chapter Eleven

'It is very doubtful,' Dominic answered stiffly.

'But possible?'

'Perhaps,' he allowed abruptly.

Caro turned away. 'Whose house is this?'

Dominic looked down at her between narrowed lids, her cheeks flushed, her mouth slightly trembling as she pulled the sheet over her nakedness. It was a little late in the day for maidenly modesty, of course, but now was possibly not the right time for Dominic to allude to that fact.

'I do not believe that to be important at this moment—'

'I do.' There was a stillness about Caro now. A wariness that bordered on anger, perhaps?

He gave a humourless smile. 'You had made it obvious from the first that you did not wish to remain at Blackstone House, and last night it became just as obvious to me that the two of us could not continue to reside under the same roof any longer—'

'At which point in last night's proceedings did this become so obvious to you, Dominic?' Caro interrupted sharply. 'Perhaps at the point where you announced the inappropriateness of seducing a female guest in your own home?' Angry colour now heightened the delicacy of her cheeks.

Looking down at her, the warmth of their lovemaking still visible upon her body, Dominic knew that she had never looked lovelier: her eyes sparkled, her cheeks were flushed, her lips slightly swollen from the passion of their kisses, and the skin across her shoulders and the exposed tops of her creamy breasts was slightly pink from the abrasion of the light stubble upon Dominic's jaw.

That jaw hardened at the accusation he heard in her tone. 'If you are somehow meaning to imply that I brought you to this house in order to seduce you—'

'Did you not?' She stood up, her movements agitated as she held the sheet tightly to her breasts to pace the bedchamber.

'Do not be ridiculous, Caro.' Dominic's quickly rising anger was more than equal to her own. Damn it, he was the one who had been in complete ignorance of her innocence until a few minutes ago!

The signs had been there if he had cared to see them, Dominic instantly rebuked himself. Caro's naïvety concerning the interest of the men who had come to Nick's night after night just to see her. The frequent indications of her being a young lady of refinement. The often imperious manner that hinted at her being used to issuing orders rather than receiving them.

That Dominic was now assured he had not been

guilty these past three days of attempting to make love to a married woman or a member of the servant class was poor consolation when he had instead robbed a young woman of the innocence she should one day have presented to her husband.

'Ridiculous?' Caro now repeated softly, eyes gleaming as dark as emeralds. 'You strode into this house earlier as if you owned it—and perhaps that is because you do?' She didn't wait for Dominic to answer before striding across the bedchamber to throw open the wardrobe doors, her expression darkening as she saw the three pretty silk gowns hanging there. She turned to shoot Dominic a scathing glance. 'The previous occupant of this house appears to have been so hastily removed that she has left several of her gowns behind!'

'There was no previous occupant of this house—'

'All evidence to the contrary, my dear Dominic!' Caro was breathing hard in her agitation—she could only hope this anger served to hide the deep hurt she really felt.

It was humiliating enough that he had not even desired her enough to complete their lovemaking once he'd become aware of her innocence, but for him to have chosen to bring her to the house he had already owned, and where another woman had obviously been hastily removed, was a much more painful insult.

Dominic was well aware that at the moment Caro did not consider him her 'dear' anything; in fact, she looked more than capable of plunging a knife between his shoulder blades if one had been readily available.

Which, thank God, it was not… 'Look at the gowns more closely, if you please, Caro,' he ordered.

Her nose wrinkled delicately at the suggestion. 'I have no wish to—'

'Look at them, damn you!' Dominic demanded impatiently. 'Look at the gowns, Caro,' he repeated more evenly as he realised that it was himself he was angry with and not her. 'Once you have done so, you will see that they are the ones ordered for you yesterday.'

Caro eyed him uncertainly for several seconds before turning her attention back to the gowns hanging in the wardrobe, frowning as she realised they were indeed the ones ordered from the seamstress yesterday. Two days dresses, one of pale peach, the other of deep yellow. The third an evening gown of pure white silk and lace.

A purity Caro was all too aware she could no longer lay claim to…

'If you care to look in the drawers in the dressing table you will find your own undergarments and new nightgowns, too.'

Caro firmly closed the wardrobe door on the mockery of that white gown. 'All that proves is that you were sensible enough, after all, to remove the belongings of your mistress and replace them with my own.'

Dominic drew in a sharp breath, knowing that engaging in their usual verbal battle of wills was not going to help this already disastrous situation. And no matter what she might choose to think to the contrary, he had not brought her here with any intention of seducing her. The opposite, in fact. He had thought—hoped—that by removing her from Blackstone House, he would be removing her from his temptation. Instead of which he had merely exacerbated the situation by bringing Caro here and making love to her before he had even had chance to explain.

'Caro, I acquired ownership of this house only this morning.'

'Now who is being ridiculous?'

Dominic knew, for all that Caro was putting such a brave face on things, that she had to be keenly feeling the loss of her innocence. 'I can take you to the office of my lawyer, if you wish,' he spoke gently. 'I am sure he would be only too happy to show you today's date upon the transfer of the deeds, if that will help to convince you I am telling you the truth?'

Her chin rose. 'You not only bought this house this morning but somehow managed to engage all those servants downstairs, too?' A flush entered her cheeks as she obviously recalled the curious gazes of those servants earlier as he'd carried her through the entrance hall and up the stairs.

An impulse he now deeply regretted when it had resulted in him taking Caro's innocence… 'They are, one and all, men and women already known to me. Men who served under me in the army, and their wives, whom I knew could be trusted to protect you,' he admitted ruefully.

Her eyes glittered, whether with anger or tears, Dominic was unsure. 'Obviously they did not feel that protection was necessary when it applied to *yourself*!'

'Caro—'

'Do not touch me, Dominic!' Her warning was accompanied by a step away from him, the knuckles on her fingers showing white as she tightly gripped the bedcover about her nakedness. 'I believe, if this truly is to be my home for the immediate future, that I should like you to leave now.'

No more so than Dominic wished to remove himself, he felt sure. At this moment, all he wanted to do was walk away from Brockle House and forget he had ever met Caro Morton. Forget especially that he had taken her innocence.

'Perhaps on your way out you might ask for a bath and hot water to be brought up to me?' Caro requested stiltedly as Dominic pulled on his pantaloons and shirt before sitting on the side of the bed to pull on his boots.

Dominic inwardly winced at the thought of the soreness she must now be experiencing following their lovemaking. 'Please believe me when I tell you I did not plan for what happened here this morning—'

'Planned or otherwise, it is done now.'

There was so much sadness in her tone, that if that knife had been available, then Dominic believed himself to be capable of plunging it into his own heart at that moment. 'I cannot express how much I…regret what has happened.'

Caro looked up at him searchingly, not sure whether she felt reassured by Dominic's claim, or insulted by it. Their lovemaking had been a mistake, of course, a shocking error on both their parts. But even so… 'I had not believed you could possibly insult to me more than you already have; I was obviously wrong.' She turned her back on him to stare sightlessly out of the window into the square below. 'I require the bath and hot water to be brought up to me now, if you please, Dominic.'

Dominic stared at the proud set of Caro's bare shoulders for several long seconds before bending to pick up the rest of his clothes from the floor. 'I will call on you later this afternoon.'

She turned sharply. 'For what purpose?'

Dominic's heart sank at the suspicion he so easily read in her expression. 'For the purpose of checking that you have not suffered any feelings of ill health from this morning's…activity.'

Caro gave a humourless snort. 'As far as I am aware, we did not indulge in anything of an unnatural nature this morning.'

A flush warmed the hardness of Dominic's cheeks. 'No, of course we did not.'

'Then I fail to see why you might think I will suffer any ill health because of it?'

'Damn it, Caro—'

'I suppose if you think it more fitting, then I could perhaps swoon or have a fit of the vapours?' she continued scathingly. 'But only if you believe it absolutely necessary.' Her nose wrinkled. 'Personally, I have always believed that women who behave in that way, seemingly at the slightest provocation, to be complete ninnies.'

Even in the midst of what Dominic considered, at best, to be an exceedingly awkward situation, he could not help but admire her courageous spirit. She truly was a woman like no other he had ever met. What had just happened between the two of them could certainly not be termed a mere 'slight provocation'. In fact, Dominic felt sure that most women in her position would be either screaming obscenities at him or alternately demanding jewels and gowns, the latter as compensation for the loss of her innocence; Caro asked only for a bath and hot water in which she might bathe the soreness from her body.

Dominic gave a rueful smile. 'I, too, would prefer that you do not swoon or have a fit of the vapours.' That smile faded as he looked at her searchingly. 'You truly are unharmed from our encounter?'

He knew himself to have been severely provoked when he'd returned to Blackstone House earlier and found Caro gone. Even more so when he'd arrived at Nick's and found her happily engaged in conversation with Nicholas Brown—even now Dominic dreaded to think what might have befallen Caro if he had not been present when she had been foolish enough to suggest walking with him in the park! For her to then taunt him as she'd done regarding his own behaviour towards Brown had been more than Dominic's already frayed nerves had been able tolerate.

An intolerance that Caro had paid for with her inno-cence…

'I am as comfortable as might be expected in the circumstances.' Caro kept her chin proudly high even as she saw the way Dominic winced at her lack of assur-ances. In truth, it was her pride that now hurt more than her body.

Caro eyed him uncertainly now from beneath her lashes, still so very aware of how handsome he looked with the darkness of his hair rakishly tousled, and his shirt hanging loosely over his pantaloons, the buttons still undone halfway down his chest and revealing the hard and muscled flesh beneath. Hard and muscled flesh that Caro now knew more intimately than she did her own…

She gave a decisive shake of her head. 'We were both in error earlier. Let that be an end to it.'

Dominic continued to look at her searchingly for several long seconds. A scrutiny that Caro was determined to withstand without alerting him to how distressed she felt inside. And not by their lovemaking, as Dominic presumed, but because of the emotions which Caro feared had instigated her own part in that wild and wonderful lovemaking.

He frowned. 'I have your promise that you will stay well away from Nicholas Brown?'

'Such a promise is completely unnecessary, I assure you.' Caro's brow creased with irritation that Dominic, after revealing to her that Brown was the person behind the attack on Lord Thorne and consequently was the excuse for her own incarceration in this house, could for one moment think she had any interest in ever meeting the villain again!

Dominic wanted nothing more than to take Caro in his arms and smooth the frown from her brow and the shadows from her eyes. Even knowing of the physical discomfort she must now be suffering following their lovemaking, Dominic was not enough in control of his own emotions at that moment to be sure that he would be able to stop himself from making love to her fully if he were to touch her again.

He was a man who had enjoyed his first physical encounter at the age of sixteen. And there had been many women since that first time with whom he had enjoyed the same physical release. It was disturbing to realise that almost making love with Caro had been completely unlike any of those previous encounters. More sensuous. More out of control. With the promise of being more wildly satisfying…

'Caro—'

'Dominic!' Her eyes flashed in warning as she turned to face him, the control she had been exerting over her own emotions obviously at an end. 'In the past two days I have been caught up in the midst of a brawl, seen an innocent man beaten within an inch of his life, been deposited in your own household against my wishes, drunk tea with the man you assure me is responsible for that innocent man being beaten, been literally carried away and deposited in this house like a piece of unwanted baggage, before then being made love to. I should warn you, I am seriously in danger of resorting to behaving like that complete ninny I mentioned earlier, if you do not soon take your leave!' Her voice quivered with emotion, an emotion she masked by crossing the room to ring for the maid.

Still he hesitated. 'I should also like your promise that you will not attempt to go out alone again, now that you are aware of the danger.'

Could Caro make Dominic such a promise? What choice did she have? The only place she wished to go was back to Shoreley Hall in Hampshire, where she might be with her sisters and lick her wounds in private. Something she most certainly could not do, now that she and Nicholas Brown had met, when it might also result in her taking the danger that man represented back home with her…

In truth, what Caro most wanted at that moment was

the privacy to sit down and cry. To scream and shout, if necessary. And after doing those things she needed the peace and quiet in which to come to terms with the loss of her innocence and the wantonness of her own behaviour this morning in Dominic's arms.

She gave a cool inclination of her head. 'You have my promise. Now, do you not think your own time would not be better spent in dealing with Nicholas Brown, rather than in lingering here to extract superfluous promises from me?'

Dominic's eyes narrowed. 'Superfluous?'

She gave a tight smile. 'Of course it is superfluous, when I so obviously have nowhere else of safety to go.'

'Caro—' Dominic broke off what he was going to say as, after a brief knock, a maid appeared in the doorway in answer to Caro's ring. 'Your mistress requires a bath and hot water,' he instructed tightly. 'Immediately,' he added firmly as the maid seemed inclined to linger in order to satisfy her curiosity rather than be about her business. He waited until the woman had gone before turning back to Caro. 'My advice is that once you have bathed you then rest quietly—'

'Why is it, I wonder, Dominic, that when you offer advice it always has the sound and appearance of an order?' Caro eyed him with exasperation.

Dominic gave a weary sigh as he ran impatient fingers through his already tousled hair. 'Caro, this situation is already difficult enough—could we not at least try to behave in a civilised manner towards each other?'

Could they? Somehow Caro doubted that they could ever be completely civilised with each other; it seemed that whenever the two of them were together their emotions ran to extremes. Arrogance. Anger. Desire.

She sighed heavily. 'Perhaps when you return this afternoon our emotions will be less…fraught than they are now,' she allowed distantly.

Dominic certainly hoped that would be the case.

But somehow he doubted it.

Chapter Twelve

'I am afraid I cannot accurately describe any of the four men who attacked me.' Nathaniel Thorne lay propped up against the pillows in one of the bedchambers at his widowed Aunt Gertrude's house, his expression regretful as he gazed across to where Dominic stood in front of one of the long picture windows.

Dominic had been shocked by the worsening of his friend's appearance when he arrived at Mrs Wilson's home a few short minutes ago, and the elderly lady's young companion showed him into Nathaniel's bedchamber. His friend's face was extremely pale except for the myriad of brightly coloured bruises and cuts that, although they were starting to heal, still looked vicious and painful. The bandage about Nathaniel's broken ribs was visible at the unbuttoned collar of his loose white nightshirt.

Nathaniel shook his head. 'As I told you at the time, I had no sooner walked outside than I was set upon by those four men wielding knives, and fists that had the force of hammers. I was immediately too busy defending myself to take note of what any of them looked like.' He grimaced at his oversight.

In truth, Dominic had not held out much hope of Nathaniel being able to add any more light on this particular subject. Regrettably, his reasons for coming here were, in fact, as much self-interest as they were concern for Nathaniel. Much as he wished to assure himself of Osbourne's well being, Dominic had been even more in need of a diversion from his own company!

Having returned to Blackstone House earlier to bathe and change his clothes, Dominic had then found himself pacing his study, too restless, his thoughts too disturbed, for him to be able to even glance at the papers concerning estate business sitting on his desktop awaiting his attention.

How could it be any other when all he could think about was Caro's stolen innocence?

'What is it, Dom?' Nathaniel's softly probing concern was the first indication he had that he might have actually groaned his self-disgust out loud.

Dominic had believed, hoped, that he could talk to Nathaniel about his present dilemma with regard to Caro. Instead he had realised since coming here that, as close as the two men were, there was no way that he could confide his despicable deed to the other man. More importantly, that he could not speak about Caro in such a way with a third party. Even one of his closest friends.

Gabriel, Nathaniel, and Dominic had always been as close as brothers, but even so, Dominic knew that he could not reveal to one of those friends what had taken place at Brockle House that morning. Osbourne, quite rightly, could not help but consider the taking of Caro's innocence as being beneath contempt. The same contempt, in fact, that Dominic now felt towards himself...

The truth of it was that he had been suffused with feelings of helplessness when he'd discovered Caro had gone from Blackstone House this morning, but instead of feeling relieved when he found her at Nick's, he had instead been filled with anger to see her calmly sitting drinking tea with Nicholas Brown. So much so that Dominic had completely lost control of the situation once they'd reached Brockle House.

How Caro must now hate and despise him—

'Dom?'

He closed his eyes briefly before focusing on Osbourne. 'I believe it is time I left; I have no doubt tired you enough for one day,' he dismissed briskly as he stepped forwards into the bedchamber, ready to take his leave. 'Is there anything I might bring to make you more comfortable?'

Nathaniel winced. 'No, as usual my Aunt Gertrude appears to have everything well in hand.'

Dominic smiled slightly at his friend's affectionate irony. 'I did not see her when I arrived earlier.'

'She has been persuaded to go out visiting this morning.' The relief could be heard in Osbourne's tone. 'Between her over-attentiveness, and her companion's sharp tongue, I am not sure I will last out the week!'

Dominic would not have thought the quiet and gracious young lady who had shown him up to Osbourne's bedchamber capable of being sharp-tongued. 'I am sure you will manage, Nate.'

'I wish I had the same confidence.' His friend gave a shake of his head. 'Of all things, my aunt is talking of removing me to the country to convalesce once I am well enough to travel.'

The idea had merit, Dominic decided after only the briefest of considerations. Nathaniel would be removed from danger, at least, if he were safely guarded by the formidable Mrs Wilson at her country home. 'It sounds a reasonable plan to me.'

'It is not at all reasonable!' Nathaniel glared. 'The Season has barely begun and Aunt Gertrude is intending to subject me to the boredom of the country when I am in no condition to protest.'

'No hardship, surely, when she is also removing you from the avaricious sphere of all those marriage-minded mamas?' Dominic reasoned drily.

'As I have reached the age of eight and twenty without as yet falling foul of those marriage-minded mamas, I am reasonably optimistic that I will have no trouble continuing to resist the allure of their beautiful daughters.' Osbourne eyed Dominic curiously. 'Speaking of which… Was I hallucinating, due to the beating I had just taken, or did your angel accompany us home in your carriage two evenings ago?'

Dominic stiffened. 'My angel?'

He knew to whom Nathaniel referred, of course; although the last time he had seen Caro, she had, quite rightly, presented him with all the warmth of a porcelain statue…

'You know exactly to whom I am referring, Dom,' Nathaniel prodded ruthlessly.

Exactly, yes. 'Do I?'

'Do you have any idea how boring it is just lying here with nothing to do but think?' Nathaniel's scowl was disgruntled to say the least.

'If you must think, then perhaps you should give consideration to Gabriel's future rather than my own?' Dominic attempted to change the subject.

Osbourne brightened slightly. 'He should be arriving in England very shortly.'

Dominic shrugged. 'But with the intention of travelling immediately to Shoreley Hall, remember.' Fortunately. If informed, Gabriel would definitely have had something to say about the situation Dominic found himself in. 'I—'

'I am sure we are very grateful for the frequency of your visits, Blackstone, but the physician has assured me that my nephew is in need of rest rather than excessive conversation.' An officious Mrs Wilson bustled forcefully into the bedchamber to begin enthusiastically plumping up the pillows beneath Osbourne's head, obviously now returned from her visiting, and not at all pleased that Dominic was once again disturbing her nephew in his sickbed.

Dominic gave her a polite bow. 'I assure you I am just as concerned for Osbourne's welfare as you obviously are, ma'am. In fact, I was about to take my leave when you came in.'

'Oh, I say, Aunt—'

'We must all take note of Mrs Wilson, Nate, if you

are to make a full and speedy recovery,' Dominic drawled mockingly over his friend's protest.

The other man shot him a narrow-eyed glare that contained the promise of retribution for Dominic's defection at some later date. A glare that he chose to ignore as he smilingly took his leave. A smile that faded as soon as Dominic stepped from Mrs Wilson's home, as he acknowledged that he could no longer put off his return to Brockle House.

And Caro…

'Lord Vaughn is here to see you, Mrs Morton.'

Caro heard the butler's words, but did not immediately respond to them.

The first thing Caro had done, once Dominic finally left earlier that morning, was to strip the soiled sheets from the bed and attempt to remove the worst of the bloodstains with some of the cold water left in the jug; bad enough that she was aware of this tangible evidence of her lost innocence, without the whole household being made aware of it, too.

Although she doubted there could be much doubt in the minds of any of the servants Dominic had engaged at Brockle House, concerning the events of this morning!

To their credit, Caro could not claim there had been any evidence of that in the demeanour of any of the servants who'd brought in the bath and hot water some half an hour after Dominic's departure, their manner both polite and attentive as the fire was lit in the hearth before the footmen placed the bath in front of it and the water was poured in.

Caro had refused the offer of help from one of the maids, however, needing to be alone as she soaked in the bath and contemplated the events of the morning just past.

Not one of those thoughts had offered any comfort to the situation in which she now found herself, Caro knew, at the very least, that she should feel angry with Dominic for having taken her innocence and yet somehow she could not bring herself to do so. Perhaps because she knew herself to be just as responsible as he—if not more so—for what had happened?

She had wanted Dominic to make love to her this morning. Had desired him as much as he had desired her, to the extent that her chief emotion had been disappointment when he had brought an abrupt halt to their lovemaking. It was a shameless admission from a young woman who had been brought up to believe that women who behaved in such a way were wantons, no better than the prostitutes who roamed the streets of any large town or city.

As to how Caro now felt towards Dominic himself…

That was a question she had considered and then shied away from answering. Whatever her feelings towards him, it would be madness indeed for Caro to care anything for the Earl of Blackstone—a man who so obviously shunned all the softer emotions in life.

That Dominic had now returned, as he had said he would, made Caro all the more determined that he not become aware of her own inner confusion of emotions. 'Show him in, please,' she instructed the butler coolly as she stood up to receive him with the same formality to be found in the sunlit drawing room in which she sat.

* * *

One glance at Caro's coolness of expression and the dignified elegance of her body was enough to tell Dominic that, even if she had not recovered from this morning, she did not intend to reveal as much by her demeanour. Aware of the presence of the butler, Dominic greeted her formally. 'Mrs Morton.'

She gave a brief curtsy in response to his abrupt bow. 'How kind of you to call again so soon, Lord Vaughn.'

Dominic wasn't fooled for a moment by the politeness of Caro's greeting, aware as he was of the utter disdain in her expression. As aware, in fact, as he was of how lovely she looked in a gown of deep lemon, with the sun shining through the window behind her and giving her delicate curls the appearance of spun gold, her light and floral perfume tantalising his senses.

He waited until the butler had left the room and closed the door behind him before answering drily. 'A visit you obviously wish I had not made.'

Caro raised her light-coloured brows. 'On the contrary, I am merely curious as to why you bothered to have yourself announced when you are the owner of this house?'

Dominic frowned his irritation. 'I may own the house, Caro, but you are the one living here—'

'Temporarily.'

'As such,' Dominic continued firmly, 'it would have been impolite of me to simply walk in unannounced.'

Her smile was more bitter than amused. 'And politeness is to be between us from now on, is it?'

Dominic's mouth compressed as he walked farther into the room. 'It is to be attempted, yes.'

'How nice.' Caro resumed her seat upon the sofa, her hands folded neatly together to rest upon her thighs as she looked across at him serenely. 'In that case, would you care to take tea with me, Lord Vaughn?'

What Dominic would rather have was a return of the old Caro. The Caro who no more cared for polite inanities than he did and who opposed him at every turn. The same Caro who had defiantly assured him on numerous occasions that she would do exactly as she pleased, when she pleased. A Caro who, as far as Dominic could tell, was nowhere to be seen in this coolly self-possessed young lady who gazed back at him so aloofly.

'Or perhaps you would care for something stronger than tea?' she prompted distantly when Dominic made no answer, not betraying by word or expression how deeply his presence here disturbed her.

She had no idea how a woman was supposed to behave towards a man who only that morning had taken her innocence, but had afterwards made it patently clear how much he considered that action to have been a mistake. She was sure, given the circumstances, that she should not be quite so aware of how magnificently handsome he appeared in a superfine of deep blue, a paler waistcoat beneath, his linen snowy-white, with buff-coloured pantaloons above brown Hessians.

Although the expression in those silver-coloured eyes, and the hard tension in his jaw, showed he was far from as confidently relaxed as he wished to appear.

The coldness that now existed between the two of them was intolerable, Caro decided heavily. Not that it was her wish for either of them to allude to the events of earlier this morning—it was, in truth, the very last thing she wished to talk, or even think, about—but she found the polite strangers they were pretending to be just as unacceptable. So much so that her emotions were once again verging on the tearful.

She stood up abruptly to tug on the bell-pull. 'You would prefer brandy? Or perhaps whisky?'

A glass of either of those held appeal, Dominic acknowledged wryly. Except he doubted that even imbibing a full decanter of alcohol would numb the feelings of guilt that had beset him as he observed the changes in Caro. 'By all means order tea for us both.' He moved restlessly to stand over by the window as she spoke softly to the butler when he arrived to take her order.

He could have been the male guest in the drawing room of any female member of the *ton*, Dominic recognised with a frown. There was the same politeness, the same formality and stiffness of manner he could have expected to receive there. The sort of polite formality that had never existed between himself and Caro!

He drew himself up determinedly once the two of them were once more alone. 'Caro, it must be as obvious to you as it is to me that we need to talk.'

'What would you care to talk about, Lord Vaughn?' she prompted brightly as she resumed her seat on the sofa to look across at him with unreadable sea-green eyes. 'The weather, perhaps? Or the beauty of the gardens at this time of year? I am afraid, never having attended one, that I cannot talk knowledgably of the balls and parties given in the homes of the *ton*—'

'You will cease this nonsense immediately.' Dominic

could no longer contain his impatience with the distance yawning between them. 'I have no more wish to discuss the weather, the garden, or the doings of the *ton*, than I believe you do.'

She raised haughty brows. 'I thought I had just assured you that I would be only too happy to converse on either of the first two subjects—'

'If you do not stop this nonsensical prattling, Caro, then I will have no other recourse but to come over there and shake you until your teeth rattle!' Dominic's hands were clenched at his sides as he resisted that impulse, a nerve pulsing in his tightly set jaw as he glared across the room at her.

She visibly bristled. 'If you even attempt to do so, then I assure you *I* will have no other recourse but to take the letter opener from the table over there and stab you with it!'

Dominic gave an appreciative grin as his tension eased slightly. Better. Much better. Almost the Caro he was used to, in fact.

He waited until the tray of tea things had been placed on the low table in front of her, and the butler once again departed about his business, before speaking again. 'I had thought you might be interested in hearing how Lord Thorne fares this afternoon?' He strolled across to make himself comfortable in the armchair facing Caro as she sat forwards on the sofa to pour the two cups of tea.

She paused to look across at him. 'He is well, I hope?'

'Slightly better, yes. But, if I read the situation correctly, he is also being thoroughly suffocated by the kindness of his doting aunt, as well as browbeaten by the sharp tongue of her young companion.'

Caro smiled slightly at the image this conjured up of the rakishly handsome Lord Thorne being fussed over by one lady and rebuked by another. 'No doubt something he considers more tiresome than his injuries.' She handed Dominic his tea before picking up her own cup and saucer and settling back against the sofa.

There was a slight pause before Dominic spoke again. 'Caro, we should have had this conversation this morning, but…' He gave a shake of his head. 'Emotions were such that I did not feel the time was right—'

'I sincerely hope you do not intend plaguing me by enquiring again after my own health, Lord Vaughn!' Her eyes flashed deeply green as she looked across at him. 'I have already assured you that I am perfectly well and do not wish to discuss this subject further.' To her dismay her hand shook slightly as she concentrated on raising her cup to her lips and took a sip of the milky unsweetened tea in order to avoid meeting the probing of that silver gaze.

It was uncomfortable to sit here drinking tea together as if they were only casual acquaintances, but Caro knew she preferred even that to the humiliation of discussing the events of this morning. Just being in the same room as Dominic was enough to make her aware of the slight aches and soreness of the different parts of her body—all of them a physical reminder of their lovemaking earlier today.

As she had hoped, the bath she had taken had eased some of her discomfort. But it seemed there had been no soothing the slight redness to her breasts from the chafing of stubble upon Dominic's jaw as it rubbed against her tender flesh, or the slight soreness between her thighs every time she moved—a constant reminder of what had happened between them.

None of them were things Caro cared to discuss with Dominic!

Or things she should think of and dwell on, when he had already made it so clear that he considered their lovemaking to have been a mistake.

If only Caro were not still so aware of him. Of the way his silky dark hair had fallen rakishly over his brow. Of how the hand he now raised to push back those dark locks had this morning been entangled in the golden curls between her thighs—

'Would that we could dismiss it so easily.' Dominic's mouth had thinned with displeasure.

She frowned as she forced her thoughts back from those memories of carnal delight. 'I do not see why we cannot.'

Could Caro really be this innocent? Dominic wondered. If so, then it was even more important that they have this discussion. 'You were the one to mention earlier that there may be consequences from our actions this morning.'

She stilled. 'Consequences I recall you saying would be extremely unlikely.'

Dominic gave up all pretence of appearing in the least relaxed as he stood up to pace restlessly on the rug in front of the fireplace. Earlier, he had been too shocked by that proof of Caro's innocence, so befuddled by the intensity of his arousal, to be in any condition to think clearly, let alone have a rational discussion on the subject.

Even now, Dominic found himself in danger of wanting to make love to her again rather than talk, as they surely must. To kiss the vulnerability of her exposed nape, to touch and caress the firm swell of her breasts, to part the soft curls between her thighs as he stroked the sensitive nubbin there before throwing up her skirts and once again thrusting his arousal into the exquisite pleasure of her!

His hands clenched at his sides. 'Consequences I said *may* be a possibility,' he corrected stiltedly.

'I do not understand?'

'Much as it pains me, Caro, there is the possibility—remote, I do acknowledge—that merely by having penetrated you, you could become with child,' Dominic explained as she looked up at him blankly.

Caro's eyes widened and all the colour drained from her cheeks as the cup and saucer she was holding slipped from her fingers and tumbled to the floor.

Chapter Thirteen

Caro could only stare down numbly at the broken cup and saucer as it was quickly surrounded by a rapidly spreading pool of milky tea that threatened to wet her satin slippers as well as the rug in front of the fire.

'Caro—'

'Ring for Denby, would you, Dominic?' Caro grabbed a napkin from the tea-tray and fell down on to her knees to wipe up the worst of the tea before starting to gather up the shattered pieces of porcelain, grateful to have this diversion as a means of avoiding answering Dominic's previous statement.

Caro was not ignorant about how babies were made; even if Diana, as the eldest, had not felt it her duty to discuss such matters with her two younger sisters once she considered them both old enough, it would have been impossible to avoid knowing about such things, when their father had often discussed the selective breeding for the deer and other livestock at Shoreley

Hall with his estate manager in the presence of his three daughters.

She had simply chosen to believe—to the point of denial—that such a thing could not possibly come about from Dominic's brief penetration.

'Leave it, Caro.' He stepped forwards to take a grip of her arm and pull her effortlessly to her feet, maintaining that hold as he turned to speak to the butler who had entered the room. 'Denby, could you see that this is cleaned up whilst I take Mrs Morton outside for a refreshing walk in the garden?' Dominic's expression was grim as Caro appeared too dazed to respond with her usual aversion to being told what to do, but instead allowed him to guide her outside into the sunlit garden. In truth, he was unsure as to whether she might have collapsed completely if he had not maintained that steadying grip upon her arm. 'Caro, I realise the delicacy of this situation, but surely—'

'Not now, Dominic,' she managed to breathe. 'I— allow me a few minutes in which to think, if you please.' She stepped away from him, releasing his hold upon her arm before turning her back on him and walking over to gaze down into the murky depths of the fishpond.

She looked so delicate, Dominic realised with a frown, so very young and vulnerable, as she stood there so still and silent. Unseeing, too, he did not doubt, knowing from the stunned expression and the pallor of her face that her thoughts were troubled ones.

As troubled as Dominic's own. 'I have come here this afternoon to assure you, that if by some mischance you do find yourself with child, I will of course feel honour-bound to offer you my hand in marriage.'

'Marriage!' Caro appeared horrified by the mere suggestion of it as she turned to stare at him.

Dominic had always been aware that he would have to marry one day. As a means of providing an heir, if for no other reason. But, if he had given the matter any thought at all, then the future bride he had imagined for himself would be selected from one of the families of the *ton*, a young lady of gentleness and obedience. She would certainly not be a stubborn and forthright young woman who refused to so much as listen—worse, who wilfully went her own way no matter what advice was offered to her.

He took a deep breath. 'It is obvious to me, despite the circumstances under which we first met, that you were obviously brought up to be a lady.'

'Indeed?' Caro's tone was icy.

'And that for reasons of your own,' Dominic continued determinedly, 'you have chosen to temporarily separate yourself from your family. Luckily, no one but Butler and Jackson…' and possibly Nicholas Brown, he mentally acknowledged '…is aware that Caro Morton and the masked lady are one and the same person. It is regrettable that you ever associated yourself with a gambling den, of course, but it cannot be changed now—'

'I assure you, if I have any desire to change *anything* about my visit to London, then it is that I ever had the misfortune to meet *you*!' Caro informed him frostily.

Dominic's mouth tightened at the deliberate insult. 'Even so, if you should indeed find yourself with child, then I am prepared, in view of the fact that I know of your previous innocence, to accept my responsibility—'

'I would advise that you not say another insulting word.' Her eyes flashed in warning. 'With child or otherwise, I would never consider even the possibility of ever marrying you,' she continued scornfully. 'Not even if you were to go down upon your knees and beg me to do so!'

Dominic could never envisage any situation in which he would ever go down upon his knees and beg any woman to marry him, although the vehemence with which Caro dismissed the very notion of a marriage between the two of them was insulting rather than reassuring.

She gave a delicate shudder now. 'I knew you to be an arrogant man, *my lord*, but I had not realised you to be one so full of self-conceit, too!'

Dominic felt the angry tide of colour in his cheeks at this further added insult. 'These character faults of mine did not seem a hindrance to the desire you felt for me earlier today!'

Caro's own cheeks became flushed at this reminder of her response to his lovemaking. But having come to London in the first place in order to escape the possibility of her guardian—another Earl, no less—being able to somehow coerce her into marrying him, Caro could not help but feel slighted by Dominic's obvious aversion to the unwelcome possibility that he might have to take her as his own Countess.

'I believe we have both of us made our feelings in this matter clear, Lord Vaughn,' she dismissed. 'And this conversation is therefore at an end. It would be better if you did not lay hands upon me again!' Her eyes narrowed as she found Dominic was now standing far too close to her for comfort and about to take a grip upon her arm.

His eyes glittered down at her just as fiercely as his fingers closed around her arm. 'And if I should choose not to heed that advice?'

Caro's chin rose challengingly. 'Then you will leave me no choice but to punch you upon your arrogant chin!'

He gave a start of surprise, then the angry glitter began to fade from his eyes to be replaced by reluctant admiration as he gave a brief laugh. 'You are without doubt the most unusual woman I have ever encountered.'

Unfortunately for him, Caro's own anger remained just as intense as it had ever been. 'Because I choose to threaten you with something you would understand rather than womanly hysteria?'

'Exactly so.' His fingers relaxed slightly upon her arm, but he did not release her. 'Caro, I meant you no insult just now when I said that I am prepared to offer you marriage should there be a child—'

'Did you not?' She tossed her head. 'Am I to understand that you expect me to feel grateful, then, by your *honour-bound* offer? Flattered when you express how *regrettable* you consider this situation to be? Suggesting that, as you are completely assured of my innocence before today, I should be happy that you are prepared to *accept your responsibility* as the father of any baby I might produce in the next nine months?'

'You are twisting my words—'

'Indeed I am not,' Caro denied hotly, her anger deepening the more she thought about Dominic's so-called proposal of marriage. At the moment, she really did feel capable of punching him upon his arrogant chin! 'Please accept my assurances, Lord Vaughn, that if I did happen to find myself unfortunate enough to be carrying your child, you would be the very last man I would ever think of going to for assistance.'

Dominic looked down at her sharply. 'Who else should you go to but me?'

Caro might have behaved recklessly in coming to London in the first place, most especially by remaining to become a singer in a gentleman's gambling club, even more so by allowing the lovemaking with Dominic this morning to go as far as it had, but none of those things changed the fact that she was in reality Lady Caroline Copeland, and the daughter of an Earl. A woman, moreover, who was Dominic Vaughn's social equal. That he had no idea of her true identity was irrelevant—the man was arrogance personified!

'I am not without friends, sir.' Caro looked down the length of her nose at him—not an easy feat when she was so much shorter than he. 'Good and faithful friends, who would be true to me no matter what I have done.' Caro considered her two sisters to be her best friends as well as her family. As such, she had no doubt that both Diana and Elizabeth would stand beside her, no matter what the circumstances.

His top lip curled. 'And where have these friends been these past two weeks?'

Her chin rose. 'Exactly where they have always been.' There had been comfort for Caro in knowing that her two sisters would be waiting for her at Shoreley Hall whenever she should choose to return to them. No doubt with a severe reprimand from Diana for having run away at all, and a whispered urging from Elizabeth to relate her adventures once they were alone together, but nevertheless, Caro had no doubt that her sisters would stand beside her come what may.

Dominic scowled darkly as his hand once again took a firm grip upon her arm. 'Damn it, Caro—'

'No doubt, by tomorrow, I will be in possession of as many black-and-blue bruises as Lord Thorne!' Caro protested, knowing full well he wasn't hurting her, but the implication that he was would make him release her immediately.

'I apologise.' As she had predicted, Dominic did indeed let her arm go abruptly. 'Caro, put your stubborn pride aside for one moment, and just consider—'

'The honour of becoming your Countess?' she flung back at him derisively. 'I have considered it, my lord— and as just quickly dismissed it!' She eyed him with the disdain of a queen.

Dominic was fast losing patience with this conversation. In attempting to be honest with her and proposing marriage if she should find herself with child, it appeared he had only succeeded in insulting her. And nothing he had said since appeared to have in any way rectified that situation. It appeared, in fact, that he could not regain favour in her eyes no matter what he did or said.

Yet did he wish to regain favour in her eyes? Surely it would be better for both of them if he left things exactly as they were? It was unpleasant to feel the lash of her tongue and coldness of manner towards him, but the alternative would no doubt only result in another of those passionate encounters. Dominic still burned with desire for her, despite knowing how ill advised a repeat of this morning's activities would be.

Just to look at Caro was to remember the silky smoothness of her skin beneath his fingers. To remember the hard pebbles of her nipples being drawn into his mouth. The burning heat of her slick and yet tight thighs as she took him deep inside her… No, perhaps it would be much safer to foster this lack of accord between them!

'As you wish, Caro,' he said haughtily as he turned away to studiously straighten the shirt cuffs beneath his jacket.

Caro was absolutely incensed as he turned his back on her. 'I cannot imagine what I could have been thinking of this morning, allowing you to make love to me, when you are so obviously everything that I most despise in a man!'

He turned back sharply, nostrils flared. 'Just as your own rebellious and outspoken nature is everything that I most dislike in a woman!'

Caro eyed him coldly. 'Then we are agreed we do not care for each other?'

His jaw tightened. 'Indeed we are!'

She gave a cool nod. 'Then I will wish you good day, Lord Vaughn.'

Dominic eyed her with frustration. He had never met a woman who could bring him so quickly to anger. To impatience. To fury. But most especially to desire…

Logical thought told Dominic that if he wished to retain his sanity, then any future protection he provided for Caro's safety must necessarily be given from a distance. Just to be with her was playing the very devil with his self-control—

'Am I to remain a prisoner here, as I was at Blackstone House, until this danger from Nicholas Brown is over?' Caro interrupted Dominic's disturbing train of thought. 'Or am I to be allowed out for a carriage ride, at least?'

He refocused on her, his instincts telling him, for the sake of her own safety, to deny her even that small pleasure. However, that same instinct was quickly overridden by the memory of how flagrantly Caro had chosen to defy those same instructions only this morning and what the result of that defiance had been!

His mouth twisted. If he denied her, she'd likely find a way to disobey him, and then all hell would be let loose. Far better that he knew what she was doing at all times. 'I believe a carriage ride is permissible.'

'How kind!' Her sarcasm was unmistakable. 'And am I to take a maid with me on this carriage ride?'

'I do not believe that to be necessary unless you especially wish to do so. The grooms and coachmen here are also old comrades of mine,' he added before she had the opportunity to make another scathing comment. 'I trust in their ability to ensure that no harm befalls you.'

'*Further* harm, I think you mean?'

Dominic flinched as that verbal arrow of hers hit its mark. How he longed to take this rebellious woman into his arms. To kiss her into submission, if he could achieve her obedience in no other way. Yet at the same time he knew he should not, could not do either of those things. 'I will call on you again tomorrow—'

'I am sure there is no need to trouble yourself on my account,' she cut in.

Once again Dominic bit back his frustration, knowing how badly he had already handled this situation. 'I will take my leave, then.'

She nodded coolly. 'Lord Vaughn.'

There was nothing more for Dominic to do or say. Nothing he could do or say, it seemed, that would make things as they had once been between them.

Even if he did not know, could not completely comprehend, exactly what that had been…

Caro was filled with a raw restlessness once she was sure that the Earl had gone from the house, aware as she was of the rest of the afternoon and the long evening alone that now stretched before her. Tomorrow, too, in all probability, now that she had told Dominic it was unnecessary for him to call on her.

He should not have made her so angry! Should not have said those insulting things to her. Insults, Caro acknowledged ruefully, that she had more than returned.

How different things could have been, if instead of offering her marriage in that insulting manner, Dominic had first made a declaration of having fallen in love with her.

And if he had? Caro asked herself. What would her answer have been then to his marriage proposal? Would she have returned that declaration of love before accepting his marriage proposal?

The thought that she might have done both of those things was so disturbing to Caro that she found herself hurrying from the drawing room, pausing only long enough in the entrance hall to instruct Denby to have the coach brought round, before hurrying up to her bedchamber to collect her bonnet and pelisse. The afternoon seemed to have grown chilly since Dominic's abrupt departure…

Quite where she intended going on her carriage ride Caro had no idea, aware only that she had to escape the confines—the memories!—of Brockle House, if only for a short time.

She instructed the coachman to drive through the same park as yesterday—perhaps with the hope that she might once again catch a glimpse of the young girl with the dog that had so achingly reminded her of Elizabeth. But if that was her wish then she was disappointed, and after only a short time she was also a little tired of the curious glances being directed towards where she travelled in the black carriage so obviously bearing the crest of the Earl of Blackstone.

Feeling in need of sympathetic company, Caro knocked upon the roof of the carriage and instructed the coachman to take her to Nick's; Drew Butler and Ben had been delighted when she had called to see them this morning, so surely a second visit would not be too unwelcome?

But they had not gone far in that direction before Caro looked up and noticed a huge black cloud billowing up into the sky, her attention fixed on that black haze as she once again tapped on the roof of the coach. 'What is that about, Daley?'

'I believe it might be smoke, Mrs Morton,' he answered respectfully.

Smoke? If there was smoke then there must be a
fire. And fire was a dangerous thing in a city the size
of London. 'Perhaps we should go and see if we can be
of any assistance, Daley?'

The middle-aged man looked uncertain. 'I doubt his
lordship would approve, madam.'

Dominic.

Smoke?

Fire!

Quite why Caro was so convinced those three things
were connected she had no idea—she only knew that
she became more convinced of it by the second!

Chapter Fourteen

'You have to stop now, Drew; there is nothing more we can do,' Dominic instructed the man wearily.

The two men were blackened from head to toe from having several times entered the burning building before them, thick black smoke now billowing out of every doorway and window of the building even as the flames and sparks shot up through a hole in the burning roof.

Butler's eyes glittered wildly in his own soot-covered face. 'Ben is still in there!'

'There is nothing more we can do,' Dominic repeated dully, his own expression grim beneath the soot and grime as he stared up at the inferno that had once been Nick's.

'But—'

'He's gone, Drew.'

The older man's arms fell helplessly to his sides, his weathered face echoing the defeat both men felt as they could only stand now and watch the fire blaze out of control despite their own efforts and that of the men who had arrived a few minutes ago to help put it out.

The fire had been well under way when Dominic himself had arrived some half an hour or so ago. Nowhere near as fierce as it was now, of course, but even so he had quickly drawn a halt to Drew and Ben Jackson's efforts as they rushed in and out of the building salvaging what they could.

Unfortunately Ben had decided to return one more time to collect some personal belongings and the account books from the desk in Drew Butler's office.

He had not come out again...

Drew's hands clenched into fists at his sides. 'I'm going to kill the bastard!'

Dominic's jaw tightened. 'Brown?'

The older man's eyes blazed with fury as he turned. 'Who else?'

It was a conclusion that Dominic had come to himself the moment he saw the fire blazing and so easily recalled Brown's air of quiet satisfaction when he had left the gambling club earlier today.

Dominic had gone into the lion's den the evening before, with the intention of ascertaining whether Brown truly was the one responsible for the attack on Osborne. The slickness with which the other man had denied all knowledge of that attack—when he was a man known to boast that he was aware of everything that happened in what he regarded as being 'his city'— had seemed to indicate those suspicions were correct.

That Brown had himself arrived at the gambling club earlier today, supposedly to pay a visit on his old friends, Butler and Jackson, as well as the guarded conversation that had transpired between Brown and Dominic in Caro's presence, was simply a measure, Dominic was certain, of the other man's audacity.

A fire in that building, only hours after Brown's visit, was to Dominic's mind tantamount to a direct challenge...

He frowned darkly. 'The law will need evidence before they will agree to act.'

The older man gave a scathing snort. 'I don't need any evidence to recognise Brown had a hand in this.'

Neither did Dominic. 'Be assured, I feel exactly the way you do about this, Drew, but nevertheless I must seriously advise against taking matters into your own hands—'

'So I'm to sit back and let him get away with murder, am I?'

Dominic had already experienced one slight on his honour in the past two days; he was not about to suffer another one. He put his hand on the older man's arm. 'I am hoping you will trust me to ensure that will not happen.'

Drew barely seemed to hear him. 'I worked for the man for almost twenty years. Had my suspicions before this of what a low-down cur he could be, but—' He gave a disgusted shake of his head. 'Brown did this as surely as my name is Andrew Butler.'

Dominic drew his breath in sharply. 'And I have assured you that I will ensure he will be made to pay for his crimes—'

'Dominic! Drew! Oh, thank goodness you are both safe!'

Dominic turned just in time to catch Caro as she launched herself into his arms.

Caro had barely been able to comprehend the sight that had met her eyes as the carriage turned into the avenue and she saw the blazing remains of the club where she had worked until two evenings ago. The whole building was ablaze, with that heavy black smoke billowing everywhere, and dozens of men hurrying back and forth as they threw water upon the blaze to prevent it passing to the vulnerable neighbouring buildings.

Her relief when she spotted Dominic, standing to one side in conversation with Drew, had been immense. So much so that she had briefly forgotten her earlier disagreement with Dominic, and simply thrown herself into his arms out of the sheer relief of seeing him safe.

Her cheeks now felt hot—and not from the effects of the fire!—as she gathered herself together and extracted herself from Dominic's embrace before turning to face the older man. 'How good it is to see that you are unharmed, Drew—'

'Never mind that now, Caro,' Dominic was the one to answer her as he pulled her firmly back from the danger of the hot timbers now starting to fall from the top of the blazing building. 'Explain what you are doing here, if you please!'

She frowned up into his dark and disapproving face. 'I had gone out for a drive, as I told you I intended, when I saw the smoke…'

'And decided to investigate,' Dominic recognised with barely restrained violence. 'Did you not realise that by doing so you might have become caught up in the blaze yourself and possibly been injured?'

She waved an airy hand. 'I hope I have more sense than to have gone close enough so that—'

'And yet here you are!' Dominic glared down at her, very aware that she was as yet unaware of Ben Jackson's absence. That when she did realise he would have another crisis on his hands; Caro's affection for the gentle giant had been obvious from the first, and once she discovered that Ben had disappeared into the blazing building some minutes ago, and not returned, she was sure to react. In truth, Dominic had no idea which direction those emotions would take, tears and cries of anguish, or anger that her friend might have perished in the fire...

She gave a pained frown. 'I was concerned—'

'And now that concern has been satisfied I want you to get back into your carriage immediately and return to Brockle House,' Dominic instructed firmly.

'But—'

'Caro, do not argue with me over this, as you seem to feel you must argue every other point in our conversations.' Dominic's jaw was as tightly clenched as Drew's fists had been minutes ago. 'You can be of no possible help here,' he added.

'Might I suggest that you leave me to continue dealing with the situation here whilst you escort Caro home?' Drew quietly drew Dominic's attention, his pointed look in the direction of some activity at the side of the building enough to tell Dominic that Ben had been found; neither man believed he could have lived through the minutes he had spent trapped in that raging inferno…

'That is unnecessary—'

'It is very necessary.' Dominic easily cut across Caro's protest even as he gave a brief nod to the older man in recognition of their silent exchange.

'To you, perhaps—'

'To me, too, Caro.' Drew gently added his own weight behind the argument as he moved forwards so that he now stood beside Dominic. 'Do as his lordship advises and return to your carriage—'

'Why are you suddenly both in such a hurry for me to leave?' Caro eyed both men suspiciously as she realised they seemed to be crowding around her. Herding her, actually. Much like her father's estate workers when they were gathering the livestock together to house them in the huge barns over the winter. 'I—where is Ben?' Her gaze moved sharply to the left and then to the right, but with Drew and Dominic standing like two sentinels directly in front of her, she found that vision limited.

Deliberately?

'Caro—'

'Where is Ben, Dominic?' Caro lifted her hands and placed one against the chest of both men with the intention of pushing them aside, nimbly stepping around them when neither man was made to move. Just in time to see that several of the men who had been fighting the fire were now carrying something from the side of the building. Something heavy. A dead weight, in fact… 'Ben?' she gasped weakly.

'No, Caro!' Dominic reached out and grasped her by the shoulders as she would have run across to where the men were now placing that cumbersome burden down upon the ground.

Her gaze was frantic as she lifted her hands to fight against Dominic's hold upon her. 'Can you not see that it is Ben?'

'We know who it is, Caro.' Once again it was Drew who spoke gently. 'If there's anything that can be done for Ben, then you can be assured that it will be,' he added grimly. 'The best thing you can do for him now is to return home without any more fuss.'

Caro became very still in Dominic's grasp as she looked first at Drew and then back to Dominic, the latter giving a slight shake of his head as he turned back from looking at the frantic activity around that scorched bundled of rags that had obviously been Ben Jackson.

Because even from this distance Caro could see that his spirit was no longer there...

An anguished cry escaped her lips even as she felt her legs buckle beneath her and began to fall slowly to the ground.

'You are perfectly safe, Caro.' Dominic's voice sounded harsher than he had intended, in the otherwise silence of the moving carriage, as he tried to still her struggles to free herself from where he held her tightly against his chest. 'Please be still, Caro,' he urged more gently.

For once in their acquaintance she heeded him, unmoving in his arms as she looked up at him with huge sea-green eyes that were rapidly filling with tears. 'Is Ben really gone, Dominic?'

He drew in a ragged breath. 'If it is any consolation

then I believe he would have died from breathing in the smoke long before the fire ever came anywhere near him.' He sincerely hoped that was the case, at least.

Although the method of Ben's death did not change the fact he was indeed dead. And as a result of a fire both Drew and Dominic believed to have been deliberately set by Nicholas Brown.

'Truly, Dominic?'

He forced the rigidity from his expression at those grim thoughts of Brown's cowardly act before looking down at Caro, knowing that she needed to believe that Ben's death had been as painless as was possible given the circumstances. 'Truly.' Dominic nodded.

He had paused only long enough, after seeing the unconscious Caro into the safety of the carriage, to converse briefly with the men who had brought out Ben's body. It seemed they had found him collapsed in the hallway leading to Drew's office situated at the back of the club, where the fire itself was the least fierce.

'He was such a kind young man.' Caro's voice caught emotionally.

Dominic had seen Ben off and on for years on his visits to the gambling club; it had been impossible not to feel an affection for the younger man's almost childlike acceptance of his lot in life.

As such, Dominic knew that it was going to be hard for all of them to accept the death of such an affable and likeable young man. 'He was,' he acknowledged flatly.

Caro pulled out of his arms to slowly sit up. 'How could it have happened, Dominic?' She gave a slightly dazed shake of her head. 'I can hardly believe I was sitting drinking tea with him only hours ago…' The tears began to fall unchecked down her cheeks.

'Yes.' Dominic's mouth tightened as he easily recalled that Brown had been seated at that table, too. 'We may perhaps have more insight into how the fire began once the flames have died down and we are able to get back inside the building.' Although in his own mind—and undoubtedly that of Drew Butler—Brown, or one of his henchmen acting on instructions, was clearly to blame.

'Do you believe Nicholas Brown to be responsible?'

Dominic was not in the least surprised at the speed of Caro's astuteness. 'Undoubtedly,' he confirmed grimly.

'As just another deliberate act to cause you as much inconvenience as possible, or do you think he really meant either Ben or Drew—or possibly both—to die?' Her face had taken on a slightly green cast as she voiced that last possibility.

As far as Dominic was aware, he had never lied to Caro; in fact, his actions, especially this morning, had possibly been too honest where she was concerned. Possibly? The whole of his behaviour today, from making love to her to the crassness of his marriage proposal, had been honest to the point of self-destruction!

That she had allowed him to hold her just now, even briefly, Dominic knew was due only to her distress over Ben's death. Once she had recovered her senses they would no doubt be back to a state of daggers' drawn.

He drew in a deep breath as he chose his words carefully. 'I believe it was the former. At the same time, I also believe Brown did not care who, or if, anyone should be hurt in the fire,' he acknowledged heavily before taking the kerchief from his pocket and wiping the worst of the soot and grime from his face and hands.

Caro breathed shakily. 'Ben would not have hurt even a fly.'

Remembering those ham-sized fists, and the several occasions upon which he had witnessed the younger man wielding them, Dominic was not quite sure of the truth of that statement! Nevertheless, he took Caro's point; there had never been any malice in Ben's actions in doing his job defending the club.

'I am sure it was pure misfortunate that Ben perished in the fire.' Dominic was not as certain of that as he sounded, aware as he was that this morning Nicholas Brown had witnessed both Ben and Drew busily at work in the gambling club so that it might re-open as soon as was possible.

Caro looked up at him closely. 'Do you honestly believe that?'

'I...believe it is a reasonable assumption, yes,' he said carefully.

'I am neither a child nor an imbecile, Dominic, and after all that has happened, I do not expect you to treat me as such!' Caro's expression had become fierce as she obviously picked up on his evasion.

He had no doubts as to her maturity or intelligence; it was simply not in his nature to confide his thoughts and feelings to another person. 'I assure you it is not my intention to do either of those things, Caro. I simply feel it is better not to voice my concerns until I can be completely sure of my facts.'

He also had no intention of allowing her to become in the least involved in the reckoning that Dominic had every intention would shortly descend upon Nicholas Brown; Caro was impetuous enough, reckless enough, to place herself in danger if she believed it was necessary to avenge Ben.

No, Dominic had every intention of dealing personally with Mr Nicholas Brown…

Caro still looked slightly ill. 'I cannot conceive of anyone doing something so…so heinous, as to have deliberately started a fire.'

Dominic was only too aware that Brown was reputed to have done much worse things than that in the past. Just as Dominic was now aware—too late to save Ben, unfortunately—that after the attack on Osbourne two nights ago, and despite Drew's assurances that he was quite capable of taking care of himself and his own family, including Ben, Dominic should have insisted on more safeguards being put in place. The reason he had not was because he had been so distracted by the need to protect Caro that he had given little thought to anything else…

A danger that now seemed more immediate than ever; Dominic had thought to make Caro safe by offering her his protection, by moving her as quickly as he could to the obscurity of Brockle House. But Brown's visit to the gambling club this morning had exposed Caro, if not as the masked singer, then certainly as a closer acquaintance to Dominic than the cousins they claimed to be. Now he feared the man might even know that Caro resided at Brockle House as from this morning…

Dominic shared Drew's eagerness to confront Nicholas Brown, to ensure that he paid for his crimes—in fact, at that moment, he knew he would enjoy nothing more than personally strangling the man with his own bare hands—but his explanation to Caro, when she had previously dared to question his honour, was also true. A soldier, an officer, did not confront his enemy until he had all of his troops in place.

And Nicholas Brown was now most certainly Dominic's enemy!

'Caro, I believe it would be best if I were to stay at Brockle House tonight.' He looked at her from underneath lowered lids.

Her own eyes widened. 'I believed we had both made our feelings on that subject perfectly clear—'

'I did not say it was with any intention of sharing your bed,' Dominic cut in impatiently. 'Only that it might be…safer, perhaps, if I were to stay at Brockle House tonight.'

Caro's cheeks warmed as she realised her mistake. Of course Dominic did not intend sharing her bed again tonight; he did not intend sharing her bed ever again! Something she should feel grateful for. And yet somehow did not… 'Is it your belief that we are both now in mortal danger from Nicholas Brown?'

Dominic shrugged. 'Perhaps.'

Caro was consumed with annoyance at Dominic's reticence, his refusal to share his thoughts and feelings with her. He had to be the most self-contained man she had ever met—and that was including her father, who had become so shut inside himself after their mother had left them all to go and live in London ten years ago, that he had never mentally been completely with his three daughters again. As far as she could tell,

Dominic shared none of his thoughts and ideas with anyone.

Least of all a woman to whom he had only offered marriage if *by some mischance*, as he'd put it, she should find herself carrying his child!

'If you feel it is necessary, Dominic, then of course you have every right to spend the night in what is, after all, your own property.' She gave a cool inclination of her head.

Dominic breathed heavily through his nose. 'In that case, until this situation has been resolved to my complete satisfaction, I feel it best if I spend all of my nights at Brockle House.'

Caro's eyes widened. 'Are you not going to find that a little…restricting?'

He scowled darkly. 'In what way?'

She shrugged. 'Would such an arrangement not… limit your own freedom to come and go as you wished?'

Dominic drew in an angry breath. 'Caro, if you are once again suggesting that I might have a mistress set up in another house in London somewhere, and with whom I might wish to spend my nights, then let me state, once and for all, that I do not now, nor have I ever, had a mistress in the accepted sense of the word!' He eyed her coldly.

'No?' Her brows rose. 'I would be interested to know why not.'

'Then it is an interest I am afraid you will just have to continue to endure,' Dominic growled. 'After only a few days of having you as a permanent fixture in my life, of feeling responsible for you twenty-four hours a day, I am more convinced than ever that my decision never to be tied down by such an arrangement was the correct one.' He meant to be insulting, and he knew he had succeeded when he saw the sparkle of anger in the deep blue-green of Caro's eyes.

A spark of anger that Dominic had deliberately incited…

'That situation can be rectified any time you choose to let me leave both your home and your company,' she came back challengingly.

'Unfortunately, it cannot.' Dominic sighed. 'Not until Brown has been brought to justice. Never fear, Caro,' he added mockingly. 'I am sure that Brockle House is large enough for us to successfully avoid spending time in each other's company, if that is what you wish?'

'I wish it more than anything!' There was an angry flush to Caro's cheeks as she turned away from him to present him with her profile as she stared out of the carriage window.

Dominic accepted that it had been cruel of him to bedevil her in this way when their lovemaking had ended so disastrously earlier today. When she had been present as they pulled Ben's body from the burning building. His only excuse was that his baiting of her had briefly cast aside her bewilderment and pain over Ben's death, to be replaced by a little of the usual fiery spirit he so admired and which was such a large part of her nature.

A spirit Dominic dearly hoped would help see her through, what he was sure, were going to be several difficult days…

Chapter Fifteen

'Caro, when I said earlier that you might avoid my company as much as is possible for the duration of my stay here, it was not with any intention that you would eat your dinner in your bedchamber whilst I am left to dine downstairs alone.'

She was completely unmoved by the impatience in Dominic's tone as she turned to look at where he stood in the open doorway of her bedchamber.

It had been almost two hours since they had arrived back at Brockle House. Dominic appeared to have bathed and changed out of the soiled clothing of earlier into a black evening jacket and snowy white linen with a meticulously tied neckcloth. Evidence, perhaps, that in the interim he had sent to Blackstone House for both his valet and his clothes.

Caro had spent those same two hours trying to come to terms with the fact that Ben Jackson was dead. To accept that her friend had perished in a fire Dominic believed had been started deliberately by Nicholas Brown or one of his close associates.

For years she had chafed and fought against the sheltered life she had been forced to lead in Hampshire, with the result that she had not hesitated to put her plan into action once she had decided to run away to London as a means of avoiding the arrival of her guardian and his unwanted offer of marriage. She had believed herself to be thoroughly capable of taking care of herself, and that spending several weeks in London would be an exciting adventure she would remember for the rest of her life.

Nothing about her previous life could possibly have prepared her for such stark reality as she had witnessed today.

She gave a slight shake of her head. 'I have not eaten my dinner in my bedchamber.'

Dominic scowled darkly as he strode forcefully into the room. 'In that case, why haven't you?'

She gave a listless shrug. 'I am not hungry.'

'Caro—'

'Dominic, please!' She stood up restlessly, also having bathed and changed into the deep rose-coloured gown. 'How can I possibly eat when every time I so much as think of poor Ben's fate I feel utterly nauseous?'

Dominic's expression softened as he realised that, while he'd had some little relief from her tempting charms in the past couple of hours, suggesting they avoid each other's company had not been particularly beneficial to her; he could see the evidence of the tears she had obviously shed once she was alone in the slight redness about pain-darkened eyes and the pallor of her cheeks. 'It will not help anyone if you make yourself ill—'

'You cannot expect me to eat when Ben is lying dead in the morgue!' Caro's voice broke emotionally over the last, and she buried her face in her hands, her shoulders shaking, as she once again began to sob piteously.

Dominic felt a tightening in his chest as he witnessed her distress, taking the two steps that enabled him to reach out and take her into his arms, her head resting against his chest as she wept. He had never been at ease with a woman's tears, and, after the intimacies they had shared, he found Caro's especially difficult to bear. Her close proximity was even more difficult as he felt her arms move about his waist and the warm spread of her fingers across his back...

Dear Lord! Desire, arousal were the last things he should be feeling when she was obviously so distraught. And yet, try as he might, he could exert no control over the stirring, the hardening of his thighs, as Caro nestled the softness of her body against his. She rested so trustingly against him—for Dominic was sure that she shared none of those same thoughts of desire as she continued to sob quietly. His own physical response to that trust was as inappropriate as it would no doubt be unwelcome should she become aware of it, and he grimaced with annoyance at his own body's betrayal.

As Caro's tears slowly began to abate she sensed a change in the mood between herself and Dominic. A tension, an intimacy, that invaded her senses with a subtlety that was as insidious as it was undeniable. The very air around them seemed to thicken, to deepen, and she was suddenly completely aware of the tense heat of his body and the ragged unevenness of his breathing, as his chest rose and fell beneath the increasing warmth of her cheek. She was also aware of the thick length of his arousal as it continued to grow and press against the softness of her own thighs.

Her breath caught in her throat as she slowly raised her head to look up at him, knowing by the glittering intensity of the silver gaze that looked down and met hers that she was not mistaken concerning his present state of arousal.

She moistened dry lips before speaking. 'Dominic, how can it be that we feel this…this desire after all that has happened today?' She was utterly bewildered— almost ashamed—by the feelings now coursing hotly through her own body.

Dominic shook his head. 'I have seen it dozens of times in soldiers following a battle,' he recalled huskily. 'I believe it is a need, a desire, to reaffirm one's own place in the mortal world following confrontation with death.'

Caro breathed shallowly. 'Is it not shocking for me to feel this way now?'

His expression softened. 'Does it feel shocking to you?'

'No.' The pink tip of her tongue swept across her lips a second time. 'I— It feels as if, as you say, I have a need to know that we both still live.'

Dominic looked down at her searchingly, a gaze that she met unflinchingly. 'Will you allow me to make love to you, Caro?' he asked gently.

Her eyes widened. 'But I thought you had made it quite clear that we could not, must not, repeat the events of this morning?'

'Neither will we.'

Her frown was perplexed. 'I do not understand...'

Dominic gave a rueful smile. 'There are many ways in which to make love, my dear. Many of them do not involve the penetration that could so easily result in you becoming with child.'

Caro's cheeks felt hot. 'I see. And will you...will you show me these other ways?' Her cheeks were flushed, her eyes fever bright.

But not with awkwardness or discomfort, Dominic noted with admiration, but instead with a curiosity and underlying excitement. He knew he should not allow this to happen, that he should refuse to acknowledge the invitation in her eyes. But as he looked down at her, he clearly saw the same desire in her that now throbbed through his own body, and he knew he would not, could not, walk away from her as he surely should.

He, too, had had time to think since they had parted after arriving at Brockle House earlier. To realise that she could just as easily have gone to visit Drew and Ben at Nick's this afternoon rather than this morning. To acknowledge that she might have been inside the club with the other two men when the fire began, and easily envisage the nightmare of what might have been—Caro lying in the morgue rather than Ben Jackson...

Which perhaps explained why he had felt it so keenly when Denby had told him a short time ago that Caro had asked him to inform Dominic she would not be joining him downstairs for dinner. Whatever the reason, no matter how much more it might complicate matters if he were to make love with her again, he knew that it was something he urgently needed to do.

Caro pulled out of his arms to turn her back on him before looking at him over her shoulder. 'I believe we should start by removing my gown?'

He drew his breath in sharply as he looked at the calm determination in Caro's expression for several long seconds before raising his hands to begin releasing the buttons down the back of her gown. Only to falter slightly once he had unfastened a half-dozen of those tiny buttons. 'Are you *sure* you want to do this?'

'I am very sure, Dominic,' she murmured even as she tilted her head forwards to reveal the fragile vulnerability of her nape.

It was more than any man could bear—more, certainly, than he could at this moment—to resist Caro's absolute conviction in what they were about to do. And once he had unfastened the rose-coloured gown, allowing it to pool on the carpet at her feet, before she stepped free of its confinement and turned to face him wearing only a shift that nevertheless revealed the firm thrust of her breasts tipped by those darker nipples, and the silky thatch of golden curls between her thighs, Dominic had no room for thoughts of resistance. His desire blazed completely out of his control as she reached up to slip the thin straps of her last garment down over the slenderness of her arms, before allowing that, too, to fall at her feet and she stood before him completely naked.

Dominic meant to be gentle with her, out of consideration for the discomfort she must still feel following their lovemaking this morning. But it was a gentleness Caro firmly rejected as she stepped boldly into his arms before raising her head so that her lips might capture his. That kiss became wild, fiercely heated, as she dispensed with his jacket and waistcoat before unfastening his shirt and pushing her hands inside the silky material to caress his bared chest.

Dominic returned the heat of that kiss even as he reached up to rend the material of his shirt in two to allow her better access to his flesh. Caro's nails scraped over the hard nubbins nestled amongst the silky dark hair that covered his chest, the hard tips of her own breasts pressed against the muscled hardness of his abdomen. He gasped into her mouth as those caressing, confident hands moved slowly downwards to stroke the length of his erection as it jutted proudly against the confinement of his pantaloons.

It did not remain confined for long as Caro easily dispensed with the six buttons at the sides of his pantaloons before peeling that flap of material aside, the fingers of one hand curling about his engorged arousal even as she cupped him beneath with the other.

Dominic broke the kiss, his groan one of aching longing as he felt her dextrous fingers sweep across the sensitive tip before moving down along the length of him. 'Yes, Caro! Oh, God, yes!'

'Tell me how to give you pleasure, Dominic,' she encouraged softly.

His breath caught in his throat. 'Kiss me there, take me into the sweetness of your mouth!' His moan was heartfelt as Caro dropped softly to her knees in front of him, that sea-green gaze looking up to steadily meet his as she slowly and deliberately opened those kiss-swollen lips and took him into the fiery heat of her mouth.

Dominic's knees almost buckled completely as he looked down at her pleasuring him, his hands moving to become entangled in her golden curls as she continued her delicious ministrations until he knew he was going to lose control. He needed to taste her before that happened, wanted to pleasure her in the same way.

Dominic ignored her slightly reproachful look as he gently disengaged himself and pulled her back up on to her feet. He swung her up into his arms and carried her over to lie her down upon the bed, gently propping her head upon the pillows. She watched him as he first drew off his boots and then threw off the rest off his clothes before moving to kneel between her legs. The darkness of his gaze briefly held hers captive before he lowered his head between her parted thighs to run his own tongue along the length of her opening before rasping moistly over and around her sensitive bud, feeling it pulse with each rhythmic stroke. 'Watch me, Caro!' he urged.

She obeyed as he gently parted her golden curls and cried out as he lowered his head once again to stroke that pulsing bud with the hard tip of his tongue, and she felt the pleasure begin to build, to grow, deep inside her. Suffusing her with heat. Turning her limbs to water. Her head fell back against the pillows even as her thighs began to undulate against that marauding mouth and tongue.

That pleasure surged out of control as his hands moved up to cup and capture both her breasts before he rolled the nipples between finger and thumb,

Caro's release hitting with the force of a tidal wave as he squeezed those roused tips at the same time as his tongue thrust into her time and time again until she lay limply back against the pillows.

Dominic moved up on to his knees to look down at Caro as she lay there, replete and naked against the pillows. 'My turn now, love,' he said throatily.

Caro was completely focused on that jutting arousal as she came up on to her knees to move down the bed and kiss him slowly from base to tip, before then taking him fully into the heat of her mouth.

It was too much, Dominic already far too aroused from both the taste of her in his mouth and her earlier attentions, and his hands tightly gripped Caro's shoulders as he climaxed fiercely, hotly, triumphantly…

Caro's hand moved in a gentle caress against the unruly darkness of the hair at Dominic's nape, his head resting lightly against her breast as they lay naked together in the aftermath of their wild and satisfying lovemaking.

She felt no awkwardness, no shame; she knew that they had both needed what had just happened between them, that he had been correct in that they had both needed to reaffirm their precarious grip on mortality, and the silence between them now was companionable rather than uncomfortable.

Dominic raised his head slightly to look at her, that silver gaze guarded. 'I was not too rough with you?'

'Not at all,' she assured without hesitation. 'Was I too rough with you?' she added, aware that she had been somewhat less than gentle herself!

He smiled slightly before lowering his head back down on to her breast. 'Not in any way I would not like you to repeat if, or indeed whenever, the mood should take you.'

Caro's cheeks felt warm as she recalled the way in which she had caressed and kissed Dominic so intimately. She had no knowledge of lovemaking between a man and a woman other than the things he had shown her these past few days, and yet she had gloried in touching and kissing the beauty of his hard arousal.

'I no longer feel quite so…empty.' Her voice was husky with emotion.

'Nor I,' Dominic acknowledged softly.

She frowned as a thought occurred to her. 'Do you know whether or not Ben had any family?'

Dominic's shoulders tensed beneath the caress of Caro's fingers. 'He has a sister, I believe. A Mrs Grey.'

'She will be deeply saddened by his death.'

'As we all are,' Dominic said heavily. 'Drew was to go and see her as soon as he was able to get away. I have asked him to convey my regrets, and also to tell her that I will call on her tomorrow to discuss the funeral arrangements if that is what she wishes.'

'I would like to attend the funeral.'

The tension in Dominic's shoulders increased. 'I am not sure that is a good idea—'

'It was not a request, Dominic,' Caro insisted. 'Have you—have you seen much of death?' she asked before he could voice any more objections.

'More than I care to remember,' he admitted harshly.

Caro breathed a sigh. 'My own mother died when I was but ten years old, and she was not at home with us when it happened.' She gave a pained frown as she remembered the circumstances under which her mother had died. 'My father died only a few months ago, but he had been ill for some time, and in truth, it was more of a happy release for him than a shock to...to his family.'

Dominic was aware that the pieces that made up Caro's life were given rarely and sparingly, but she had said enough just now for him to know it was no more a father that she hid from than a husband.

He could not resist looking up at her and teasing her a little. 'I believe you told Drew that it was a maiden aunt who had died a few months ago, and in doing so left you homeless as well as penniless.'

Two bright wings of colour now brightened Caro's cheeks. 'I did say that, yes.'

'And...?'

She gave an irritated little snort. 'What difference does it make whether it was a father or a maiden aunt?'

'None at all—except maybe to that father or aunt.' Dominic placed a slow and lingering kiss upon the side of her breast in apology for his teasing of what they both knew to be a complete fabrication of her previous life. But he felt too relaxed, too satiated, to seriously question it at this moment. That relaxed contentment rendered him ill prepared for Caro's next question...

'Obviously you are the Earl, so your own father is no longer with us, but what of the rest of your family? Your mother, for instance?'

All relaxation fled, all contentment, as Dominic sat up sharply. 'Also dead. They both died when I was but twelve years old.'

Caro gasped. 'Both your parents?'

'Yes.'

'Together?'

'No. Caro—'

'Please do not go, Dominic!' She reached out to grasp his arm as he would have stood up, her gaze pleading as he paused to look down at her. 'If you do not wish to talk of your parents, then we will not do so,' she promised huskily.

Dominic concentrated on how her loosened curls looked, all spread out on the pillow behind her. Her eyes were a beautiful, luminous sea-green, her lips slightly swollen from the kisses they had shared. Her cheeks were flushed, as was the delicate skin of her breasts, the tips all pouting and rosy from his attentions. His expression softened as he slowly exhaled his tension away before once again lowering his head to rest against one of those kiss-reddened breasts, his hand moving to lightly cup its twin. 'There is nothing more to say about my parents other than that they are both dead.'

'But your mother, at least, must have been quite young when she died?'

Dominic sighed. 'She was but two and thirty at the time of the accident. My father was eight and thirty when he chose to follow her only days later.'

Caro stilled, her heart pounding loudly beneath Dominic's head. 'He *chose* to follow her?'

Dominic had learnt early on in their acquaintance not to underestimate Caro's intelligence, and with this question she once again proved he had been wise not to do so. 'Yes.'

Caro's throat moved convulsively as she swallowed

before speaking. 'Can you possibly mean that he took his own life?'

Dominic made no attempt to halt his movements a second time, instead sitting up and moving away from her. Caro was sensible enough—or too stunned still—not to try to stop him, either by word or deed. He shrugged. 'He loved my mother very much and obviously saw no reason to continue living without her.'

'But he had a young son to care for!'

'Obviously he did not feel I was reason enough to continue living.' Dominic stood up and began pulling on the pantaloons he had discarded so eagerly only minutes ago.

Caro reached down and pulled the bedsheet up to her chin as she watched him with huge, disbelieving eyes. 'My own father loved my mother very much, too, and was devastated when she died. But even so, I do not think he ever contemplated the idea of taking his own life; he accepted that he had other responsibilities—'

Dominic's scathing snort cut off her halting words. 'Obviously your father was made of sterner stuff than my own.'

'I do not believe it was a question of that—'

'And I believe we have talked of this quite long enough for one evening!' His eyes glittered a pale and dangerous silver.

Caro lowered her gaze. 'It is just that I do not understand how any man, no matter how devastated he is by loss, could deliberately take his own life at the cost of leaving his twelve-year-old son alone in the world.'

'I have *told* you why!' Dominic paused to glare across at her once he had pulled on the tattered remnants of his shirt. 'He loved my mother so much he had no desire to live without her.'

The compassion in her eyes as she looked up at him was almost his undoing. As it was, the painful memories this conversation evoked felt like a heavy weight bearing down upon him. 'I am sure my father felt justified in his actions, Caro,' he said.

Caro looked stubborn. 'I do not believe there can be any justification for leaving a twelve-year-old boy alone and without either of his parents.'

Dominic's dark brows lifted, his expression hard and uncompromising; eyes a steely grey, cheekbones as sharp as blades beneath the tautness of his skin, that vicious scar livid from eyes to jaw, and his mouth a thin line. 'Not even if you hold that twelve-year-old boy—your own son—responsible for the death of the woman you loved?'

Caro gave a shocked gasp, all the colour draining from her cheeks as she stared up at Dominic with those huge sea-green eyes.

Chapter Sixteen

Dominic knew that the look of horrified disbelief on Caro's face was perfectly justified; no doubt that was exactly the emotion she was feeling, at even the suggestion that a twelve-year-old boy could be responsible for killing his own mother. Let alone that it might actually be the truth…

Not that Dominic had caused his mother's coach to leave the road and plunge into the river. Nor had he wedged the door of that carriage shut so that it was impossible for her to escape when the carriage began to sink and the water to flood inside it. And neither had he physically held his mother's head beneath the water until she'd drowned.

No, he had not personally done any of those things. Nevertheless, he knew he was as much to blame for his mother's death as if he had done every one of them.

Caro shook her head. 'It is utterly ridiculous to even suggest you might have done such a thing.'

'Is it?'

'Utterly,' she spoke with conviction.

'You do not believe me capable of killing someone?' He eyed her tauntingly.

'Of course you have killed in the heat of battle,' she said. 'It is the way of things. But I do not believe you capable of harming any woman, let alone killing your own mother.'

'Come now, Caro, I am sure you must know me well enough by now to realise that I am capable of all manner of things. Seducing, not once, but twice, the young woman I have taken into my care is only one of them.' He looked disgusted with himself.

'I was as instrumental as you in both those seductions.' Caro's cheeks warmed with guilty colour as she quickly stood and collected her wrap, securing the belt of that robe around her waist. 'I also believe you are only saying these things about your mother in order to shock me.'

His mouth twisted. 'Am I succeeding?'

'I am more disappointed that you feel you have to say things that cannot possibly be true—'

'Oh, but they are true,' he cut in, his voice silkily soft, eyes narrowed to challenging slits as she looked across at him. 'I, and I alone, am responsible for the death of my mother.'

Once again Caro could see the ruthlessness in Dominic's expression; yes, she had no doubt that if he deemed it necessary for someone to die, then he would be cold and decisive, even savage, in the execution of that death. But the underlying edge of gentleness, of love, she had heard in his voice as he spoke of his mother told her that he could not have had a hand in her death. Besides which, what would a twelve-year-old boy know of killing anyone?

'Tell me how she died, Dominic,' she urged.

'What difference does the manner of her death make?'

'It makes all the difference in the world,' Caro said crossly. 'Why did you tell me these things if you did not wish me to question you?' Although she might take a guess on it having something to do with him thinking that he deserved to have people—women, most especially—feeling no affection for him.

But also an indication, perhaps, that he might also fear that she was falling in love with him? Caro winced inside. That he was determined to foil any such softness of emotion, if it existed, was humiliating. Worse than humiliating, if he'd guessed her feelings correctly.

In contrast, Dominic was a difficult man to read. That was deliberate, she felt sure. On the surface he was an arrogant, hard and uncompromising man, who outwardly scorned all the softer emotions. Yet, at the same time, he'd shown a deep concern over the attack on his friend, Lord Thorne. And instead of being furious earlier at the loss of his gambling club, as many gentlemen might have been, Dominic had instead only revealed a deep sorrow and anger at the death of poor Ben.

And Dominic's concern for Caro's own safety and welfare was just as undeniable, even though he took great pains to claim he had been forced into saving her from her own reckless behaviour!

He might give himself all sorts of reasons for his behaviour, but Caro had seen the man beneath and would have no part of it. 'I will know the truth, Dominic, if you please!'

He arched mocking brows. 'And will you then reveal to me the truth about yourself?'

Caro was in a quandary. No doubt he considered such an exchange of information fair. And it probably was. Except she could not confide her own situation to him, especially now when, having thought long and hard earlier this evening, Caro had decided that, guardian or not, she must return to Shoreley Hall as soon after Ben's funeral as possible.

Once back at Shoreley Hall she would assume the mantle of Lady Caroline Copeland. That being so, there was absolutely no reason for him to know anything further concerning Caro Morton, a woman who did not exist out of the small circle of acquaintances she had made in London.

She drew in a deep breath. 'I must refuse.'

Dominic's lip curled. 'Then it would seem we are at an impasse.'

'The two situations are completely different,' Caro snapped her impatience with his stubbornness. 'I have not just laid claim to killing someone!'

'How do I know that you did not see off this "maiden aunt" or your father before making your escape to London?' Dominic eyed her mockingly.

Because there was no maiden aunt, and of course Caro had not been involved in her father's death! But the second part of his statement, concerning her having made her escape to London, was too close to the truth for comfort...

'I believe you are merely trying to fudge the issue by making ridiculous accusations,' she said.

'You may think what you please,' Dominic retorted. 'As far as the subject of my mother, and the manner of her death, is concerned, I have no wish to discuss the matter further. With you or anyone else.' The finality in his tone did not allow for further argument. 'I believe I will wish you goodnight now, Caro.' He gave her a brief bow before striding across the room, pausing briefly when he reached the door. 'If you wish it, I will have some supper brought up to you.'

'That will not be necessary, thank you.' Caro felt even less like eating now than she had earlier. Ben was still dead, and contemplating food after the intimacies she and Dominic had just shared was impossible. Also, his refusal to further discuss his mother's death had left Caro with more questions than answers, especially as she now feared she might indeed have fallen in love with him!

Dominic's face darkened in fury when he returned to Brockle House late the following morning, accompanied by Drew, and was informed by a concerned Denby that Mrs Morton and Mr Brown were taking tea together in the Gold Salon.

The fact that Nicholas Brown had come here at all was disquieting. That Caro had chosen to receive him, knowing all that she did about the other man, was more disturbing still in view of what Dominic knew to be her often reckless and impulsive nature!

'Damn it, Denby.' He glared at the man who had once been his batman in the army but was now, for the sake of expediency, posing as his butler. 'What is the good of my installing you here to protect Caro when you then let the biggest threat to her calmly walk through the front door?'

The other man gave a pained frown. 'Mrs Morton had been for a walk in the park across the way—she was accompanied by my wife,' he added quickly as Dominic looked set for another explosion. 'It was apparently as she was returning to the house that she saw Mr Brown stepping down from his coach and stopped to engage him in conversation.'

Which sounded exactly the sort of thing Caro would do, Dominic realised frustratedly. He also realised that Brown must have had the two of them followed yesterday to know to find Caro at Brockle House at all. 'That still does not explain why you allowed the man to accompany her into the house?'

'I tried to prevent it from happening—'

'Obviously you did not try hard enough!'

'My wife is in the Gold Salon with them, my lord.'

'I am relieved to see that you have not completely lost your senses!' Dominic barked.

'We are wasting time here, my lord.' Drew put a steadying hand upon Dominic's arm. 'Brown can be a wily cur at the best of times, and I really don't think we should leave Caro to deal with him alone any longer. She is also likely to say more than she ought to him.'

'Caro has no more sense than a—'

'She is merely idealistically young,' the older man interrupted diplomatically.

'Nothing a sound beating would not cure!' Dominic assured the other man grimly as he strode across the entrance hall to thrust open the door to the Gold Salon, taking in at a glance the determined expression on Caro's face as she sat on the sofa looking up at a relaxed and nonchalant Nicholas Brown as he stood beside the unlit fireplace.

'I apologise for you having to receive our guest alone, Caro.'

She gave a self-conscious start at the icy coldness of Dominic's tone, one glance at the fury so clearly evident upon his face enough to show her how displeased he was at having returned to Brockle House to find that, despite all his warnings, she had chosen to invite Nicholas Brown inside when he'd had the audacity to arrive outside in his carriage some minutes earlier.

Dominic was no doubt perfectly aware that her sole purpose for inviting the other man to join her for tea, knowing him to be responsible for both Ben's death and the attack upon Lord Thorne, was to confront him with his perfidy! Something she had been just about to do when Dominic had arrived accompanied by Drew Butler.

In truth, Caro knew a certain relief in the timely arrival of the two men. Every attempt on her part to challenge the villain with his terrible deeds had been smoothly and charmingly foiled by him as he had kept up a stream of polite gossip and inanities from the moment they had entered the Gold Salon. Caro had even begun to doubt both her own and Dominic's conviction that Brown was responsible for anything more than having the misfortune to have gained a bad reputation!

'To what do we owe the pleasure of your visit, Brown?' Dominic obviously felt no such doubts as he kept the icy coldness of his gaze firmly fixed upon the older man.

Brown raised dark and mocking brows. 'I merely called to pay my respects to Mrs Morton.'

'Indeed?' Dominic's teeth showed in a predatory smile.

'I understand she was present when the fire occurred yesterday afternoon?' Brown said smoothly.

Dominic's jaw clenched. 'What of it?'

'I, of course, wished to assure myself of her good health.' Brown's smile was lazily confident. 'Women are such fragile creatures, are they not?'

It was impossible for Dominic to miss the underlying threat in that single remark. For him not to feel an icy chill in his veins at the thought of this man harming one golden hair upon Caro's head. His mouth thinned. 'Which is why men were, presumably, put on the earth to protect them.' Two could engage in this particular game of veiled threats. And when that game now so obviously involved Caro it was one that Dominic had every intention of winning.

As was to be expected, Caro was unable to stop herself from commenting on Dominic's remark. 'I am sure I am perfectly capable of protecting myself, Dominic.'

'All evidence to the contrary, my dear,' he said grimly.

Her cheeks flushed prettily. 'You—'

'I, too, am pleased to see that you are quite recovered from yesterday's ordeal, Mrs Morton,' Drew cut in tactfully.

Caro gave him a grateful smile. 'And I you.'

'Oh, I believe you will find that it's going to take

more than a fire to be rid of me,' he said, at the same time shooting a telling glance in Brown's direction.

'My compliments on your lucky escape, Drew,' the other man taunted.

'Would that Ben had been so lucky,' Drew said pointedly.

Hard brown eyes glittered with satisfaction. 'Such a waste of a young life…'

'A needless waste,' Drew agreed harshly.

'It would appear that you have had a busy morning, Brown?' Dominic felt it was time to intercede, before Drew's anger became such that he spoke or acted incautiously and this situation deteriorated whilst Caro was still present. Dominic and Drew had talked of this earlier and had agreed it must not be allowed to happen; if she were not present now, the conversation would no doubt have ceased being polite long ago!

Even the thought of Caro being anywhere near when that veneer of politeness was stripped from this situation, to reveal the ugly truth they all knew lurked beneath, was enough to send a cold rivulet of fear down Dominic's spine; he had no doubt, for all Brown looked so elegant in his perfectly tailored clothes, that the other man had a knife, or possibly even a small pistol, concealed somewhere about his person. Just as Dominic also believed that Caro would be Brown's target if this situation were to explode into violence now…

'Indeed?' Brown drawled.

Dominic nodded. 'I am informed by Ben's sister, Mrs Grey, that you have assisted her by financing tomorrow's funeral arrangements.'

He gave a dismissive shrug. 'It seemed the least I could do in the circumstances.'

'And what *circumstances* might they be?' Dominic asked.

Nicholas Brown met his gaze unblinkingly. 'Ben was my employee, and as such was loyal to me, for far longer than he was to you.'

It was tantamount to a declaration that it had been this change of loyalty on Ben's part—and no doubt on Drew's, too—which had ultimately brought about the young man's demise. That Brown would have been more than happy if both Drew and Ben had perished in yesterday's fire, as retribution for the fact that they had chosen to continue being employed by the new owner of Nick's rather than leave.

Just as Brown's visit to Caro was yet another veiled threat? That the villain had so clearly shown that he was fully aware of exactly where Caro resided now was, to Dominic's way of thinking, tangible evidence of that threat…

'I believe it is time you took your leave, Brown.' Dominic had had quite enough of even attempting to be polite to this man. 'Caro is looking a little pale. No doubt she is in need of rest following the events of yesterday and all this talk of death and funerals today.' He rang the bell for Denby.

Caro knew she might look less than perfect, but she had not, as yet, had the opportunity to say all that she wished to say to Mr Nicholas Brown! Added to which, she had been rendered almost speechless by the politeness—at least on the surface—of the conversation between the three men. Why did Dominic or Drew not just confront the man? Tell him of their suspicions and demand an explanation? It was what she had intended doing until she had found herself rendered tongue-tied by the man's smooth charm!

'Having now assured myself as to your welfare, Caro, I believe I will also take my leave,' Drew said smoothly.

But not smoothly enough that Caro was not aware of the hard edge beneath the blandness of his tone. 'No doubt I will see you again at Ben's funeral tomorrow.'

Brown raised surprised brows. '*You* will be attending?'

Caro looked at him coldly. 'But of course I shall—'

'It has yet to be decided.' Dominic was the one to cut in as he stepped forwards to lift one of Caro's hands and place it firmly in the crook of his arm so that the two of them now stood side by side as they faced Brown.

The gesture was so obviously one of possession that Caro could not help but be aware of it. Just as she was aware of the warning of Dominic's fingers firmly gripping her own as he kept her hand anchored in the crook of his arm. 'Dominic—'

'It is time to say goodbye to Mr Brown and Drew now, Caro,' he instructed her tautly.

Just as if she were a child who needed reminding of her manners! Or as if Dominic meant to silence her before she had the chance to do or say something that would totally strip away even this tense veneer of social politeness. Her mouth firmed determinedly. 'Perhaps before he leaves, I might ask Mr Brown—'

'I am sure, Caro, that whatever queries you might have for Mr Brown, they can surely wait until another day.' Those long fingers again pressed down on Caro's.

'Perhaps tomorrow at Ben's funeral?' she persevered.

Silver eyes glittered down at her in warning. 'Perhaps.'

Caro's cheeks flushed in temper. 'This is utterly ridiculous—'

'Ah, Denby.' Dominic turned to the butler as he quietly entered the room. 'Mr Brown and Mr Butler are leaving.'

'But—'

'Say goodbye to our guests, Caro.' The dangerous glitter in Dominic's eyes dared her to do anything more than that.

Much as she longed to accuse Nicholas Brown, Caro had enough wisdom to know when Dominic had been pushed to the limit of his patience. And the hard tension of his body as he stood next to her informed her that he had reached that limit some time ago.

Her parting comments to the other two men were made distractedly, her agitation now such that she could barely restrain herself.

It was a lack of restraint that Dominic clearly echoed, as he waited only long enough for Denby to close the door firmly behind himself, his wife and their departing visitors, before releasing Caro's hand and rounding on her furiously. 'What did you think you were doing by calmly inviting Brown in here? No, do not tell me, I know exactly what your intentions were!'

'Someone must confront Mr Brown—'

'And someone will,' Dominic assured her fiercely. 'But not you, Caro. *Never* you! And if you dare—so much as *dare*,' he grated, 'accuse me of behaving in a cowardly manner by not confronting him myself just now, then I must warn you, Caro, that I really will have no recourse but to administer the beating someone should have given you long ago!'

Her cheeks were pale. 'I had no intention of accusing you of being cowardly!'

'That is something, I suppose,' Dominic muttered darkly.

Caro knew him well enough now to know that he could be every bit as dangerous as Nicholas Brown if he chose to be. Nor had she missed the lethal purpose in the gaze Dominic had directed at Brown when he entered the salon a few minutes ago.

The difference between the two men was, of course, that Dominic was undoubtedly a man of honour. Of integrity. A gentleman. A gentleman who had caused her to behave as less than the lady she was from the moment they had first met!

Which thought had absolutely no place in their present conversation! 'That is not to say I understand why neither you nor Mr Butler did not challenge Mr Brown, both over the attack on Lord Thorne, and the setting of the fire that resulted in Ben's death.' A frown creased the creaminess of her brow.

'Perhaps because we were both endeavouring to protect *you*?'

'Me?'

Dominic gave a rueful shake of his head at the surprise in Caro's expression. Despite the week she had spent singing in a gentlemen's gambling club, and after all that had happened these past few days—including their lovemaking—she remained an innocent. She could not conceive, it seemed, that Nicholas Brown was more than capable of killing her where she stood, and to hell with the consequences.

Yet Dominic now feared that Brown's visit here today meant that he had decided, by implication, if not yet deed, to now turn the focus of his malevolent attentions upon Caro herself...

Chapter Seventeen

It was a threat Dominic intended taking very seriously indeed. 'I have decided, now that Brown has made it so obvious he knows of your whereabouts, that for your own safety it would be a good idea if I were to remove you immediately from London and place you at my estate in Berkshire.'

Caro's eyes widened, initially in shock, quickly followed by indignation. She had already spent a night at Blackstone House, followed by another in Brockle House, both properties owned by the Earl of Blackstone; for her to now be seen to move into his estate in Berkshire was unacceptable. Besides which, there was the added insult that Dominic had not even bothered to consult her before making this decision.

She gave a firm shake of her head. 'No.'

He became very still, his eyes narrowed to silver slits. *'No?'*

Caro shrugged her slender shoulders. 'No, Dominic. I must have a say in where I go and what I do—and this makes me feel like an unwanted relative you must needs move from house to house in order to avoid their company.'

If Caro really were a relative of his then Dominic would have put her over his knee and spanked her pretty bottom days ago. For the sheer stupidity, her complete lack of caution, in coming alone to London at all, and therefore placing herself firmly in the midst of this highly volatile situation. As it was, Dominic was currently perceived—by Brown, if by no other—as being Caro's protector. 'When it comes to the subject of your safety, Caro, I feel you must do as I ask.'

'No, Dominic, I must not.' Her unblinking gaze challenged him, her chin raised in haughty disdain. 'I have not had opportunity to tell you before this, but it is already my intention to leave London once I have attended Ben's funeral tomorrow.'

'To go where, may I ask?' Dominic glowered down at her.

'No, you may not ask—Dominic!' She protested as he reached out and took a tight grip of her wrist. 'You will not be able to force my compliance simply by the use of brute strength.' She spoke calmly and clearly, her gaze reproachful as she looked up at him.

Dominic had no wish to force her compliance or hurt her in any way. But just the thought of the likes of a man like Brown ever being in a position to cause her harm caused a painful tightening in his chest.

As did the thought of Caro leaving London. Leaving *him*…

He also wondered, if not for their present heated conversation, whether she would have even bothered to inform him of her intention to leave London, let alone confide where he might be able to find her if he wished to see her again.

If he wished to see her again?

Dominic released his grip on Caro's arm to step sharply away from her, a frown darkening his brow as he studied her between guarded lids. There was no doubting that she was a breathtakingly beautiful young woman. Or that just looking at her now in that green gown, and imagining the naked curves beneath, filled him with the need to once again make love to her. But surely that was all she was, or ever could be, to him? Just a beautiful young woman who—for the moment— he felt a need to protect? To imagine she might mean any more to him than that was unacceptable to a man who had long ago decided he did not want or need one particular woman in his life. Especially if that woman was one he might care for enough that her death would drive him to the same brink of madness his father had suffered after the death of Dominic's mother.

He shook his head. 'You know I cannot allow it, Caro.'

'Why not?' For Caro to dare to hope that he might feel some of her own regret at the thought of them parting would, she knew, be too much to ask.

He looked irritated now. 'Because Brown is still a threat.'

'To me?'

'Caro, how do you imagine Brown even knew to visit you here at Brockle House?'

Her eyes slowly widened. 'He had us followed yesterday?'

'Exactly,' Dominic bit out curtly. 'And until he is…
dealt with, I must insist, if you will not agree to go to
my estate in Berkshire, that you at least agree to remain
at Brockle House for now.'

Caro looked at him searchingly, noting the grim
determination of his expression, the light of battle in
his eyes. 'You intend to deal with Mr Brown yourself,
do you not?'

Dominic drew in a harsh breath, wishing not for
the first time that Caro were not as astute as she was
beautiful. Or so forward in voicing her shrewd opinions
and observations. 'It is for the law—'

'Dominic, I have asked several times that you not
treat me as a child or an imbecile!'

He sighed deeply at her obvious irritation. 'Very
well, then. Yes, if the law is not enough to bring Brown
to justice, then I will feel no hesitation in dealing with
him myself.'

'How?'

'I think it best if you do not know the details.'

'Dominic.'

'Caro!' he exclaimed in exasperation. 'Is it not
enough to know that I respect you, admire you, even
like you?' he added ruefully. 'And that it is because
I feel all of those things for you that I do not wish to
involve you any further in this mess than you already
are.'

Caro knew from the implacability of his tone that
Dominic really would tell her no more on that subject.
Just as she knew that having his respect, admiration and
liking, whilst being secretly cherished, could never be
enough for her. She wanted him to feel so much more

than that. Needed him to love her in the same way she had realised she loved him. Completely. Irrevocably.

Who could have ever known that, in coming to London in this way, she would meet the man she was to fall so deeply in love with? Certainly not Caro. She had thought only to avoid being coerced into a marriage she did not want. Instead she had met the man whom she would love for the rest of her life and *he* didn't want to marry *her*…

Caro stepped away from him, her trembling hands clasped tightly together in front of her, knowing that her pride would never allow her to let him see how deeply she had fallen in love with him. 'I accept that for the moment it is best that I remain here. But I do wish to leave as soon as you feel it is safe for me to do so,' she added firmly.

Dominic looked at her between narrowed lids. 'With the intention of returning to your family?'

'Yes. And please do not ask me where or who that family is,' she said ruefully as she could see that was exactly what Dominic was about to do. 'As with your own actions concerning Mr Brown, it serves no purpose for you to know the details of my destination.'

He straightened abruptly. 'And if you need to talk to me at some point in the future?'

If she found herself with child, he meant… 'Then I will know where to find you,' Caro dismissed evenly.

Dominic sighed. 'You know, Caro, I do not have so many people I consider friends that I can simply allow one of them to just up and leave London and for ever disappear.'

Dominic thought of them as being friends?

Knowing how and why, after hearing the sad tale of his parents' deaths, Dominic shunned emotional attachments of any kind, she could not help but feel flattered that he should think of her as a friend. Unfortunately, she wanted to be so much more to him than just a friend!

'I am sure that you have many more friends than Lord Thorne, Drew Butler and myself,' she said lightly.

'Perhaps,' Dominic conceded drily. 'Osbourne and I have just spent the past month in Venice with one of our oldest and closest friends.'

Venice?

Caro stiffened, barely daring to breathe as she looked searchingly at Dominic now. He had recently spent a month in Venice? Where Lord Gabriel Faulkner, Earl of Westbourne since the death of Caro's father, and now the guardian of all three sisters—the very same man who had sent his lawyer with the offer of marriage to one of the three Copeland sisters, without so much as having met any of them—had resided for the past two years, at least?

Caro was well aware that Venice was a large city with an even larger population, Venetians as well as other people simply visiting. Nevertheless, she could not help her feelings of disquiet at the knowledge that Dominic had just spent a month there. Where he had no doubt met and socialised with both the Venetian aristocracy and those members of English society currently residing there. Possibly including Lord Faulkner?

'Perhaps you will have the chance to meet him,' Dominic continued. 'Westbourne is due to arrive back in England himself in the next few days,' he explained at Caro's questioning glance.

Westbourne!

Caro's fears had just been realised!

Not only did Dominic know Lord Faulkner, but the two of them had obviously been close friends for a number of years. Worst of all, Dominic was expecting Westbourne to arrive back in England any day! No doubt one of the first things he would do was pay a visit to his friend, Lord Vaughn—and Dominic had just told her that he would introduce the two of them!

Caro moved carefully over to a chair and sat down, knowing her legs were in danger of no longer supporting her. What was she to do? If, as Dominic said, he was expecting the Earl of Westbourne to arrive in England within days—possibly even today—then Caro could not afford to linger in London any longer if she wished to avoid detection, no matter what she might have assured Dominic earlier.

Not that Lord Faulkner would recognise her as anyone other than Caro Morton here in London. But she had never intended her absence from Shoreley Hall, and the separation from her beloved sisters, to be a permanent one, which meant that Westbourne must one day be introduced to his ward, Lady Caroline Copeland. If he had already been introduced to Caro Morton, the repercussions to all of them when that happened would be great indeed!

Caro had dearly wanted to attend Ben's funeral before returning to Shoreley Hall, and the thought of leaving Dominic so soon was worse than painful, but the knowledge of her guardian's imminent arrival in England meant that she had no choice but to leave immediately.

Caro Morton must cease to exist forthwith.

'Caro?'

She straightened, schooling her features into the polite social mask recognisable as Lady Caroline Copeland as she looked up and saw the concern in Dominic's expression. 'Yes?'

'Will you promise me not to leave the house unaccompanied until this matter is settled?'

She could not give such a promise and mean it. Not now. 'I trust I am not so foolish as to even attempt it now that you have alerted me to the fact that Nicholas Brown is watching my every move,' she answered.

Dominic nodded, apparently sensing none of the evasion in her reply. 'I will be out for the rest of the day, but should hopefully be back in time for us to dine together this evening.'

'I will look forward to it.' They had become almost like strangers in these past few minutes, Caro recognised heavily, Dominic's friendship with Lord Faulkner, and her knowledge of her own imminent departure from London, seeming to have severed the tenuous bonds of their own friendship.

Caro could feel the hot burn of tears in her eyes. 'I believe I will go upstairs to rest.' Dominic must be made to leave. Now. Before those threatening tears started to fall and he demanded an explanation as to the reason for them. She doubted he would appreciate hearing that it was because her heart was breaking at the very thought of being parted from him.

Now that the time had come, Dominic felt an uncharacteristic reluctance to part from Caro, even for a few hours.

Damn it, apart from the friendship he had long held

with Osbourne and Westbourne, he had never been a man who allowed himself to become entangled in emotional attachments. And yet he was aware he had formed a friendship of sorts these past few days with both Drew Butler and Ben Jackson.

And he had formed a friendship with Caro, too…

A friendship that Dominic knew had come into being because he had ultimately been unable to deny the respect and admiration he felt for the courage and determination she had shown him from their very first meeting. He would feel Caro's loss all the more keenly once she was allowed to return to her home and family. But it was a friendship Dominic could not, would not, allow to control either his actions or his judgement.

He drew himself up stiffly. 'Until this evening, then.' He nodded to her before turning on his heel to stride determinedly from the room.

Caro waited only long enough to be sure that he had truly gone before she allowed the tears to fall. Hot and remorseless tears that almost brought her to her knees. At the thought of never seeing Dominic again. At the knowledge that she would never again know the warmth of being held in his arms. Kissed by him. Never again know the wonder, the beauty, of their lovemaking.

Caro cried until there were no more tears inside her to be shed. Until all that was left was the knowledge that she must leave this house immediately.

Must leave London.

And Dominic…

Once outside Dominic dismissed the carriage he and Butler had arrived in earlier, deciding that the walk to

Mrs Wilson's to check on Osbourne one last time before his aunt whisked him off to the country to recover from his injuries would be far more beneficial in helping to clear his head of the disturbed thoughts that had been plaguing him ever since he had realised how deeply he would feel it when Caro left London for good.

Except Dominic's thoughts remained distracted, for the duration of his walk, and whilst he chatted with the disgruntled but resigned Osbourne. And they continued to plague him after he had taken his leave and stood outside on the pavement outside Mrs Wilson's home.

He had intended lunching at his club, before returning to Blackstone House for the afternoon to deal with estate business, leaving him free to once again spend the night at Brockle House.

Yet he did none of those things, as instead, his feet took him back in the direction of Brockle House. Back to Caro.

His behaviour was totally illogical. Totally unprecedented. He felt a longing to be with her that he knew he should strongly resist. But could not…

Just as he could not believe his own eyes as he neared Brockle House and saw Caro hurrying towards him. Alone. Dressed in her dark cloak and that unbecoming brown bonnet, which should have been consigned to the incinerator along with those unbecoming gowns, but somehow had not. And carrying the bag in which her few belongings had been packed to transport them to Brockle House.

Caro came to an abrupt halt, her eyes widening in alarm, as she saw a furiously angry Dominic striding forcefully towards her. It could not be! Dominic had gone off for the day to see to other business. He was not really here at all, was a figment of her imagination, brought about by the chasm of misery Caro had fallen into at the thought of being parted from him.

'Where do you think you are going?' The grip of his hands on the tops of her arms felt real enough, as did the fierceness of his scowl as he glowered down at her. 'Answer me this instant, Caro!'

Dominic was real! He was really here!

Caro could not breathe. Could not think. Could only stare up into Dominic's face and know that she loved him past all bearing...

'You little fool!' He shook her, eyes glittering in the harsh handsomeness of his face as he glared down at her. 'Do you not realise the danger you have put yourself in by venturing out alone like this?'

'Why are you here?' She gave a dazed shake of her head. 'You told me you had other business to attend to for the rest of the day. You said—'

'I am well aware of what I said, Caro,' he grated. 'Just as I am aware that you *lied* to me when you said you would be resting in your rooms for the rest of the morning. You have obviously taken advantage of my absence to pack your bag and make your escape without so much as a word of goodbye!'

'I—' Caro moistened her dry lips.

'Where were you going?' Dominic demanded harshly as he shook her slightly again. 'What—?' He broke off abruptly, his eyes suddenly wide and staring.

'Dominic?' Caro could only look up at him uncomprehendingly as those silver-grey eyes turned up into his head before glazing over completely, his mouth becoming lax, and his hands losing their grip upon her arms as he began to sink slowly to the ground.

Revealing to her frightened gaze the hefty and brutish-looking man who stood behind him, some sort of cudgel raised in his hand, before something was thrown over her head to cut off all sight and she felt herself being lifted and carried away...

Chapter Eighteen

Caro had no idea how long she had been held a prisoner in this opulently furnished bedchamber. It had seemed like hours, and yet it could equally have been only minutes. Time had become unimportant to her since she had seen Dominic fall to the ground after receiving that blow to the back of his head.

None of her anguished thoughts since that time had been for herself; she was far too worried whether that blow to Dominic's head had been heavy and hard enough to kill him.

A world without Dominic was unthinkable. Unimaginable. Making a complete nonsense of any concerns Caro might have for her own welfare. She had become the prisoner of Nicholas Brown, of course. There could be no other possible explanation for what had occurred. But none of it mattered to Caro in the slightest if Dominic were now dead.

She stood up and moved restlessly around the room to end up standing in front of the window. It was barred on the outside and looked out over a walled and secluded garden, with a sheltering of surrounding trees that made it impossible for anyone in any of the neighbouring houses to see either into the garden or the house.

It was a seclusion she was already aware of, because the window had been the first place she had checked for escape, once she had managed to untangle herself from the blanket that had been kept about her as she was bundled inside a coach and transported to this house.

There had been two men inside the coach with her, and although the blanket did not allow her to see their faces, she could easily guess that one of them had struck Dominic, and the second was the man who had stood behind Caro and thrown the blanket over her head. Neither of them had deigned to answer her repeated demands during the journey to know whether or not they had killed Dominic.

So far she had seen nothing of Nicholas Brown…

Caro knew that she should be afraid of the man. That the men he employed were responsible for Ben's death and the severity of the injuries Lord Thorne had received several nights ago. That those same men might also have now slain Dominic…

And yet Caro felt too contemptuous and angry towards Brown to be in the least afraid of him. Contempt, because all of those acts had been cowardly, administered in such a way that neither Brown nor any of his men were ever in any real danger of injury themselves. Anger, because if Dominic did indeed lie dead somewhere, then Caro felt fully capable of administering that same fate to Brown, if she were given the slightest opportunity.

A choking sob rose in her throat. Dominic could

not be dead! It was a possibility too horrific to even contemplate—

Caro turned sharply as she heard the key turning in the lock of the door, her chin raised proudly high, sea-green eyes full of the contempt she felt as Nicholas Brown stepped into the room.

'Mrs Morton,' he greeted with his usual relaxed charm—for all the world as if they were exchanging pleasantries in a drawing room! 'You're comfortable, I hope?' he added courteously as he remained standing in the doorway of the bedchamber.

Her chin lifted disdainfully. 'I have witnessed a man being…felled before my eyes.' Caro gathered her courage after that slight falter as she talked of the attack on Dominic, determined to show this man no weakness whatsoever. 'I have suffered being covered in a rough and smelly blanket, abducted in a coach, and held a prisoner in this bedchamber for some time. Yes, Mr Brown, I am perfectly comfortable, thank you.'

Grudging admiration entered that calculating brown gaze. 'I understand now why Blackstone became so besotted with you,' he murmured.

It was an admiration Caro did not value in the slightest. Any more than she believed Dominic had ever been besotted with her. But the thought of it was enough to give her the courage to continue in the same vein. 'Unfortunately I consider you so far beneath contempt that you do not even have the right to breathe Lord Vaughn's name.'

A tightness appeared around those brown eyes as his gaze narrowed. 'We will see how wonderful you still consider him to be when he fails to rescue you in time from my "contemptuous" clutches.'

The only part of that statement that mattered to Caro was the indication it gave that Dominic was still alive! She sagged inside. If that could only be true, if Dominic could still but live, then whether or not he succeeded in rescuing her did not matter; Caro just wanted him to be safe.

She raised scornful brows. 'Dominic is worth a hundred—no, a thousand!—of you.'

Brown scowled darkly. 'Perhaps you should wait to make comparisons as to who is the better man until after I have bedded you?'

Caro's eyes had widened before she had a chance to control her reaction to this shocking statement. 'You will not find me a willing bed partner, Mr Brown,' she assured cuttingly, her chin still raised defiantly high.

His mouth twisted derisively. 'I am counting on it, Mrs Morton,' he drawled mockingly. 'Blackstone took my prized possession from me and now I am very much enjoying the anticipation of availing myself of his,' he jeered before stepping out of the room, and relocking the door behind him.

Caro sank weakly down on to the bed, wondering how she could ever have been deceived into thinking Nicholas Brown was anything other than what he was: a low, despicable man, with no honour, or, indeed, any virtues to recommend him.

She could only hope that, if Dominic truly were still alive, he would look for her—as he surely must?—and find her, before Brown decided to carry out his threat.

'Everyone is in position, my lord.' Drew Butler spoke softly at Dominic's side as the two men stood hidden in a doorway further down the road from the house in Cheapside belonging to Nicholas Brown.

The house where Dominic hoped and prayed that he would find Caro. Alive. And unharmed. Anything else was unacceptable to him.

What he would say and do to Caro once he had delivered her safely back at Brockle House, Dominic had not dared think of as yet. He had still not got over the shock of regaining consciousness earlier only to find Caro was nowhere to be found.

'Are you sure you are up to this, my lord?' Drew voiced his concern. 'The blow to your head was severe, and—'

'Let's get this over with, Drew,' he said grimly as he raised the two pistols in his hands ready for breaching Brown's front door. 'There will be time enough to worry about the blow I received to my head once we have found Caro and I am assured she has come to no harm at Brown's hands.' The expression on his face was enough to show what would happen to said man if Caro had been harmed in any way...

Dominic had downed a single glass of brandy earlier in order to put him back into his right senses, after which he had sent for Drew Butler, and then taken him and the men who had formerly been under his command into the study at Brockle House, in order that they might devise a plan to effect a rescue without injury to Caro.

Spending over two hours observing the comings and goings of Brown's men to his house in Cheapside, so that they might count the number of adversaries they would have to deal with once they were inside, had stretched Dominic's patience to breaking point. Enough so that now he could not wait to get inside the house and have this thing between himself and Brown over and done with once and for all.

And, far more importantly, to know that Caro was indeed safe and unharmed…

Caro felt both thirsty and hungry as she lay upon the bed, several more hours having passed without anyone offering her refreshment of any kind. Something she did not feel inclined to bring to anyone's attention when she had not seen Nicholas Brown again for that same length of time.

It was—

Caro sat up abruptly as she heard the sound of several unnaturally loud bangs, taking several seconds—and a few more of those loud bangs—before she realised that what she was hearing was gunfire.

Dominic!

She rose hastily from the bed to run across to the locked door, pressing her ear against it to see if she could hear anything of what was taking place on the other side. Men shouting. Feet running. More shots. And then an unnatural and eerie silence…

Caro stepped back from the door, unsure as to whether Dominic and the men who had accompanied him were the victors of the battle or whether it was the despicable Nicholas Brown and his men. If it was the latter—

The key was being turned in the lock!

The handle was turning.

The door being pushed open—

'Dominic!' Caro cried gladly as he stood so tall and

in command in the doorway, that gladness turning to horror, and her face paling, as Caro saw the blood staining the front of his jacket and shirt. She ran across the room. 'You are hurt!'

'It is not my blood, Caro,' he had time to reassure her before his arms wrapped about her and he held her tightly against his chest.

She leant back slightly to look up at him with wide, haunted eyes. 'Is it Nicholas Brown's?'

Dominic's jaw tightened. 'We struggled, and the gun between us went off. He is dead, Caro,' he added hoarsely.

'I am glad!' she assured him fiercely. 'He meant to—he threatened to—'

'Do not think of it again, my dear.' Dominic could not bear just now to know what Brown had threatened to do to Caro if she had not been rescued. Any more than he wanted to think of the battle, the deaths, that had just occurred.

All talk, explanations, could come later. It was enough for now that he held her safely in his arms…

'The physician would not approve of you imbibing brandy so soon after receiving that severe blow to your head!' Caro stood in the doorway of the study at Brockle House as she glowered at Dominic disapprovingly.

In truth, his head was pounding worse than it had this morning. But whether the physician who had been called would have approved of his actions or not, Dominic knew that a glass of best brandy, his first since returning Caro back to Brockle House two hours earlier, was necessary if he was to get through the necessary conversation with her. Indeed, that he might need more of it before the evening was through…

It had been a difficult afternoon for all of them—explanations to be made to the representatives of the law, arrangements made for the removal of Brown's body and those of his men.

With so many witnesses to what had taken place, and Caro's own testimony of her abduction and Brown's intentions towards her, it had not been too difficult to persuade the authorities that Brown and his men were the guilty parties, and Dominic and his men merely effecting a rescue. In truth, he had a suspicion that certain members of the law were pleased to be relieved of the presence of the troublesome Nicholas Brown, once and for all.

Caro, as Dominic might have expected, had stood up wonderfully well under all the strain!

'Come in and close the door, Caro,' Dominic requested softly now as he leant back against the front of the leather-topped desk.

She stepped lightly into the study and closed the door behind her, disturbed by how ill Dominic now looked; there was a grey cast to his skin, his eyes sunken in the dark shadows above the high blades of his cheekbones. His mouth was a grimly thinned line and his jaw was clenched tensely.

'Did…the events of this afternoon disgust you?' he asked huskily.

She raised startled eyes to look at him searchingly, but was unable to read anything of his mood from his expression. 'How could I possibly feel disgust when I know that if you had not succeeded in killing Brown then it would be you and I who now lay dead?'

His mouth quirked. 'There have been several occasions when you have given me the impression you would not consider my own death to be such a bad thing.'

'I was young and silly—'

'And now you are mature and so much wiser?' he teased.

Caro felt the warmth of the colour that entered her cheeks. 'I feel…older than I was this morning, certainly.'

Dominic's frown was pained. 'I am sorry for that.'

'Why should *you* be sorry?' She looked at him quizzically. 'It is Nicholas Brown who is responsible for my new maturity, Dominic, and not you. He—if you had not rescued me, he told me that he intended to—'

Dominic stepped forwards and took her firmly into his arms. 'I have already told you that it will do you no good to think of that any more,' he urged. 'Bad enough that I have to think of it, imagine it, without knowing it hurts you, too.' His arms tightened almost painfully about her.

Caro raised her head to once again look up at him. 'Does the thought of it hurt you so badly, Dominic?'

His eyes glittered a pale silver. 'Almost as much as the knowledge that you were leaving me.'

'I was not leaving you, Dominic.' She sighed. 'I merely thought it best that I return home—'

'Without so much as a goodbye? Giving me no idea how I would ever find you again?' His expression had become fierce, those silver eyes glowing with repressed emotion as he looked down at her.

Caro swept the tip of her tongue lightly over the dryness of her lips, a hope, a dream, starting to build and grow inside her. 'Would you ever have wanted to find me again?'

'How can you even ask me that?' Dominic shook her slightly in exasperation. 'Do you not know—have you not guessed yet how much I love you?'

'What did you say?' Caro hardly dared to believe the emotions she could now read in those glowing silver eyes. Warmth. Admiration. Love!

'I love you, Caro,' he repeated huskily. 'Do you think, after all that has happened, that if I were to get down on my knees and beg, you might one day be able to love me in return and consider becoming my wife?'

Her cheeks warmed as she remembered the occasion upon which she had said those words to him. 'As I recall, you had just finished telling me that our love-making was a mistake—'

'Then it was a most wonderful, glorious mistake!' he assured her fiercely as he cupped the sides of her face between gentle hands. 'I have been a fool, Caro. An arrogant fool. My only excuse—if there can ever be one!—is that I have never met a woman like you before. Never known any woman with your courage, your generosity of spirit, your honesty. I love you truly, Caro, and if you could one day learn to love me in return, I promise you I will love you for the rest of our lives together. Will you, Caro? Will you give me the chance to show you how much I love you? A chance to persuade you into learning to love me?' he added less certainly.

It was that uncharacteristic uncertainty that convinced Caro she could not be dreaming, after all; even in a dream she would not have bestowed uncertainty upon a man she knew to be always confident and sure, of both his own emotions and those around him!

And yet Dominic was not sure of her and seemed to have no idea that she had fallen in love with him, too. 'My dear…' her voice was gentle, tentative '…I am already in love with you—'

'My darling girl!' Dominic swept her ecstatically up into his arms before claiming her mouth with his.

Caro was still so overwhelmed by his declaration of love and his proposal of marriage, that for several long and pleasurable minutes all she could do was return the passion of his kisses.

It was some time later before her sanity returned. 'I realise that the Earl of Blackstone could not possibly marry a woman such as Caro Morton—'

'I can marry whom I damned well please,' he told her with a return of his usual arrogance. 'And I choose to marry you, if you will have me,' he added determinedly. 'I do not care who or what you are, Caro. Or what you are running away from. I love you. And it is my dearest wish—my only wish—to make you my wife.'

This, more than anything else, finally convinced Caro of the depth of Dominic's love for her. He was a lord, an Earl, and yet he was proposing marriage to a woman he had only known as a singer in a gambling club. A woman he had already made love to. Twice!

She chewed briefly on her bottom lip. 'I should tell you that my mother ran away with her lover when I was a child, and was later shot and killed by him when he caught her in the arms of yet another lover.'

Dominic's thumb moved lightly across her bottom lip, his eyes ablaze with the love he claimed to feel for her. 'I have said I do not care about your past, my love, and I truly do not,' he vowed. 'Besides, you are not responsible for your mother's actions.'

'Any more than you are to blame for the death of your own mother.'

Dominic released his breath in a deep sigh. 'I have always felt responsible…'

Caro gently touched his cheek with her fingertips. 'Tell me what really happened.'

He gave a pained wince. 'I do not believe I could bear it if, once I have done so, you decided you did not love me, after all.'

'It will not happen,' she vowed with certainty. 'Dominic, I know you to be a man who is honest and true. A man who cares deeply for others in spite of himself— Lord Thorne, Drew, Ben, myself, to name only four. I absolutely refuse to believe that you would ever have harmed your own mother.'

'I hope you still think that once I have told you what happened.' Dominic kissed her slowly and lingeringly before speaking again. 'I went away to school when I was twelve years old. I was not a good pupil. I resented being sent away, and got into all manner of scrapes in an attempt to be sent home again. I do not even remember what the last one was.' He grimaced. 'Only that it resulted in my mother having to travel to the school shortly after the Christmas holidays in order to stop the headmaster from expelling me.'

Caro could hear his heart beating rapidly in his chest, the harshness of his breathing as he was obviously beset by the memories that had haunted him into adulthood. 'I love you, Dominic,' she encouraged gently.

His arms tightened about her as he continued. 'Her coach slipped on the icy roads and into an even icier river. The doors became stuck fast and she could not get out as the water—'

'Do not say any more!' Caro sat up and placed her fingertips over his lips as she gazed down at him. 'You were a child, Dominic. A child who felt hurt and rebellious because he felt he had been sent away from those he loved. You were no more responsible for the death of your mother or your father than—than I am.'

Strangely, as Dominic looked up into Caro's compassionate and love-filled eyes, all of the guilt, the feeling that he was unworthy of being loved, quietly and for ever slipped away.

She shook her head. 'It is sad that your father felt he could not go on living without her but—loving you as I do, I believe I know something of how he must have felt,' she added shyly; if Dominic really had been killed earlier today, then Caro knew she would have found it difficult to go on living, too...

He gave a choked groan as he pulled her tightly against him and buried his face in her hair. 'How was I ever lucky enough to find you, Caro? How?'

Caro did not want him to be sad any more; he had already suffered enough, believed himself unworthy of love for long enough. 'But you do not know yet whom you have found,' she reminded him teasingly.

He raised his head to smile at her. 'First tell me that you will marry me, whoever you are.'

'I will.'

'Caro...' Dominic kissed her for several more love-filled minutes, the happiness on his face when he at last raised his head, making him look almost boyish as he grinned down at her.

'But before that can happen,' Caro murmured ruefully, 'you will have to obtain the approval of my guardian.'

Dominic's smile faded slightly. 'Your guardian?'

'I am afraid so.'

He frowned. 'Tell me who this guardian is and I will go to him immediately, assure him that I am a reformed character since meeting you and solicit him for his permission to marry you.'

'It is not necessary for you to go to him.' Caro's eyes glowed with laughter. 'I believe that he is coming to you.'

'To me?' Dominic frowned his confusion. 'But how—?' His eyes widened as he became still. *'Westbourne?'* he breathed in disbelief.

'I am afraid so,' Caro admitted.

Dominic stared down at her, absolutely dumbstruck for several long seconds, and then he began to smile, and then finally to laugh. 'Westbourne!' He sobered suddenly. 'It is because I had told you I was expecting him to arrive in England any day that you were leaving London so hurriedly earlier,' he realised incredulously.

'Yes.'

'What I should have added is that Gabriel does not intend to remain in London, but travel almost immediately to Shoreley Hall.'

'Oh dear!' Caro cringed now at the thought of what her sister Diana would have to say to Dominic's friend when he arrived.

Dominic seemed to suffer no such worries as he

chuckled, once more diverted by the thought that he had stolen a march on his friend and whipped one of his possible choices of bride out from under his nose. 'And which Lady Copeland will I have the pleasure of making my wife?'

'Caroline—I am the second daughter.'

'And you decided to run away to London after refusing to even contemplate becoming Westbourne's bride?'

She gave a delicate shudder. 'I could not possibly marry a man I do not love.'

'And your sisters? Have they run away, too?'

'Oh, no, I am sure they have not.' Caro shook her head, firmly pushing away the flicker of doubt in her mind about that girl in the park who had looked so like Elizabeth. 'I am the rebellious one, I am afraid.'

'Something I will be grateful for until the day I die,' Dominic assured her lovingly.

Dominic loved her just as much as Caro loved him—and she was blissfully certain that he would obtain his friend's permission for the two of them to marry as soon as it could be arranged.

She wound her arms about his neck as she arched up into him. 'Would you care to show me how much you are grateful, Dominic?'

'Gladly!' he groaned as his head lowered and his mouth once again captured hers, the two of them quickly forgetting everything and everyone else but the love they felt for one other, now and for always.

* * * * *

The Lady Forfeits

CAROLE MORTIMER

Chapter One

'Good God, Nathaniel, what have you done to yourself?' Lord Gabriel Faulkner, Earl of Westbourne, exclaimed with less than his usual haughty aplomb.

Gabriel had come to an abrupt halt in the doorway of the bedchamber on first sighting his friend as he lay prostrate upon the bed. Lord Nathaniel Thorne's, Earl of Osbourne's, face was an array of cuts and rainbow-coloured bruises; a wide bandage about the bareness of his muscled chest attested to the possibility of several ribs also being broken.

'Begging your pardon, ma'am.' Gabriel recovered himself enough to turn and give an apologetic bow to the lady standing in the hallway beside him.

'Not at all, my lord,' Mrs Gertrude Wilson, Osbourne's aunt, dismissed briskly. 'I suffered the same feelings of shock upon first seeing the extent of my nephew's injuries four days ago.'

'Would the two of you stop discussing me as if I were

not here?' The patient was obviously less than pleased with this development.

'The physician said you are to rest, Nathaniel,' his aunt instructed sternly before turning that same steely-eyed attention on Gabriel. 'I will leave the two of you to talk now, my lord. But for no longer than ten minutes,' she warned. 'As you see, Nathaniel is more in need of peace and quiet than conversation.' She turned back into the hallway. 'Come along, Betsy,' she added. 'It is time for Hector's walk.'

Gabriel was rendered completely mystified by this last comment until another figure stepped out from the shadows of the hallway: a young, slender girl, with ebony curls surrounding the pale oval of a face made beautiful by huge blue eyes, clutching a small white dog in her arms.

'If I have to suffer much more of this mollycoddling I will very likely resort to wringing someone's neck,' Nathaniel grumbled as soon as his aunt and her companion had departed and the two gentlemen were at last left alone in the bedchamber. 'It is so good to see you, Gabe,' he added more warmly as he struggled to sit up, the grimace on his face evidence, despite his denials, that it was a painful business.

'Stay where you are, man.' Gabriel crossed to his friend's bedside, the usual look of determination now back upon a haughtily handsome face dominated by shrewd midnight-blue eyes. Tall and dark, and dressed in a perfectly tailored black superfine, silver waistcoat and grey pantaloons above black Hessians, the Earl of Westbourne gave every appearance of being the fashionable English gentleman, despite having spent the last eight years roaming the Continent.

Osbourne relaxed back against the many pillows behind him. 'I had thought it was your intention to go straight to Shoreley Park when you arrived from Venice, rather than come up to London, Gabe? Which begs the question—?'

'I believe your aunt has advised that you rest, Nate,' Gabriel murmured, arching one arrogant brow.

Osbourne scowled. 'Having summarily removed me from my own home and into her own cloying care, I believe if my Aunt Gertrude were to have her way she would now have me tied to the bed and all visitors refused entry.'

Despite his friend's grumbling, Gabriel realised Nate's aunt had done the correct thing as Nate so obviously found any movement extremely painful and couldn't fend for himself. 'What happened to you, Nate?' he asked as he folded his elegant length on to the chair placed beside the bed.

The other man grimaced. 'Well, despite what you said when you first saw me, I certainly did not do this to myself.'

But having served with Osbourne in the King's army for five years, Gabriel knew better than most how proficient Osbourne was with both sword and pistol. 'So how did it happen then?'

'A little…disagreement outside Dominic's new club, with four pairs of fists and the same amount of hobnailed boots.'

'Ah.' Gabriel nodded. 'And would these four sets of fists and hobnailed boots have any connection to the gossip now circulating about town concerning the sudden demise of a certain Mr Nicholas Brown?'

The other man gave him an appreciative grin. 'You have seen Dominic, then?' He referred to their mutual friend, Dominic Vaughn, Earl of Blackstone, who had won a gambling club called Nick's off a rogue named Nicholas Brown, who had then tried to sabotage and threaten Dominic any way he could until Dominic had had to deal with him in no uncertain terms.

'Unfortunately not. I called at Blackstone House on my arrival in town earlier this morning and was informed that Dominic was not at home. That he has, in fact, gone into the country for several days.' Gabriel looked thoughtful.

The three men had been friends since their school-days together, that friendship continuing despite Gabriel's sudden banishment to the Continent eight years ago. He dearly hoped that Dominic's sudden departure from town did not mean his friend was about to face the same fate after being forced to shoot dead that scoundrel Nicholas Brown…

'It is not at all what you think, Gabe.' Nathaniel's grin had widened as he reached for the letter on the bedside table and handed it to the other man. 'The authorities have accepted Dominic's account of what took place between himself and Brown; it would appear that Dominic is even now travelling into Hampshire with the intention of visiting the family of the woman he has every intention of making his wife. Look, see what he wrote to me before he left.'

Gabriel quickly scanned the contents of the missive from their friend. A brief, unhelpful letter, obviously written in a hurry, with little real information—apart from the news that Dominic had indeed gone into Hampshire with the intention of asking permission from this woman's guardian for the two of them to marry. 'And who, pray, is Miss Morton?' He placed Dominic's letter lightly back on the bedside table.

'An absolute beauty.' Osbourne's eyes lit up appreciatively. 'Not that it was apparent immediately, of course, because of the jewelled mask and ebony wig she wore when I first saw her. But once they had been removed—'

'She was wearing a *mask* and *wig*?' Gabriel repeated in astonishment.

Osbourne looked less sure of himself in the face of that Gabriel's utter incredulity. 'She was singing at Nick's the evening the fight broke out, and so Dom and I had no choice but to step in and—' He broke off as Gabriel raised a silencing hand.

'Let me see if I have understood you correctly,' Gabriel said grimly. 'Are you really telling me that Blackstone is about to ask for the hand in marriage of a woman who, until a short time ago, sang in a gentlemen's gambling club disguised in a jewelled mask and ebony wig?' His tone had gone positively icy with disapproval.

'I—well—yes, I suppose I am…' Osbourne confirmed uneasily.

'Has Dominic completely taken leave of his senses? Or perhaps he also received a blow to the head from one of those fists or hobnailed boots?' Gabriel exploded. He could envisage no other explanation for his incredibly eligible friend even contemplating proposing marriage to a singer in a gambling club—no matter how beautiful she was!

Nathaniel gave a shrug. 'His letter says he will explain all upon his return to town.'

'By which time it will no doubt be too late to save him from this reckless venture; no guardian of such a woman would even consider turning down an offer of marriage from an earl. In fact, I would not be at all surprised if Dominic does not return to town already married to the chit.' Gabriel scowled his displeasure at the thought of his friend's obvious entrapment by this "absolute beauty".

'I had not thought of it in quite that way.' Nathaniel frowned his own concern. 'She seemed very much the lady of quality when I spoke with her.'

'My dear Nate, I may have been absent from London society for some years,' Gabriel drawled drily, 'but I do not believe it has changed so much that ladies of quality now seek employment in gentlemen's gambling clubs.'

'Hmm.' Nathaniel considered the matter further. 'Perhaps, as you are travelling into Hampshire yourself, you might seek Dominic out and—'

'My original plan to go to Shoreley Park no longer stands.' Gabriel's mouth tightened at the thought of the conversation that had taken place earlier that morning in the offices of his lawyer, that had succeeded in altering all his plans. 'I arrived back in England only hours ago, to find an envoy from my lawyer awaiting me upon the quayside in possession of a letter requesting that I come to town immediately and meet with him. It would appear that the three Lady Copelands—having, as you are well aware, all decided to refuse my offer of marriage—have now chosen to absent themselves from Shoreley Park completely. No doubt in anticipation of my arrival there.'

It was an occurrence that did not please Gabriel in the slightest. Insult enough that his offer of marriage to one of his wards had been refused, sight unseen, without his now being put to the trouble of having to seek out all three of the rebellious chits!

The previous two Westbourne heirs having died at Waterloo, Gabriel had surprisingly come into the title of the Earl of Westbourne six months ago, along with guardianship of the previous earl's three unmarried daughters. In the circumstances, and as he had a complete lack of interest in taking any other woman as his wife, Gabriel had deemed it appropriate to offer marriage to one of those daughters. Not only had they all refused him, but, to add insult to injury, they had now all taken it into their heads to defy even his guardianship. A defiance Gabriel had no intention of tolerating!

'I called upon Dominic earlier with the intention of taking him up on his offer that I stay at Blackstone House with him when I returned to town.' Gabriel shrugged. 'It appears, in light of his disappearance into the country, that I shall have to make Westbourne House my home, after all.'

'It's been closed up these past ten years,' Nathaniel grimaced. 'It's nothing but a mausoleum and it's probably full of mice and other rodents, too.'

Gabriel was well aware of the dereliction of Westbourne House. It was the very reason he had been putting off his arrival there all morning. Once he had finished talking to his lawyer he had first called upon

Dominic at Blackstone House, only to learn of the other man's disappearance into the country. A similar visit to Nathaniel's residence had garnered the information that he was currently residing at the home of his aunt, Mrs Gertrude Wilson, meaning he couldn't stay with him either.

'There's absolutely no reason why you cannot stay at Osbourne House in my absence,' the earl assured him, as if suddenly aware of his thoughts. 'We could have both moved back there if my aunt had not taken it into her head to remove me to the country later this afternoon.' He looked less than happy with the arrangements. 'Take my advice, Gabe—never let a woman get the upper hand; she's apt to take advantage while a man's down.'

Gabriel had no intention of allowing a woman, any woman, to take advantage of him ever again, having learnt that hard lesson only too well eight years ago…

'Oh, I say!' Osbourne instantly looked contrite. 'I did not mean to imply—'

'No implication taken, Nate, I assure you. And kind as your offer is, I fear, as I must take up residence at Westbourne House at some time, it may as well be now.' Gabriel rose languidly to his feet. 'I will see if I can find someone suitable to go into Hampshire and locate Dominic, and hopefully return him to his senses before it is too late,' he added darkly.

Society, as Gabriel knew only too well, did not, and would not, ever forgive such a social indiscretion as an earl aligning himself in marriage to a woman who had previously been a singer in a gentlemen's gambling club.

'Now I believe it is time I took my leave—before Mrs

Wilson returns and has me forcibly ejected from the premises!' He fastidiously straightened the lace cuff of his shirt beneath his superfine.

'Can't see it m'self,' his friend snorted as he rang the bell for one of the servants to escort Gabriel down the stairs. 'My Aunt Gertrude may have me at a disadvantage for the moment, but I very much doubt she would ever have the same effect on you.'

In truth, Gabriel had found Mrs Wilson's polite if cool attitude towards him something of a relief after the years of being shunned by society. Obviously coming into the title of earl did make a difference! 'Think it lucky that you have a relative who feels enough affection for you to bother herself about you,' he said drily. His own family, such as it was, had not troubled themselves to even learn of Gabriel's whereabouts this past eight years, let alone enquire about his health.

As Gabriel travelled in his coach to Westbourne House he considered the possibility, now he was in possession of the old and much respected title of the Earl of Westbourne, with all the wealth, estates and power that title engendered, as to whether there might be a sea change in the attitude of the family that had chosen to banish him from their sight all those years ago. Even if there was, Gabriel thought coldly, he was indifferent to becoming reacquainted with any of *them*.

Gabriel's air of studied indifference suffered a severe blow, however, when he arrived at Westbourne House some minutes later.

The front door was opened by a perfectly liveried butler who, upon enquiry, informed Gabriel, "Lady

Diana is not at home at the moment, my lord, but is expected back very shortly."

Lady Diana Copeland? One of the previous Earl of Westbourne's rebellious daughters who was supposedly missing from home? And, if so, exactly how long had she been in residence at Westbourne House?

'The earl requests that you join him in the library immediately upon your return, my lady,' Soames stiffly informed Lady Diana Copeland as he opened the front door to admit her. Instead the butler succeeded in bringing her to an abrupt halt so that she now stood poised upon the threshold.

'The Earl of…?'

'Westbourne, my lady.'

The Earl of Westbourne!

Lord Gabriel Faulkner?

Here?

Now?

And apparently awaiting her in the library…

Well, who had more right than Lord Gabriel Faulkner, the newly titled Earl of Westbourne, to be awaiting Diana in what was, after all, now *his* library, she scolded herself. Besides, had she not been anticipating just such an opportunity in which to personally inform the new earl exactly what she thought of both him, his blanket offer of marriage to herself and her two sisters, and the serious repercussions of that preposterous offer?

Diana stiffened her spine in preparation for that conversation. 'Thank you, Soames.' She continued confidently into the entrance hall before removing her bonnet and handing it and her parasol to the maid who had accompanied her on her morning errands. 'Is my Aunt Humphries still in her rooms?'

'She is, my lady,' the butler confirmed evenly, his expression as unemotionally non committal as a good butler's should be.

Nevertheless, Diana sensed the man's disapproval that Mrs Humphries had taken to her bed shortly after they had arrived at Westbourne House three days earlier and that she had chosen to remain there during the uproar of Diana's efforts to ensure that the house was cleaned and polished from attic to cellar.

Diana had been unsure as to what she would find when she reached Westbourne House. Neither she, nor her two sisters, had ever been to London before, let alone stayed in what was the family home there. Their father, the previous earl, had chosen not to go there either for all of ten years before his death six months ago.

The air of decay and neglect Diana had encountered when she'd first entered Westbourne House had been every bit as bad as she had feared it might be—as well as confirming that the new earl had not yet arrived from his home in Venice to take up residence here. The few servants who remained had fallen into almost as much decay and neglect as the house in the absence of a master or mistress to keep them about their duties. An occurrence that Diana had dealt with by immediately dispensing with the servants unwilling or unable to work and engaging new ones to take their place, their first task being to restore the house to some of its obvious former glory.

A task well done, Diana noted as she looked about

her with an air of satisfaction. Wood now gleamed.
Floors were polished. Doors and windows had been left
open for many hours each day in order to dispel the last
of the musty smell.

The new earl could certainly have no complaints as
to the restored comfort of his London home!

And, Diana knew, she had delayed that first meeting
with the new earl for quite long enough…

'Bring tea into the library, would you, please,
Soames,' she instructed lightly, knowing that all the
servants, old as well as new, now worked with a quiet
and competent efficiency under the guidance of this
newly appointed butler whom she has interviewed and
appointed herself.

'Yes, my lady.' He gave a stiff bow. 'Would that be
tea for one or two, my lady? His Lordship instructed
that a decanter of brandy be brought to him in the
library almost an hour ago,' he supplied as Diana looked
at him questioningly.

Diana could not help a glance at the grandfather
clock in the hallway, noting that the hour was only
twelve o'clock—surely much too early in the day for
the earl to be imbibing brandy?

But then what did she, who had lived all of her one-
and-twenty years in the country, know of London ways?
Or, the earl having lived in Venice for so many years,
were they Italian ways, perhaps?

Whichever of those it was, a cup of tea would do Lord
Gabriel Faulkner far more good at this time of day than
a glass or two of brandy. 'For two, thank you, Soames.'
She nodded dismissively before drawing in a deep and
determined breath and walking in the direction of the
library.

* * *

'Enter,' Gabriel instructed tersely as a knock sounded on the door of the library. He stood, a glass half-full of brandy in his hand, looking out at what was undoubtedly a garden when properly tended, but at the moment most resembled a riotous jungle. Whoever had seen to the cleaning and polishing of the house—the absent Lady Diana, presumably?—had not as yet had the chance to turn her hand to the ordering of the gardens!

He turned, the sunlight behind him throwing his face into shadow, as the door was opened with a decisive briskness totally in keeping with the fashionably elegant young lady who stepped determinedly into the library and closed the door behind her.

The colour of her hair was the first thing that Gabriel noticed. It was neither gold nor red, but somewhere in between the two, and arranged on her crown in soft, becoming curls, with several of those curls allowed to brush against the smooth whiteness of her nape and brow. A softness completely at odds with the proud angle of her chin. Her eyes, the same deep blue colour of her high-waisted gown, flickered disapprovingly over the glass of brandy he held in his hand before meeting Gabriel's gaze with the same challenge with which she now lifted her pointed chin.

'Lady Diana Copeland, I presume?' Gabriel bowed briefly, giving no indication, by tone or expression, of his surprise at finding her here at all when his last instruction to the three sisters was for them to remain in residence at Shoreley Park in Hampshire and await his arrival in England.

Her curtsy was just as brief. 'My lord.'

Just the two words. And yet Gabriel was aware of a brief *frisson* of awareness down the length of his spine on hearing the husky tone of her voice. A voice surely not meant to belong to a young lady of society at all, but by a mistress as she whispered and cried out words of encouragement to her lover…

His gaze narrowed on the cause of these inappropriate imaginings. 'And which of the three Lady Copelands might you be in regard to age?' In truth, Gabriel had not been interested enough in the three wards that had been foisted on him to bother knowing anything about them apart from the fact they were all of marriageable age! Time enough for that, he had decided arrogantly, once one of them had agreed to become his wife. Except none of them had, he recalled grimly.

'I am the eldest, my lord.' Diana Copeland stepped further into the room, the sunlight immediately making her hair appear more gold than red. 'And I wish to talk with you concerning my sisters.'

'As your two sisters are not in this room at the moment I have absolutely no interest in discussing them.' Gabriel frowned his irritation. 'Whereas *you*—'

'Then might I suggest you endeavour to *make* yourself interested in them?' Diana advised coldly, the narrowness of her shoulders stiff with indignation.

'My dear Diana—I trust, as your guardian, I may call you that?—I suggest that in future,' he continued smoothly without bothering to wait for her answer, 'you do not attempt to tell me what I should and should not interest myself in.' A haughty young miss too used to having her own way presented no verbal or physical challenge for Gabriel after his years spent as an officer in the King's army. 'As such, *I* will be the one who decides what is or is not to be discussed between the two of us. The most immediate being—why it is you have chosen to come to London completely against my instructions?' He stepped forwards into the room.

Whatever sharp reply Diana had been about to make, in answer to this reminder of the arrogance with which she viewed Lord Gabriel Faulkner's "instructions", remained unsaid as he stepped forwards out of the sunlight and she found herself able to see him clearly for the first time.

He was, quite simply…magnificent!

No other word could completely describe the harsh beauty of that arrogantly handsome face. He possessed a strong, square jaw, chiselled lips, high cheekbones either side of a long blade of a nose, and his eyes— oh, those eyes!—of so dark a blue that they were the blue-black of a clear winter's night. His dark hair was fashionably styled so that it fell rakishly upon his brow and curled at his nape, his black jacket fitted smoothly across wide and muscled shoulders, the silver waistcoat beneath of a cut and style equally as fashionable, and his grey pantaloons clung to long, elegantly muscled legs, above black and perfectly polished Hessians.

Yes, Lord Gabriel Faulkner was without doubt the most fashionable and aristocratically handsome gentleman that Diana had ever beheld in all of her one-and-twenty years—

'Diana, I am still waiting to hear your reasons for disobeying me and coming up to town.'

—as well as being the most arrogant!

Having been deprived of her mother when she was but eleven years old, and with two sisters younger than herself, it had fallen to Diana to take on the role of mother to her sisters and mistress at her father's home; as such, she had become more inclined to give instructions than to receive them.

Her chin tilted. 'Mr Johnston merely advised that you would call upon us at Shoreley Park as soon as was convenient after your arrival from Venice. As, at the time, he could not specify precisely when the date for that arrival might be, I took it upon myself to use my own initiative concerning how best to deal with this delicate situation.'

Haughty as well as proud, Gabriel acknowledged with some inner amusement at the return of that challenging tilt to Diana Copeland's delicious chin. She had also, if he was not mistaken, already developed a dislike for him personally as well as for his role as guardian to herself and her sisters.

The latter Gabriel could easily understand; as he understood it from his lawyer, William Johnston, Diana had been mistress of Shoreley Park since the death of her mother, Harriet Copeland, some ten years ago. As such, she would not be accustomed to doing as she was told, least of all by a guardian she had never met.

The former—a dislike of Gabriel personally—was not unprecedented, either, but it usually took a little longer than a few minutes' acquaintance for that to happen. Unless, of course, Lady Diana had already taken that dislike to him before she had even met him?

He quirked one dark, mocking brow. 'And what "delicate situation" might that be?'

A becoming blush entered the pallor of her cheeks, those blue eyes glittering as she obviously heard the mockery in his tone. 'The disappearance of my two sisters, of course.'

'What?' Gabriel gave a start. He had known the Copeland sisters had chosen to absent themselves from Shoreley Park, of course, but once he was informed of Diana's presence at Westbourne House, he had assumed that her sisters would either be staying with her here, or that she would at least have some idea of their whereabouts. 'Explain yourself—clearly and precisely, if you please.' A nerve pulsed in his tightly clenched jaw.

Diana gave him a withering glance. 'Caroline and Elizabeth, being so…alarmed by your offer of marriage, have both taken it into their heads to leave the only home they have ever known and run off to heaven knows where!'

Gabriel drew in a harsh breath as he carefully placed the glass of brandy down upon the table before turning his back to once again stare out of the window. While he'd known the three Copeland sisters had absented themselves from Shoreley Park, to now learn that his offer of marriage had actually caused the two younger sisters to run away, without so much as informing their older sister of where they were going, was not only insulting but, surprisingly, had also succeeded in affecting Gabriel when he had believed himself to be beyond reacting to such slights.

He had been forced to live in disgrace all these years, always knowing that of all the people Gabriel had previously loved or cared about, only his friends Blackstone and Osbourne believed in his innocence. It had meant he hadn't particularly cared, during his five years in the army, as to whether he lived or died. Ironically, it had been that very recklessness and daring that had succeeded in making him appear the hero in the eyes of his fellow officers and men.

Realising that two young, delicately bred ladies had been so averse to even the suggestion of marriage to the infamous Lord Gabriel Faulkner that they had chosen to flee their home rather than contemplate such a fate had laid open a wound Gabriel had believed long since healed, if not forgotten…

'My lord?'

Gabriel breathed in deeply through his nose, hands clenched at his sides as he fought back the demons from his past, knowing they had no place in the here and now.

'My lord, what—?' Diana recoiled from the icy fury she could see in Gabriel's arrogantly handsome features as he turned to glare across the room at her with eyes so dark and glittering they appeared as black as she imagined the devil's might be.

He arched a dark brow over those piercing blue-black eyes. 'You did not feel the same desire to run away?'

In truth, it had not even entered Diana's head to do so. It was not in her nature to run away from trouble and she had been too busy since discovering her sisters' absence for there to be any time to think of anything else. But if she had thought of it, what would she have done?

Ten years of being the responsible daughter, the practical and sensible one, had taken their toll on the light-hearted and mischievous girl she had once been, until Diana could not recall what it was to behave impetuously or rashly, or to consider her own needs before those of her father and sisters. She would definitely not have left.

'No, I did not,' she stated bluntly.

'And why was that?' An almost predatory look had come over his face.

Diana straightened her shoulders. 'I—'

Quite what she had been about to say to Gabriel she could not be sure as the butler chose that moment to enter with a tray of tea things and place them on the table beside the fireplace. A tray of tea things set for two, Gabriel noted with some amusement; obviously, from that flicker of disdain he had seen on the fair Diana's face a few minutes ago, she did not approve of the imbibing of strong liquor before luncheon, if ever.

To hell with what the Lady Diana approved of!

Gabriel moved with deliberation as he picked up the glass of brandy he had been enjoying earlier and threw the contents to the back of his throat before replacing the empty glass down upon the table beside the tea tray, the smooth yet fiery liquid warming his insides, if not his mood.

He waited until the butler had left the room before speaking again. 'I believe you were about to tell me why it is you did not choose to run away as your sisters have done?' he asked.

'Would you care for tea, my lord?'

His eyes narrowed at this further delay. 'No, I would not.'

Blonde brows rose. 'You do not care for tea?'

'It is certainly not one of the things I have missed in all these years of living abroad,' he said drily.

Diana continued to calmly pour a cup of tea for herself before straightening, her gaze very direct as she looked across at him. 'I trust your journey from Venice was uneventful, my lord?'

He gave an impatient snort. 'If you are intending to distract me with these inanities, Diana, then I believe I should warn you that I am not in the habit of allowing myself to be distracted.'

'I have heard you were considered something of a war hero during your years in the army,' she commented.

She had heard of his time in the army? Had she heard something of those other, much more damaging rumours of his behaviour eight years ago, too?

Gabriel's expression became closed as he observed Diana through narrowed lids. 'And what else have you heard about me?'

Guileless blue eyes met his unblinkingly. 'In what context, my lord?'

Over the years Gabriel had faced down enemies and so-called friends alike, without so much as even the slightest possibility of any of them ever getting the better of him, but this young woman, who had lived all of her life in the country, nevertheless showed no hesitation in challenging him.

'In any context, madam,' he finally replied.

Slender shoulders lifted in a dismissive shrug. 'I make a point of never listening to idle gossip, my lord. But even if I did,' she continued, just as Gabriel felt himself starting to relax, 'I fear I have not been in town long enough, nor is my acquaintance wide enough as yet, to have had the time or opportunity to be made privy to any...confidences.'

If Diana Copeland feared anything, then Gabriel would be interested to learn what that something was. She had certainly shown no hesitation as yet in speaking her mind, clearly and often! And if Gabriel had his way, this young lady would be returning to the country long before she had the opportunity to become "privy to any confidences"...

She raised one delicately arched brow. 'Perhaps you would care to enlighten me?'

She was good, Gabriel recognised admiringly. Very good, in fact. She showed just the right amount of calm uninterest to indicate that the subject on which they spoke was of little or no relevance to her. If Gabriel had been less sensitive to the subject himself, he might even have been fooled by her...

'Not at this moment, no.' His jaw tightened. 'Nor have I forgotten our original subject.'

'Which was...?'

He drew in a deep and controlling breath, even as his hands flexed impatiently at his sides. 'I wish to know why, instead of disappearing before my arrival in England as your sisters have obviously chosen to do, you have come to stay at Westbourne House instead?'

She straightened haughtily. 'Are you, as the new

owner of this property, expressing the sentiment that I no longer have that right?'

Gabriel made another attempt to regain control of the conversation. Something he was finding it harder and harder to do the longer it continued! 'No, I am not saying that. As my ward you are, of course, perfectly at liberty to continue using any of the Westbourne homes or estates. It is only that, in this case, you must have been aware that once I had learnt you weren't in Shoreley Park, Westbourne House was sure to be my first choice of residence?'

'I was aware of that, yes.'

'Well?' Gabriel found himself becoming more and more frustrated with this conversation.

She sipped her tea delicately before answering. 'Surely the reason for my being here is obvious, my lord?'

'Perhaps to make enquiries about your two sisters?'

'That was my first concern, yes.'

'And your second?' That nerve was once again pulsing in Gabriel's jaw, and if he was not mistaken, he was developing a twitch in his left eyelid too!

Diana sat forwards to carefully place her empty teacup down upon the silver tray, that slight adjustment in her pose revealing more of the deep swell of her creamy breasts. Full and plump breasts, Gabriel noted admiringly, and slightly at odds with the slenderness of the rest of her revealed by the cut of her gown. Born and raised in the country or not, Diana Copeland was every inch a lady, he noted as his gaze trailed down her graceful slim arms and her elegant hands in their white-lace gloves. A self-confident and outspoken young lady who—

'My second reason for awaiting your arrival here is, of course, that I have decided to accept your offer of marriage.'

If Gabriel had still been enjoying his brandy at that moment, then he would surely have choked on it!

Chapter Two

Diana remained outwardly calm as she stood up to cross the room with purpose and rearrange the flowers in the vase that stood upon the small table near the window, having averted her face, she hoped, before any of the inner trepidation she felt in having voiced her acceptance of this man's offer of marriage could be revealed.

His lordship's surprise on hearing that acceptance had been all too obvious in the way those midnight-blue eyes had widened incredulously, followed by his stunned silence.

At any other time Diana might have felt a certain satisfaction in having rendered speechless a man of Lord Gabriel Faulkner's obvious arrogance and sophistication. Unfortunately, in this case, and on this particular subject, she would have welcomed almost any other response from him.

Perhaps, as Diana had initially refused his offer, the earl had now decided to withdraw it? In which case, she would not only have caused herself embarrassment, but also placed him in the awkward position of having to extricate himself from an unwanted engagement.

If that incredulity was for another reason, such as now that he had actually met her, the new Earl of West-bourne found either her looks or her character unsuitable in his future countess, then Diana was not sure—following other hurtful events of this past week—that she would be able to withstand the humiliation.

'Correct me if I am wrong, but did you not say you are the eldest of the Copeland sisters?' he finally managed to say.

A frown creased Diana's brow as she turned. 'I did, yes…'

He looked a little bemused. 'My lawyer led me to believe that the eldest of Copeland sisters was already betrothed. Is that not correct?'

Diana drew in a sharp breath even as she felt the warmth colouring her cheeks. 'Then he was misinformed, my lord. I am not, nor have I ever been, formally betrothed. Nor do I have any idea how Mr Johnston could even have heard such a thing,' she added waspishly.

Gabriel studied her closely, noting that high colour in her cheeks, the proud almost defiant tilt to her chin, and the challenging sparkle in those sky-blue eyes. He wondered as to the reason for them. Just as he also questioned the precise and careful way in which she had dismissed the existence of any betrothal…

His mouth firmed. 'I believe Johnston was told of the betrothal by one of your sisters.'

'Indeed?' Blond brows rose haughtily. 'Then it would

seem that the man was not misinformed, after all, but merely misunderstood the information given to him.'

Somehow he did not think so... He had inherited William Johnston, along with the title, estates and guardianship of the three Copeland sisters, from their father, Marcus Copeland, the previous Earl of Westbourne. The lawyer was a precise and self-satisfied little man whom Gabriel did not particularly like, but at the same time he believed the lawyer would make it a matter of professional pride never to be misinformed or mistaken concerning information he gave to one of his wealthy and titled clients. So why was this betrothal no more?

Gabriel looked at her directly. 'Was it you or the young gentleman who had a change of heart?'

'I have just told you there was no gentleman!' she protested.

'A young man, then. One who no doubt found the prospect of marriage to a titled young lady whose fortunes now rested on the goodwill of her guardian a far different marriage prospect than the eldest daughter of a wealthy earl?' Gabriel enquired, eyeing her knowingly.

Diana withstood that gaze for as long as she could before turning away abruptly, determined he should not see the tears that now glistened in her eyes and on her lashes.

Damn the man!

No—damn *all* men!

And most especially Malcolm Castle for having the backbone of a jellyfish!

She and Malcolm had grown up together in the village of Shoreley. Had played together as children.

Danced together at the local assemblies once they were old enough to attend. They'd taken walks together on crisp winter days and fine summer evenings. Diana had even allowed Malcolm the liberty of stealing her very first kiss after he had declared his love for her.

She had believed herself to be equally as smitten. Her father had shown no disapproval of their deepening friendship. Malcolm's parents, the local squire and his wife, were obviously thrilled at the idea of a possible match between their son and the eldest daughter of the wealthy Earl of Westbourne. All had seemed perfect.

Except, as his lordship had just pointed out so cruelly, the penniless eldest daughter of the previous Earl of Westbourne had not been nearly as appealing as a prospective wife to Malcolm, or to his parents. Diana's father had not expected to die so suddenly and had not set his affairs in order with regard to his daughters. Financially, they were completely at the mercy of the new earl's goodwill—and as he had been away from society for so long, Lord Gabriel Faulkner was an unknown quantity.

Diana had, of course, noted that Malcolm's visits to Shoreley Park had become less frequent after her father died. There had been no suggestions of their walking out together, let alone the stealing of a kiss or two, and of course there had been no attending the local assemblies because Diana and her sisters were in mourning. But Diana had not been concerned, had believed Malcolm's absence to be out of consideration for her recent bereavement and nothing else.

Until the previous week when Diana had learnt— from inadvertently overhearing two of the housemaids indulging in idle gossip—of the announcement of Malcolm's betrothal to a Miss Vera Douglas, the daughter of a wealthy tradesman who had recently bought a house in the area.

To add insult to injury, Malcolm had called to see Diana that very same afternoon, full of apologies for not having told her of the betrothal himself, and insisting that it was his parents who had pushed for this other marriage rather than himself, and that, in spite of everything, it was still Diana that he loved.

Diana could perhaps have forgiven Malcolm if he had found himself smitten with love for another woman, but to hear from his own lips that he was only marrying this other wealthy young woman because his parents wished it was beyond enduring. A jellyfish, indeed! And one that she knew she could inwardly congratulate herself on being well rid of.

Except Malcolm's defection had left her pride in tatters and made her the object of pitying looks every time she so much as ventured out into the village. So she had decided, with her usual air of practicality, that the perfect way in which to dispel such gossip would be if she were to accept, after all, the offer of marriage from Lord Gabriel Faulkner, seventh Earl of Westbourne. Marriage to any man—even taking into account that past scandal connected to Gabriel, which Diana's neighbours had hinted at, but never openly discussed—surely had to be better than everyone believing she had been passed over for the daughter of a retired tradesman!

'Am I correct in thinking that the dissolution of your previous engagement is the only reason you have now decided to accept my own offer of marriage?' that taunting earl now prompted irritatingly.

How could Diana have known, when she so sensibly made her decision to accept his lordship's offer, how wickedly handsome he was? How tall and muscular? How fashionably elegant?

How irritatingly perceptive to have guessed within minutes of her announcing her acceptance of his offer as to the real reason for her change of mind!

'It was made more than clear that one of us must accept your offer if we wished to continue living at Shoreley Park,' she informed him defensively.

Gabriel frowned darkly. 'Made clear by whom, exactly?'

'Mr Johnston, of course.'

Gabriel could see no 'of course' about it. 'Explain, if you please.'

She gave an impatient huff. 'Your lawyer stated on his last visit to us that, if we all continued to refuse your offer, we might find ourselves not only penniless, but also asked to remove ourselves from our home.'

Gabriel's jaw tensed and he felt that nerve once again pulsing in his cheek. 'Those are the *exact* words he used when speaking with you?'

Diana gave a haughty inclination of her golden-red head. 'I am not in the habit of lying, my lord.'

If that truly were the case—and Gabriel had no reason to believe that it was not—then William Johnston had far exceeded his authority. It was not the fault of the Copeland sisters that they had no brother to inherit the title and estates, or that their father had not seen fit to secure their futures himself in the event of his death.

Damn it, Gabriel had only made his offer of marriage at all out of a sense of fairness, appreciating that, but for fickle fate, one of the Copeland sisters' own cousins would have inherited the title rather than a complete stranger. A cousin, one would hope, who would have treated the previous earl's daughters as fairly as Gabriel was attempting to do.

His mouth thinned. 'I have *no* intention of asking you or your sisters to leave your home, either now or in the future.'

Diana looked confused. 'But Mr Johnston was very precise concerning—'

'Mr Johnston obviously spoke out of turn.' Gabriel's expression was grim as he anticipated his next conversation with the pompous little upstart who had so obviously put the fear of God into the Copeland sisters that they had felt as trapped as cornered animals. 'This is the reason your two sisters have run away?'

'I believe it was…the catalyst, yes.'

Gabriel eyed her curiously. 'But only the catalyst?'

Diana grimaced. 'My sisters have found life at Shoreley Park somewhat limiting these past few years. Do not misunderstand me,' she added hastily as Gabriel raised his brows. 'Caroline and Elizabeth were both dutiful daughters. Accepted the reasons for our father's decision not to give any of us a London Season, or indeed his wish to not introduce us into London society at all—'

'Am I right in thinking your father made that decision based on your mother's behaviour ten years ago?' he interrupted gently.

Blond lashes lowered over those sky-blue eyes. 'Our father certainly blamed the…excesses of London society for my mother having left us, yes.'

Circumstances meant that Gabriel himself had not been part of that society for a number of years, but nevertheless he could understand Copeland's concern for his three no doubt impressionable daughters. 'He did not fear that keeping you and your sisters shut away in Hampshire might result in the opposite of what he intended? That one or all of you might be tempted into doing exactly as your mother had done and run away to London?'

'Certainly not!' Her reply was both quick and indignant. 'As I have said, Caroline and Elizabeth found life in the country somewhat restricting, but they would never have hurt our father by openly disobeying him.'

'They obviously did not feel the same reluctance where I am concerned,' Gabriel pointed out with a rueful grimace. 'Your presence here would seem to imply that you believe your sisters to have finally come to London now.'

In truth, Diana had no idea where her sisters had gone after they'd left Shoreley Park. But having searched extensively locally, with no joy, London, with all its temptations and excitement, had seemed the next logical choice. Except Diana had not realised until she arrived here quite how large and busy a city London was. Or how difficult it would be to locate two particular young ladies amongst its sprawling population.

'I believed it to be a possibility I might find at least

one of them here. My sisters did not leave together, you see,' she explained as Gabriel once again raised arrogantly questioning brows. 'Caroline disappeared first, with Elizabeth following two days later. Caroline has always been the more impulsive of the two.' She gave an affectionate if exasperated sigh.

Gabriel's face darkened ominously. 'They had the good sense to bring their maids with them, I hope?'

Diana winced. 'I believe they both thought that a maid might try to hinder their departure—'

'You are telling me that they are both likely somewhere here in London *completely* unprotected?' The earl looked scandalised at the prospect.

Diana was no less alarmed now that she had actually arrived in London and become aware of some of the dangers facing a young woman alone here—overfamiliarity and robbery being the least of them. 'I am hoping that is not the case, and that the two of them had made some sort of pact to meet up once they were here.' Rather a large hope, considering Elizabeth had seemed as surprised as Diana—and resentful—by Caroline's sudden disappearance. 'In any case, I am sure they will have come to no harm. That we may even one day all come to laugh about this adventure.'

Gabriel was not fooled for a moment by Diana's words of optimism and could clearly see the lines of worry creasing her creamy brow. It was a worry he, knowing only too well of the seedy underbelly of London, now shared. 'I trust *you* did not also come to London unchaperoned?'

'Oh, no,' she assured him hurriedly. 'My Aunt Humphries and both our maids accompanied me here.'

'Your Aunt Humphries?'

'My father's younger sister. She was married to a naval man, but unfortunately he was killed during the Battle of Trafalgar.'

'And am I right in thinking that she now resides with you in Hampshire?'

'Since her husband's death, yes.'

Good Lord, it seemed he did not have just three young, unruly wards to plague him, but an elderly widow he was also responsible for! 'And where is your aunt now?'

She looked apologetic. 'She does not care for London and has stayed in her rooms since our arrival.'

Thereby rendering her of absolutely no use whatsoever as a chaperon to her niece! 'So,' Gabriel announced heavily, 'if I am to understand this correctly, your two sisters having run away, you have now decided to offer yourself up as a marital sacrifice in the hopes that, once they learn of our betrothal, they will be encouraged to return home?'

Diana met his gaze steadily. 'It is my hope, yes.'

Gabriel gave a hard and humourless smile. 'Your courage is to be admired, madam.'

She looked startled. 'My courage?'

'I am sure, even in the relative safety of Hampshire, that you cannot have remained unaware of the fact that you are considering marriage to a man that society has wanted nothing to do with this past eight years?'

'I have heard…rumours and innuendo, of course,' she admitted gravely.

Gabriel would wager that she had! 'And this does not concern you?'

Of course it concerned her. But if no one could be persuaded to tell her of this past scandal, what was she expected to do about it? 'Should it have done?' she asked slowly.

He gave a bored shrug. 'Only you can know the answer to that.'

Diana frowned slightly. 'Perhaps if you were to enlighten me as to the nature of the scandal?'

Those sculptured lips twisted bitterly. 'And why on earth would you suppose I'd ever wish to do that?'

Diana stared up at him in frustration. 'Surely it would be better for all concerned if you were to inform me of your supposed misdeeds yourself, rather than have me learn of them from a possibly malicious third party?'

'And if I prefer not to inform you?' he drawled.

She gave him a frustrated look. 'Did you kill some-one, perhaps?'

He smiled without humour. 'I have killed too many someones to number.'

'I meant apart from in battle, of course!' Those blue eyes sparkled with rebuke for his levity.

'No, I did not.'

'Have you taken more than one wife at a time?'

'Definitely not!' Gabriel shuddered at the mere sug-gestion of it; he considered the taking of one wife to be ominous enough—two would be utter madness!

'Been cruel to a child or animal?'

'No and no,' he said drily.

She gave another shrug of those slender shoulders. 'In that case I do not consider what society does or does not believe about you to be of any relevance to my own decision to accept your offer of marriage.'

'You consider murder, bigamy and cruelty to children or animals to be the worst of a man's sins, then?' he asked with a bleak amusement.

'I have no other choice when you insist on remaining silent on the subject. But, perhaps, having now made my own acquaintance,' she suddenly looked less certain of herself, 'you have decided you would no longer find marriage to me acceptable to you?'

Was that anxiety Gabriel could now see in her expression? Had the young fool who had rejected her, no doubt because of that change in her circumstances, also robbed her of a confidence in her own attraction? If he had, then the man was not only a social-climbing fortune-hunter, but blind with it!

Diana Copeland was without doubt beautiful—certainly not 'fat and ugly' as Osbourne had suggested she might be when he'd first learnt of Gabriel's offer for one of the Copeland sisters without even laying eyes on them! Not only were her looks without peer, but she was obviously intelligent, too—and capable. Gabriel was fully aware he had her to thank for having arrived at a house that was not rodent infested and musty smelling, and with servants who were quietly efficient. She was, in fact, everything that an earl could ever want or desire in his countess.

Also, having now 'made her acquaintance', Gabriel had realised another, rather unexpected benefit if he should decide to make her his wife... No doubt that golden-red hair, when released from its pins, would reach down to the slenderness of her waist. Just as those high, full breasts promised to fit snugly into the palms of his hands and the slenderness of her body would benefit from a lengthy exploration with his seeking lips.

Obviously it was an intimacy that Diana's cool haughtiness did not encourage Gabriel to believe she would welcome between the two of them at present—because she was still in love with the social climbing fortune-hunter, perhaps?—but she would no doubt allow it if she were to become his wife.

Diana felt her nervousness deepening at the earl's continued silence. Nor could she read anything of his thoughts as he continued to look at her with those hooded midnight-blue eyes.

Was she so unattractive, then? Had her role as mistress of her father's estate and mother to her two younger sisters this past ten years rendered her too practical in nature and, as a result, plain? Was Gabriel Faulkner even now formulating the words in which to tell her of his lack of interest in her?

'You realise that any marriage between the two of us would require you to produce the necessary heirs?'

Diana looked up sharply at that softly spoken question and felt that delicate colour once again warming her cheeks as she saw the speculative expression in those dark eyes. She swallowed before speaking. 'I realise that is one of the reasons for your wishing to take a wife, yes.'

'Not one of the reasons, but the *only* reason I would ever contemplate such an alliance,' Gabriel Faulkner bit out, his arrogantly hewn features now cold and withdrawn.

Diana moistened her lips with the tip of her tongue. 'I am fully aware of a wife's duties, my lord.'

That ruthless mouth compressed. 'I find that somewhat surprising, considering your own mother's complete lack of interest in them.'

Her eyes widened at the harshness of his remark. Her chin rose proudly. 'Were you acquainted with my mother, sir?'

'Not personally, no.' His disdainful expression clearly stated he had not wished to be either.

'Then you can have no idea as to why she left her husband and children, can you?'

'Is there any acceptable excuse for such behaviour?' he countered.

As far as Diana and her sisters were concerned? No, there was not. As for their father... Marcus Copeland had never recovered from his wife leaving him for a younger man and had become a shadow of his former robust and cheerful self, shutting himself away in his study for hours at a time, and more often than not taking his meals there, too, when he bothered to eat at all.

No, there was no acceptable explanation for Harriet Copeland's desertion of her family. But Diana did not appreciate having Gabriel Faulkner—a man with an acknowledged, if unspoken, scandal in his own past— point that out to her. 'I am not my mother, sir,' she said coolly.

'Perhaps that is as well...'

She frowned her resentment with his continued needling. 'If, having considered the matter, you have now changed your mind about offering for me, then I wish you would just say so. It is not necessary for you to insult my mother, a woman you admit you did not even know, whilst you are doing so!'

In truth, Gabriel had no interest whatsoever in the marriage of Marcus and Harriet Copeland; he was well aware that marriages amongst the *ton* were often loveless affairs, with both parties tacitly taking lovers once the necessary heirs had been produced. That Harriet had chosen to leave her family for her young lover, and was later shot and killed by that same lover when he'd found her in the arms of yet another man, was of no real consequence to the present situation.

No, the coolly composed and forthright Diana Copeland, whilst as head-turningly beautiful as the infamous Harriet, was most certainly not the mother!

'Your mother produced only daughters,' he drawled drily.

Those blue eyes once again sparkled with temper. 'And if she had not, then you would not be here now!'

Gabriel gave her an appreciative smile. *'Touché.'*

'Nor is it possible for anyone to predict what children will be born into which marriage,' she argued.

'Also true.' He inclined his head. 'I was merely questioning as to whether or not you are prepared for the physical intimacy necessary to produce those children? If we have girls to begin with, we will keep trying until we have a boy.'

Diana drew in a sharp breath. It had taken several days after Malcolm's defection, accompanied by too many of those pitying looks of neighbours and friends, for her to come around to the idea of seriously considering the offer of marriage from Lord Gabriel Faulkner.

Accepting such an offer would not only salvage some of her own pride, she had assured herself, but would also help to persuade her two sisters to return home now that the possibility of marriage to a man they did not love had been removed.

Both of them were good and practical reasons, she had decided, for her to be the one to accept Gabriel's offer. Except she did not feel in the least practical now that she was faced with the flesh-and-blood man...

She looked at him now beneath lowered lashes, appreciating the way his perfectly tailored clothing emphasised the width of his shoulders, his muscled chest, the narrowness of waist, and his powerful thighs and long legs, before raising her gaze back to that wickedly handsome face, heat suffusing her cheeks as she saw the look in the dark and taunting eyes that stared unblinkingly back at her. A quiver of...something shivered down the length of her spine as she found herself unable to look away from those mesmerising midnight-blue eyes.

Whether it was a shiver of apprehension or anticipation she could not be sure. Although the tingling sensation she suddenly felt in her breasts would seem to indicate the latter.

Diana found that slightly shocking when he had not so much as touched her. She had only ever known a pleasant warmth when Malcolm kissed her, not this blazing heat at just a look from Gabriel... 'As I have stated, I believe I know, and am willing to participate in, all the duties expected of me as a wife,' she said stiffly.

'Perhaps we should test that theory before making any firm decision?' he drawled.

Diana did not at all care for the return of that predatory glint to his navy-blue eyes. 'Test that theory how?'

He raised speculative brows. 'I suggest we try a simple kiss to begin with.'

She gave a start. 'To *begin* with?'

'Exactly.'

Diana swallowed hard, pride and pride alone preventing her from taking a step back as Gabriel crossed the room with a catlike tread until he stood only inches in front of her. So close, in fact, that she was totally aware of the heat of his body and the clean male smell of him that tantalised and roused the senses, her breath catching in her throat when she finally looked up into his compelling face.

Those midnight-blue eyes were hooded by lids fringed with long, dark lashes, his beautiful high cheekbones as sharp as blades on either side of his aristocratic nose, sculptured lips slightly parted, his jaw square and uncompromising.

In contrast, Diana's own lips had gone suddenly dry, her breathing non-existent—in fact, she was starting to feel slightly light-headed from a lack of air in her lungs! She knew instinctively that any kiss she received from this man would be nothing like that chaste meeting of the lips she had infrequently shared with Malcolm Castle.

Diana could feel her pulse start to race and a welling of excitement rising up within her breast as those powerful arms moved firmly about her waist before she was pulled up against the hardness of Gabriel's chest and his head began to lower towards hers.

She was perfectly correct. Being kissed by Gabriel Faulkner was absolutely *nothing* like being kissed by Malcolm…

His arms about her waist crushed her breasts against that hard chest even as he took masterful possession of her lips with his own. His mouth moved over hers in a slow, lingering exploration before the sweep of his tongue parted her lips and he kissed her more intimately still, that skilful tongue seeking entrance in gentle, flickering movements.

Diana's pulse continued to race, to thunder; she felt both hot and shaky as their kiss continued, her hands moving up to Gabriel's chest with the intention of pushing him away, but instead clinging to the width of his shoulders, able to feel the flexing of muscles beneath his jacket as she did so. No doubt he could feel her own trembling, as his hands moved caressingly down the length of her spine before cupping her bottom to pull her thighs up against his muscular ones.

Nothing that had gone before—not Malcolm's kisses, or the talk Aunt Humphries had given concerning the marriage bed on Diana's sixteenth birthday; a talk Diana had dutifully passed on to her two sisters once she'd considered them both old enough to understand— had prepared her for the heat of Gabriel's kisses, or her complete awareness of that hardness that throbbed between his thighs.

Gabriel began to draw the kiss to a close as he sensed Diana's rising panic at the intimacy, knowing by the shyness of her responses that the fool who had passed her over had never even bothered to so much as kiss her properly, let alone introduce her to physical pleasure.

He looked down at her beneath hooded lids, having firmly assured himself of his own willingness to introduce her to every physical pleasure imaginable, before allowing his arms to drop from about the slenderness of her waist. He stepped away from her, his expression deliberately unreadable. 'Perhaps now would be the appropriate time to tell you that you did not ask me the correct question a few minutes ago when you were asking me for details of that past scandal.'

She blinked up at her, her cheeks still flushed. 'No?'

Gabriel's expression was grim. 'No.'

She shook her head as if to clear it. 'Then what should I have asked you?'

'Whether I have ever been accused of taking a young girl's innocence and then refusing to marry her when she found herself with child?'

Diana's throat moved convulsively as she swallowed, knowing that her cheeks were no longer flushed, but deathly pale. 'And have you been accused of that?'

'Oh, yes.' His teeth showed in a humourless smile.

She knew a brief moment's panic, the blood pounding in her veins, the palms of her hands suddenly damp inside her gloves, her legs feeling slightly shaky. There was no possibility of her, or of any decent woman, marrying a man so unfeeling, so without honour— No, wait one moment, she told herself sternly. Gabriel had said he'd been accused of such a heinous crime; he had not admitted to being *guilty* of it…

She looked up at him searchingly. His was a hard and implacable face, the face of a man who would not suffer fools gladly. Those midnight-blue eyes were equally as cold and unyielding. But it was not a sly or malicious face—more one that defied anyone to ever question him or his actions. As he was now daring her to do?

She drew in a shaky breath. 'You said you were accused of it, not that you were guilty.'

Those dark eyes narrowed. 'I did say that, yes,' he allowed softly.

'And so are you indeed innocent of that crime?'

Gabriel gave a small, appreciative smile. Not a single member of his family had bothered to ask him that question eight years ago, choosing instead to believe Jennifer Lindsay's version of events.

His friends Osbourne and Blackstone had not bothered to ask it either, but that was because they both knew him too well to believe he could ever behave in so ungentlemanly a fashion if he were indeed truly guilty of taking a young woman's innocence.

That Diana Copeland, a young woman he had only just met—moreover, a young woman Gabriel had deliberately kissed with passion rather than with any consideration for her own innocence—should have asked that question was beyond belief.

Gabriel looked her straight in the eye. 'I am.' His gaze narrowed to steely slits as she continued to frown. 'Having asked and been answered, you are now doubting my word on the subject?'

'Not at all.' She shook her head. 'I just— What could this young girl, any young girl, possibly hope to gain by telling such a monstrous lie?'

'As an only child I was heir to my father's fortune and lands,' Gabriel explained.

'Was...?'

His mouth firmed. 'That fortune and lands were instead left completely in my mother's care on my father's death six years ago. Fortunately I was not left destitute as my grandfather's estate had been left in trust and could not be taken away from me.'

'And this young girl's lies are the reason your family and society treated you so harshly all those years ago?' she pressed.

'Yes,' he grated.

She gave him a sympathetic look. 'Then I can only imagine it must have been a doubly bitter pill to swallow when you knew yourself to be innocent of the crime.'

'You only have my word for that,' he pointed out grimly.

'And is your word to be doubted?' she asked delicately, eyeing him quizzically.

Gabriel frowned. 'My dear Diana, if I truly were the man almost everyone believes me to be, then I could simply be lying again when I say, no, it is not.'

She smiled gently. 'I do not believe so. You are a man, I think, who would tell the truth and—excuse me—to the devil with what anyone else chooses to believe!'

Yes, he was. He had always been so, and this past eight years had only deepened that resolve. But, again, it was surprising that this woman already knew him well enough to have realised and accepted that…

'And the—the young girl,' she spoke hesitantly. 'What became of her?'

His mouth tightened. 'My father paid another man to marry her.'

'And the babe?'

That nerve pulsed once again in Gabriel's tightly clenched jaw. 'Lost before it was even born.'

Diana's expression was pained. 'How very sad.'

'Knowing all of this, are you still of the opinion you wish to become my countess?' he asked her directly.

Her cheeks were pale, her hair in slight disarray from their kisses, but there was still that familiar light of resolve in those sky-blue eyes. 'You are no more responsible for what people may wrongly choose to believe of you than I can be held accountable for my mother having left her husband and three daughters.'

Gabriel's mouth quirked. 'The announcement of a betrothal between the two of us would certainly give society much to talk about!'

She smiled a little sadly. 'No doubt. Perhaps, if you hope to become reconciled to society you should not, after all, contemplate taking one of Harriet Copeland's daughters as your countess?'

Gabriel's expression hardened. 'I have absolutely no interest in becoming reconciled to society, or in having society be reconciled to me. Nor do I care what any of them may choose to think of me or the woman I take as my countess.'

'Then we are in agreement?' Diana held her breath as she waited for his answer.

'I will have the announcement of our betrothal appear in the newspapers as soon as is possible.' He gave a sharp inclination of his arrogant head.

This was what Diana had wanted, what she knew was necessary to salvage her own pride after Malcolm's defection, and to encourage her sisters to return home. Yet the reality of being betrothed to the hard and unyielding Lord Gabriel Faulkner, a man beset with a past scandal that rivalled even that of Diana's mother—

worse, a man who had kissed her with such passion only minutes ago—caused her to inwardly tremble.

Whether that trembling was caused by apprehension or anticipation she was as yet unsure...

Chapter Three

'I am seriously starting to doubt that your Aunt Humphries exists,' Gabriel commented drily the following morning as he and Diana sat together in the small dining room, eating their breakfast attended by the quietly efficient Soames.

The previous afternoon had been taken up with various visits to the newspaper offices, the Westbourne lawyer, William Johnston, and to an old comrade in connection with Dominic Vaughn's disappearance into the country. But Gabriel had returned home in time to change for dinner before joining Diana downstairs. Only Diana. Mrs Humphries had sent her apologies. Those same apologies had been sent down again in regard to breakfast this morning.

Diana smiled. 'I assure you she does exist, but suffers dreadfully with her nerves. In fact, she did not wish to come to London at all and only did so because I insisted on coming here,' she added affectionately.

Gabriel raised dark brows. 'I am relieved she had

enough sense to agree to accompany you, at least. But taking to her rooms the moment you arrived, and remaining there, is certainly not helpful. In fact, it is totally unacceptable now that I am residing here, too.'

She looked enquiringly at him. 'Surely there can be no impropriety when you are my guardian?'

'A guardian who is now, officially, your betrothed.' Gabriel passed the open newspaper he had been reading across the table to her.

Diana's hands trembled slightly as she took possession of it, searching down the appropriate column until she located the relevant announcement. *The betrothal is announced between Lord Gabriel Maxwell Carter Faulkner, seventh Earl of Westbourne, Westbourne House, London, and his ward, the Lady Diana Harriet Beatrice Copeland, of Shoreley Park, Hampshire. The wedding will take place shortly at St George's Church, Hanover Square.*

There was nothing else. No naming of who Gabriel Faulkner's parents were, or her own, just the announcement of their betrothal. Nevertheless, there was something so very real about seeing the betrothal printed in the newspaper and knowing that it would no doubt be read by hundreds of people all over London this morning as they also sat at their breakfast tables.

Not that Diana had even considered changing her mind about the betrothal since they had come to their agreement yesterday. Nor did she baulk at the comment that the marriage was to 'take place shortly'—the sooner the better as far as she was concerned, preferably before Malcolm Castle and Miss Vera Douglas walked down the aisle together!

No, Diana had no regrets about her decision; it was only that seeing the betrothal in print also made Gabriel Faulkner so very real to her too. Not that there could really have been any doubts in her mind about that, either, after being held in his arms and kissed so passionately by him yesterday.

Just thinking about that kiss had kept her awake last night long after she had retired to her bedchamber…

Nothing in Aunt Humphries's talk all those years ago, concerning what took place in the marriage bed, had prepared Diana for the heady sensations that had assailed her body as Gabriel had kissed and held her. The heat. The clamouring excitement. The yearning ache for something more, something she wasn't sure of, but believed that marriage to a man of his experience and sophistication would undoubtedly reveal to her…

Gabriel watched beneath hooded lids as the colour first left Diana's creamy cheeks before coming back again, deeper than ever. That rosy flush was practically the same colour as the gown she wore this morning, accompanied by an almost feverish glitter in those sky-blue eyes as she raised heavily lashed lids to look across the breakfast table at him. 'You are concerned by the word "shortly" in the announcement, perhaps?' he asked.

'Not at all,' she dismissed readily. 'I would like to find my sisters first, of course, but can see no reason why the wedding should not take place immediately after that.'

'No?' Gabriel looked at her wickedly. 'I had imagined that perhaps you might wish to give your young man—I trust he is a young man?—the appropriate time in which to rush to your side and admit to having made a mistake as he proclaims his everlasting love for you?'

Irritated colour now darkened Diana's cheeks at Gabriel's teasing tone. 'He is a young man, yes…as well as a very stupid one. And even if he were to do that, I would not believe or trust such a claim.' Her mouth—that deliciously full and tempting mouth—had firmed with resolve.

Gabriel leant back in his chair to look across at her speculatively. That Diana was beautiful could not be denied. That she had a firmness of will could also be in no doubt. That her nature was unforgiving where this young man was concerned he found surprising. Especially considering she had accepted Gabriel's own claim of innocence the previous day without his having produced so much as a shred of evidence to back up that claim. Except his word…

He set his jaw. 'Perhaps I should know the name of this young man? So that I might send him about his business if he should decide to come calling,' he added as Diana gave him a sharp glance.

'I trust I am perfectly capable of dealing with such a situation myself if it should ever arise,' she retorted snippily.

Gabriel was well aware of the strength of Diana's character—how could he not be when he knew she had acted as both mistress of her father's house and mother to her two sisters since the age of eleven?

No, his reason for wishing to know who the young fool was who had turned away from Diana when her fortunes had changed was a purely selfish one; having secured her agreement to marry him, he had no intention of now allowing her to be persuaded into changing her mind. Firstly, because they would both be made to look incredibly foolish if the betrothal ended almost before it began. And secondly, because kissing her yesterday had shown him that marriage to her would not be the hardship he had always envisaged matrimony to be…

Beneath the coolness, and that air of practicality and efficiency she had displayed so ably by preparing Westbourne House for habitation, Gabriel had discovered a warm and passionate young woman that he would very much enjoy introducing to physical pleasure. He certainly had no intention of allowing some fortune-hunting young idiot to reappear in her life and steal her away from under his very nose. Or any other part of his anatomy!

Gabriel's mouth compressed. 'Nevertheless, you will refer any such situation to me.'

Diana looked irritated. 'I feel I should warn you, my lord, that I have become accustomed to dealing with my own affairs as I see fit.'

He gave an acknowledging inclination of his dark head. 'An occurrence that I believe our own betrothal now renders unnecessary.'

It was Diana's first indication of how life was to change for her now that she had agreed to become Gabriel's wife. A change she was not sure she particularly cared for. Ten years of being answerable only to herself had instilled an independence in her that she might find hard to relinquish. Even to a husband. 'I am unused to allowing anyone to make my decisions for me,' she reiterated.

Gabriel did not doubt it; it was because Diana was no simpering miss, no starry-eyed young debutante looking to fall in love and have that man fall equally as in love with her, that he could view their future marriage with any degree of equanimity. 'I am sure that, given time, we will learn to deal suitably with each other.'

Diana gave a knowing smile. 'I think by that you mean, with time, *I* will learn to accede to *your* male superiority!'

Gabriel found himself returning that smile. 'You do not agree?'

She shook her head. 'I do not believe you to be in the least superior to me just because you are a man. Nor is my nature such that it will allow for subservient and unquestioning obedience.'

Since meeting Diana, Gabriel had come to realise that the last thing that he desired in a wife was subservience or obedience. When he had told Osbourne and Blackstone a week or so ago of his plans to marry, Gabriel had assured them both that his marriage was a matter of obligation and expediency. Firstly, because he needed a wife, and, secondly, because of a sense of obligation to the Copeland sisters, because they had all been left without provision for their future when their father had died so unexpectedly. As such, subservience and obedience in his future wife had seemed the least that Gabriel could expect.

Having glimpsed the fire hidden beneath Diana's cool exterior yesterday, Gabriel knew that in their marriage bed, at least, he required neither of those things!

'My lord…?' Diana gave him a searching glance as the silence between them lengthened uncomfortably.

Had she said too much? Been too frank about her character? But surely it was better for him to know the worst of her before they embarked on a marriage together, rather than learn of it after the event?

She had certainly believed so. But perhaps she had been a little too honest? 'I could perhaps attempt to… quell, some of my more independent inclinations.'

'There is no need to do so on my account, I assure you,' he said with a twinkle in his eye before turning to dismiss the attentive Soames, waiting until the butler had left the room before continuing. 'Diana, I had expected to be bored, at the very least, in any marriage I undertook; it is something of a relief to know that will not, after all, be the case.'

Her eyes widened. 'You do not think it preferable to wait and perhaps marry a woman whom you love?'

'Love?' He managed to convey a wealth of loathing in that single word.

'You do not believe in the emotion?' she asked cautiously.

His top lip curled back disdainfully. 'My dear Diana, I have discovered that love comes in many guises—and all of them false.'

She could perhaps understand Gabriel's cynicism towards the emotion when he had been so completely ostracised after being falsely accused of taking advantage of an innocent young lady. Had he loved the young lady before she had played him false?

Yes, Diana could sympathise with him—possibly even shared his cynicism towards love. Malcolm Castle had certainly made nonsense of that emotion when he'd professed to still love Diana, but had every intention of marrying another woman!

She sighed. 'Perhaps you are right and a marriage such as ours, based on nothing so tenuous and fickle as love, but on common sense and honesty instead, is for the best.'

Gabriel frowned as he heard the heaviness in Diana's tone. One and twenty was very young for such a beautiful young lady to have formed such a pragmatic view on love and marriage. But perhaps, with the experience of her parents' marriage, and her young man's recent abandonment of her, she was perfectly justified in forming that opinion. After all, Gabriel had been but twenty years old himself when he learnt that hard lesson.

'Which is not to say…' he stood up slowly to move around the table to take Diana's hand in his before pulling her effortlessly to her feet '…there will not be other…compensations in our marriage to make up for that lack of love.'

She blinked up at him as she obviously realised it was his intention to kiss her once again. 'I—my lord, it is only nine o'clock in the morning!'

Gabriel threw back his head and laughed. 'I trust, my dear, you are not about to put time limitations on when and where I may make love to you?'

Not at all. Indeed, she would dare anyone to put limitations on a man such as Gabriel Faulkner. It was only that his behaviour now deviated drastically from her Aunt Humphries's description of what marriage would be like.

Her aunt had led her to believe that it was usual for a husband and wife to go about their daily lives separately—for the husband that involved dealing with business and correspondence in the morning and visiting his club in the afternoon, for the wife it meant dealing with the household responsibilities, such as menus of the day, answering letters, receiving visitors and returning those visits in turn, along with needlework and reading. Evenings would possibly be spent together, either at home or attending social functions, followed by returning home and retiring to their separate bedchambers.

On one, possibly two nights a week, the husband might briefly join the wife in her bedchamber, during which time it was the wife's duty to do whatever her husband required of her. Aunt Humphries had been a little sketchy as to what that 'whatever' might entail, with the added advice that a husband had 'needs' a wife must satisfy, 'silently and without complaint'...

Luckily, Diana had some idea as to what those 'needs' might entail; her father had bred deer on the estate in Hampshire—no doubt what took place between a husband and wife in their marriage bed was not so very different from that process. Such an undignified business that it was not surprising her aunt had chosen not to discuss it!

But at no time had Diana's aunt mentioned that a husband—or, in this particular case, a betrothed—was in the habit of stealing kisses throughout the day. Most especially the type of kisses that yesterday had made Diana's toes curl in her satin slippers!

She straightened. 'As I assured you yesterday, I believe I know my duty towards my future husband, my lord.'

Gabriel's brow lowered. Damn it, he did not wish

Diana to allow him to kiss her out of a sense of duty; he wanted her to now give freely what he had taken so demandingly yesterday. 'Gabriel,' he encouraged huskily.

That pulse was once again beating intriguingly in the slender column of her throat. 'It would be improper of me to be so familiar until after we are wed, my lord,' she said, her eyes lowered demurely.

His jaw clenched. 'I believe you know me well enough by now to realise that I have no care for what is considered "proper".'

She gave a nervous smile. 'I am not sure—' Her words were cut off abruptly as Gabriel lowered his head and took possession of her lips.

Full and sensuous lips that had tempted him unbearably this past hour as Diana had first sipped her tea and then bit into a slice of buttered toast smothered in honey. He'd found himself imagining heatedly what other uses those deliciously plump lips might be put to…

She tasted of that honey she had spread so liberally over her toast earlier, deliciously sweet, with an underlying heat that encouraged him to kiss her more deeply. His tongue appreciated the honey upon her lips before moving past that plumpness and into the hot, moist cavern of her mouth.

There had been no shortage of women in Gabriel's life during his years spent on the Continent: blondes, redheads, dusky-haired and dusky-skinned Italian women, young and slightly older, all experienced, and all initially intrigued by his scandalous past, but choosing to linger after once sharing his bed in the hopes of being invited to share it again.

He had become an expert lover during those years, able to give satisfaction to even the most demanding and experienced of women. That he had never personally enjoyed anything more than the immediate satisfaction of the flesh was not the fault of any of those women; Gabriel had only allowed his physical emotions to become engaged in those trysts.

Holding Diana in his arms, moulding the soft curves of her body against his, tasting, feeding from her lips and experiencing the sweetness of her instinctive response, brought out a gentleness in Gabriel, a need to protect that he had long thought forgotten, if not completely dead—emotions that he knew from experience could be called incautious at best and dangerous at worst. Slowly introducing Diana to the pleasures of their marriage bed, melting that cool exterior, was one thing, feeling anything more than that physical pleasure himself was something Gabriel did not intend to allow to happen. No matter how tempting the honeypot!

Not liking the trend of his own thoughts one little bit, he swiftly removed his mouth from hers and raised his head before putting her firmly away from him. 'I think we should stop there, don't you, Diana?'

Diana felt too dazed at first to wonder why he'd ended their kiss so abruptly, but as his words penetrated that daze she instantly felt the embarrassed flush that heated her cheeks. Had her enthusiasm in responding to his love-making perhaps been inappropriate in his future countess, after all?

She stepped back, her expression becoming cool despite feeling her legs tremble slightly from the effects of that passionate kiss. 'I believe *you* were the one who initiated that kiss, sir.'

He looked down his arrogant nose at her. 'Are you questioning my right to do so?'

Diana suddenly realised that once she was Gabriel's wife, she would have no right to question him about anything he might choose to demand of her. Could she bear that? Could she stand being nothing more than this man's possession, his to do with whatever he wished?

If it succeeded in salving her wounded pride following Malcolm's betrayal of the love they had professed to feel for each other, then yes, she could, she thought defiantly. 'I apologise if you feel I lacked…decorum just now,' she said stiffly. 'I—I am overset, I believe, and far too emotional, both from Caroline and Elizabeth's disappearance and seeing the announcement of our betrothal this morning.'

Gabriel felt a moment's regret, guilt even, for what Diana evidently believed. But only for a moment—the tender emotions he had briefly felt towards her whilst kissing her were not for someone as disillusioned as he. Far better to keep some distance between them. For as much as he believed he would enjoy introducing her to all the pleasures of the flesh once they were wed, he had no wish to do so if there was any danger she might give in to romantic flights of fancy. It would only result in her knowing a worse disillusionment than she had already suffered at the hands of her fickle young man.

Gabriel stepped away and placed his hands firmly behind his back to withstand the temptation to touch her again. 'No doubt we will receive an avalanche of visiting cards and invitations this morning following the announcement of our betrothal.' His mouth twisted derisively. 'The socially polite and the simply curious, all anxious to claim they were the first to receive Lord Gabriel Faulkner upon his return to London after an eight-year absence. Needless to say, I do not expect you to accept any invitations without first consulting me,' he added.

Diana bristled with obvious indignation. 'I may have lived all my life in the country, but even so I trust I know the correct way to behave. As such, of course I will not receive visitors, or accept any invitations, without first discussing them with you.'

He gave a hard smile. 'My request has little to do with behaving correctly and more to do with the fact that I do not care for most of society.'

Diana was well aware of the reason for Gabriel's dictate— 'request' was not at all a fitting description! She also empathised with it; as the daughter of a notorious countess, Diana would no doubt come in for her own share of curiosity where society was concerned following the announcement of their betrothal. As such, she was more than happy to leave the choice of deciding which invitations they would accept or decline to Gabriel's superior knowledge on the subject; left to her own devices, she might make a social gaffe.

She stifled a sigh. 'I believe I will go upstairs and check upon my aunt.'

'Perhaps whilst there you might suggest it would be a good idea if she were to join us for dinner this evening?'

Diana was aware that this was no more a 'suggestion' than Gabriel's earlier dictate had been a 'request'. 'I will certainly enquire if she is feeling well enough to join us this evening,' she answered coolly. She might as well start as she meant to go on; she had no intention of allowing Gabriel to simply dominate every aspect of her life, however arrogant he was.

He frowned slightly. 'And I suppose that is the best I can hope for?'

'It is.' Diana met his dark gaze unblinkingly.

Gabriel gave her an appreciative smile. One thing he could say for Diana—she did not back down from any of his challenges. 'It is my intention this morning to make discreet enquiries concerning your two sisters. I will obviously need detailed descriptions of them both...' He listened attentively as Diana eagerly supplied him with those details. 'Is there anything else you need to tell me before I go?'

She looked confused. 'Such as?'

His mouth quirked ruefully. 'Such as could either of your sisters have run off to be with a young man?'

'Certainly not!' Diana's denial was immediate.

Gabriel held up his hands defensively. 'I had to ask.'

There were high wings of indignant colour in her creamy cheeks now. 'My sisters may have behaved rashly by running away, but I do not believe they would have been so rash as to have totally ruined their reputations, my lord.'

Gabriel wished he felt the same certainty about that as she did. Unfortunately, even if neither Caroline nor Elizabeth had initially run off to be with a man, he knew that situation could have changed. Caroline had, according to Diana, now been missing for over two weeks, and her sister Elizabeth only two days less than that. Plenty of time for unscrupulous men to have noted and taken advantage of two young women alone and unprotected.

'I am glad to hear it,' was all he said, as he didn't want to distress her further. 'Please pass along my respects to your aunt.'

Diana watched as he crossed the breakfast room in long and forceful strides, noting the way his dark-brown superfine moulded to the width of his shoulders and narrow waist, his buff-coloured pantaloons doing the same for his long and muscled thighs. Physical attributes, along with those sensually pleasurable kisses, which set her pulse racing just to think of them, indicating that the best—and certainly the safest—course was not to think about them at all!

'I had almost forgotten…' Gabriel suddenly said as he came to a halt in the doorway to turn and look back at her standing so elegantly in the centre of the room. 'I realise that Hampshire is a large county, but do you by any chance know of a family named Morton?' He had already sent several old comrades into Hampshire in search of Dominic Vaughn and the woman he had announced it was his intention to marry, but it would be negligent on his part not to enquire if Diana knew of the woman's family. Something he had almost forgotten to do since kissing her earlier.

'Morton?' She looked momentarily startled. 'The butler at Shoreley Park is named Morton, but, apart from that, I'm not aware of any family of that name.'

Gabriel's expression became guarded. 'Indeed? And does he possess a family? In particular, a daughter of marriageable age?'

'Not that I am aware of… No, I am sure he does not,'

she said firmly. 'Morton has been with us for years. I am sure I would have heard of a daughter if he had one.'

'Hmm,' Gabriel murmured softly. 'Still, it is curious that your butler also possesses that name…'

'Why is it curious, my lord?' Diana looked puzzled.

'I am not sure.' He scowled darkly, the pieces of that particular puzzle becoming more obscure the deeper he delved into it. 'It is a start at least,' he muttered. 'It may be that this butler has a niece of that name.'

'I do not recall him ever mentioning one…' A frown creased Diana's creamy brow. 'What is this woman to you, my lord?'

Gabriel became suddenly still. 'Why should you assume she is anything to me?'

A delicate blush coloured her cheeks. 'I thought, as you asked about her—'

'Did you think that because I said the woman is young I must, either now or some time in the past, have had some personal interest in her?' he queried with a gleam in his eyes she wasn't at all sure of.

Diana had no idea what to think. In fact, this whole conversation was somewhat confusing to her. Indeed, she still felt slightly befuddled by her response to his kiss earlier and its abrupt and slightly hurtful ending.

She suddenly became aware how little she really knew of the man she had agreed to marry. She had believed him yesterday when he'd told her that he was not responsible for seducing that young girl and leaving her pregnant. However, she had to acknowledge that his past might appear in a somewhat different light to her if she were to learn that the allegedly wronged woman from eight years ago, and the one he now sought, were one and the same...

Chapter Four

Gabriel's lids narrowed over glittering dark blue eyes as he watched the emotions flickering across Diana's expressive face. Puzzlement. Alarm, quickly followed by wariness. 'Well?' he demanded harshly.

Her throat moved as she swallowed before speaking. 'I have no idea what to think, my lord.'

'Then perhaps it would be prudent if you were to remain silent on the subject until you do know,' he rasped angrily. He had taken all the suspicion and accusations he could stand eight years ago. He had no intention of suffering them again from the young woman he intended to make his countess.

Even if that young woman had accepted nothing more than his word on it yesterday when he'd claimed his innocence of that past misdeed? his conscience whispered to him.

He eyed Diana in some frustration, nostrils flared, jaw clenched. He was not used to explaining himself to anyone, but…'If you must know, I am seeking this woman in connection with a friend rather than having any interest in her myself,' he said tautly.

'A friend, my lord?'

Gabriel gave a humourless smile at her continued uncertainty. 'Believe it or not, I do still possess some. Men who have remained loyal and true all these years despite what my family and society may have chosen to believe of me.'

Diana had not meant to imply otherwise; she had merely been curious to know who this young lady might be and exactly what she meant to Gabriel. For instance, could she be his mistress? When she had so coolly and practically decided to accept his offer of marriage, she had done so without consideration for the fact that he might already be involved with another woman And if he was, would he want to continue seeing her even after he married Diana?

Her aunt had mentioned to her how both the married men and women of society, once the heirs had been born, often chose to go their own way in regard to bed partners. That Diana's own marriage might become so sordidly complicated was a situation she found too unpleasant to even contemplate.

'I am glad to hear it.' She gave an inclination of her head. 'And you say it is for one of these friends that you are seeking this lady named Morton?'

'I have said so, yes.'

She looked at him searchingly as she heard the challenge in his tone. A challenge that was reflected in the hard glitter of those midnight-blue eyes as they easily met her gaze. 'Then I hope that your enquiries are successful.'

So did Gabriel. Otherwise Dominic could find himself married to the chit and socially ruined; having experienced that for himself, it was not something Gabriel would wish upon one of his closest friends.

That was not to say he would easily forget Diana's suspicions of him just now…

'You cannot possibly have become betrothed to such a disreputable rake as Gabriel Faulkner!' Aunt Humphries goggled up at her from where she lay resting upon her *chaise* in the sitting room that adjoined her bedchamber.

A room Diana found both cluttered and hot, warmed as it was by both the fire in the hearth and the sun shining in through the huge bay window. 'He is Lord Gabriel Faulkner, seventh Earl of Westbourne, now, Aunt,' she said quietly.

'Well…yes. And his mother was a gracious and lovely woman, to be sure…'

'You were acquainted with Mrs Faulkner?' Diana asked curiously.

'Felicity Campbell-Smythe and I were the greatest of friends thirty years ago.' Her aunt smiled affectionately at the memory of that friendship. 'We lost touch when we both married, of course,' she continued briskly. 'But I recall that her son was involved in the most dreadful scandal some years ago—'

'His lordship and I have spoken of that.' Her tone was stiffly disapproving; she loved her aunt deeply and she'd helped to fill the place of the mother who had left them all those years ago. But even so, Diana did not intend to discuss Gabriel's past with her or anyone else. He had spoken of the matter to her in confidence, and it was a confidence she would not, could not, break.

Her aunt sat up agitatedly, her greying blond curls bouncing about her thin and lined face. 'But—'

'It is not polite of us to discuss either Mrs Faulkner or the Earl in this way.' Much as Diana might wish to learn more about Felicity Faulkner, she knew that to do so would only lead to more questions and comments about Gabriel from her aunt. 'All that is important for now is that you know I am betrothed to him, and that we will very shortly be married.'

'But—'

'There is nothing more to be said on the subject, Aunt,' she added firmly as she moved away from the *chaise* to stand in front of the window, looking out at the square below.

There was a nursemaid and her small charge in the park across the road and a footman walking a large black dog, with a maid hurrying along the pavement carrying several brown paper-wrapped parcels. All of them such normal, everyday occurrences. It was so very strange when Diana felt as if her own life would never again be what she had considered normal…

She was to be married soon. Was to become the wife of the forceful and arrogant Earl of Westbourne. The changes in her life had started before that, of course. They had begun with the death of her father six and a half months ago. If not for that, Gabriel would not have inherited the title. There would have been no reason for her sisters to have run away from home. No reason for

Diana to have agreed to marry a man she did not know and who did not know her either.

How strange fate was. How fickle. A few months ago, Diana's life had seemed settled. Malcolm Castle would become her husband, and after their wedding they would reside in the gatehouse to Castle Manor, only moving into the manor itself after Malcolm's own father had died.

Diana had been able to envisage it all in her mind's eye. Her future, certain and sure, stretching out before her. She would marry Malcolm. They would have several children together, followed by grandchildren. With her two sisters also perhaps married to men who lived locally, the three of them would meet often to gossip and laugh together.

Instead, Diana now found herself in London. Malcolm was to marry another woman and was no longer even a part of her life. Her two sisters were missing, heaven knew where. And she was betrothed to a man of mercurial moods at best, and cold and unapproachable at worst.

A handsome and exciting man, whom she privately admitted caused her pulse to race just by being in the same room with her…

'Is it bad news, my lord?'

Gabriel scowled as he looked up from the letter he had been reading to see Diana standing in the doorway of the study. It was one of the many letters and visiting cards that had been delivered to the house since the announcement of their betrothal in the newspapers two days ago.

Diana had not been in evidence when he'd returned late that afternoon from yet another fruitless attempt to locate the missing Copeland sisters, an enquiry from Soames eliciting the information that she was with the housekeeper consulting on the menus for the week. Menus that would no doubt have to be changed once he had sifted through the invitations that had arrived these past two days and decided which, if any, of the social engagements they would attend.

For himself, Gabriel had absolutely no interest in attending any social functions, having no wish to place himself in the position of being the visible focus of the *ton*'s gossip. But to refuse them all would be unfair to Diana when he knew she had lived all of her one-and-twenty years shut away from the class of people to which she rightly belonged. Bad enough that she was to become the wife of the scandalous Gabriel Faulkner, without, as her father had already done, denying her the company of her peers.

'It's not news that concerns either of your sisters, if that is your worry.' Gabriel placed the letter he had been reading down upon the desk in front of him as he looked at her with appreciation.

She wore a gown of pale and misty blue, the red lights in her hair seeming more prominent against its muted colour. Her cheeks were slightly flushed, with a bright sparkle to those sky-blue eyes, the whole endowing her with a vibrancy of beauty that was extremely easy on Gabriel's somewhat jaundiced eye.

He raised an eyebrow. 'Perhaps we might begin discussing the arrangements for the wedding? I had thought next week would be—'

'Next week!' she echoed breathlessly, those blue eyes widening.

Gabriel frowned. 'You said you had no objections to it taking place shortly?'

'And I do not,' she explained. 'It is only that I had not thought to be married until after we have found my two sisters.'

Gabriel sighed. 'But we have no idea when that might be.'

Diana looked unhappy. 'You were again unsuccessful in your enquiries?'

He stood up impatiently. 'It would seem that your two sisters have succeeded in appearing to have completely disappeared from the face of the earth—I trust you are not about to faint, Diana?' Gabriel said as he swiftly crossed the room in three long strides to grasp the tops of her arms as she swayed.

He cursed himself for speaking so frankly to her about her sisters. His mood had been terse and irritable for the past two days as he first went about the business of retaining a new lawyer after dispensing with William Johnston's services—but not before Gabriel had first left the other man in no doubts as to his displeasure concerning his treatment of the Copeland sisters. That had been followed by the seeking out of half a dozen of the men who had once served with him in his regiment and instructing them to search every inch of London for the two missing women.

He had risked having lunch at his old club today too, not a wise decision as it turned out, as he was forced to fend off the curiosity of several of the other members who had obviously been instructed by their wives to elicit whatever information they could about him and his bride-to-be.

Returning to another avalanche of invitations and letters—and one of those letters in particular—had not improved his temper, with the result that now he had upset Diana.

She shook her head in denial, her face still very pale. 'My sisters have to be somewhere!'

Gabriel's hands dropped back to his sides as he stepped away from her. 'Indeed they do,' he reassured her heartily, although privately he was not sure that 'somewhere' necessarily had to be in London. He had been thinking that Diana revealing the butler at Shoreley Park was named Morton was surely too much of a coincidence to actually be one. 'Tell me, Diana, do either of your sisters sing?'

She looked a little bewildered by the question. 'I—they both do. Caroline has the finer voice of the two, but they are both perfectly competent. Why do you ask?'

'I merely wish to know as much about them both as possible,' Gabriel said vaguely, storing this piece of information away with the rest of what he now knew of Caroline and Elizabeth Copeland. Information, on Caroline at least, that was leading him to a conclusion he could barely credit!

'Of course,' Diana accepted ruefully. 'I am very grateful for all your help in this delicate matter.'

His mouth compressed grimly. 'Time enough for thanks once they have both been found.'

Something Diana was beginning to doubt might ever happen. She had been in London a week now without any success; it really did seem, as Gabriel had pointed out so succinctly, as if Caroline and Elizabeth had completely disappeared from the face of the earth!

She firmly dismissed such negativity from her mind. Her sisters would both be found, safe and sound. 'You seemed…distracted by your letter, when I first came in, my lord,' she commented.

'Did I?' A shutter seemed to come down over his face before he turned to stroll back to the desk. 'Perhaps it is at the thought of having to reply to all these letters and invitations,' he said drily.

There were indeed a large number of them; Diana had been surprised at just how much correspondence had been delivered this past two days when Gabriel had been ignored for all these years. The sheer volume of post seemed to indicate his past sins had indeed been forgiven, if not totally forgotten, now that he was the wealthy Earl of Westbourne.

She sighed. 'Perhaps we should just refuse them all? With my sisters still missing, I do not feel particularly sociable, and we have the added excuse that I am still in mourning for my father.'

Gabriel leant back against the desk as he regarded Diana through narrowed lids. She was a beautiful and gracious young woman, and would no doubt make something of a stir in society. Amongst the males, especially—the women, old as well as young, would no doubt envy her beauty. A beauty that deserved to be seen, if not touched…

'No, I am afraid we cannot do that, Diana.' He groaned inwardly at the thought of the posing and posturing he would no doubt be forced to endure during these necessary forays into the *ton*'s ballrooms. 'It is over six months since your father died and our betrothal has been announced. We will have to attend some of the quieter social events together, at least.' He stood up to resume his seat behind the desk, his expression becoming grim as he once again glanced at one of the letters he had received today.

Diana moved closer to the desk. 'Will you not share your news with me, my lord?'

Should he show her the letter that had so disturbed him? Perhaps it was better that she have absolutely no illusions about the man that he was and would continue to be once they were married? 'It would appear that the announcement of our betrothal in the newspapers has not just alerted the *ton* to my presence here at Westbourne House.' He held up the letter.

Diana gave him a searching look before taking the single sheet of notepaper from him, able to sense the tension in his lithe and athletic body. She glanced down at the signature at the bottom of the letter she held, but was none the wiser for reading that signature. 'Who is Alice Britton?'

'She was my mother's companion.'

Diana raised one silky brow. 'Was?'

He gave a terse inclination of his head. 'It would seem she retired some months ago and is now living in Eastbourne.'

She quickly read the contents of the letter, very soon realising the reason for Gabriel's tension. 'We must both prepare to travel into Cambridgeshire immediately—'

'No.'

She gave him a startled glance. 'Of course, I will understand if you would prefer that I not accompany you—'

'Diana, whether I would prefer you to accompany me is of absolutely no relevance when I have absolutely no intentions of going anywhere near Cambridgeshire, now or in the future.' Gabriel's expression remained grim as he began to pace the room.

'I—but Miss Britton says that your mother's health was fragile when she last saw her four months ago.'

His eyes glittered as he glared at her. 'Then my rushing into Cambridgeshire to see her would only result in making it even more so.'

Diana realised he believed that statement to be the truth. She just found it hard to accept that his own mother would not want to see him if her health was so poor. 'I am sure you are mistaken, Gabriel—'

'Are you?' Gabriel looked at her bitterly. 'I have not received a single card or letter from any member of my family since I left. And what do you make of the fact,' he continued remorselessly when Diana would have pointed out that his family could not have written to him when they did not know where he was, 'that when I learnt of my father's death six years ago, I wrote to my mother immediately, expressing my sorrow, and with the added request that I might visit her. A letter to which she did not even bother to respond.'

Diana's heart ached at the emotion she so clearly heard in his tone. 'That does seem damning, yes—'

'It is no more than I might have expected,' he rasped harshly. 'Yet my mother's ex-companion now requests that I hasten to visit my mother because her health is "fragile"? I think not.'

'She also states that your mother has longed to see you for some time—'

'Something I find extremely unlikely. Nor will she receive any forgiveness from me to ease her conscience.'

Diana eyed him compassionately. 'It was not concern for your mother's mortal soul I was considering when I suggested we should both go and see her.'

Gabriel's eyes narrowed. 'What then?'

'Your own,' she said gently.

'Mine?' he barked. 'You claimed to believe me when I told you I have done absolutely nothing for which I need feel ashamed.'

Diana had believed him. She still believed him. Indeed, this past two days in his company made her more convinced that Gabriel Faulkner was a man it was impossible not to believe when he claimed something was so! 'Do you not see that, if your mother dies, now or some time in the future, without the two of you having reconciled, then *you* will be the one who is left alive to suffer the torment, possibly for the rest of your life, knowing that you could have set things right between you, but your pride would not allow you to do so?'

He stopped his pacing, his gaze suddenly shrewd as he looked down at her. 'And is that what happened to *you*, Diana? Did your mother ask for your forgiveness for leaving you all and you refused her?'

Diana's heart skipped several beats. 'We were not discussing me or my mother—'

'We are now,' Gabriel cut in. 'Tell me, did your mother come to regret leaving you all for the arms of her young lover? Did you refuse her your forgiveness?' he persisted ruthlessly.

Diana knew that her cheeks had grown pale at the memories that assailed her of that terrible time they had all suffered after her mother had left them: her father a white and ghostly figure as he wandered from room to room in Shoreley Park, as if he might somehow find his wife in one of them if he just looked hard enough; her two sisters crying constantly at night until they fell into an exhausted sleep, only to wake again screaming or crying, and demanding to know why their mother did not come and comfort them as she'd used to do when they were beset with bad dreams.

And through it all, as Diana had done the best that she could to comfort all of them, she had felt her anger towards her mother growing for having so selfishly hurt them all, until it seemed her heart had become utterly consumed with hatred for her.

Her throat moved convulsively now as she swallowed down the bitter bile that had risen in her throat. 'My mother never wished to return to us or ever asked for our forgiveness, so how could I have refused her?' Her voice was flat, emotionless.

He frowned darkly. 'Diana—'

'If you will excuse me, my lord?' She held her head regally high, her gaze deliberately avoiding his. 'It is time that I go upstairs and change before dinner.' Even if the thought of eating now made her feel ill.

She very rarely thought of her mother any more. There seemed little point.

'You are standing in my way, my lord,' she said stiltedly as Gabriel effectively blocked her escape by moving to stand in the open doorway of the study.

'Will you allow me to apologise, Diana?' Gabriel

looked down at her searchingly, knowing by the pallor of her face and the haunted look in those sky-blue eyes that he had hurt her with his taunts about her mother. Even though he himself was hurting after receiving that letter concerning his own mother, it was not an acceptable reason for his having upset Diana.

He reached up to lightly clasp the tops of her bare arms. 'I am sorry for my churlishness just now,' he said huskily. 'It is only—' His mouth tightened. 'I am sure that Alice Britton meant only to act for the best, but the past is better left alone. By both of us, it would seem,' he added gently.

Diana raised long-lashed lids, those sky-blue eyes over-bright. With unshed tears? Had Gabriel hurt her that much? Had he really become so unfeeling this past eight years? So selfishly absorbed in his own disillusionment that he had ceased to care if, or when, he hurt others with his coldness and cynicism?

'You are forgiven, Gabriel.'

He drew in a sharp breath at Diana's softly spoken absolution, for once in his life not sure what to do or say next. Any more of his arrogance or sarcasm was likely to cause the glitter of tears he could see in her eyes to overflow, and yet to do anything else would be—

'As I hope you will forgive me for my intrusion into something that is so very personal to you.'

It was too much. Diana apologising to *him*, when he was the one who had behaved so churlishly, was too much. He released her arms to pull her into his embrace, the top of her golden-red curls now resting under his chin and smelling of lemons. 'I am a brute for hurting you.'

The warmth of her cheek rested against his chest. 'I should not have attempted to interfere.'

'No one has more right to do so,' Gabriel grated fiercely. 'You are to become my wife. My countess.' And it was only now, holding her in his arms and totally aware of the vulnerability she was usually at such pains to hide behind that veneer of practicality and determination, that he realised the enormity of what his betrothal to this woman meant.

He had renewed his offer of marriage in the belief it was to be an arrangement of mutual expediency, she needing a sop to her injured pride following her young man's defection, and he needing a suitable wife to act as mistress in his homes and provide the necessary heirs. All well and good.

Except he had not expected to actually like the woman whom he married. Or to desire her to the extent that holding her in his arms again like this was a physical torture. But as Gabriel refused to run the risk of his heir perhaps making his appearance only seven or eight months after the wedding and therefore causing even more unwanted gossip for them both, he knew he'd have to continue to suffer the torture a little longer unless he removed the temptation.

He took a firm hold of her arms and moved her away from him, dark eyes hooded by lowered lids as he looked down at her. 'As you say, it is time we both went upstairs and changed for dinner.'

Diana blinked up at him, momentarily stunned by the sudden return of his previous coldness. But what had she expected? That talking of their mutual hurt at their mothers' hands would somehow forge a bond between the two of them? That it would bring about an understanding between them, a closeness that would make their betrothal seem less daunting to her?

If that had indeed been her hope, then one glance at his haughtily remote expression, at the coolness in those dark blue eyes as he looked down at her, was enough to tell her that such a warmth of understanding did not, and never would, or could, exist between them.

Her own expression was as proudly distant as she gave a stiff inclination of her head. 'Until dinner then, my lo—' Diana broke off abruptly, startled into silence as she heard the sound of voices raised outside in the hallway. 'What on earth…?'

'Indeed.' Gabriel's expression was suddenly tense as he heard the commotion.

She frowned. 'Perhaps we should go and see what is wrong?'

'Perhaps we should.' He brushed lightly past her to walk swiftly in the direction of those raised voices.

Diana almost had to run to catch up with those long strides, so intent on doing so that she almost crashed into his broadly muscled back as he came to a sudden halt in front of her to stare across the wide hallway to where there were three people standing in the open doorway.

The butler, Soames.

A tall and handsome dark-haired man, with icy grey eyes and a livid scar down his left cheek that did nothing to detract from that handsomeness, but instead gave him an almost dangerous air.

And standing beside him, her beautiful face animated, was Diana's sister Caroline…

Chapter Five

If there had been any doubts in Gabriel's mind as to the identity of the young woman who stood beside his friend Dominic Vaughn, the Earl of Blackstone, then they were instantly dispelled as Diana gave a choked sob before moving past him to run quickly across the hallway on slippered feet.

She threw herself into the other woman's arms with a loud cry of 'Caroline!', her joy obvious as she began to both laugh and cry at the same time.

Caroline joined in as they held each other tightly, causing Gabriel and Blackstone to exchange a look that involved raised eyebrows and wry smiles, before Gabriel then turned his attention back to studying Lady Caroline Copeland. Seeing how his friend looked at her, no doubt she was none other than "Miss Morton"—the same young woman who until a few days ago had been singing in Dominic's gambling club wearing a jewelled mask and ebony wig in order to disguise her appearance! He'd started to suspect the truth after learning the Copelands' butler's name was Morton—truly no coincidence.

Slender and elegant in a gown of sea-green beneath her grey cloak, Caroline Copeland's hair was pure golden rather than the reddish-gold of Diana's, her eyes that same beguiling sea-green as her gown, her complexion alabaster, her pointed chin bearing the determination of her older sister.

A determination that, in Caroline's case at least, had led to her both risking her reputation and putting herself in danger rather than ever marry Lord Gabriel Faulkner, he thought bleakly. His reputation had much to answer for.

'How good it is to see you back in England at last, Westbourne!' Dominic Vaughn came forwards to grasp the other man's hand. 'Not now, Gabe,' he bent forwards to murmur softly to his friend before stepping back, the brightness of his smile lending his usually austere features a boyishness that Gabriel had not seen in him for some years. 'We travelled all the way to Shoreley Park in order to see you, only to arrive and find that you had not gone there, after all.'

'You have come from Shoreley Park, then?'

Gabriel turned to see a somewhat bewildered Diana standing beside her sister, their arms about each other's waists as Diana stared across at the two men. Just as she no doubt wondered what Caroline was doing in the company of such a dangerous-looking man. Injured in the Battle of Waterloo, Dominic Vaughn had a scar the length of his left cheek, from his eye down to his arrogant jaw line. A scar that gave him a somewhat sinister appearance.

Gabriel turned to the stony-faced butler. 'Bring tea for the ladies and brandy for the gentlemen to the study, if you please, Soames.'

'Very well, my lord.' The elderly man bowed stiffly before leaving, giving no indication, by word or demeanour, that he had moments ago been involved in a verbal exchange with a man and woman who were obviously known to his employer.

'What—?'

'We will wait until we are in the study to talk further, Diana,' Gabriel instructed before standing back to allow the ladies to precede them, his bride-to-be obviously still dazed by the sudden and unexpected appearance of her sister in the company of Dominic Vaughn and Caroline eyeing Gabriel somewhat challengingly as she walked at her sister's side.

'You are going to have your work cut out with that one, Dom,' he murmured drily to his friend as the two of them fell into step behind the women.

Dominic gave him an unconcerned smile. 'It already is.' He sobered slightly. 'You intend to give us your blessing, then, Gabe?'

'From the little I have already learnt of this business from Nathaniel, I believe I had better!' He gave a rueful shake of his head as he followed the ladies into the study.

As expected, Diana instantly demanded to know how and why her sister came to be here at all, let alone accompanied by a man such as the Earl of Blackstone.

What followed, once Soames had delivered the requested tea and brandy, was almost certainly a truncated version of what Lady Caroline Copeland had been up to since her arrival in London, totally for Diana's benefit, so she need not worry about the potential risks to her sister's reputation, and also to place Dominic in the most positive light possible.

'It seems I have you to thank for my sister's safe delivery back to her family, my lord.' Diana's gratitude to Dominic for ensuring her sister's safety since her arrival in London was tinged with concern. That he had been a close friend of Gabriel's for some years had been made obvious to her during this past conversation, but grateful as Diana was to have Caroline restored to her, she could not help but think her sister travelling about the countryside in the company of such a man as the earl was highly improper.

She turned to Caroline. 'Why did Elizabeth not travel back with you?'

Her sister looked surprised. 'With *me*? But I assumed she had travelled up to London with you and Aunt Humphries.'

Diana's trepidation grew. 'She left Shoreley Park two days after you did.' Caroline's face paled.

'You mean she may have been in London alone these past weeks? Dominic!' Her expression was slightly panicked as she turned to grasp the arm of the stern-faced Earl of Blackstone.

Diana was no less concerned at having her worst fear confirmed—that Elizabeth and Caroline had not, as she had hoped, arranged to meet up in London...

'One of your sisters has been returned to you unharmed, my dear; there is every reason to believe the same will prove true regarding your other sister.'

Diana barely heard Gabriel's words of comfort as he walked into her bedchamber uninvited when she had not responded to his brief knock upon the door.

The initial shock of realising that Elizabeth was still missing had resulted in there being more questions than answers. The hour becoming late, Gabriel had suggested that Lord Vaughn also stay here for the night at least, and that Caroline's and the earl's luggage be taken upstairs, so that they might all retire and change for dinner before resuming the conversation.

Except Diana had been too upset to do more than collapse upon her bed once she'd reached her bedchamber.

She now sat in a ball of misery on the side of that bed, her eyes red and sore from crying, her cheeks still damp with those tears as she looked up at Gabriel. 'I would not call finding Caroline alone in the company of such a man as Dominic Vaughn having her returned to me unharmed.'

Gabriel stiffened. 'Blackstone has been one of my closest friends since childhood. Moreover, he is a man I would trust with my life. In fact, I believe I have done so on several occasions.'

Diana gave a despairing shake of her head. 'Caroline is but twenty years old—'

'Blackstone is only eight and twenty—'

'In years, perhaps. But anyone looking at him could see that in experience and worldliness he is a man of much greater years.' She gave a delicate shudder. 'That he is—'

'Have a care, Diana.' Gabriel eyed her icily now. 'After you and your sister had left the study earlier,

Blackstone formally offered for Caroline and I have given them my blessing.'

Diana stood up abruptly, her eyes wide with shock. 'You cannot be serious!'

He nodded. 'Completely.'

'But—'

'Do not be naïve, Diana, one need only look at the two of them together to see how things stand between them.'

Yes, Diana had felt the undercurrents of heated awareness between her sister and the Earl of Blackstone. Felt them, and at the same time feared for her impetuous sister. 'Caroline has led such a sheltered life—'

'Diana.' Just her name, but spoken in such a reproving tone that it would be unwise to ignore it.

Except she was feeling less than wise at this moment! 'Caroline has always been strong-willed and headstrong, but in this instance she cannot possibly be sure of her feelings. She and the earl haven't known each other for that long—'

'And we had known each other for less than a day when you accepted my own offer of marriage,' he pointed out.

'That is not the same at all!' she said impatiently. 'You know as well as I that the only reason I accepted your offer of marriage was so that neither of my sisters need do so.'

Yes, Gabriel knew of Diana's reasons for accepting him. But knowing them and having Diana state them so bluntly were two entirely different things...

Something she also became aware of as she glanced across at him almost guiltily. 'I did not mean to imply—'

'I am well aware of what you meant, Diana,' Gabriel

said frostily. 'But our own reasons for marrying should not reflect on Dominic and Caroline. Whether you like or approve of the match, they are in love with each other and intend to marry.'

And Gabriel's own opinion hadn't mattered either! His conversation with his friend, once the two ladies had retired to their bedchambers, had been brief and to the point; Dominic intended to marry Caroline Copeland as soon as it could be arranged for them to do so. His gruff advice that Gabriel not object to the match or the swiftness of the upcoming nuptials had been enough of an indication to him as to the intimacy of their relationship.

Although Gabriel doubted Diana would welcome hearing of that…'I had the impression during our conversations about your sisters that you wished only for them to be free to choose who they fell in love with?'

'Yes, of course I do.'

'But you do not accept, because they have not been long acquainted, that Caroline is as deeply in love with Dominic as he is with her?'

Did Diana accept that? Caroline had always been the most stubborn and rebellious of the three sisters, the one always caught out in some mischief or another when they were growing up. Never seeming afraid of seeing a notion through once she had set her mind on it—Caroline's flight to London two-and-a-half weeks ago was evidence of that!

But to accept that Caroline was in love with Dominic Vaughn, the fierce-looking Earl of Blackstone, and that he was in love with her, that the two of them wished to marry, could not be attributed to either mischief or stubbornness. And yet Diana had seen the love shining in Caroline's eyes every time her sister so much as glanced at Dominic, as it was in his when he returned those glances. Indeed, Diana would have to be blind not to see the way the two constantly touched and looked at each other. Or how Caroline, usually so independent, had instantly turned to him for comfort the moment she realised Elizabeth was missing…

Could Diana possibly be jealous of that closeness? Oh, not of the love that so obviously glowed between the couple—having suffered what had proved to be the shallowness of Malcolm Castle's love, Diana had no intention of trusting in a man's declaration of love ever again, hence the expediency of her betrothal to Gabriel.

But could her misgivings now be because she resented the fact that Dominic Vaughn had now taken her place as the stalwart in Caroline's life? Could that possibly be the reason for her doubts about the match? If that was the case, then they were selfish doubts and did not deserve to so much as be acknowledged, let alone voiced!

Besides which, there was that air of intimacy between her sister and the earl that implied her concerns might already be too late…

She drew herself up determinedly. 'I will offer them both my warmest congratulations when we all meet downstairs for dinner.'

Gabriel looked admiringly at her. Whatever doubts and misgivings she still had concerning the suddenness of her younger sister's betrothal, she now had them firmly under control. No doubt the same firmness of control that had governed Diana's decision to accept his own offer of marriage. 'Perhaps, once they learn of our own betrothal, they will offer those same warm congratulations to us?' he teased.

'Of course.' It was obvious from the way Diana's cheeks had paled slightly that she had momentarily overlooked her own hasty engagement in her concerns for her sister.

'Then we are agreed that your sister and Blackstone will marry soon?' he asked.

'I did not think you required my agreement to the match,' she replied.

'I do not,' he acknowledged. 'But I am sure that your sister does.' Gabriel straightened and turned to leave.

'My lord, what do you intend to do concerning our earlier conversation?'

Gabriel's eyes narrowed. 'Which earlier conversation would that be, Diana?'

She moistened those pouting and sensuously full lips before speaking. 'I—in regards to the letter you received from Miss Britton about your mother, of course.'

Of course. He should have known, been prepared for the fact that the conscientious Diana could not simply let the subject be. 'Nothing, Diana. I intend doing absolutely nothing in regard to that letter.'

'Perhaps you might travel to Eastbourne first and talk to Miss Britton in person—?'

'I have already written back to Alice Britton informing her that I am far too occupied in town at the moment to spare the time to travel into Cambridgeshire.' He gave an impatient snort as Diana looked less than satisfied with this reply. 'I wish I had never shown you the damned letter!' Indeed, he wished he had never placed the announcement of their betrothal in the newspapers at all, if by doing so he had provided Alice Britton with an address where she might write to him.

Blue eyes widened. 'Miss Britton's letter was so filled with warmth and affection for your mother...'

'Yes, she was with my mother for many years.'

'She also seems most concerned that your mother is now living alone at Faulkner Manor apart from the servants and a Mr and Mrs Prescott,' she pressed.

With good reason—given a choice Gabriel would not have trusted one of his horses to the care of said Mr and Mrs Prescott! 'My mother's younger brother Charles and his wife,' he told her tersely.

Diana eyed Gabriel curiously, aware of the harshness of his expression and the increase in tension in that tautly muscled body; his wide shoulders were stiffly set back, his arms rigid and his hands clenched at his sides. 'Do you have a large family?' In truth, Gabriel was a man who, by his very nature, gave the impression of complete self-containment; so much so that it had never occurred to her that he might have family other than his mother and deceased father.

'I have no family.' Those midnight-blue eyes were utterly implacable.

'But—'

'At least, none that I care to acknowledge,' he added. 'Nor any who have cared to acknowledge me for the past eight years, either.' There was no missing the dangerous edge of warning in his tone now.

Even so, she found herself curious to know more about the family he dismissed so easily. 'Is Mr Charles Prescott your mother's only brother or—?'

'I have said I do not wish to discuss this with you any further, Diana.' He looked down at her with fierce eyes.

The past few hours had been fraught with emotion, to say the least, and as such she did not feel inclined to humour his usual arrogance. 'Does your desire not to discuss a certain subject usually meet with success?' she came back tartly.

'Invariably, yes.' Gabriel raised amused brows as he saw the light of battle deepen in those sky-blue eyes; whether she realised it or not, Diana was every bit as headstrong and strong-willed as she claimed Caroline was!

'What a pity, then, that it has failed in this instance.' Her chin jutted out stubbornly.

He grinned. 'I trust, Diana, that you are not about to disobey me before our marriage vows have even been made?' He could not resist teasing her.

Those blue eyes sparkled rebelliously. 'Indeed, at this moment it crossed my mind to request that part of the marriage service be omitted altogether, my lord!'

Gabriel gave an appreciative chuckle. 'Personally, I have always preferred the part of the vows that say "with my body I thee worship",' he drawled and instantly had the satisfaction of seeing two wings of colour heat her cheeks. In embarrassment? Or at the memory of the times Gabriel had already taken her in his arms and kissed her?

Something, against his previous better judgement to the contrary, he felt more than inclined to repeat now. Perhaps he might allow himself a little—just a little enjoyment of her graceful, desirable body?

Diana's eyes widened in alarm as he moved stealthily towards her. 'I—what are you doing?' Her voice came out as a breathless squeak as he now stood so close to her she could feel the heat of his body through the thin material of her gown.

He quirked dark brows. 'I thought, following the tensions of the past hour or so, that perhaps a little demonstration of how I intend to worship you with my body once we are married might be beneficial to us both.'

She swallowed hard, at the same time aware that her heart had begun to pound so loudly she was sure that he must hear it too. 'We are alone in my bedchamber, my lord…'

Those sculptured lips curved into a smile that added warmth to the intensity of those compelling midnight-blue eyes. 'The perfect time and place, I would have thought, for such a private demonstration—wouldn't you agree?'

Diana was more than alarmed now—she was light headed, both from his proximity, and the delicious intent reflected in those dark blue eyes fixed so purposefully upon her parted lips. 'That will not be necessary, my lord.'

'I do not recall saying it was necessary, Diana,' he murmured. 'Just something we might both enjoy.'

Diana would only be deceiving herself if she did not admit to having enjoyed the times Gabriel had already taken her in his arms, as she had noticed their absence this past two days. And perhaps the intimacy that so obviously existed between Caroline and Dominic Vaughn was having an effect on her own sensibilities—

because she wished for nothing more at that moment than for Gabriel to repeat those earlier kisses.

She moistened her lips with the tip of her tongue. 'I am not sure my guardian would approve.'

Gabriel's grin could only be described as wolfish. 'On the contrary, your guardian is in complete agreement with your participating in the exercise.'

'Then how can I refuse?' She smiled up at him shyly.

As before, Diana felt light and very feminine as Gabriel took her in his arms, with that smell of lemons and flowers, her lips against his soft and yielding, the womanly curves of her body moulded against his much harder ones. Gabriel couldn't help deepening the kiss, becoming more demanding as he parted her lips with a slow sweep of his tongue before dipping into the moist cavern of her mouth to become even more aroused by her heat.

Dear God! He should not have played this dangerous game, should have heeded his earlier warnings and avoided taking her in his arms again at all until they were safely wed. At the very least, he should find the strength to put her away from him now.

Instead he found himself groaning low in his throat as desire surged through him with the speed of a lit taper igniting paper, engorging his shaft until it throbbed with the same rapid heat as his heart pulsed. The kiss became even more passionate as his lips now devoured hers, crushing the full roundness of her breasts against his chest.

Diana's breath caught and her neck arched as Gabriel wrenched his mouth from hers to travel the length of her throat, his tongue a rasping caress as he tasted her, a trembling beginning in her knees and climbing to between her thighs as one of his hands moved restlessly across her back and hips before moving up to cup the softness of her breast.

'Perfection,' he groaned huskily, his hand tightening, fingers seeking, squeezing, plucking at the sensitised tip through the thin material of her gown even as his lips and tongue continued their sensual exploration of her throat.

Diana's fingers moved from the broad width of Gabriel's shoulders to become entangled in the heavy thickness of the hair at his nape, feeling on fire, her skin hot, sensitive to his every touch, every caress. His lips were moist and warm against her heated flesh as he kissed his way down to the bare swell of her breasts above her gown, causing those already aroused nubbins at their tips to pucker and harden and ache even more. For what exactly, Diana was still unsure.

Gabriel tugged down the soft material of her gown to bare one of her breasts, satisfying that ache as he drew the tight tip into the heat of his mouth hungrily, his tongue sweeping across it, making it tingle and burn at the same time.

Diana had never known such pleasure as this existed, a hot and pulsing pleasure that caused a flood of moisture between her thighs so that she now ached there too. An ache that increased as Gabriel's fingers curled about her hips to pull her into the hardness between his thighs, moving rhythmically against her. Each stroke of that hardness sent a fierce pulse of desire deep inside her as he continued to pay attention to her breast, causing that pleasure to build higher and higher until she suddenly felt as if she were about to explode.

'Gabriel?' She was unsure if that gasp was a plea for him to stop or to continue, her fingers curled tightly into his hair as she held him to her at the same time as she wanted to put an end to the torment of emotions that surged throughout her body.

Hearing the uncertainty in her voice was enough to bring Gabriel to his senses and realise exactly what he was doing, and with whom. This was no woman of experience, no woman he could take to his bed, to freely explore and pleasure, then forget all about her. Diana was to become his wife. His countess. The mother of his children. Children he fully intended would be born securely inside the parameters of their marriage so that no breath of scandal could be attached to them. Until Elizabeth was found, Diana wouldn't marry him, and he had no idea how long it would take to find his last runaway ward. He dared not risk bedding her until the knot was securely tied.

He drew in a hissing breath as he pulled away from her and held her at arm's length. Just the sight of her plump and bared breast, slightly reddened from the ministrations of his lips and tongue, was enough to make his thighs throb uncomfortably. 'I believe that is enough enjoyment for one evening,' he said unevenly as a red-faced Diana hastily straightened her gown and looked up at him with bewildered blue eyes.

Gabriel was starting to feel just as bewildered and unsure of himself whenever he was alone in Diana's company, and he didn't like it one little bit!

'I believe it is time that you changed for dinner,' he said, attempting to regain control of the situation.

'But—'

'Now, please, Diana.'

If she carried on standing there, tempting him, looking at him with her beautiful wide blue eyes, he might just have to take her in his arms again and that would be a disaster. Good sense and experience told him not to allow this woman beneath the guard he had so carefully erected about his emotions this past eight years. But just holding her in his arms was enough to force all those good intentions completely from his mind. What on earth was happening to him?

Chapter Six

'You have seemed somewhat preoccupied, all evening, Gabe.'

Gabriel looked down the length of the dining table to where Dominic was sitting, his expression uncharacteristically inquisitive as he sipped his after-dinner brandy now that the two men were alone in the dining-room.

In actual fact, Gabriel had found his friend's whole demeanour to be out of character this evening, as the four of them had eaten dinner together before the two ladies had retired to leave the men to enjoy their brandy and cigars. Mrs Humphries had once again sent her apologies; apparently she had been rendered prostrate at the sudden reappearance of her niece Caroline in the company of the twelfth Earl of Blackstone!

Dominic was certainly a changed man. For one thing Gabriel had never seen his friend smile as much as he had this evening, let alone indulge in the lovingly teasing banter that seemed to be such a part of his relationship with Caroline Copeland.

It was a sharp contrast to the stilted politeness that now existed between Diana and Gabriel!

To make matters worse, the announcement of the betrothal between the two of them had not been met with warm congratulations at all, but with astonishment from Caroline and concerned silence from Dominic— the same concern with which he still looked at Gabriel now.

'You and Caroline did not seem particularly pleased earlier at the announcement of my betrothal to Diana,' Gabriel commented, sipping his brandy.

The other man grimaced. 'Obviously I have not had chance as yet for private conversation with Caro, but I fear she may believe that her sister has only agreed to the marriage because she and Elizabeth made clear their own reluctance to do so.'

Gabriel raised dark brows. 'And what is your own opinion on the subject?'

Dominic breathed in deeply before answering. 'Recalling your own comments in Venice a little over a week ago, I cannot help but think that may indeed be the case. You said yourself you only offered marriage to one of the Copeland sisters because you felt it was the correct thing to do as they had been left so badly off by their father—as well, of course, as providing you with the necessary heirs.'

Both, Gabriel considered, very sound reasons for his offer of marriage to the Copeland sisters. Except he had not known Diana when he made that offer. Had not held her in his arms. Kissed her passionately. Caressed her bountiful curves...

He sat back in his seat abruptly. 'And if it is purely a marriage of convenience?'

His friend sighed heavily. 'I completely sympathise with your reasons for wanting to avoid emotional involvement, Gabriel. I should; I felt exactly the same way until I met and fell in love with Caro,' he added ruefully.

'Yes, I would be very interested to hear exactly how that came about…' Gabriel eyed the other man speculatively.

'No doubt you would,' Dominic drawled drily, 'but, as you are well aware, a gentleman does not kiss and tell.'

Gabriel raised dark brows. 'Not even when the lady in question happens to be my own ward?'

'Most especially then!' Dominic grinned. 'I would hate to have to put you in the position of having to call me out. Especially as I should win.'

Gabriel laughed. As, no doubt, he was expected to do; both men knew that of the two them Gabriel was the superior swordsman, as Dominic was the superior shot. Just as both men knew that there were no circumstances under which Gabriel would ever lay such a challenge before one of his two closest friends…

He smiled. 'On the contrary, I wish you and Caroline every happiness together.'

Dominic gave an acknowledging inclination of his head. 'And will you and Diana be as happy together, do you think?'

He glanced away. 'We can only hope.'

'Gabriel—'

'Dominic, no matter what you may or may not think

to the contrary, I did not in any way coerce Diana into our betrothal.' He scowled darkly. 'In truth, I was as surprised as you when she decided to accept my offer.'

'Caro led me to believe that Diana was to marry a son of the local Hampshire gentry. What happened to that?'

Caroline was probably also the person who had revealed that fact to William Johnston. 'I believe you will find that it was the gentleman's change of heart that has prompted her to accept my own offer,' Gabriel admitted curtly.

Dominic looked regretful. 'So this really is to be a marriage of convenience for both of you?'

'What else?' he said flippantly.

'Gabe—'

'We have been friends a long time, Dominic, and it is a friendship that I value highly, but in this particular circumstance I will thank you to keep your opinion to yourself,' Gabriel cut in, eyeing his friend warningly.

Dominic returned that gaze for several long seconds before allowing the tension to slowly ease from his wide shoulders. 'You do realise that at this moment Caro is probably engaged in a similar conversation with Diana?'

Gabriel nodded wryly. 'I'm sure Caroline is advising Diana to inform me she has changed her mind and will not marry me after all.'

The other man looked intrigued. 'And your reaction if Diana *were* to do that?'

What would he feel if that should happen? Gabriel wondered. Annoyance, certainly, at having to retract the announcement in the newspapers. But what else would he, personally, feel…?

He would feel nothing else, *nothing*! Diana was no more necessary to his happiness than any woman had been. If she should change her mind about marrying him, then no doubt he would find another quickly enough who would accept; from the mountain of invitations he had received these past two days it would appear that inheriting the earldom of Westbourne had made him as eligible to the ladies of the *ton* as it had assured his place back in society.

Besides…'Diana will not change her mind.'

'You sound very sure of that fact,' Dominic murmured.

Gabriel gave a slight smile. 'When you have come to know your future sister-in-law only a little longer you will realise that Diana is not a woman to go back on her word.' The abruptness with which he stood put an end to that particular conversation and Gabriel moved down the table to replenish both men's glasses before speaking again. 'Dominic, there is something else I would talk to you about…'

The other man's gaze sharpened. 'Yes?'

'I received a letter earlier this today from my mother's companion, Alice Britton.'

'The devil you did!' Dominic burst out incredulously.

'Indeed.' Gabriel made no effort to resume his seat at the table, but instead began to pace the room.

'For what purpose?'

He ran a hand through his hair. 'To inform me that my mother's health has been fragile since my father died.'

'I am sorry for that, Gabe.'

'As am I,' he admitted. 'She also wished me to know

that my Uncle Charles and his wife have resided at
Faulkner Manor with my mother this past six years.'

'Good God!'

'Yes.'

'What do you intend to do about it?'

'You are the second person this evening to ask me
that.' Gabriel sighed.

'Diana?' Dominic said knowingly.

'Exactly.'

'Shall you go into Cambridgeshire, then?'

Gabriel looked at him. 'What do you think?'

His friend snorted. 'I think that you are as likely to
return to Faulkner Manor with Charles and Jennifer
Prescott in residence as you are to consign yourself to
the fires of hell!'

'Exactly,' Gabriel confirmed.

'Does Diana know? Is she conversant with what happened eight years ago?'

'I am not a complete blackguard, Dominic,' Gabriel
said. 'I felt it only fair that Diana be made aware of
the…basics of that past scandal.'

'But not the details?' Dominic asked shrewdly.

'No.'

'Such as the *name* of the lady you supposedly
ruined?' his friend pressed.

'We both know that I never laid so much as a finger
on her.' Gabriel's mouth had thinned into a grim line.
'And I dispute the claim that she ever was, or ever could
be, considered a lady!'

'Gabriel—'

'No, I have not informed Diana of her name.' His

hand was now clasped so tightly about his brandy glass that Gabriel was surprised it did not shatter.

Dominic looked wary. 'Do you not feel that perhaps you should?'

Gabriel shook his head. 'I don't feel it's necessary that I do so at this point in time, no.'

And if he had his way, it never would be…

Caroline was distraught. 'I cannot even bear the thought of you marrying a man you do not love. Even one who has surprised us all by being so sinfully handsome,' she allowed grudgingly.

Diana smiled affectionately at Caroline now as she paced Diana's bedchamber energetically. 'He is rather handsome.'

'Even so—'

'If, like our Aunt Humphries, you are about to raise the subject of the past scandal attached to the earl's name, then I think you should know that he has already discussed it with me.'

Her sister's eyes widened with curiosity. 'He has?'

Diana smiled ruefully. 'If we are to have nothing else between us, then I believe we are to have honesty, at least. But only between the two of us,' she added firmly as she saw Caroline's interest. 'I have no intention of breaking the earl's confidence by discussing the subject with you or anyone else.'

'But to even think of marrying without love—'

'Caroline, I am not looking for love and romance in my marriage.' She sighed.

'Why on earth not?' her sister demanded, outraged.

Diana smiled sadly. 'Possibly because I have good reason to know how fickle those two things can be?'

'I do not understand.' Caroline halted her pacing to shake her head. 'I was sure that you and Malcolm Castle were to be married.'

'Malcolm is no longer a part of my life.' It was Diana's turn to stand up restlessly.

'But why not? What on earth happened?'

'He is to marry another. And that is an end to it, Caroline,' she added decisively as her sister would have demanded to know more. 'Now I am happy to settle for marriage to a man who makes no false declarations of love, but has stated firmly and clearly exactly what he expects of me.'

'He expects you to become nothing but a brood mare,' her sister snorted.

Diana stiffened. 'You are being unfair—'

'Forgive me, Diana!' Caroline stepped forwards to hug her impulsively. 'It is only that to love, and know that I am as deeply loved in return, is the most joyful experience of my life: I simply cannot bear the thought of your settling for less.' The light of rebellion shone in her sea-green eyes.

'I am not like you, Caroline.' She smiled gently. 'I do not require that a man be as wildly in love with me as your earl obviously is with you. A mutual respect and liking will suit me just as well.'

'And do you respect and like Gabriel Faulkner, Diana?' her sister probed softly.

Did she like and respect Gabriel? Diana wondered, her cheeks feeling suddenly warm. She respected his honesty, at least, and he was, as Caroline proclaimed, sinfully handsome. He was certainly not a man to be overlooked under any circumstances. She had also found his kisses and caresses to be thrillingly pleasurable— But did those things all add up to a liking for him?

'I have every confidence that Lord Faulkner and I will deal very well together in our marriage,' she finally said evasively.

Caroline eyed her. 'That does not answer my question.'

No, it did not, because she had no idea whether or not she liked the man she had agreed to marry. Surely liking someone was a comfortable feeling, an easy relationship, and did not involve the knife-edge of awareness that Diana experienced whenever she was in his company?

'It is enough for now that I respect both him and the honesty he has given me,' she reiterated with such finality that even the impulsive Caroline knew not to probe any further.

'We appear to have caused something of a stir when we announced our betrothal to Dominic and Caroline yesterday evening,' Gabriel commented, glancing across the breakfast table at the coolly composed Diana.

Neither Caroline nor Blackstone had made an appearance as yet this morning, causing Gabriel to wonder privately whether the pair were not together in one of their bedchambers indulging in the intimacy that had been so apparent between them yesterday evening. Not that he was overly concerned if they were; Dominic had made it more than plain yesterday that his marriage was to take place at the earliest convenience.

How different, how much more acceptable to Gabriel was Diana's air of capable calmness than her younger sister's obvious fiery and impulsive nature; he certainly did not envy Blackstone his choice of wife. Although he did have doubts as to whether Diana's cool composure was not merely a thin veneer this morning.

'Perhaps, having had opportunity to talk with your sister, you have decided that you do not wish our own betrothal to continue,' he suggested.

'If one more person dares to suggest that to me, then I fear I might actually scream!' Diana pierced him with over-bright blue eyes as she glared across the small table at him.

Somehow Gabriel did not think so. 'Caroline?'

'Yes.'

'And your Aunt Humphries was less than warm to the idea when she was informed, was she?'

Diana lifted that stubbornly pointed chin. 'I have given my word, Gabriel, and I will not break it.'

His mouth quirked as she repeated the claim he had made to Blackstone the previous evening. It seemed his reading of her character was correct. 'No matter what terrible tales you are told about me?'

'Not even then.'

Gabriel looked at her admiringly. 'If we'd had a dozen women like you beside us in the fight against Napoleon, then the war would no doubt have ended much sooner than it did.'

'If that situation had been left in the hands of women,

then there would not have been a war at all,' Diana returned waspishly.

Gabriel gave an appreciative smile. 'You are determined to go ahead with our marriage, then?'

Diana's outward confidence wavered slightly at the caution she sensed in Gabriel's manner. 'Unless you are having second thoughts on the matter?'

'Not at all,' he dismissed easily.

She felt somewhat reassured by that ease of manner. 'In that case, I suggest we turn our discussion as to what we are to do about the disappearance of Elizabeth.'

The earl's good humour instantly evaporated. 'Tell me, is she as without fear as Caroline?'

Diana's expression softened with affection. 'Despite appearances, I believe Elizabeth's character to be less headstrong, certainly. Her initial impulses are invariably tempered by caution,' she explained at Gabriel's look of enquiry.

'That is something to be grateful for, at least!'

Diana laughed. 'I only met Lord Vaughn yesterday, but I believe him to be more than capable of curbing the more dangerous of Caroline's excesses.'

'Let us hope so.'

'They are so very much in love, are they not…?'

Gabriel wondered if she was aware of how wistful she both sounded and looked. Probably not—her own foray into romantic love had not had such a happy ending. Any more than a marriage between the two of them would? he wondered.

'They are, yes.' Gabriel resolutely shook off any doubts he might have about Diana becoming the wife of a man who was incapable of feeling love. 'With

Blackstone's help I intend to intensify the search for Elizabeth this very morning.'

A frown creased her creamy brow. 'Do you really think it possible she followed Caroline here?'

'I am sure of it.' Just as sure as he was that it would be too much to hope that the youngest of the Copeland sisters had faired as well as Caroline, who had fallen into a safe pair of hands.

She gave him a quizzical glance. 'And you are still as determined this morning not to travel into Cambridgeshire to see your mother?'

His mouth thinned. 'Oh, yes.'

'Very well.' She gave a cool inclination of her head. 'If you should change your mind—'

'I will not.' Gabriel threw down his napkin and stood, a nerve pulsing in his cheek. He had succeeded in distracting both Diana's attention and his own from this subject the previous evening by taking her in his arms and kissing her. A course of action that had, if anything, backfired on himself. 'The subject is at an end, Diana. I advise you not attempt to discuss it with me again.'

Diana knew, from the ruthless resolve she could see in his expression as he left the room, that she would have little choice but to do as he asked.

Or, at least, Diana *would* have had little choice if a second letter had not arrived from Alice Britton the following morning, care of Westbourne House, and addressed to her this time…

'Caro is becoming most displeased at our lack of progress in regard to our search for Elizabeth.' Dominic grimaced as the two men strode back into the entrance hall of Westbourne House.

Gabriel shot his friend a disbelieving glance after handing his hat and cane to the attentive Soames. 'I cannot believe how quickly you have fallen beneath that young lady's beautiful thumb.'

Dominic gave an unconcerned grin. 'It is not the beauty of Caro's *thumb* under which I have fallen!'

Gabriel snorted with laughter. 'I would find you quite nauseating if it were not for your obvious happiness with the arrangement.' In truth, he had never seen his friend so happy or contented; even these few brief hours Dominic had spent away from Caro's company were chafing the other man's patience.

Dominic grinned unabashedly as he turned from handing over his own hat and cane. 'I cannot recommend the arrangement strongly enough.'

Gabriel looked down the length of his nose. 'I am perfectly content with my own betrothal to Diana, thank you very much.'

'As you please,' Blackstone shrugged.

'I do please,' Gabriel replied before turning to the butler. 'Where are the ladies, Soames?'

'I believe Lady Caroline is upstairs with her aunt, my lord.'

'And Lady Diana?'

'She and her maid departed in the carriage more than an hour ago, my lord.'

'Departed?' Gabriel repeated softly, a terrible sense of foreboding settling over him.

'Yes, my lord.'

'To go where?'

'She did not say, my lord.' The butler placed the two hats and canes upon the stand in the hallway. 'She was in somewhat of a hurry when she left, but she did ask me to keep this note about my person to give to you as soon as you returned.' The butler produced the slightly crumpled missive from the breast pocket of his jacket.

Gabriel took the note before striding into the privacy of the parlour and breaking the seal. It was a letter from Diana, explaining where she was going and why. Along with a second letter tucked inside the first, from Alice Britton and addressed to Diana, entreating her to exert her influence upon Gabriel to encourage him to visit his mother at his earliest convenience.

Gabriel read Diana's letter three times. Disbelievingly. Incredulously. She had gone to Cambridgeshire! The colour drained from his cheeks and a furious glitter entered his eyes, his fingers finally clenching about the paper before he crushed it into the palm of his hand.

Chapter Seven

Diana's nervousness at her decision to travel to Faulkner Manor in Cambridgeshire accompanied only by her maid increased the further they travelled away from London, aware as she was that Gabriel was sure to be most displeased when he returned to Westbourne House and learnt what she had done.

Displeased enough, she hoped, to follow her...

In view of his determination not to even discuss the subject any further, there had seemed no other way in which to ensure that he travelled to see his mother, something she felt even more strongly that he should do upon receipt of that second letter from Alice Britton. The elderly woman was obviously deeply concerned for Felicity Faulkner.

Except Diana had quickly realised the glaring fault with her plan: there was no guarantee Gabriel *would* follow her. Indeed, he had not done so in the almost twenty-four hours since she had departed London.

Nor had Diana slept during her overnight stay at a coaching inn, as she instead worried about the force of Gabriel's anger when they next spoke. Yet he still had not arrived.

Diana's decision to travel to Faulkner Manor had not been made lightly, torn as she was between worry over her youngest sister's whereabouts and the obligations she felt were expected of her as the future wife of the Earl of Westbourne. Indeed, she would not have even contemplated such a journey as this had she not been reassured concerning Elizabeth's welfare by the fact that Caroline and Lord Vaughn, now that they were aware Elizabeth was missing, were just as single-minded in their determination to find her.

That particular concern put to rest, Diana was able to concentrate on her duties as Gabriel's future wife; as such, she had made her preparations to leave for Cambridgeshire.

Only now was she beset with such trepidation, both at her temerity in having requested Gabriel's valet pack a trunk of the earl's clothes to travel in the carriage with her, and the anger she knew to expect from Gabriel for her having gone at all. She very much doubted that he would appreciate her explanation that she considered their betrothal to mean that his family was now as much her responsibility as it was his!

It was too late to do anything else now but continue her journey, Diana told herself with a determined straightening of her shoulders. Gabriel might even now—she could only hope—be somewhere on the road behind her, in hot and angry pursuit…

* * *

'I trust there is some good reason why you have not already followed Diana?'

Gabriel slowly turned from where he had been standing, watching stony-faced out of the window in his study as what seemed to be an army of gardeners set to work putting order back into the overgrown lawn and tangled flowerbeds; he had no doubts that the work was being carried out under the exact instructions of Lady Diana Copeland…

Lady Caroline Copeland stood imperiously in the open doorway, Gabriel's gaze cool and unemotional as he looked down the length of his nose at her; he had been aware of her brief knock upon the door several seconds ago, but had chosen not to acknowledge it. 'I do not recall giving you leave to enter.'

She stepped fully inside the room and closed the door behind her. 'I do not recall having asked for it.'

No, she had not, Gabriel acknowledged with grudging admiration. Petite and beautiful in a gown of pale grey, aged only twenty, Caroline nevertheless had a determination of will that exceeded both those attributes—was it any wonder that she had managed to bedazzle the arrogant and cynical Earl of Blackstone?

Nevertheless…'I am not in the habit of discussing my movements, or lack of them, with anyone.'

'Indeed?' She gave an inelegant snort. 'Might I suggest, where Diana is concerned at least, that you *become* used to it?'

Gabriel raised arrogant brows. 'You *suggest*?'

'Insist,' she said crisply.

'As I thought.' Gabriel suppressed a small smile as

he turned fully into the room, the afternoon sunlight warm upon his back, a warmth that did nothing to dispel the coldness of the anger he felt towards Diana.

He was also, he acknowledged ruefully, still somewhat nonplussed at having learnt of her departure for Faulkner Manor. The years he had spent as an officer in the King's army had resulted in his being used to issuing orders and having them obeyed. That the woman he had been betrothed to for only six days, a beautiful and elegantly composed young woman whom he knew to possess a regard for duty far beyond her years, had none the less completely disregarded his wishes was beyond belief.

Perhaps he should have taken more notice of Diana's previous remark concerning having the word 'obey' removed from their wedding vows!

'Well?'

Gabriel frowned as he refocused his attention on Diana's sister. 'As I have already stated, I see no reason to explain myself, to you or to anyone else.'

She gave an exasperated sigh. 'You are as stubbornly proud as Dominic.'

He raised an eyebrow at her. 'No doubt the reason we have remained friends for so many years.'

'No doubt,' she muttered. 'Your own shortcomings aside, it is Diana who concerns me.'

He looked taken aback at this second insult in as many minutes. 'I fail to understand why?'

Sea-green eyes flashed her impatience as she stepped further into the room. 'Perhaps you are not aware of it, but my sister has always put her own desires and needs aside in favour of others—'

'Considering your own recent actions, I am surprised to hear that you are at all aware of Diana's selflessness!' Gabriel's mouth was tight with disapproval.

Warmth coloured her cheeks at this more-than-obvious rebuke concerning her own recent waywardness. 'How could I not be aware of it when it is obviously the only reason she has agreed to marry you?'

Dark eyes narrowed in warning. 'Have a care, Caroline.' His voice was silkily soft. 'I have deliberately not mentioned your own recent scandalous behaviour in running off and becoming a singer in a gambling club to Diana, because of her deep love for you and my own friendship with Blackstone, but I assure you—both those things will cease to matter if you continue to berate me in this unacceptable way.'

The colour as quickly faded from her cheeks, but she gamely continued. 'I know little or nothing of past happenings, of course, but you cannot seriously mean to leave Diana to face your family alone!'

'I believe I would be perfectly within my rights to do so when she has so blatantly disobeyed my wishes,' Gabriel drawled back. 'But, no,' he relented at Caroline's outraged expression, 'that is not my intention.' He had known from the moment he read her letter earlier that he would have to follow her, that by lingering in London in this way he was only putting off the inevitable.

'Oh?' Caroline now looked less certain of her indignation on her sister's behalf.

Gabriel explained. 'Even as we speak my horse is being saddled in preparation for my own departure.'

Caroline visibly relaxed the tension in her shoulders.

'Why did you not just say so immediately I came in the room?'

Gabriel gave a rueful smile. 'You seemed so determined to be outraged on Diana's behalf that I did not like to disappoint.'

She tossed her head. 'You and Dominic are so much alike you could be brothers!'

He grinned. 'Considering that you and he are shortly to be married, I will take that as a compliment.'

'I should not if I were you,' Caroline said honestly. 'A certain arrogance in one's beloved may be acceptable, but it is not so attractive in the man set to marry one's sister.'

'I will try to bear that in mind,' Gabriel replied, inwardly warmed by Caroline's obvious love for her sister and her open declaration of loving Dominic as much as he loved her; it boded well for a marriage between the two.

She eyed him uncertainly. 'I trust you will not be too displeased with Diana when you see her again?'

He gave her a straight look. 'On the contrary, Caroline—I am very much looking forward to demonstrating the depths of my displeasure to your sister.' He was anticipating that very much indeed!

Diana was cold, tired, and feeling extremely irritable by the time the carriage came to a halt at the end of the long gravel drive in front of Faulkner Manor early on the second evening after her hasty departure from Westbourne House.

The cold and tiredness were explained by the long hours of travelling in the carriage whilst the rain fell steadily outside, that rain dampening her pelisse and bonnet when they risked a brief stop at a reputable road-side inn in order to enjoy a light luncheon.

The reason for the feelings of irritation lay firmly upon Gabriel Faulkner's broad shoulders.

Her initial nervousness at the thought of his anger, once he discovered where she had gone, had first changed to relief when there came no sound of the thundering of horse's hooves in angry pursuit. But that relief had then turned to puzzlement as a day and night passed, and then another day, still with no sign of him. Finally, she had become irritated when she had to accept that he really had decided not to follow her.

She had felt sure he would—so why hadn't he? Obviously their betrothal was a matter of convenience for both of them, but nevertheless she had believed any gentleman's sense of honour would dictate he at least show loyalty to the woman he intended to make his wife.

Apparently in Gabriel's case that sense of honour did not come into play when it might involve seeing any of his family again. What was she to say to them concerning his absence? To his mother?

She came to an abrupt halt as the groom offered his hand to assist her in stepping down from the carriage, her senses suddenly humming as she became aware, alerted, by a feeling of—of something—

It was pure instinct that caused her to turn and look down the length of the gravel drive, her cheeks paling, eyes widening, as she saw the huge black stallion silhouetted there in the last of the sun's evening rays, the rider upon its back equally as huge and daunting and dressed all in black, with his hat pulled low over his brow and his black cloak swirling behind him.

Diana knew with certainty the identity of that rider. Gabriel!

Even as she stood in arrested stillness, a sheet of lightning flashed across the darkening sky behind him and caused the horse to rear up on its back legs, clearly revealing his face, accusing dark eyes visible beneath the brim of his hat, his expression stony as the horse's hooves clattered back down upon the gravel.

The horse galloped towards where she stood, its rider bent low upon its back, giving him the appearance of the archangel of the same name about to swoop down vengefully upon his enemy.

Diana…

It had been Gabriel's hope that he would succeed in meeting up with Diana before she arrived at Faulkner Manor and, in doing so, prevent either of them going there. Unfortunately his malingering in London meant that was not the case. He easily recognised the black coach that had come to a halt—he should; it was now one of his own and bore the Westbourne crest of an angel and a rampant unicorn upon its doors. A groom wearing the Westbourne livery had opened one of the doors, lowered the steps and was waiting to assist Diana in alighting from the carriage.

She turned a startled face in Gabriel's direction even as she stepped down on to the gravel, blue eyes widening with alarm as she obviously recognised him seated upon the back of the glossy black stallion.

An alarm she would find was well deserved as soon

as the two of them were alone together, he thought in grim satisfaction!

It had been a long and uncomfortable ride from London, despite an overnight stay at a mediocre inn, and he was now tired and hungry and very wet; it had been raining for most of the day, but the heavens had opened up completely five miles back, and succeeded in soaking him through to the skin in the process.

But none of those things were as unpleasant to him as finding himself back at Faulkner Manor after all these years. Nor was he in any doubt as to who was to blame for that.

Lady Diana Copeland. The woman to whom he had recently become betrothed. The interfering young lady who would very shortly be made aware of the penalty for disobeying him…

Gabriel pulled Maximilian to a halt mere feet away from her before sliding from the saddle to throw the reins into the hands of the waiting groom. He marched across to where she still stood in transfixed alarm beside the coach, her eyes becoming wider still as he reached out and grasped her arm.

The length of her creamy throat moved convulsively as she swallowed before speaking. 'How good it is to see you, my lord, when I had thought you said that commitments in town would not allow you to join me until tomorrow.' Her voice was smoothly composed, despite her obvious discomfort.

This last was said for the listening servants, Gabriel knew. As far as Diana was aware, he had not intended coming with her at all; indeed, he still wished himself anywhere but here! 'I could not bear to be parted from you for even so short a time,' he replied to save her face. 'Especially when you took it upon yourself to bring most of my clothes with you,' he grated for her ears alone.

Diana knew that his initial words must sound lover-like to those listening, but there was no missing the promise of retribution in his next comment, or those dark and piercing eyes that glittered down at her so intently. 'I am gratified to know you feel that way, my lord.'

'Let us hope that you feel as *gratified* once we are alone together,' he murmured.

Diana's nervousness grew. 'Did you not receive my letter of explanation?'

'I would not be here at all if I had not,' he bit out.

'Then—'

'What on earth is all the fuss about? Good God, is that you, Gabriel?' a female voice said.

Gabriel gave Diana one last quelling glance before a shutter came down over all his emotions as he turned to look at the obviously shocked young woman who was standing at the top of the steps leading up to the house, only the tightening of his fingers upon her arm betraying that he was not as composed as the blank expression on his face meant to imply.

Diana turned slowly to look up at the woman who still gazed at Gabriel with utter disbelief.

She was young, possibly only a few years older than Diana's one and twenty, and possessed of a smooth perfection of beauty: a wide and creamy brow, fine brown eyes, a small and perfect nose, her lips full above a delicately vulnerable jaw. Her hair was a pure raven-black and arranged in fashionable curls and the slenderness of her figure was shown to full advantage in a fashionable gown of pale peach.

'Your powers of perception have not failed you, madam,' Gabriel said smoothly, answering the other woman.

Her cheeks paled even as she fought for composure in the face of his biting sarcasm. 'I see that the years have done little to reduce your unbearable arrogance.'

'Did you expect them to have done?'

'I did not expect to see you at all!' she exclaimed.

'Obviously not,' he murmured.

The woman glared at him. 'If you had bothered to inform us of your visit, then I would have told you that you are not welcome here.'

A nerve pulsed in Gabriel's rigidly clenched jaw. 'For some inexplicable reason I seem to have had several conversations recently concerning my lack of need to inform anyone of my actions.'

Diana knew that was a little dig at her, too…

'If you would not mind?' He now eyed the other woman coldly. 'Diana and I will join you in the house in a moment.' It was unmistakably a dismissal.

The young woman looked as if she were about to continue arguing his right to enter the house at all, but then obviously thought better of it after another glance at his expression, instead satisfying herself with one last glare before turning away to hurry back inside.

Diana could only surmise that the haughty young beauty was another of Gabriel's relatives—perhaps the daughter of Mrs and Mrs Charles Prescott? Her

manner towards Gabriel had certainly been familiar—
and insulting—enough to be that of a cousin.

'All will shortly be revealed, Diana,' Gabriel assured
her as the threatening rain began to fall once again. He
took her arm and began to swiftly ascend the steps.

'But—careful, Gabriel!' Diana protested as she has-
tened to accommodate those steps and instead stumbled
over the hem of her gown.

Gabriel's impatience, his anger, was such that he was
beyond being reasoned with. Diana had brought them
both into this scorpions' den, and he had little sympa-
thy for her if she now found his resentment not to her
liking. 'I am already very wet and weary from spending
unnecessary hours in the saddle; I would advise you not
to add another soaking to my list of discomforts.'

She pulled her now-soiled skirts away from her
slippered feet before looking up at him from beneath
lowered lashes. 'I can see that you are angry with me,
Gabriel, but I assure you I thought only of you when I
decided to come here.'

'On the contrary, I believe you to have acted completely *without* regard or consideration towards my feelings when you made that decision,' he corrected her
curtly, not so much as sparing her another glance as he
pulled her up the last of the steps.

She gasped. 'How can you possibly say that when
I abandoned my search for Elizabeth in order to come
here?'

'So that I would not be beset with guilt and regret
when I one day learn of my mother's demise,' he
reminded her witheringly.

'Yes.'

Gabriel's eyes glittered down at her darkly. 'That was *my* decision to make, not yours.'

'But—'

'I will allow you plenty of time later in which to explain yourself.'

She felt the sting of icy coldness in his tone. 'With any intention of actually listening to what I have to say?'

'Probably not.'

'Then I see little point—'

'Will you, for the love of God, just be silent, Diana!' he said, coming to a sudden halt, his breathing harsh as he paused outside the home he had left so ignominiously eight years ago.

The anger he had felt towards Diana had sustained him through the arduous journey into Cambridgeshire, as he'd mentally listed the many and varied ways in which he intended to make her suffer for putting him to the trouble of following her here. To now find himself standing outside the front door of the home he had been so cruelly banished from, the family he had never thought to return to, filled him with a desolation that struck to his very heart.

'Gabriel?' Diana could not help but feel concerned at the bleakness of his expression as he gazed up at the house that had once been his home. Their acquaintance was of such a nature that it had been fraught with tension from the onset, but as she now looked up into the face above her own she knew that this man was not even the arrogant and dictatorial one she had known for the past six days, but one who was a complete stranger to her…

She swallowed hard, knowing in that moment that she should not have forced Gabriel into following her here, that by doing so she had painfully lanced an old and festering wound that would have been better left alone. 'It was never my intention to cause you discomfort, my lord,' she whispered.

'Your apology comes too late and is too little, Diana.' Gabriel looked down at her with the eyes of the stranger he now seemed to her. 'There is no turning back or away now,' he muttered for her ears alone before taking the step forwards that would take them both inside the house.

As Diana stepped inside the cavernous marble entrance hall, she was instantly struck by a chill that sent rivulets of cold down her spine. It was not a chill of temperature, but of atmosphere, as if the very walls of the house had absorbed a malignance of spirit for so long and so intensely that it now existed in the very fabric of the bricks and mortar of which it was built.

Which was in itself fanciful; bricks and mortar did not absorb emotions, any more than could the opulent statuary and paintings upon the walls, she told herself. It had to be her own tiredness and hunger—and not a little trepidation at the thought of the promised conversation with Gabriel when they once again found themselves alone together—that was to blame for these imaginings.

Nevertheless, Diana found herself holding the folds of her cloak more tightly about her in an effort to ward off that chill.

'Is my mother well?' Gabriel rasped as the dark-haired beauty hurried down the wide and sweeping staircase, her beautiful face slightly flushed from the exertion.

She ignored his question and instead spoke to the waiting butler as she reached the bottom of the staircase. 'Bring tea to the brown salon, if you please, Reeve.'

'Bring tea for the ladies by all means, Reeve, but I would prefer something stronger,' Gabriel turned to address the butler, at the same time noting that the passing of the years had not been kind to the elderly man; he looked twenty years older rather than the eight it had been since Gabriel last saw him.

Nevertheless there was a warmth of welcome in the butler's gaze as he realised Gabriel's identity. 'Very good, my lord.'

'And have the green-and-gold bedchambers prepared for both Lady Diana and myself,' Gabriel added as he handed his hat and cloak to him, along with Diana's cloak and bonnet.

'You cannot just walk in here and issue instruction to the servants as if you owned the place!' the woman exclaimed.

'I believe it is my mother who still owns Faulkner Manor?'

'I—yes.'

'Then do it, please, Reeve,' Gabriel said before once again turning his glacial gaze on the dark-haired beauty, who glared at him so resentfully. 'I suggest, madam, that we continue this conversation where it is warmer.'

'You—'

'Now,' he demanded.

With a flounce of her skirt the young beauty turned

and preceded them into a room decorated in browns and golds, the fire burning in the hearth doing little to alleviate the chill in the atmosphere, however.

Gabriel's eyes narrowed to glittering slits. 'I believe I asked after my mother's health.'

The woman's mouth thinned. 'Felicity is as well as can be expected.'

'What exactly does that mean?' he asked.

She shrugged creamy shoulders. 'Felicity has become fragile since your father died. In fact, she retired to her rooms following his funeral. She now rarely, if ever, leaves them.'

'No doubt giving you leave to take over as mistress here?' Gabriel said contemptuously.

'How exactly like you to blame others for what we all know to be the results of your own misdeeds!' she came back waspishly.

Gabriel did not react by so much as a twitch of an eyebrow at the mention of his father's death, or of how his mother's grief at that death had been so extreme that she had retired completely from all society, although both pieces of information managed to pierce the shield he had placed so firmly about his emotions. His father had always been something of a strict adherent of the rules of society, and his mother more of a social butterfly, but it had been an attraction of opposites, their deep and abiding love for each other obvious to all around them.

Was Gabriel to blame? If he had not allowed himself to be banished eight years ago, would things be different now? Would his father still be alive and his mother's joy of life still touch everyone and everything around her?

'Would you care to make the introductions, Gabriel?'

He dragged himself back from those thoughts of the past with effort at this gentle reminder of his manners from Diana, looking first at the woman who eyed him so hostilely from across the room, and then down at his bride-to-be as her hand rested lightly upon his arm.

'Diana, this is Mrs Jennifer Prescott, the wife of my Uncle Charles. Mrs Prescott, I present my betrothed, Lady Diana Copeland.' He made the introductions brief and to the point.

Diana stared at him blankly for several long seconds, before turning to look at the other woman, unable to hide the incredulity in her gaze at the realisation that the young, incredibly beautiful woman standing beside the fireplace was married to his uncle. A woman Gabriel had wished never to see or hear of ever again…

Chapter Eight

'Mrs Prescott.' Diana's curtsy was perfunctory at best as she tried to dismiss her previously formed opinion that Mrs Charles Prescott would be a plump and matronly woman. Had Gabriel not told her that his uncle was his mother's brother; surely implying that he would be a gentleman in his forties at the very least? The beautiful woman who had now been introduced to her as that gentleman's wife was aged only in her mid to late twenties.

'Lady Diana.' Mrs Prescott gave a terse inclination of her head rather than returning her curtsy.

Diana was very aware of Gabriel's tension as her hand rested in the crook of his arm, like that of a wild beast prepared to spring in defence should the need arise. Did he fear that it might? She felt the return of those misgivings she had experienced when first entering this house, knowing she had been wrong to dismiss them; there was something seriously amiss in this household, something that lay quiet and patiently waiting in its darkest corners.

She longed to escape, if only briefly. 'Gabriel, I believe I would prefer to freshen up after our journey rather than take refreshment.'

He appeared not to hear her for several long seconds, his gaze locked in silent battle with that of his beautiful aunt by marriage, then slowly Diana felt some of the tension ease from his arm as he turned to look down at her between hooded lids.

Even so, his jaw remained tightly clenched as he answered her. 'I am sure that Mrs Prescott will be only too happy to excuse us both.'

Irritation flickered across that beautiful face even as she rang for the butler. 'I would be happier if you had never come here at all,' she spat.

'And why is that?'

'You know why.'

'Perhaps,' he allowed. 'I take it my mother still occupies the same suite of rooms?'

'Of course.' Mrs Prescott frowned. 'But I do not advise that you attempt to visit her this evening, Gabriel. Felicity always dines early and she has already been settled for the night—'

'I believe it is for me to decide if and when it is advisable that I visit my mother this evening and not the empty-headed woman married to my uncle,' he said savagely.

'You are insolent, sir!' she said in outrage.

He quirked challenging brows. 'How clever of you to realise that I am not the same idealistic young man you knew so long ago who was forced to have to leave.'

She glared at him. 'It was by your own choice, sir.'

'I found the alternative contemptible,' Gabriel said silkily.

Jennifer Prescott released a hissing breath. 'You—'

'Where is my dear Uncle Charles this evening?' Gabriel interrupted, aware of how unfair it was to Diana to continue this conversation in which she had no part.

Mrs Prescott's chin tilted. 'My husband departed for London yesterday with the intention of spending several days there.'

'For business or pleasure?'

'Business, of course.'

There was no 'of course' about it in Gabriel's eyes; his uncle had always been an inveterate gambler. 'I had not realised that my uncle still had any business interests in town.' Having no interest in accidentally meeting his uncle or his young wife at some *ton*nish affair, Gabriel had made discreet enquiries about Charles since returning to England, unsurprised to learn that he spent most of his time in Cambridgeshire and ventured to town only occasionally. Occasions when he invariably lost at the gambling tables.

'He does not.'

'Then—'

'Charles and I gave up our own home after your father died and your mother took to her rooms; we moved here so that I might take over the running of the house and Charles could manage Felicity's estates and business interests,' Jennifer Prescott informed him haughtily.

Gabriel continued to view her with scorn. There was no doubting that she was more beautiful than ever or that her youthfully slender curves had matured into those of a voluptuous and desirable woman. But it was a beauty that held no appeal for him, however, distrusting as he did every word and gesture the woman made. Yet having made the mistake of underestimating her once, he had no intention of doing so a second time.

'No doubt Charles has taken every opportunity in which to line his own pockets,' Gabriel said drily. It seemed that Alice Britton's politely worded letters concerning the state of affairs at Faulkner Manor had perhaps underestimated the situation, after all.

The colour faded from Jennifer Prescott's cheeks as she gasped. 'You go too far!'

His mouth tightened. 'Do I?' Dark blue eyes warred silently with those liquid brown ones until Reeve's entrance, in answer to her earlier summons, abruptly broke that tension as she was forced to turn away and issue the instruction to take Gabriel and Diana to their bedchambers.

The brief respite allowed Gabriel several seconds in which to regain his now habitual remoteness. He had not wanted to come here. Would not have come here if it were not for Diana's interference.

A fact she no doubt now regretted almost as much as he!

'There must be a vast number of years between your Uncle Charles and his wife.' It was a statement rather than a question. Diana looked on in concern as Gabriel paced the bedchamber with restless energy.

It had been something of a surprise to Diana to learn that the green-and-gold bedchambers Gabriel had requested be made ready for them were actually adjoining rooms, the door between the two rooms standing open, a fact that he had taken advantage of the moment the butler departed.

There was no doubting that the arrangement was slightly improper, implying as it did an intimacy between them that did not exist. But at the same time, still disturbed by the undercurrents in this household, Diana felt comfortable with the knowledge that Gabriel was but a room's width away if she should need him.

Neither of them had as yet taken advantage of the warm water that had already been brought up to the bedchambers along with their luggage; instead, Diana had dismissed her maid before sitting down heavily upon the bed to watch Gabriel begin that silent pacing.

He glanced at her now. 'Almost thirty, I believe.'

'You do not seem particularly fond of your aunt…'

'How very astute of you to notice!'

She frowned at the sarcasm in Gabriel's tone. 'Why did you not simply explain to me, when we received Miss Britton's first letter, the complexity of the situation here?'

He became suddenly still. 'What situation?'

'To begin with, that your uncle's wife was not the contemporary of your mother that I had thought her to be?' Diana grimaced. She knew it was not so unusual to find elderly men of the *ton* married to much younger women, but even so…

'As I have already stated—to you, to Caroline and to Mrs Prescott—I believe I am not in the habit of explaining myself to anyone.'

Diana could only imagine the circumstances under

which he had told the outspoken Caroline that! 'Surely you must have known I would be surprised to find Mrs Prescott so young in years?'

'Perhaps.'

There was no 'perhaps' about it in Diana's eyes. 'And she and your uncle have resided here with your mother since your father died?'

'So it would seem.' His mouth twisted with distaste.

'But surely it was kind of your aunt and uncle to give up their own home in order to live here and care for your mother?' she said uneasily.

'A word of advice, Diana—do not believe everything that you hear here.' Gabriel looked down at her intently. 'Most especially do not believe anything that Mrs Prescott has to say.'

Diana's eyes widened. 'I do not understand…'

'Then permit me to explain,' he said. 'Mr and Mrs Prescott did not give up their home and move here out of concern for my mother. I made it my business to know that their house, along with everything else of value, was reclaimed by the bailiffs in order to pay off Charles's considerable gambling debts.'

Diana blinked. 'And now you believe him to be lining his own pockets with your mother's inheritance?'

'Let us hope not too deeply.' He frowned. 'I believe my father knew his brother-in-law well enough to have left his will in such a way as to make it impossible for anyone but my mother to touch the capital.'

'I realise this situation is not ideal, Gabriel, but perhaps, now that we have come here,' Diana ventured softly, 'we should try to make the best of it.'

'Is there a best of it?' Gabriel came to an abrupt halt

in front of her. 'If there is, then I wish you would tell me what it is.'

Diana gave an inward wince, knowing she fully deserved his displeasure when she had flouted his wishes and succeeded in bringing them both to this cold and inhospitable household to which he had once belonged.

Indeed, she could see only one positive aspect to this mess.

'Hopefully, you will be able to make your peace with your mother, at last.'

He sighed. 'How youthfully naïve you are, Diana.'

She looked at him searchingly, sensing a wealth of pain beneath his words. 'May I...would you like me to come with you when you visit with your mother?'

He raised an eyebrow. 'For what purpose?'

'Gabriel—'

'Diana?'

She frowned at the unmistakable mockery in his rebuke. 'If I am to become your wife, then surely my place is at your side?'

He looked down at her between narrowed lids. 'When you are my wife your place will not be at my side, but beneath me in my bed!'

Diana felt the warmth of the colour that darkened her cheeks at his deliberate crudeness. 'I understand the reason for your anger, my lord—'

'Anger?' he repeated incredulously. 'I assure you, what I feel at this moment is far too fierce to be called anything as lukewarm as anger!'

Once again she was aware of a rivulet of sensation down the length of her spine as she looked up into the burning intensity of those indigo-coloured eyes. But it was not just that icy shiver of apprehension she had experienced earlier. She and Malcolm had been friends and then sweethearts for years. Her acquaintance with this man had been only a matter of days, and yet in that brief time Diana had felt more of a sexual awakening than she had ever known in Malcolm's youthfully inexperienced arms. In years Gabriel was not so much older than Malcolm, yet he far outstripped him in sophistication and experience; he had kissed Diana more deeply, touched her more intimately, than anyone else had ever dared to do.

As she gazed at him beneath lowered lashes, Diana knew they were kisses and caresses that she had secretly longed would be repeated and his comment just now about being in bed together had only intensified that longing…

Instead of retreating from his anger, she instead raised her hand to lay her fingers lightly against his clenched cheek. He felt warm to the touch, his cheekbones rapier sharp beneath the skin, his eyes now so dark they appeared an inky liquid black.

'I am not a cat or a dog you might tame into docility with a stroke of your fingertips, Diana!' His voice sounded harsh in the sudden stillness that surrounded them, a nerve now pulsing in that clenched jaw.

Her gaze softened. 'I am not so foolish as to believe anyone could ever tame you, Gabriel,' she said huskily.

That nerve continued to pulse. 'Then what is it you are attempting to do to me?'

What was she doing? Diana questioned herself silently. She had forced him to follow here against his will. They were in a household with an unpleasant atmosphere, she was uneasy in the brittle company of the young and beautiful Mrs Prescott and she had yet to meet Gabriel's reclusive mother. And yet at this moment, here and now, only his obvious pain seemed of any relevance to her.

'I believe I am attempting to show you, no matter what you may think to the contrary, that I am not your enemy,' she said.

'I am aware of exactly what you are, Diana.'

'Which is…?'

He snorted. 'A naïve and idealistic young lady who, despite her own experiences to the contrary, still somehow believes the situation that exists in this house could have a happy ending.'

Gabriel had set out to wound with his harshness and knew he had succeeded as she gave a pained flinch and her fingers left his cheek to slowly drop back to her side. At the same time, he realised with a frown, removing the warmth he had briefly experienced beneath the concerned compassion of her touch.

Damn it, he did not need anyone's pity, least of all hers.

Sexual passion, however, he knew from experience, allowed for very little thought other than the satisfaction of aroused desire. And he was aroused, Gabriel realised wryly; all of his recent anger and frustration was suddenly channelled into sexual awareness as he looked down at Diana beneath hooded lids. As he admired the slight dishevelment of the red-gold curls that threatened to escape their pins, the paleness of her cheeks, her neck a delicate arch above the light flush that coloured the swell of her breasts, which were visible above the low neckline of the rose-coloured gown she wore. Gabriel could easily imagine her graceful neckline adorned with pearls that bore the same delicate rosy hue as the full and tempting swell of her breasts.

'Gabriel?' Diana asked uncertainly as she obviously sensed, if not completely understood, the sudden sexual tension that had sprung up between them.

He raised a languid gaze, noting there was now a flush to her cheeks and a brightness in her eyes, her tongue moist and pink as it swept nervously across the sensual swell of her bottom lip. 'Are you afraid of me, Diana?' he voiced softly—aware, at this moment, that his raw emotions had stripped away his previous caution in regard to making love to her.

Her breasts quickly rose and fell, her throat moving above them as she swallowed before speaking. 'Should I be?'

He gave a rueful smile. 'Undoubtedly.'

She shook her head, unwittingly releasing several of her curls from the pins keeping them precariously in place. 'I do not believe you would ever hurt me, Gabriel.'

His smile became wolfish. 'I assure you, at this moment, I am more than capable of causing someone harm.'

Her gaze remained unwaveringly on his. 'I did not say you were not capable of harming me, Gabriel, only that I do not believe you would ever choose to do so.'

Then she knew more than he did himself—because at this moment he could envisage nothing he would enjoy more than to pick her up in his arms, throw her down upon the bed and rip the clothes from her body before ravishing her where she lay.

Or, alternatively, laying her down upon the bed before releasing her hair completely and then leisurely removing every item of clothing that she wore before slowly exploring with his lips, tongue and hands every perfect, delectable inch of her.

His hands clenched at his sides as he could almost taste her pleasure. 'You are awakening the beast that exists in myself and every other man,' he warned her, knowing he was seriously in danger of casting all sense aside and kissing her passionately.

For once in her well-ordered life she did not want to behave cautiously, only wished to banish the coldness that existed between herself and Gabriel even as she hungered for the promise of passion she saw in those piercing blue-black eyes as he looked down at her so intensely.

Many years ago her father had shown her a picture in one of the books he kept in his study of a sleek black panther; at this moment Gabriel reminded her of that big cat. Feral and sleek. Predatory. Dangerous.

She reached up once again and this time touched the silky black softness of his hair as it fell rakishly across his forehead. Long seconds passed and she held her breath in anticipation as he looked deep into the depths of her clear and steady blue gaze, down over the delicacy of her nose and across the creamy pallor of her cheeks, before lingering, settling, on the parted swell of her lips.

She felt the intensity of that gaze almost like a caress as her heartbeats quickened and a warmth spread from her breasts down to between her thighs. She wanted, needed, to be close to him, wanted so much to hold him, to banish, even briefly, the pain he was obviously suffering—

'No, damn it!' Gabriel suddenly grasped the tops of her arms and put her firmly away from him, his expression savage as he continued to glare down at her.

Diana stumbled slightly as she felt the coldness of his rejection, her humiliation complete as he turned his back on her to walk across the room and stand in front of one of the huge bay windows looking out over the stables.

What had she expected? That they would somehow be united by the uncomfortable atmosphere that existed in this household? That she would be the one to whom Gabriel turned for comfort because of the strain he felt at being back here?

If Diana had expected either of those things to occur, then she obviously was as naïvely idealistic as he had just accused her of being; he had made it more than clear that he would not be here at all if not for her interference. Something he was very unlikely to forgive her for...

She straightened her shoulders. 'Perhaps now might be a good time for you to leave me the privacy in which to wash and change for dinner.'

Gabriel drew in a deep and laboured breath as he clearly heard the hurt beneath the coolness of Diana's tone, a hurt he knew had been caused by his rejection of the warmth and comfort she had so freely offered him.

As much as he might long to accept that offer, to just

accept the comfort of Diana's body and forget everything but their mutually satisfying physical release, he could not bring himself to do it—and not just because he wished to wait until after they were married.

The mere thought of consummating their relationship for the first time in the oppression of this house was enough to dampen all arousal. No, better by far that she should suffer a little hurt now than that either of them should ever be haunted by that particular memory.

He drew in a ragged breath. 'You still have absolutely no idea what is going on in this house, do you, Diana?'

She looked confused. 'You have told me some of it and I know there is an unpleasantness of atmosphere here.'

Gabriel gave a hard, humourless laugh. 'If only that were all it was.'

'Then talk to me, Gabriel,' Diana encouraged. 'Let me share this with you.'

'So that you can attempt to fix it? Just as you have fixed so many other things for your own family since your mother abandoned you so cruelly?'

She flinched, stepping away from him. 'You are the one who is being deliberately cruel.'

'I'm sorry, Diana. This house and the people in it make me feel like being cruel.' Gabriel ran an agitated hand through the heavy thickness of his hair.

Diana's heart instantly softened again at this explanation. 'I understand—'

'You understand nothing!' He gave a sudden hard bark of derisive laughter. 'God, I have been back in this house only a matter of minutes and already I feel as if I am suffocating!'

'Then confiding in me can surely only help to ease your suffering.' Her hand once again rested on the rigid tension of his arm as she looked up at him pleadingly.

'Do you seriously believe that?'

'It cannot do any harm.'

'You are wrong, Diana. So very wrong.' Gabriel shook his head, at the same time knowing that if they were going to stay here, even if only for tonight, then it would not be fair to leave her in ignorance of the past any longer. There was another person in this household who would be only too delighted to regale her with a different version of events. 'Very well.' He became very still. 'You have asked to know and said that you wish to share this with me.'

Diana could not help but notice how his mouth had become an uncompromising line, his eyes once again like hard onyx. Knowing that he was not in possession of his usual arrogant control at this moment, she thought that his mood was now such that his previous taunt about her mother's abandonment was likely to fade into insignificance under the avalanche of what he was about to tell her.

Gabriel gave a wry smile as he saw the apprehension in her gaze. 'Or perhaps you have changed your mind and would now prefer not to know?'

Diana swallowed hard, a small cowardly part of her wishing to say, yes, she had changed her mind, that she did not want to hear what he was about to tell her, yet at the same time knowing that nothing in this household would make sense until she heard what he had to say...

Her chin rose proudly. 'I trust I have never shied away from hearing the truth, my lord.'

He bared his teeth in a pained grimace. 'I have no doubt you will want to run from this particular truth.'

Her apprehension grew even as she continued to meet his gaze with steady resolve. 'Nothing you tell me now will change my opinion of you.'

'Which is?' he asked curiously.

She moistened her lips before answering. 'I know you to be a man who feels a deep obligation in regard to your guardianship of my two sisters and myself. That Lord Vaughn, who was an officer and is a gentleman, holds you in high regard.'

'None of what you have said so far is your own opinion of me,' he pointed out.

Perhaps that was because it seemed wiser, with their own acquaintance so new, for Diana to acknowledge how others regarded him. Her own feelings towards the man to whom she was betrothed were still too tenuous to be voiced. That Gabriel was both arrogant, and impatient of the foibles of others, Diana already knew. That he chose to keep his own emotions firmly hidden from prying eyes behind a wall of hauteur, she was also aware—but as to how she *personally* felt towards him?

She found herself drawn to his unmistakable good looks. Quivered when he took her into his strong arms and pressed her body against his hard and muscled one. Trembled when he kissed her with those sensually sculptured lips. Was filled with a yearning desire when he touched and caressed her with assured and yet gentle hands.

Things that she had no wish to share with him right at this moment!

'Do not trouble yourself to look for an answer when

it is obviously so difficult for you to find a suitable one,' Gabriel said bitterly as he saw how Diana was struggling to find an answer that was not too insulting.

She looked uncomfortable. 'Perhaps you should just tell me what you feel it is I need to know?'

'Where to start?' he mused darkly.

'The beginning?'

Gabriel looked at her. 'That would be eight years ago.'

Eight years ago? At the time of the scandal that had ripped Gabriel's life, and that of his family, apart?

His jaw was tightly clenched. 'I have told you of the scandal that resulted in my being disgraced and disinherited.'

'Yes…'

He nodded tersely, no longer looking at her. 'What you also need to know, if you are to make sense of the tensions that now exist in this household, is—' He broke off, suddenly breathing quickly.

'Gabriel, if you would rather not—'

'The fact that you forced us both to come here no longer leaves me any choice in the matter,' he said grimly.

Diana gave a shiver of apprehension. Gabriel had been honest with her from the first; he had not hesitated to tell her the worst of himself as well as the best, but even so she knew from the fierceness of his manner now that what he was about to tell her was so extreme, so immense, that it could destroy her regard for him for ever…

Chapter Nine

'Jennifer Prescott, the wife of my Uncle Charles, is the same woman I was accused of seducing and then later abandoning when she announced she was expecting my child.'

Diana felt as if she had received a heavy blow to her chest as she took an unsteady step backwards, her breath arresting in her throat, all the colour draining from her cheeks as she stared up at Gabriel in dazed incomprehension. Then she stumbled until the backs of her knees hit the bed and she sat down abruptly upon its softness.

It could not be true—could it?

The young and beautiful woman married to Gabriel's uncle was the same woman who had accused Gabriel of seducing her eight years ago? Worse, Charles Prescott was the man his father had paid handsomely to marry her in Gabriel's stead because he believed that woman was expecting his son's child?

It was too incredible.

Unbelievable.

And yet, was it really so unbelievable a solution? By marrying Charles Prescott, that young woman had still married into Gabriel's family, thereby resulting in her child being born into the family, too. Except the child had not survived…

Besides which, this knowledge now made perfect sense of the open hostility between an icily scathing Gabriel and the outraged Jennifer Prescott.

She raised startled lids to find Gabriel looking across at her with a watchful and narrow-eyed intensity, his jaw arrogantly challenging, his shoulders stiff and his hands tense at his sides.

That wary tension told her more clearly than anything else could have done that the words she spoke next were crucial, not just to the here and now, but to any continuing relationship between them.

But imagining Gabriel and the beautiful Jennifer Prescott engaged together in intimacy was—

No!

Having seen the other woman for herself, and acknowledged her beauty, did not mean Diana should now not believe Gabriel's claim of innocence. Admittedly, it was difficult to imagine any man being immune to that dark and exotic beauty, but if he said he was, then once again she had no reason to doubt his word. Just as she had assured Caroline two days ago, if there could not be love between herself and Gabriel, then surely they must at least have honesty?

Diana either trusted and believed in the word of the man to whom she was now betrothed, or she did not. It was that simple. She stood up to cross the room and stand in front of the window that looked out over the stables and extensive grounds, her thoughts racing as she attempted to come to terms with what she'd been told.

Gabriel's insistence that he was innocent of that past scandal had not changed. It would, she was sure, never change; he was a man who stated the truth, and be damned with whether anyone chose to believe him or not.

She chose to believe him. She must!

Her gaze was very clear and direct when she finally looked across at him still tensely waiting for her response. 'I believe I owe you an apology, Gabriel.'

'*What?*'

Diana gave a slight nod at his shocked explosion. 'I should have realised that you had another reason other than the past tensions between your mother and yourself for refusing to visit Faulkner Manor.'

Gabriel stared at her wordlessly. For such a coolly composed and self-contained young lady, Diana succeeded in surprising him far more often than he would have wished. He had expected her initial shock at his disclosure concerning Jennifer Prescott, and in that he had not been disappointed. However, he had expected either tears or angry accusations to follow, not that she would apologise to him!

In acting so maturely, she had made a mockery of his own anger and resentment at once again finding himself at Faulkner Manor...'My uncle's marriage to Jennifer Lindsay, as she was then, is not a subject on which I have ever wished to dwell,' he told her.

She looked at him sympathetically. 'I can understand that.'

'Can you?'

'But of course,' she said. 'Not only were you not believed eight years ago, but the woman who made the accusation was accepted into your family whilst you were banished. That must have seemed doubly cruel.'

Cruel to the point that Gabriel had left, vowing never to step foot inside the Manor again. And yet here he was, not only back in his childhood home, but welcomed back—if Jennifer Prescott's obvious shock and dismay at his reappearance could be called a welcome—by the very woman who had once set out to completely destroy his life.

'Yes, it was,' he agreed.

'Were your uncle and aunt acquainted before your father arranged their marriage?'

'I presume so,' he said.

'But you do not know for sure?'

'I don't see how that's important, to be honest,' Gabriel said. 'Charles has always been a frequent visitor to Faulkner Manor and Jennifer's family lived nearby. Usually he came to ask my father to make him a loan they both knew would never be repaid. But what could my father do? Charles was always in debt to the loan sharks, but he was my mother's brother and her only living relative.'

'Those circumstances would have made it difficult for your father to refuse him, certainly.'

'Impossible,' he reiterated.

'And is your uncle a handsome man?' she asked pensively.

Gabriel frowned. 'I fail to see what my uncle's looks have to do with anything.'

Diana shrugged creamy shoulders. 'I was merely curious as to whether or not there is a family resemblance between you and him.'

'Why?' Gabriel's impatience with her questions was barely contained.

Why, indeed? Diana mused. Things were so much more complicated than she could ever have realised before coming here. Jennifer Prescott was an undoubted beauty. The fact that both she and her husband resided at Faulkner Manor, running the house and estates whilst Gabriel's mother remained in her rooms did, as Gabriel had accused earlier, make his aunt the mistress of this household. And the other woman's obvious shock and dismay when she realised Gabriel had come here had been plain to see.

But as well as all of those things was a question that no one seemed to have provided an answer to as yet...

Now that Diana had met Jennifer Prescott—and, she admitted uncomfortably, taken an instant dislike to her—it was a question that greatly intrigued her. Namely, if Jennifer Lindsay had not been expecting Gabriel's child eight years ago, then whose child had it been?

She smiled at the enormity of her imaginings. 'No doubt your uncle is a portly gentleman of middle years—'

'On the contrary, he's an extremely handsome rogue of middle years,' Gabriel drawled drily. 'In fact, I believe Charles was considered something of a catch until his penchant for gambling put him beyond the pale as far as the marriage-minded mamas of society were concerned.'

'I see…'

He gave her a frustrated look. 'What exactly do you see?'

Diana was not entirely sure; she needed to spend more time here, to observe Mrs Prescott—and perhaps her husband if he should return to Faulkner Manor whilst they were still here—to fully put into words what was at this moment only the beginnings of a suspicion.

She shook her head. 'Perhaps we have spoken of this enough for now. There is still some time before we are expected downstairs for dinner—would this not be a good time for you to visit your mother?'

'It would, yes.' In truth, whilst Gabriel now wished very much to see his mother again, he also admitted to an inner feeling of reluctance to do so. His relationship with his mother had always been closer than the one with his father, but it was a closeness that had ceased to exist the moment he'd left home. Not a word or a letter had been exchanged between the two of them in all that time. As such, and in spite of Alice Britton's assurances in her letter that his mother longed to see him again, he still had his doubts.

'I shall be perfectly content in your absence, Gabriel,' Diana assured him briskly. 'Indeed, I would welcome the time in which to wash and change before dinner. After all…' her lips curved in anticipation '…Mrs Prescott must not be allowed to think you are to marry an unfashionable young lady!'

Gabriel scowled. 'Mrs Prescott can go hang herself for all I care about her opinion on anything, least of all the woman I am to marry.'

Diana's smile was rueful. 'This is something between us two ladies, I believe, Gabriel.'

'Have a care, Diana.' He looked troubled. 'She is a woman whom I have learnt at my cost it is dangerous to cross.'

'I may have lived all of my life in the country, Gabriel, but I assure you that I am not without a certain knowledge of my own sex. As such, I believe Mrs Prescott will quickly learn that I am not a woman without thoughts and ideas of my own.'

Gabriel looked at her admiringly. He could not help but be aware of the steely determination in her manner, the same strength of character that had stood her in such good stead during all those years of caring for her father and two sisters and had encouraged her to accept his own marriage proposal. The same force of will that had enabled Diana to travel into Cambridgeshire completely against his wishes.

To his surprise, he suddenly found that he could no longer feel any anger towards her in that regard, accepting the explanation that she had believed she was acting in his best interests. And perhaps she had...

And perhaps Gabriel had delayed his visit to his mother for long enough! 'Your fortitude is to be admired, my dear.'

She gave him a confident smile. 'We may be marrying for convenience rather than love, my lord, but that does not make me any less loyal to you and our betrothal.'

He had no doubts about that when he acknowledged that Diana had travelled into Cambridgeshire alone, but for her maid, simply because she considered it was the right thing to do. Just as she showed every indication of remaining here, despite now knowing of the true unpleasantness of the situation that existed here.

Gabriel could not help but feel scornful of the young man who had so recently rejected the love and regard in which Diana had so obviously held him, even more so because his own respect for her was growing by the minute.

'I am not sure I deserve such loyalty, Diana,' he murmured huskily as he reached down to take her hand in his before lifting it to his lips and placing a kiss upon her lace-covered palm, folding her fingers about that kiss before releasing her hand.

'I live in the hopes that you may eventually do so!' Her eyes sparkled up at him mischievously.

He found himself returning the warmth of her smile. That smile fading again as he grimly considered the task in front of him. 'As you suggest, I will visit my mother now and leave you to change for dinner.'

Diana had not even realised she had stopped breathing until Gabriel left the bedchamber and she felt that breath released in a shaky sigh. Simply because he had taken her hand in his and kissed it? Ridiculous. Dozens of men, young as well as old, had kissed her hand in the past—but it had always been the back of her hand, never her palm…

There had been an unmistakable intimacy in Gabriel having placed that kiss in her palm before then folding her fingers about it. Diana could still feel the warmth of his lips through the lace of her glove. She was just so totally aware of everything about him, from his dishevelled black hair to his rain-spattered Hessians. There was no doubting that, perfectly groomed and tailored, Gabriel was one of the most devilishly handsome men she had ever met. But he was even more so slightly dishevelled and less than his usual arrogant and assured self.

None of which was in the least relevant to their present dilemma! Well…it was mostly Gabriel's dilemma, Diana admitted, but one to which she had assured him she had no intentions of abandoning him.

Alice Britton's concerns for Felicity Faulkner, for the strangeness of the situation here, had, Diana considered, been completely justified. There was indeed something bizarre about this household.

'Gabriel?'

Having only seconds ago entered his bedchamber, Gabriel now looked up to see Diana standing in the open doorway between their two rooms, the heavy weight he felt pressing down upon him momentarily dissipating as he took in the beauty of her appearance.

As she had intended, she had obviously taken advantage of his hour's absence in which to wash and change before dinner, her cream silk-and-lace gown perfectly complimenting the magnolia of her skin, her eyes a clear blue, her lips a full and strawberry blush, and her red-gold curls kept in place by two pearl-encrusted combs.

The picture she looked was breathtakingly beautiful.

His expression softened somewhat. 'You look…very lovely, Diana.'

'As intended.' Her manner was brisk as she stepped into his bedchamber. 'How was your mother?'

Gabriel sobered instantly. 'It is difficult to tell when

she remained asleep the whole time I was in the room.'
Nevertheless, he had been shocked at how much older
his mother looked; her face was much thinner and paler
than it used to be, and there was an abundance of grey
amongst the darkness of her hair as it lay in loose curls
about her shoulders.

Diana frowned. 'She was not aware of your presence
at all?'

'No.'

'Did you attempt to make her aware?'

'Of course I did!' Gabriel said. 'I both held my mother's hand and talked to her, but she remained completely
oblivious to my presence.'

Diana could see by the harshness of his expression
how much it pained him to admit it. No doubt, having
prepared himself for the meeting, it had been something
of a disappointment that she had not even woken long
enough to acknowledge that her only son was in the
room with her.

She moved forwards to place her hand lightly on his
jacket-clad arm, at once able to feel his tension beneath
her fingertips. 'No doubt you will have better luck in
the morning.'

'Let us hope so.' In truth, he had been very disturbed by his mother's condition and wished he had
not remained away as long as he had. A fact he must
needs relay to Alice Britton at the earliest opportunity,
along with his apology for having written back to her
so tersely two days ago. If anything, his mother's old
companion had understated the situation that existed
here, so much so that Gabriel felt inclined to remove
his mother as soon as she felt well enough to travel.

Always supposing that Felicity would agree to leave with him, that was…

'I am sure, when she wakes, that your mother will be overjoyed to see you again, Gabriel,' Diana said, smiling at him encouragingly.

His answering smile was less assured. 'Let us hope so.'

'Were you and your mother close once?'

'Very.' Gabriel's father had already been aged one and thirty when he and the twenty-year-old Felicity had married thirty years ago. He'd been a man very set in his ways and not inclined to visit the nursery much after his son was born. He'd only really taken an interest in Gabriel once he reached an age where it was possible to put him up on a horse or teach him how to shoot a gun.

Not so Gabriel's mother, who had spent much of her day in the nursery with her only child. Consequently, Gabriel's relationship with his mother had always been that much closer; to now see her looking old and frail was hard indeed for him to bear.

Diana nodded. 'Then I cannot doubt you will become so again.'

Gabriel eyed her ruefully. 'It is as well that one of us is an optimist.'

'Not only that, but I have laid your evening clothes out ready on the bed for you!'

Gabriel turned to look at where his evening clothes were indeed laid out ready for him to change into once he had washed and tidied his appearance.

'I felt it was the least I could do considering I am the

one responsible for depriving you of your valet.' Her
smile became impish.

He eyed her quizzically after noting that even his
shirt studs lay neatly beside his necktie. 'Most women
would have no idea what was required.'

Her expression saddened. 'My father decided to dispense with the services of his valet two years before he
died, so it was left to me to see that he did not appear
downstairs every morning and evening dressed in his
nightclothes.'

Gabriel frowned as she avoided meeting his searching gaze by removing her hand from his arm to turn
away and look out of the window. She was so young
to have needed to take upon her own shoulders the
responsibility of her increasingly reclusive father and
two younger, impulsive sisters. Even so, he could detect
no resentment towards her family in her tone or expression—only love and acceptance.

Diana was like no other woman Gabriel had ever
met.

Like no other woman he was ever likely to meet.

And she was very shortly to become his wife.

He seriously doubted that he was deserving of such
luck, considering the haphazard way in which he had
chosen that wife. He would be nothing but a fool if he
were to take that luck for granted.

Gabriel looked admiringly at the fragile arch of
Diana's nape. The softness of the hair that fell in enticing curls against her skin. The creamy softness of her
shoulders and arms revealed by the wide neckline and
short sleeves of her cream-silk gown. The delicate

length of her spine. The implied curves of her body beneath the drape of that silk.

And he knew that he no longer cared about where they were and why they were here.

He wanted—no, needed—this connection with Diana like he'd never needed anything before in his life.

Chapter Ten

From the weighty and lengthy silence behind her, Diana believed that she had somehow displeased Gabriel. By putting his evening clothes out ready for him to change into once he returned from visiting his mother? Or perhaps she was mistaken, and it was not she who had displeased him, but the unsatisfactory visit to his mother that still troubled him?

'My lord—oh!' She came to a startled halt as she turned to find him standing just behind her.

So close she could now feel the heat of his body through the thin material of her gown. So close that as she slowly raised her gaze to look at him, she could see the black ring that encircled the dark indigo of his eyes, giving them the appearance of that intriguing and mesmerising midnight-blue.

Her own eyes dropped from the intensity of his stare, only to come to rest on the sensual curve of his mouth, firm and sculptured lips that she knew would feel soft and compelling against her own.

She suddenly pulled herself up short. These were not thoughts, memories, she should be having when they were alone together in his bedchamber!

'Diana?'

She raised heavy lids as a quiver of awareness ran the length of her spine at the husky compulsion in his tone. It seemed she had been mistaken, that Gabriel was not displeased with her at all, that his emotions were something else entirely...

She moistened her lips with the tip of her tongue before attempting to speak. 'It really is time you considered changing for dinner.'

His own lids dropped, the expression in his eyes hidden by long, dark lashes. 'Gladly—if you would care to continue to act as my valet?'

She swallowed hard, her mouth having suddenly become dry as even the air seemed filled with heated expectation. 'Of course I will help if you feel it necessary.'

He smiled slightly. 'Not necessary, exactly, but I believe we might perhaps enjoy the intimacy?'

Betraying heat suffused her body as she responded to the lazy sensuality in Gabriel's voice. Everything else, everyone else, receded to the back of her mind, as she could see and feel only him. 'If you would care to turn around?'

He held her gaze with his own for long, timeless seconds before he gave the slightest of nods and turned the broad width of his back towards her. Something, she believed, that he did not choose to do with many people...

Gabriel could feel how Diana's hands trembled

slightly as she raised them to the neckline of his jacket, her fingers lightly brushing against the soft darkness of his hair as it curled on to the high collar, causing him to almost groan in response.

The visit to his mother's bedchamber had been totally unproductive: he had not so much as been able to speak with her, let alone gauge how she felt about him being here. Returning to find Diana waiting for him had filled him with a strange and unfamiliar feeling of gladness. Of unaccustomed warmth.

It was the oddest sensation for a man who had spent the past eight years coldly shunning friends as well as enemies.

Gabriel was so much taller than Diana that it was not easy to slide the perfectly tailored jacket from his shoulders and down the length of his arms. She was very aware of everything about him as she inadvertently touched the width of his shoulders, his muscled arms and finally the bare skin of his long and elegant hands.

She felt decidedly hot—and very bothered—by the time he turned to face her, obviously intending her to now unbutton his waistcoat. Evidence, if she should need it, that this had very little to do with her acting as his valet and everything to do with the intimacy he had mentioned earlier.

She was so aware of his gaze upon her that she fumbled slightly with unfastening the buttons on the silver-brocade waistcoat, her fingers coming into contact with his shirt-covered chest as she slipped this garment down his arms before discarding it on .to the bed beside his jacket.

She hesitated, then asked, 'Would you like me to

remove your necktie and shirt, too, or do wish to do that for yourself?'

'Which would you prefer?' he growled softly.

Diana's heart leapt in her chest at the mere thought of unbuttoning and removing his shirt and, in doing so, laying bare the wide expanse of firm and muscled flesh beneath. Her gaze flickered up before as quickly moving away again as she saw how focused his own gaze was on the rapid rise and fall of her breasts. 'Is this altogether wise, Gabriel?' she murmured huskily.

'Does everything between us have to be wise?' he countered.

She raised startled lids. 'We will be expected downstairs for dinner shortly.'

'It is not my dinner for which I feel hungry.' There was an incredible heat in his gaze as he continued to look down at her.

Diana found she could no longer look away from the intensity of those dark and compelling eyes, instead becoming lost in the warm invitation he made no effort to hide. Despite all the recent conflict, they had found a closeness here at Faulkner Manor that was very precious. Alone in his bedchamber there existed only the two of them, so close, so very aware of each other.

Assisting him to undress did not feel at all like it did when she helped her father—

'I would hope not.'

'Surely I did not say that aloud?' Hot colour suffused her cheeks as he teasingly answered the comment she had believed existed only inside her head, but which she had obviously voiced aloud.

'You did,' he confirmed, liking those bright wings

of colour in her cheeks, her eyes a bright and sparkling blue as she looked up at him. 'How does it feel then, Diana?' he asked gruffly.

'I—different. So very different.' Her voice was soft and breathy and almost made him shiver in response.

'But not unpleasant?' he pressed.

'I—no, not at all.'

'Then I see no reason why we should not continue…' Gabriel reached out to take both of her hands before lifting them and placing them flat against his shirt-covered chest.

Touching him, able to feel the muscled hardness of his chest through the fine silk material of his shirt, the firm beating of his heart and his warmth, Diana saw every reason why they should not continue.

And every reason why they should!

Her trembling fingers moved to unfasten the meticulous knot of his necktie before placing it on the bed with his jacket and waistcoat, aware of his intense regard as she slowly released the four buttons at the throat of his silk shirt.

The two sides of the shirt fell apart to reveal that the skin beneath was indeed firm and lightly tanned; there was a light dusting of dark hair upon his chest.

'Would you scream in protest if I were to remove my travel-worn shirt completely?'

Diana raised blonde brows. 'I never scream, my lord.'

There were several scenarios in which Gabriel could imagine that she might—scenarios in which his lips and hands were upon the most intimate parts of her body.

He reached up to pull the shirt over his head before discarding it untidily to the floor. 'Leave it,' he instructed as she would have picked it up. 'For God's sake, Diana, would you just touch me?' His jaw was tightly clenched as he steeled himself for the first sensation of those slender fingers upon his naked flesh.

He watched as the moist tip of her tongue moved nervously across her lips even as she raised those hands and placed her fingers lightly against his skin, hesitantly at first, and then more assuredly as she slowly traced the firm contours of his chest. Gabriel sucked in his breath and held it there as her fingernails scraped lightly across the hardened nubs nestled amongst the dark dusting of hair.

Diana stilled, eyes wide as she looked up at him. 'You seem to like that as much as—' She broke off with a self-conscious gasp.

'As you did?' Gabriel finished throatily. 'Oh, yes!'

'I had no idea.' She touched him again, delight now warming her cheeks as she saw the way those hard nubbins became harder in response, the tension in his shoulders and clenched hands also revealing the intense pleasure he felt from the caress of her fingertips.

As a child Diana had used to love sitting in her father's library, looking through the hundreds of books he had there, and Gabriel's wide and muscled chest, the flat contours of his stomach, were so very much like the drawings of the Greek gods in one of those books.

It was also exhilarating, she discovered, to be able to return some of the pleasure she'd experienced when Gabriel touched her and placed his mouth on her. Ah, yes…

'Diana, what are you doing?'

Her lips and tongue were now against the tautness

of Gabriel's flesh, her mouth curving into a smile of satisfaction at she both heard and felt his arousal. She glanced up at him beneath lowered lashes, noting the tension in his jaw and the nerve pulsing in his throat. 'Do you wish me to stop?'

'Dear God, no!' he groaned and one of his hands moved up to become entangled in the curls at her nape as he held her to him.

She needed no further invitation to continue to place open-mouthed kisses on his chest even as her hands moved lower, lightly caressing the muscled flatness of his stomach above the hardness of his arousal pressing against his pantaloons.

It surprised her that there was an answering warmth between her own thighs, her breasts becoming full and aching, the hardened tips chafing against the soft material of her shift.

It was a revelation to Diana that she received as much satisfaction in giving Gabriel physical pleasure as she did in receiving it—

'You might have considered locking the bedchamber door if you had intended bedding your future wife, Gabriel!' There was absolutely no apology in the scornful voice that sliced coldly through their intimacy.

Diana had sprung guiltily away from Gabriel at the first sound of that horribly familiar voice, her face paling as she saw Jennifer Prescott standing in the doorway that adjoined the two bedchambers. Humiliated colour brightened Diana's cheeks as the other woman looked across at her in utter contempt.

'And perhaps *you* should have considered knocking before entering,' Gabriel rasped into the chilling silence,

Diana able to feel the blazing heat of his body against her spine as he held her firmly in front of him.

His aunt's mouth sneered at them. 'You may rest assured I will make a point of doing so in future.'

'A better idea would be for you not to come to either of these bedchambers again whilst Diana and I are staying here,' Gabriel bit out. 'Now that you are here, perhaps you might like to tell us what it is you wanted?'

'You had been up here so long I thought it best to come and tell you both that dinner is ready to be served.'

'I had no idea that Faulkner Manor was so depleted of servants that you needed to behave as one yourself,' he jeered.

Jennifer gasped in outrage. 'You are so insulting, Gabriel!'

'I have not even begun to be insulting as yet,' he drawled.

There was an angry glitter in the other woman's eyes as her gaze first raked over Diana's dishevelled appearance before moving to his obvious state of undress, her dark gaze lingering avidly on the bare expanse of his muscled chest.

Gabriel's stomach roiled with distaste as he recognised the avaricious heat in her lingering gaze. 'You have satisfied your curiosity, now get out,' he ordered.

Her dark eyes blazed with fury. 'You will go too far one day,' she warned him.

He eyed her dismissively. 'Your threats hold no interest for me, madam.'

'Indeed?' Her dark gaze settled very briefly on the young woman who stood so still and silent in front of Gabriel. 'Does the same hold true for Lady Diana?'

Gabriel pulled Diana more firmly against the warmth of his chest. 'Be warned, madam, that I will view any attempt on your part to hurt Diana—by word or deed—as a personal attack on me. And I will respond accordingly.'

'Whoever would have thought you would become so sickeningly love-struck, Gabriel?' she openly mocked him now.

His gaze was positively glacial. 'I believe just knowing you has soured me to such tender feelings.'

Diana was now fully recovered from her embarrassment at being discovered in such an intimate situation with Gabriel; in fact, she felt emboldened, by both his responses and the protectiveness he now showed towards her. Or, rather, it was an illusion of protectiveness that would surely be rendered useless if he were to continue in his present vein. 'Was there something you wished to say to me, Mrs Prescott?' Her gaze was unwavering as she looked across the bedchamber at the other woman. 'Something I do not already know, that is,' she added caustically.

'Nothing that I am sure cannot wait until a more... convenient time, no,' his aunt said.

'Which this almost certainly is not,' Gabriel bit out.

Those brown eyes narrowed on him speculatively. 'I have no idea why you are in such a lather, Gabriel. After all, it is far from the first time I have seen you unclothed.' Triumph shone in her face as Diana was unable to repress her startled gasp. 'Admittedly you are more muscular than you used to be, but no doubt the brown birthmark upon your left thigh remains unchanged?'

'Get. Out.' Gabriel said through gritted teeth.

'A word of advice, Lady Diana,' the other woman ignored him to drawl mockingly. 'I believe you will come to realise that Gabriel has something of a selective memory.'

'When it comes to you it is very selective indeed,' Gabriel snarled. 'In fact, it is non-existent.'

Jennifer smiled tauntingly. 'Choosing not to remember something does not mean it did not happen.'

'And imagining something does not mean that it did,' he retorted.

Her smile remained triumphant. 'No doubt I will see you both downstairs shortly.' She turned back into the adjoining bedchamber, the sound of the outer door closing quietly behind her seconds later, evidence that she had gone.

Diana remained standing stiff and unmoving within the circle of Gabriel's arms, her earlier confidence shaken in the face of that barrage of scornful comments, her head awhirl. Admittedly the woman had meant to wound—where Diana was concerned, she had undoubtedly succeeded!—but that did not mean there was not some truth in her remarks, did it?

Jennifer Prescott claimed to have seen Gabriel unclothed in the past and had remarked how he was more muscular than he used to be. Even more damning, she'd revealed that he possessed a birthmark upon his left thigh. How did she know that piece of damning information when Diana herself did not?

'What are you thinking?'

Diana was very aware of how his body remained pressed so firmly against the length of her spine. But the earlier euphoria she had felt had very definitely faded! Gabriel's closeness now made her aware of the shallowness of his breathing and of the hardness in his body as he waited for her answer.

She drew in a ragged breath. 'Is it true that you have a birthmark upon your left thigh, my lord?'

'Damn it!' he snarled.

'Do you?'

'Yes!'

'Dear God…' She pulled out of his arms and moved away from him, uncaring if she upset him, just needing to distance herself from him. To be allowed to think.

Gabriel gave her no time in which to do that. 'Diana, this is not what it seems.'

'Then tell me what it is!' She looked up at him with bewilderment. 'I trusted you, Gabriel, I put my faith in you…'

He immediately became aloof and distant. 'Nothing that has happened here should prevent you from continuing to do so.'

'Then please explain to me why it is that woman knows of a birthmark upon your thigh which you admit does exist?' A small part of her brain realised she was acting very illogically, but the jealousy that was rushing through her was making her ignore rationality and go straight to heated accusation!

Gabriel ran a frustrated hand through the heavy darkness of his hair. He was not accustomed to being questioned in this way. In fact, he had sworn long ago that he would never try to explain himself to anyone ever again.

Except…Jennifer's taunt had sounded so very damning and he realised that Diana had already accepted so much on his word alone. She had absolutely no reason to trust him so blindly, beyond the belief that Gabriel had no reason to lie to her...

Damn Jennifer Prescott! Damn her to hell and back!

His jaw clenched. 'Did you never escape the confines of the schoolroom when you were a child to swim in the local river in your underclothes with the children from the village?'

'No.'

Somehow Gabriel had known that would be Diana's answer; she had been far too occupied, from a very young age, with the care of her father and sisters, to have the time or inclination to behave like a child herself.

'I did,' he said evenly. 'Often.'

'And your uncle's wife was one of the children from the village who also swam there?'

'She was Jennifer Lindsay then, of course, but, yes, she was one of the children who came from the village to swim.' Gabriel's tone was challenging rather than apologetic.

As if he expected Diana to immediately doubt him...

She was still too shaken by her own wildly see-sawing emotions to know what to think. What to believe.

Until she came to Faulkner Manor the young woman from Gabriel's past had been faceless and nameless. To discover that woman was now married to Gabriel's uncle was disturbing enough. To now learn that Gabriel had shared much of his childhood with the youthful Jennifer Lindsay was even more unnerving.

He would have been aged only twenty when the

scandal occurred. A young buck, no doubt eager for adventure and physical conquest. Jennifer Prescott was an incredibly beautiful and sensual woman now, and there was no reason to suppose she had been any less so eight years ago. How could the younger, virile and more adventurous Gabriel have possibly resisted her?

Diana had been so certain earlier that his word was to be trusted. That he had no reason to be untruthful. Indeed, that he was not a man who cared enough about anyone or anything enough to ever feel the need to lie or prevaricate.

But she could not deny that Mrs Prescott's taunts had shaken her confidence somewhat concerning Gabriel's version of past events. She desperately wanted to believe him. She needed to do so if there was to be any future for the two of them.

Yet, at the same time, she had to admit to the fact that a few seeds of doubt had been sown in her mind…

She shook of her head in an attempt to rid herself of unwanted thoughts, her gaze no longer able to meet Gabriel's. 'We can talk of this later—'

'We will talk of it *now*, Diana, or never.' He appeared a complete stranger to her, even the bare expanse of his chest and arms doing little to lessen the chasm widening between them.

Diana frowned. 'There is so much more now for me to consider…'

'Such as?'

'Mrs Prescott's beauty is undeniable…'

He scowled darkly. 'I have no interest in that woman. I never did, nor will I ever have any interest in her. You either accept my word on that or you do not.'

Diana looked at him closely. His expression was totally uncompromising: his eyes glacial, cheekbones drawn tight, his mouth a hard and unforgiving line above the arrogance of his jutting jaw.

Yes, totally uncompromising, and if Diana should doubt him, she knew he would be unforgiving.

She sighed. 'It is most unfair of you to pressure me in this way when so much has already happened since our arrival here.'

Was it unfair? Gabriel considered. Diana had learnt so much more about the past since arriving at Faulkner Manor. Was it too much for her to simply take his word this time that something was so, simply because he said that it was?

Perhaps, he acknowledged grudgingly.

But Gabriel had not sought, or wanted, anyone's good opinion of him for the past eight years. Pride dictated that he could not ask for it now, even from the courageous young woman who had agreed to become his wife.

'Will you not consider, Gabriel,' Diana continued huskily, 'how you would feel if the roles were reversed? If, perhaps, Malcolm Castle was to reveal to you his knowledge of a mole upon my left breast?'

'I am already acquainted with that mole myself,' Gabriel pointed out tautly.

Her cheeks warmed delicately. 'Yes, you are…'

His eyes narrowed. 'And if that gentleman and I *were* to converse on the subject, would he indeed be able to reveal his own knowledge of such an item?'

'Certainly not!' Her cheeks were now awash with colour.

'Then I fail to see the significance of such a comparison,' Gabriel said, hiding his relief at the news he was the first to gaze upon the beauty of Diana's naked breast.

He had not cared for hearing that Castle might have beaten him to it. He had not liked in the slightest even the thought of another being so intimately acquainted with the tender curves of her body. His violent feelings on the subject seemed to indicate an engaging of emotions that was completely unacceptable to him.

He straightened swiftly. 'I believe it is time you left now and allowed me to wash and change in preparation for dinner.'

Diana was no longer sure she even wished to go downstairs for dinner. Untrue! She knew that she had absolutely no desire at all to sit through a meal that promised to be uncomfortable at best and unpleasant at worst! But to make her excuses now would not only make her appear weak in the eyes of Jennifer Prescott, but unsupportive of Gabriel too.

Of course, Diana knew that the other woman had deliberately set out to cause dissention between herself and Gabriel, and she had undoubtedly succeeded; the earlier closeness that had existed between them had been badly shaken by the seeds of doubt that had been deliberately and maliciously put into Diana's mind. Doubts she dearly wished that she could dismiss as easily as she had everything else Gabriel had told her. But with the unreasoning jealousy still raging through her, she felt unable to do so.

That her feelings had been warming towards Gabriel she could not deny—how could she when she melted into his arms every time he so much as touched her! Yet it seemed that every tentative step they made towards a closeness, a regard for each other, was immediately nullified by something, or someone, which then resulted in a complete lack of understanding between them.

She had so enjoyed being given the freedom to touch and kiss him earlier, his masculine beauty so very exciting, his skin beneath her fingertips having the texture of steel encased in velvet—

'Diana!'

She gave a start as Gabriel's rebuke cut through her remembered enjoyment of those earlier caresses. 'As you suggest, I will leave you now.' She was deliberately dignified as she walked to the adjoining doorway.

'Perhaps you would like to wait for me in your bedchamber and we can go downstairs together?' he suggested. 'Unless you would prefer to go down alone and see whether my uncle's wife does not have some other remembered anecdotes of our idealistic childhood that she wishes to share with you?' he added caustically.

Diana barely repressed a shudder at the thought of any private conversation, on any subject, taking place between herself and that woman. 'I will wait in my bedchamber for you.'

'I thought perhaps you might.' Gabriel's soft taunt followed her from the room.

Her head remained high, her composure only deserting her once she had closed the door behind her and crossed the room to sink gracefully down upon the side of the bed.

She should not have come to Faulkner Manor!

Would she have preferred to remain in ignorance,

then? To have married Gabriel, only to learn later of Mrs Charles Prescott's identity as the woman from his past?

She just didn't know the answer to that question yet…

Chapter Eleven

'What on earth are you doing, Gabriel?' A frowning Jennifer Prescott, attired in a silk gown the same deep brown as her eyes, halted in the doorway of the dining room.

Gabriel barely glanced at her. 'What does it look as if I am doing?'

'I am sure that the table was perfectly set as it was!'

She glared her irritation at him, but he was unconcerned. He had requested Reeve to remove his place setting from the head of the table to the middle, so that he would now sit opposite a pale-faced Diana rather than down the length of the table at his uncle's wife.

He had been aware of her scheme as soon as he entered the dining room with a quietly composed Diana upon his arm. The obvious intention had been to make it appear that Jennifer and Gabriel were the host and hostess and Diana a mere guest.

'If I am to look across the table at anyone, then I would prefer it to be my fiancée.' He pulled Diana's chair back and saw her comfortably seated before strolling around the table to wait to take his place once the attentive butler had seen to the seating of Mrs Prescott.

Gabriel was completely aware of Diana's continued silence and how her cheeks still retained their earlier pallor. He had reluctantly accepted that it was he, even more than the vindictive Jennifer Prescott, who was to blame for her distress. The time it had taken him to wash and change before coming downstairs for dinner had also given him the opportunity to rid himself of his anger and consider things from Diana's viewpoint. He had behaved badly earlier, when he'd continued his stubborn stance that she could believe him or not about Jennifer Prescott's knowledge of his birthmark. It was no excuse for his arrogance that he had reacted out of habitual self-defence after eight years of keeping his own counsel.

He also admitted to feeling disquieted by Diana's mention of the man from her past. The more he considered Malcolm Castle, the less he liked him. He certainly had not appreciated hearing even the suggestion that he might have such intimate acquaintance with her body! So, much as he might still baulk at any further need to explain himself, he knew that, having realised his errors, he should have apologised to Diana before they came down for dinner. It was an apology that would now have to wait until this interminable dinner was over. He sighed inwardly.

'I realise that you have been…busy with other things this evening, Gabriel,' Jennifer said, waiting until after the soup course had been served and the butler had left the room before attempting to engage him in conversation. 'Too busy, I am sure, to have found the time in which to visit your mother?' Her smile appeared smugly complacent.

Gabriel glanced at her with distaste. 'Then you would be wrong, madam.'

'Oh?'

He frowned at the unmistakable sharpness in her tone. 'I was with my mother for some time earlier.'

'And how was Felicity this evening?'

He had not imagined it; there was now a definite defensive edge to her manner. 'Sleeping, as you said she might be,' Gabriel answered slowly, aware of Diana's frown as she glanced across the table at him. Because she, too, realised there was something strange about his aunt's behaviour?

'No doubt you found her much changed in appearance?' Jennifer continued to probe.

Gabriel's jaw clenched. 'No doubt.' He gave up all pretence of eating as he instead turned in his chair to face his uncle's wife. 'What interested me more was why, when my mother is so obviously not well, there was no nurse in attendance in her bedchamber?'

'Charles dismissed both the nurse and doctor some months ago. Felicity is so much better now that they were both deemed an unnecessary expense,' she explained airily as he glowered.

His eyes narrowed. 'Deemed unnecessary by whom?'

'By Charles, of course.'

'I was not aware he was a medical expert?'

'Do not be ridiculous, Gabriel—'

'I do not consider it in the least ridiculous to be concerned as to the lack of care my mother has been receiving these past few months.'

'Exactly what are you implying?' Angry colour now mottled Jennifer's cheeks. 'That Charles and I are somehow responsible for your mother's retreat from society?' She gave a disgusted snort. 'You know as well as I do the reason for Felicity's malaise is that her only son was forced to leave the country in disgrace, thereby causing her husband to sicken and die only two years later.'

One of Gabriel's hands clenched on his thigh beneath the table. He had to fight to stop himself getting up, placing his hands about Jennifer Prescott's throat and then squeezing the very life out of her! No one had ever before dared to even hint at what she just had openly stated.

Was he to blame? He could believe past events might have affected his mother that way, but he remembered his father's rigid, emotionless stance only too well to be convinced his own departure for the Continent could have had anything to do with his premature death.

'But perhaps you would prefer to discuss this matter later and in private?' Jennifer suggested. 'I am sure it is not necessary that Lady Diana be made privy to all the family scandals in one evening.'

It was impossible for Diana not to detect the note of triumph in the older woman's tone at Gabriel's pallor at being accused of causing his parents' suffering. But Diana did not believe it for a moment; her own father had been deeply in love with her mother and been broken-hearted when she left him. However, it had not killed him and neither had Gabriel's absence killed his father. It was deliberately cruel of his aunt to imply that he was at fault.

She also realised she had been thrown temporarily off balance earlier by Mrs Prescott's spiteful remarks about Gabriel's birthmark, but just this past few minutes spent in her vindictive company had finally enabled Diana to see it for exactly what it was; a means of hurting Gabriel, as well as driving a wedge of misunderstanding between the betrothed couple.

And she had so nearly succeeded…

Her gaze was cool as she looked down the length of the table at the other woman. 'I am sure that every family has its secrets and scandals, Mrs Prescott. Including my own,' she added drily. 'But our relationship is such that Gabriel and I do not have secrets between us.' She reached across the table to lightly touch the back of his hand, her heart aching as she saw the agony of emotion in the depths of his eyes as his gaze flickered across to her.

'I somehow find that very hard to believe,' Jennifer said scornfully.

'Perhaps that is because you have always found dishonesty so much easier to understand?' Gabriel rallied to toss the insult at her.

He had foolishly allowed himself to be momentarily shaken by his aunt's taunts—a loss of his normal control that Diana had not only masked by deflecting Jennifer's attention with her own conversation, but acknowledged privately by offering him her tacit and gentle support with that light touch upon his hand. Considering how disagreeably he had behaved towards her earlier, that support was breathtaking. He was fast discovering she was indeed a diamond amongst women.

He turned his hand and captured the slenderness of her fingers within his grasp, the intensity of his gaze holding hers when she looked across at him in shy enquiry. He gave her fingers a reassuring squeeze as he reiterated his resolve to apologise to her as soon as possible for his earlier bad temper.

'Might I remind you *I* am not the one who was disowned by my own family!'

He should have known that Jennifer would not have allowed his insult to go unchallenged. 'There is only your father, the rector, and he was ever blind to your faults.' Gabriel eyed her disdainfully. 'Can my uncle be equally as blind, I wonder?'

She bristled defensively. 'Charles and I are very happy with our marriage.'

'Indeed?'

Angry colour once again darkened those creamy cheeks. 'You will see for yourself when he returns from town.'

Gabriel snorted. 'I have absolutely no intention of still being in Cambridgeshire when my uncle returns.'

'No?'

'No.'

'Because you are too much the coward to face my husband, perhaps?'

Gabriel's eyes glittered fiercely at this slur upon his honour. 'If you were a man, I would call you out for such an insult!'

'If I were a man, there would be no reason for the insult!'

'You—'

'Gabriel.' It was Diana's softly spoken warning that brought an end to what was rapidly becoming an intolerable heated row.

He drew in a deep, controlling breath and forced himself to calm down. 'Diana is quite correct; we are digressing from the point.'

'And what point was that?'

His mouth tightened ominously at Jennifer's obvious sarcasm. 'That there was not so much as a maid present when I visited my mother's rooms earlier and I am not satisfied with the level of her care.'

'I have told you—'

'I would also be interested to learn why and by whom my mother's companion was pensioned off four months ago. Perhaps it was another of those decisions Charles made so arbitrarily?'

'How on earth do you know about Alice Britton?' she gasped.

'I believe I asked why and by whom, not how I happen to know of it.'

Dark brows rose haughtily. 'Charles decided she had become too old to perform her duties any longer and sent her away.'

'But did not replace her?' he pressed.

'There's was no need when I am here to keep dear Felicity company,' his uncle's wife simpered.

Gabriel would as soon see his mother in the daily company of a venomous viper! 'And when Charles decided to dismiss Miss Britton, did he also provide her with a suitable pension?' As Gabriel was well aware, Alice Britton had been with his mother since Felicity was a small child, first in the nursery, then as lady's maid and latterly as her companion. Not only was it doubtful that the elderly woman would have the means to keep herself in retirement, but now that he had seen the situation here for himself, he could not believe that his mother would ever have agreed to her companion's dismissal.

Jennifer gave a derisive smile. 'As you know, what happens in this household ceased to be any of your business long ago—'

'I will take that to mean he did not.' Gabriel's jaw was tight with disapproval.

'Take it as you wish,' she shot back as the butler returned to remove their soup dishes.

The more he learnt of the happenings in this household the past four months, the more he began to fear that Miss Britton's concerns for his mother were fully justified.

'I can see how concerned you are for your mother, Gabriel.' Once again it was the softly spoken Diana who took charge of the conversation after the butler had left the room. 'As such, I am sure that my own maid will be only too happy to sit with your mother until other, more permanent arrangements can be made.'

'That is not necessary, Lady Diana—'

'I do not wish to seem rude, Mrs Prescott…' Diana's voice became firm as she turned to address the older woman; she had suffered quite enough of this woman's opinions for one evening! '…but I believe you will find my remark was actually addressed to Gabriel.'

She flushed at the obvious put-down. 'Even so, I am

sure it is completely unnecessary for you be inconvenienced like that.'

'My dear Mrs Prescott, I assure you I do not consider it in the least an *inconvenience* to relinquish my maid to the comfort of my future mother-in-law.' She steadily met the older woman's gaze.

Diana had become firmly convinced during dinner that the atmosphere she had sensed in Faulkner Manor since their arrival was caused by the malice of Jennifer Prescott. Admittedly, having Gabriel return so unexpectedly must have been something of a shock, but that still did not explain why she was so determined to ruin any chance of happiness for him, especially as Diana was now utterly sure that Gabriel had not been guilty of any past seduction of her.

The other woman did not appear to be unhappy in her marriage; on the contrary, her earlier claim that her marriage to Charles Prescott was a happy one, despite its unusual beginnings, seemed to indicate the opposite was true, spoken as it was so convincingly. So what had happened eight years ago and why had Jennifer Prescott lied about it?

Diana turned to look across the table at Gabriel. 'Perhaps we might consider taking your mother back to London with us when we leave? I am sure that a change of scenery might help—'

'Felicity's health is far too precarious for such a long and arduous journey!' Jennifer protested sharply.

'Again, I do not wish to sound rude.' Diana unblinkingly returned the older woman's resentful gaze. 'But I believe it is for Gabriel to decide whether or not his mother is well enough to travel back to London with us.'

'My husband is now the master of this household, not Gabriel.'

'Forgive me. I was led to believe it was Mrs Faulkner's home, and that you and your husband were but guests in her household,' Diana remarked.

Jennifer gave up all pretence of politeness as she rose angrily to her feet. 'How dare you question me in this way?' The skirts of her dress swished as she stalked around the table towards Diana. 'Just because you have a title and a grand manner does not mean—'

'That is *quite* enough.' Gabriel rose to his feet to step in between Diana and the rapidly approaching harpy. 'I advise you to regain control of your emotions forthwith, madam, or I will be forced to do it for you,' he warned her.

It took several moments for his aunt to regain her composure. 'I apologise for my outburst, Lady Diana. I was merely…concerned that you do not seem to understand the fragility of Mrs Faulkner's condition.' This condescending adage completely negated her apology. 'I am sure it would be most inadvisable to even think of moving her at this time.'

Gabriel had to admit—in view of his mother's lack of consciousness when he'd visited her earlier—to being somewhat surprised himself at Diana's suggestion that they remove his mother to London. He watched his wife-to-be stand up and move gracefully to his side, her fingers resting lightly in the crook of his arm as she turned to answer the other woman smoothly. 'I apologise for speaking out of turn, Mrs Prescott.' She turned to him. 'I am sure your aunt is wise to advise caution in regard to your mother, my dear. And no doubt she is also correct in her opinion that your mother does not need the services of my maid, either.'

Remarks that were very odd, considering that Diana had been the one to make both the suggestion that her maid sit with his mother and that they should take her to London in the first place. What was going on here?

Jennifer visibly relaxed. 'Now that tempers have cooled, I suggest we all sit down and resume eating our dinner.'

'An excellent idea.' Diana smiled brightly as she removed her hand from Gabriel's arm and retook her seat at the table. 'One always develops such an appetite when one is in the country.' She placed her napkin lightly across her silk-covered knees before looking up to smile at the now-seated Jennifer Prescott.

Gabriel resumed his own seat at the table far more cautiously. His uncle's wife had just seriously insulted Diana, in both word and deed, and yet the smile that curved his fiancée's delectable lips could not have been sweeter. Not because she was not fully aware of the personal nature of the attack, he felt sure; as he had learnt to his cost, it was most unwise to underestimate the woman he was betrothed to.

Undoubtedly something was seriously amiss with Diana's contradictory behaviour, but Gabriel had no idea what it was. He intended to find out at the earliest possible opportunity, though.

He was none the wiser by the time the meal finally came to an end almost two hours later. An excruciating and long two hours for Gabriel, although the ladies appeared to suffer no such discomfort as they conversed on such subjects as London fashions and the difficulty of acquiring the correct silks and lace. The capabilities of the cook at Faulkner Manor were also extolled as each delicious course was served to them. Diana had briefly excused herself from the table to go off in search of a handkerchief after the main course was finished, leaving Gabriel and Mrs Prescott to enjoy an uncomfortable silence. Diana had resumed control of the inane conversation upon her return, this time asking about the comfort and size of the congregation that attended the church in the village of which Jennifer's father was still rector.

All of them innocuous subjects—and so totally boring Gabriel found himself in danger of falling asleep over his dessert.

'That is two hours of my life that I hope never to live through again,' he muttered as he and Diana ascended the wide staircase together. Gabriel had requested that his after-dinner brandy be delivered to the privacy of his bedchamber rather than run the risk of having to suffer any more of his uncle's wife's company.

Diana could not help but laugh at his disgruntled expression. She agreed; it had been a most tedious evening. Worse than tedious, in fact. 'Never mind, Gabriel.' She patted his hand sympathetically. 'This evening has served one purpose at least—I now completely accept your explanation as to how Mrs Prescott has knowledge of your birthmark.'

He raised surprised brows. 'You do?'

'Oh, yes.' Diana snorted. 'I am sure that even at a

very young age you would have required at least some intelligence in the women you bedded.'

Gabriel stiffened. 'I am not at all sure this is a correct conversation—'

'Oh, don't be so pompous.'

He scowled. 'I have just suffered the most agonisingly boring evening of my entire life and now you dare to call me pompous?'

She turned to eye him teasingly as they reached the top of the staircase. 'It is not in the least flattering that you include the apparently boring company of your future wife in that sweeping statement.'

'Damn it, I was not referring to you!'

'Now you are swearing in front of your future wife, too.'

'I shall do a lot more than that if you do not soon explain your previous remark,' he vowed as she continued to walk along the hallway to their bedchambers, leaving him no choice but to follow her, as he carried the candle to light her way. 'In fact, I wish you would explain the whole of this peculiar evening to me. I would be interested to learn, for example, at what point in the evening you became convinced that Jennifer Prescott has, and always did have, the intellect of a pea?'

'I believe you may be insulting the pea!' Diana laughed. 'And I believe it became apparent to me when she first described your mother's health as being nothing more than a simple malaise that did not require the attendance of a doctor or nurse, before only minutes later claiming your mother was far too fragile in health to be removed to London.' She pursed her lips. 'It has always been my belief that one is in need of a certain amount of intellect in order to be a successful liar.'

'But—' Gabriel was left standing outside in the hallway as Diana entered her bedchamber without so much as a backward glance, meaning he had to follow her if he wished to continue this conversation. 'Are you telling me you had decided over two hours ago that she is an unmitigated liar?'

She remained completely composed as she removed her long lace gloves. 'Oh, no, Gabriel, I decided that several days ago. Before I had even met her. Think, Gabriel,' she urged as he looked totally dumbfounded by her admission. 'I could hardly claim to believe your own version of past events without at the same time acknowledging that the young woman involved must therefore be a liar. As Jennifer Prescott is that young woman, ergo Jennifer Prescott must be a liar. Once I had that firmly established in my mind—and, once again, I apologise for my slight wobble over doubting your word earlier—'

'It is I who should apologise to you for behaving so boorishly,' he inserted swiftly.

'Let us not now argue about who should apologise to whom,' she dismissed with her usual briskness. 'In regard to Mrs Prescott's lack of honesty… Once I remembered that she *is* inherently dishonest, it became so much easier for me to realise I must disbelieve anything she had to say. She has also been very cunning, of course—'

'You just claimed that she lacks intellect!' Gabriel eyed her with some considerable exasperation.

'Really, Gabriel, I am sure you must be aware that true intelligence and the slyness of a cunning vixen are not at all the same thing.' Diana shot him a chiding glance.

'I must?'

'But of course,' she said. 'You are, I am glad to say, the most intelligent gentleman—apart from my father— that I have ever met.'

Gabriel was not feeling particularly intelligent at this moment; in fact, this whole conversation seemed to have run away from his understanding!

Diana, on the other hand, seemed cheerfully satisfied with her evening. And in her happy state of contentment, she was even more desirable to him. He suddenly realised that, although he still did not want to make love to her properly for the first time under this roof and before they were legally married, there *were* other ways he could satisfy the desire that ignited between them every time they touched. And he was pretty sure he knew them all…

Diana was so caught up in thoughts of the positive results of her evening that she did not even notice as Gabriel placed the lighted candle upon the dressing table before locking the bedchamber doors, only becoming aware once he stood very close to her, the warmth in his eyes unmistakable as his arms moved about her waist and he pulled her gently but determinedly into the heat of his body.

Her eyes widened. 'What are you doing, Gabriel?'

'I am sure you, at least, are far too intelligent a

woman for me to need to explain.' His head lowered, his lips nuzzling against the rapidly beating pulse in her throat.

She was undeniably flustered by the warmth of those lips against her flesh. 'But—'

'I have decided that this evening does not have to be a complete waste of time.' Those lips now moved the length of her throat, slowly, pleasurably. 'I also admit the only thing that made this evening at all bearable for me was the thought of reacquainting myself with the mole upon your left breast once we were finally alone together…' His hands were at her back as he began to unfasten the buttons of her gown that ran the length of her spine.

A quiver of anticipation travelled down that spine at the mere thought of his previous familiarity with her breasts; breasts that now tingled in awareness beneath the silk of her gown, the now familiar warmth growing between her thighs. 'And is it also your intention to acquaint me with the birthmark upon your thigh?'

His husky laugh reverberated throughout her body. 'It might be, yes. With your agreement, my dear?'

She lifted her head to look up at him and saw the desire that burned in the dark-blue depths of his eyes and the laughter lines fanning out from the corners. The slant of his cheekbones seemed less severe than usual, too, and his lips, those firm and sculptured lips, were curved up into a lazily amused smile.

This was a question to which Diana could have only one answer…

Chapter Twelve

It was the very gentleness in Gabriel's expression—an emotion so at odds with his usual uncompromising arrogance—which succeeded in melting the very bones in Diana's body. 'I believe I should enjoy that very much,' she responded huskily.

'I am much relieved to hear it.' He had finished unfastening the buttons at the back of her gown and now allowed that garment to slide down the slenderness of her arms before dropping it softly to the floor to pool silkily at her slippered feet, leaving her clothed only in her short shift and a pair of white stockings held in place by pretty white garters decorated with tiny pink rosebuds.

Gabriel's breath caught in his throat as he looked down at her, the fullness of her breasts visible beneath the thin material of her shift, the tips of those breasts already aroused and pouting as they pressed invitingly against it, a darker vee of golden curls also visible between her silky thighs.

His gaze glowed hotly as it moved back up to her face. 'So much has happened since coming into this household, I have discovered that it is only your beauty and honesty which seems real to me.'

Diana felt a wealth of emotion growing, swelling, inside her chest. Gabriel had stated clearly at the time of their betrothal that he did not love her and that he never would, but to have won the regard and the respect of a man as jaded as he was, was a pearl beyond price.

The joy of that lit her eyes as she reached up to begin unfastening the buttons of his waistcoat. 'In that case, allow me to act as your valet again, my lord…'

There was no slow and agonisingly pleasurable removal of his clothes this time, as he aided her in their removal before throwing them on to the carpeted floor beside the bed.

Diana smiled in satisfaction as the small brown birthmark was revealed only several inches above his knee after he had sat down on the bed to remove his boots and then peel off his pantaloons. 'Most respectable, my lord.'

Gabriel grimaced. 'That woman is a vindictive witch—'

He was silenced from further comment as Diana placed her fingertips lightly across his lips. She gave a gentle shake of her head. 'She has no place here with us now.'

'No.' He was completely unconcerned by his nakedness as he stood up before reaching to remove the pins from Diana's hair.

Gabriel drew in a sharp breath as those tresses were finally released to fall, as he had once imagined they might, in a warmth of reddish-gold curls that reached down to the tender curve of her waist, several of those delicate curls framing the creamy warmth of her flushed cheeks and brow.

His hands shook slightly as he raised them to cradle each side of her face before gazing deeply into her eyes. 'You are beauty incarnate, Diana. A veritable goddess come to earth.'

Diana felt almost overwhelmed by their intimacy, the nakedness of his body more perfect, more wonderfully masculine than she could ever have imagined; the muscled hardness of his shoulders and chest was beautifully, gloriously sculptured in the glow of candlelight, and tapered down to the flatness of his stomach and leanly muscled thighs. Those drawings in the book of the Greek gods in her father's library, which Diana had once looked at so admiringly, had not prepared her for the physical evidence of the arousal of a flesh-and-blood man—but then, in all fairness to those Greek gods, none of them had been drawn fully and magnificently aroused!

Diana was unable to stop staring at Gabriel's arousal, steel encased in velvet. What would it be like, she wondered, to kneel down in front of him and place her lips about that—?

She stopped, stunned at herself and her fantasies. She had no idea where they had even come from! Except she knew it was something that she felt compelled to do; she was sure he would enjoy it as much, if not more, than she would...

'Your turn will come later, little goddess.' Gabriel reached out to grasp her arms before she could sink to her knees in front of him, having seen the direction of her hungry graze. Experienced as he was, perhaps even jaded from the women he had bedded this past eight years, if she so much as touched his aching and throbbing shaft with her mouth at this moment, then he would lose all control. And he wanted to please her first.

'I wish to give you pleasure, Diana.' He slipped one thin strap from her shoulder, then the other, allowing her shift to fall softly down about her hips revealing the deliciously full, naked thrust of her breasts. 'Ah, my familiar friend.' He ran the tip of his finger across the tiny mole now visible just slightly above her left nipple.

She trembled from the pleasure of that single caress, her legs beginning to shake almost uncontrollably as he lowered his head to run the tip of his tongue across that mole before he moved lower, his tongue now a moist rasp across the aching crest of her breast, the nipple standing erect even as his lips parted, his breath hot against her skin before he took that rosy tip fully into the heat of his mouth.

Pleasure coursed from her breast down to between her thighs. She reached out to grasp on to the flexing muscles of his shoulders as she felt her core burning as he drew harder on her nipple even as his other hand cupped its twin and the soft pad of his thumb moved across its tip with the same delectable rhythm.

Diana was so lost in wonder, in pleasure, that she barely noticed as he discarded her shift altogether, only becoming aware that he had done so as he moved his hand to caress a path from her breast, over the slight curve of her stomach, before cupping her lower, the press of his palm sending quivers of pleasure coursing through her even as his fingers began a skilful caress of her moist and sensitive opening.

She gasped, her hands moving up and allowing her own fingers to become entangled in the dark thickness of Gabriel's hair as ecstasy unlike anything she had ever known before claimed and rocked her in a crescendo of ever-increasing waves.

She groaned achingly at her release before collapsing weakly against him.

He released her breast slowly before raising his head to see that Diana had not just collapsed but truly fainted, her lashes resting long and silkily upon her flushed and creamy cheeks, her breathing soft and shallow.

Gabriel frowned with concern even as he swung her up into his arms and carried her towards the bed. He had, he realised, made love with women too numerous to count, but none of them had ever fainted away after climaxing. Had he hurt her? Perhaps she was too delicate, too ladylike to enjoy such pleasures? That had to be it! What a fool he was!

'Gabriel?'

His gaze sharpened on her face, his expression softening in relief as he saw that she was looking up at him with dreamy satisfaction rather than horrified accusation.

She frowned slightly at his continued silence, one of her hands lifting to cradle the side of his sharply etched jaw. 'I had no idea that lovemaking would be so—so gloriously overwhelming.'

'Neither did I,' he assured her huskily as he knelt on the bed to lay her gently down upon the bedcovers.

'But you are a man of experience,' she said wonderingly.

'I would rather not talk about that now, my dear,' he said uncomfortably. He realised the women he had bedded in the past had all ceased to matter, been forgotten, had faded into insignificance after holding Diana in his arms and making love with her. Why that should be he had no idea.

'I believe it is now my turn to—explore,' she said shyly.

Gabriel's heart leapt in his chest at Diana's reminder that he had brought a halt to her caresses earlier. 'Perhaps we have explored enough for one night,' he said gently, recalling how overwhelmed she has just been. This was, after all, her first experience of lovemaking.

'Oh, no, Gabriel.' Diana sat up, the long length of her golden hair falling silkily about her shoulders, the naked pout of her breasts peeping through those curls, the nipples as full and ripe as the berries they resembled.

His breath caught in his throat at the sight of those juicy orbs, his shaft aching as he imagined feasting on them once again. 'Diana—'

'You will lie still, please,' she instructed as she moved up on to her knees to push him down on to the pillows, appearing not at all abashed that she wore only her stockings and garters as she knelt between his parted legs.

'Lie still,' she said—and how in the blazes was he supposed to do that when she first bent to place a soft kiss against that damned birthmark before straightening to run her tiny hands the length of his thighs? His head fell back on to the pillows as he finally felt the warmth of her lips closing about his hard and throbbing arousal and her hair fell about her like a golden curtain before spilling softly down on to his thighs.

Diana was encouraged in her caresses by Gabriel's throaty groans and the hot leaping of his arousal as she took him deeper into the heat of her mouth. She had never tasted anything so succulently addictive in her life before.

'Diana!' Gabriel sounded short of breath, his voice a low and fervent appeal.

She raised her head to look at him, concerned to see an agonised expression on his face. 'Am I hurting you?'

'Dear God, no, not at all! It is too much pleasure, Diana. Much more of it and I shall disgrace myself completely,' he explained even as he reached down for her.

She evaded his grasp, emboldened by his admission. 'How so? You must tell me, Gabriel, else how will I ever learn how I am to please you?' she pleaded.

He looked rueful. 'If you please me any more than you already have, then I shall lose control and spill myself like some callow youth.'

'Ah.' She nodded in understanding, even as her avid gaze returned to the long, hard shaft she still cradled in her hand. There was a tiny bead of moisture on its glistening tip and she bent slightly and licked it with the slow rasp of her tongue before once again taking him fully into her mouth.

'Diana…' His hands were clenched at his sides, his body completely taut.

Only minutes ago he had introduced her to undreamt-of pleasure, one she now wished to give back to him.

'Dear God!' Gabriel's groans became a litany as—almost against his will, it seemed—his hips began to rise and fall in a distinctive rhythm. Previously innocent of such intimacy, she nevertheless knew the exact moment that he lost all control and became utterly consumed in his own ecstasy.

Minutes passed; all Gabriel could hear was the sound of his own ragged breathing as he lay completely boneless, sprawled back upon the bedcovers, one of his hands still lightly entangled in the gold of Diana's curls as they cascaded across him in wild disarray, her breath a warm caress against his thighs.

Somehow he had found heaven in a place he had come to think of as hell. Somehow this woman had lifted him out of the dark and taken him into a golden paradise. It was as if—

A knock sounded softly on the bedchamber door to halt his wandering thoughts, followed by an enquiring whisper. 'Miss? Miss, you told me I should call you if—well, if I should need you?'

'What the—?' Gabriel was too satiated, too physically replete, to do more than turn and frown in the direction of the locked door.

Diana's response was much more immediate as she sat up quickly to push back the wildness of her hair from her face before running across the room to pull on and belt her robe. 'Dear Lord, how could I have allowed myself to forget?' she muttered wildly.

'Diana?' Gabriel eyed her sharply as the fog of his physical repletion began to abate.

She shook her head. 'I meant to go immediately after dinner— oh, I should not have allowed myself to become so distracted!' she told herself crossly as she hurried to unlock the door and open it just enough so that she could talk with the person outside in the hallway, but whoever it was could not see inside the bedchamber to whcrc Gabriel still lay naked upon the bed.

He sat up, a dark and heavy scowl on his brow as he watched her at the doorway. He had just been transported to some hitherto-unknown plateau of pleasure and she had just referred to their intimacy as being a distraction from some more important purpose!

She had no experience with which to compare their lovemaking, of course, and could have no idea how rare and beautiful it had been. But he was fully aware of it.

She was utterly incapable of artifice. She was the most honest and forthright young woman he had—

'We must both dress immediately.' Diana appeared flustered as, her conversation concluded, she closed and relocked the door, not sparing him so much as a glance as she hurried across the room to fling open the wardrobe doors and began searching through the array of gowns that hung there. She halted as she turned back into the room, blue woollen gown in hand, and found that he had not moved. 'Did you not hear me, Gabriel?' She frowned her impatience with his inactivity as she removed her robe and replaced it with her shift. 'You must dress. We cannot dally here a moment longer.' She stepped lithely into her gown.

Gabriel looked taken aback at her increasing agita-tion. What on earth was going on? 'I have no intention of dressing or going anywhere until I know exactly where it is I am going and why,' he said with some annoyance.

Of course he had no idea where they were going or why, Diana admonished herself as she finished pulling on her gown. How could he possibly know when she had found no opportunity—had been too lost to the wonder of what had just happened—to tell him what actions she had put into play earlier this evening?

It was far from an ideal end to the ecstasy of their earlier intimacy, but no doubt Gabriel would thank her once he knew what she had done.

'My maid has been sitting with your mother for several hours now, with instructions to come for me should she receive any visitors,' she started to explain hurriedly.

'Your maid has been sitting with my mother?' he repeated slowly.

Diana nodded. 'Do you recall that I left the dining table earlier in search of a handkerchief?'

'Yes.' Of course he remembered that, and a damned long time she had taken about it too. Over ten minutes of absolute silence between himself and Jennifer, as they glared their glittering dislike at each other, knowing that if he said one word to the witch then an avalanche of them would follow, all of them unpleasant. She had seemed to know that too and for once in her life had remained silent.

'I had no real need of a handkerchief.' Diana smiled triumphantly. 'It was merely a ruse to allow me the time in which to arrange for my maid to go to your mother's rooms.'

Gabriel raised an eyebrow. 'I thought you had agreed

with Jennifer that there was no need for your maid to sit with my mother?'

'I only gave the appearance of agreeing,' Diana corrected, moving to stand in front of the mirror on the dressing table in order to study her reflection as she pinned her hair neatly into place.

'Did you?' he asked, thoroughly confused.

She turned to eye him impatiently. 'Really, Gabriel, I am sure I am making myself perfectly clear. I lied when I appeared to take Mrs Prescott's word for it that your mother didn't need my maid's company.'

Gabriel became very still. 'I was led to believe you were incapable of lying.'

'The very reason it is easier to be believed when one is left with no other choice but to do so!'

Gabriel stared across at her wordlessly. He had just been mentally praising Diana for her honesty, for her utter lack of artifice, and all the time she was as skilful at deception as the next woman.

No doubt she had a good reason for it, he told himself. She had good reason for most things she did. Even so, it was unsettling to realise she was as capable of lying as anyone else. 'Would you care to tell me why it was you felt the need to lie on this occasion?'

'Surely that is obvious?' she said incredulously.

'Not completely, no,' he said through gritted teeth. 'Explain, if you please.' He stood up and began to gather up his clothes.

Diana blinked. She was not sure how she was supposed to even think, let alone explain, when Gabriel stood before her in all his naked glory! Their lovemaking had been a revelation to her. A wonder. A joy beyond imagining. And just looking at the magnificence of his unclothed body was enough to bring the warmth back into her cheeks. And other places too. Private, intimate places of her body that he now knew more intimately than she did herself.

Gabriel had been beautiful in his arousal, and he was no less so now, the candlelight giving his flesh a golden hue as it caressed the hard planes of his body and revealed that thatch of black hair surrounding his now-softened shaft. Even in repose it was far more impressive than those sketches of the Greek gods in that book—

'Diana!'

She gave a slightly dazed shake of her head, closing her eyes briefly before lifting her gaze to concentrate Gabriel's scowling face rather than the magnificence of his body; she might perhaps be able to concentrate on the matter in hand if she did not look at all that male beauty! 'Could you dress whilst I explain?'

'Willingly, if it is going to speed up the proceedings,' he said. He turned his back on her to sort through the clothes he had amassed on the bed.

Even his sculptured back was beautiful, Diana acknowledged achingly, longing to reach out and touch those wide and muscled shoulders, which tapered down to a narrow waist, to fondle his nicely curved buttocks—

'You do not appear to be explaining anything as yet, Diana,' Gabriel reminded her impatiently, his back still towards her as he pulled his shirt on over his head and instantly covered at least part of his nakedness.

But still not enough for her to focus on coherent

thought, the intimacy of the situation rendering her temporarily speechless.

'I swear I will come over there and shake you if you do not begin this explanation in the next ten seconds!'

Diana gave a guilty start as she heard the savagery in Gabriel's tone. It was understandable—she needed to pull herself together. 'When I left the dining room earlier in search of a handkerchief, I first visited your mother's rooms—I wished to satisfy my curiosity before taking any further action,' she explained as he stared at her incredulously.

'And did you? Satisfy your curiosity!' he rasped as Diana looked at him blankly.

'Your mother was still sleeping,' she said.

'Perhaps that is as well when she would have had absolutely no idea who you were if she had been awake.' Gabriel was dressed in his pantaloons and boots now, as well as his shirt, although he had left the latter unfastened, and the darkness of his hair was dishevelled as he looked across at her with accusing eyes. 'I had intended to introduce the two of you tomorrow.'

'Obviously, as she was asleep when I entered her bedchamber, you are still free to do so—'

'How kind!'

She crossed the room to stand before him. 'Gabriel, I believe you are missing the point...'

'Perhaps that is because you have not told me the point, as yet.' His increasing frustration with this situation was obvious in the dangerous glitter of his eyes.

Diana sighed. 'Despite her alleged malaise, I do not believe that a lady who must not yet be fifty should be asleep as much as Mrs Prescott claims your mother has been in recent months.'

'And?'

'And so when I entered her rooms earlier I took it upon myself to check the contents of the medicine bottle, which stood upon her dressing table. Amongst other, less innocuous substances, I discovered—as I suspected that I might—that it contained laudanum. It is a substance I am familiar with because my father took it in the last years of his life in order to help him sleep,' she said.

'Are you saying that all this time my mother has been taking a sleeping draught?' Gabriel asked slowly. That made absolutely no sense to him when his mother's problem seemed to be an over-abundance of sleep, not a lack of it. Unless, of course, her life was now so hellish that she preferred to sleep most of the time rather than live in that hell?

'I am afraid there is no more time for me to explain this situation just now.' Diana moved hurriedly across the room to pick up the lighted candle. 'I had meant to go immediately to your mother's rooms as soon as dinner was over.' Her cheeks became flushed as she obviously recalled exactly why she had not done so. 'May—my maid—came to tell me that Mrs Prescott had attempted to visit your mother's rooms only a few minutes ago.'

'And?' he pressed.

'When she couldn't gain entry through the locked door, she knocked upon it. May ignored that, of course, as I had instructed her to do should the need arise. Mrs

Prescott has now gone back down the stairs to collect a second key from the housekeeper.' She grimaced. 'May took advantage of her absence to leave your mother's rooms to quickly come and inform me of events.'

'Considering you are a visitor, newly come into this house, you appear to have taken rather a lot upon yourself,' Gabriel commented. To him, at least, things were still incomprehensible; fortunately, Diana gave every appearance of knowing exactly what she was doing and why.

'I would have preferred to discuss it with you first, of course—'

'Of course,' Gabriel muttered somewhat sarcastically.

'But as we were seated at dinner all together there was obviously no opportunity for me to do so,' she continued. 'As I have already explained, there really is no time to lose,' she added firmly as Gabriel would have pressed her for more details. 'May has been with me for years and is very loyal, but it would be unfair to expect her to deal with Mrs Prescott's unpleasantness twice in one evening.' She turned upon her heel with the obvious intention of leaving.

Gabriel reached out and took hold of her arm. 'Not so fast! First, at least tell me the purpose of keeping Mrs Prescott from entering my mother's rooms?'

'Surely that is obvious?'

His mouth tightened. 'Humour me.'

She glared at him. 'For the purpose of allowing your mother to awaken, of course, and so enabling her to speak to the son she has not seen in eight years.'

Gabriel was so surprised by this explanation that he relaxed his grip on her arm. A fact she did not hesitate to take advantage of as she rushed from the bedchamber.

Chapter Thirteen

By the time Gabriel had collected his addled wits enough to hurry from the now-darkened bedchamber in pursuit, he was just in time to see Diana's skirts disappearing round the end of the hallway in the direction of his mother's rooms, the candle disappearing with her and once again plunging him into darkness.

A darkness that was not only physical, but also emotional.

The depth of their lovemaking had been so consuming that even now he found it difficult to comprehend exactly what she was about from the little she had told him—not an altogether pleasant experience for a man who had always prided himself on his mental and emotional acuity!

Outside his mother's suite of rooms, Diana had placed the lit candle on the hallstand and was standing in front of the door, her arms extended and her expression defiant as Jennifer used every means she could to dislodge her from that protective stance.

One of which was to now reach out and grasp a handful of Diana's hair. 'How dare you?' his uncle's wife ranted shrilly as she tugged viciously on those golden curls. 'You have absolutely no authority to stop me from entering my sister-in-law's rooms—'

'Diana may not—but I certainly do,' he announced.

Diana turned gratefully to look at Gabriel as he approached them quickly, once again looking every inch as vengeful as his angelic namesake with his unfastened shirt billowing about him. Although, thankfully, this time the cold fury glittering in his eyes was not directed at her, but at the young woman married to his uncle.

'Release Diana immediately.' He towered over both women, but it was Jennifer who remained the focus of his ruthless gaze. 'Do not put me to the trouble of having to repeat the instruction, madam,' he warned in an intimidating voice that sent a shiver of apprehension down Diana's spine.

An apprehension that Jennifer also felt, if the suddenness with which she released her grip upon Diana's hair was any indication, although the defiance in her expression remained as she looked up at him, hands now resting challengingly upon her hips. 'Perhaps you should see to restricting the behaviour of your fiancée rather than remonstrating with me.'

Gabriel raised dark brows. 'Diana is more than capable of deciding for herself what she will and will not do.'

The dryness underlying his tone gave Diana the courage to state exactly what she intended doing at this moment. 'I have just informed Mrs Prescott that the two of us will sit with your mother tonight, thus leaving her free to enjoy an untroubled sleep.'

He looked at her searchingly for several long seconds, a shutter coming down over his expression before he turned back to Jennifer. 'I can see no reason why you would have any objection to that?'

Jennifer's beautiful face became flushed with her displeasure. '*I* have seen to Felicity's care this past four months—'

'And a right mess—'

'And now you are deserving of an unbroken night's sleep,' Diana smoothly interrupted his angry outburst; a justified outburst, she felt sure, but one guaranteed to further inflame this already heated situation. 'I assure you,' she continued firmly, 'Gabriel and I are more than happy to sit with Mrs Faulkner tonight.'

'And if I object?' Those brown eyes flashed Jennifer's displeasure with the proposal.

'It is not a matter open for discussion, madam.' Gabriel looked down the long length of his nose at her. 'Nor do I expect to ever witness you treating Diana in that disgraceful manner ever again.'

'But—'

'If you have nothing of interest to say, then I would appreciate it if you would remove yourself from this vicinity altogether.' His expression was full of his undisguised disgust.

Diana knew that she would cringe in mortification if Gabriel should ever look at her in that way and Jennifer Prescott was not proof against it either; she looked less than her usual defiant self. 'Charles shall hear of your highhandedness the moment he returns.'

Gabriel's top lip curled back disdainfully. 'I shall look forward to it,' was all he said.

Brown eyes flashed furiously. 'You have no right—'

'If nothing else, I have the right of being my mother's son,' he said harshly. 'You, on the other hand, are no more than a guest in my mother's house, with no authority to say who shall or shall not visit with her.' He looked down at her scornfully. 'Now, if you would kindly remove yourself, Diana and I wish to go inside and sit with my mother.'

Jennifer bristled with rage. 'If I chose, I could make life so uncomfortable for you that you would wish you had never been born.'

'Madam, if such an occurrence meant I never had to set eyes upon you again, then I would be happy for you to try!'

'You liked me well enough once,' she sneered.

'You are mistaken, madam.' Gabriel's tone was one of boredom now. 'That I succeeded in tolerating your presence when we were both children would be a more apt description.'

Jennifer's cheeks now become deathly pale. 'How I have always hated you,' she spat. 'With your "Lord of the Manor" attitude and your oh-so-superior manner!'

He eyed her mockingly. 'At last we are in agreement on something, madam—our heartfelt dislike of each other.'

If Diana had needed any further confirmation—which she did not—that Jennifer Prescott had lied about the happenings of the past, then the other woman had just given it to her. So she had always hated Gabriel, had she? That was very interesting...

'It is late and tempers are becoming fractious.' Diana spoke calmly as she turned to the other woman. 'Please do not trouble yourself any further concerning Mrs Faulkner. I assure you, having nursed my father for the last few years of his life, I am more than up to the task of caring for Gabriel's mother.' Having—hopefully—left Jennifer with absolutely no further argument to make, Diana put an end to their conversation by knocking softly on the door of the bedchamber and requesting that May unlock the door and admit her.

Gabriel continued in a silent battle of wills with Jennifer for several seconds after Diana had entered his mother's bedchamber, before finally his uncle's wife gave a frustrated snort and flounced off down the hallway, leaving him to slowly follow his fiancée into the muted illumination of his mother's rooms.

Diana stood beside the bed in whispered conversation with her maid, who then dropped them a light curtsy before she vacated the bedchamber, and Gabriel crossed the room to stand beside his mother's bed.

He had spoken the truth earlier when he admitted to finding his mother much changed from when he had last seen her. Well…perhaps when Gabriel had last seen her was not a good comparison to make; his mother had been distraught the day he'd left Faulkner Manor, her face deathly pale, her eyes red from hours of crying in the face of his father's implacability regarding Jennifer Lindsay's accusations.

But his mother had always been a beauty, a glowing ever-young beauty it had always seemed to him. Now she looked every one of her two-and-fifty years, the darkness of her hair showing strands of grey, her face so white and thin and lifeless it was much like one of the masks worn during the time of carnival in Venice.

'I am sure the changes you see in your mother are only superficial, Gabriel.'

He glanced across the bed to where Diana looked back at him so compassionately. A compassion he found it hard to accept, even from the woman he had so recently been intimate with.

He looked away. 'Perhaps, having now dispatched my uncle's wife, you might care to give me an explanation as to why we have done so?'

'Of course.' She smiled briefly. 'But perhaps we should go through to your mother's private parlour so that we do not disturb her?' She indicated the adjoining room, the door standing open to reveal that it was furnished comfortably. 'We can leave the door open so that we will still hear her if she should stir.'

Gabriel looked at her through narrowed lids. 'From what you already said to me in your bedchamber, I thought disturbing my mother enough so that she awakens is our main purpose for being here?'

Diana felt her cheeks warm at this reference to when they had been in her bedchamber such a short time ago, when Gabriel had touched her with an intimacy and a skill that still took her breath away. When she had returned those caresses in a way that shocked her to even think of it…

Her gaze avoided meeting his. 'I have every hope that your mother will wake very soon,' she said abruptly. 'I simply think it would be better if this conversation were not the first thing she hears when she does so.'

He raised dark brows. 'Why not?'

Diana looked pained. 'Gabriel, when I came to your mother's rooms earlier this evening—'

'You mean when you *said* you were fetching a handkerchief?'

'Yes.' Diana squirmed at this pointed reminder of her duplicity—her only excuse was that she had done what she thought was for the best. 'The laudanum in your mother's medicine really is of a very high dosage, much more than it needs to be if it is only taken as an aid to help her sleep. Besides,' she added, 'Mrs Prescott has several times confirmed that she alone has been responsible for your mother's nursing care this past four months. And that care will have no doubt have included administering her medicine.' Diana chose her words carefully, but purposefully.

Gabriel stared at her levelly for several seconds before nodding. 'You are right, Diana—this conversation would be much better taking place in the privacy of my mother's parlour.' He left the room without waiting to see if she followed him.

Which she did, of course; if Diana's suspicions proved to be correct, then this was not going to be a particularly pleasant conversation, even if it was a necessary one.

Gabriel delayed continuing this conversation with her for some minutes by putting a taper to the fire laid in the hearth, staring down at the flames that quickly caught the kindling alight before then bending down to add some of the coal from the bucket beside the fireplace. And all the time his thoughts were racing. Mulling over the things Diana had already said. The suspicions arising from those observations.

It took him several minutes to regain control of his emotions enough to draw in a deep breath before turning to face her, his hands tightly gripped together behind his back. 'Very well,' he said stiltedly. 'You may continue your explanation now.'

She grimaced. 'You understand it is only a theory as yet?'

'At this point in time a theory is more than sufficient.' His jaw was so tightly clenched he felt as if the bones might crack. Dinner had been hellish, the time in Diana's bedchamber had been paradise; only God knew what the next few minutes were going to be like.

She began to pace the parlour. 'I have found Mrs Prescott's behaviour most unusual, since our arrival earlier today. Do you recall that she was not waiting for us in the hallway when we finally entered the house, but was in fact hurrying down the staircase, her face flushed from exertion? As if she were returning from some urgent errand?'

'Yes, I do.'

'I had thought, once you told me of your…past connection—'

'There's *no* past connection!'

'No. Well. Just so.' Diana felt slightly unnerved by the force of Gabriel's protest. 'I believed at first that might be a possible explanation for Mrs Prescott's flustered behaviour, but I have had a chance to rethink her actions since and now believe that she hurried back into the house in order to go up to your mother's room and administer another dose of her medication.'

'Perhaps my mother's medication was due?'

'Then Mrs Prescott's dedication to her patient, at a

time when she was in such an obvious state of personal turmoil, would indeed be admirable.' Diana found it impossible to keep the derision out of her tone; she was usually a forbearing woman, usually only too happy to see the good in others, but she simply could not find a single thing about Mrs Prescott to like.

His eyes narrowed. 'Then we are to take it there was another reason for the administration of my mother's medication at that particular time?'

'I believe so, yes.'

'I am sure you are about to tell me what that reason was?' he drawled as she hesitated.

Then, 'None of Mrs Prescott's behaviour would have struck me as odd if it were not for the strangeness of her conversation at dinner. After first assuring us that your mother was not ill enough to require the care of a doctor or a nurse,' she explained at his questioning glance, 'she then went on to claim that your mother was too frail to sustain the strain of a coach journey back to London with us. Those two statements were in complete contradiction of each other. Rather than simply allowing my imagination to run riot at the possible reasons for that, I excused myself with the intention of checking your mother's health for myself.' She pursed her lips. 'You will recall, no doubt, that Mrs Prescott showed the first signs of agitation at dinner after you had told you that you had found the time to visit your mother's rooms earlier?'

'I do recall that, yes,' he admitted.

'I now believe that your mother did not wake during that visit for the simple reason that she was too deeply drugged by the laudanum in her medicine.'

'For what purpose?' he asked curiously.

'I believe to ensure that your mother was not awake to converse with you if you were to visit her this evening.'

Gabriel felt himself blanch as the full import of her suspicions began to take root in his own imaginings. One of them being that his uncle and his wife would already have been in residence here six years ago when he'd written to his mother and requested that he be allowed to visit her following his father's death. A letter he now wondered if his mother had ever received… Alice Britton's letter three days ago had certainly claimed that it was his mother's dearest wish to see him again, and had been for some time. The dismissal of his mother's doctor, nurse, and companion by Charles in the past four months was also suspect, leaving his mother completely alone and at the far-from-tender mercies of the Prescotts.

Diana's heart ached as she saw from the bleakness of his expression exactly how her disclosures were affecting him. 'I am so sorry, Gabriel—'

'You have done absolutely nothing for which you need to apologise,' he assured her.

Maybe not, but she was not enjoying saying any of these things to him. Especially as it had resulted in a return of that cold, emotionally closed-off man from their first meeting.

'If ensuring that your mother remained asleep truly was Mrs Prescott's intention earlier, then I knew from experience that another dose of laudanum would need to be administered some time this evening to maintain that unconscious state,' she continued gently. 'I placed my maid in here, with the door firmly locked, in order to prevent such an occurrence.'

Gabriel drew in a ragged breath. 'Jennifer cannot have seriously believed she could keep my mother asleep for the whole of my visit here.'

'Surely it needed only to succeed until such time as your uncle returned from London?' she suggested. 'At which time Mrs Prescott no doubt intended to pass the responsibility for the delicacy of this situation on to him.'

He snorted. 'Charles is no match for me, I assure you.'

She could well believe that. Just as she knew Gabriel would have succeeded in seeing the danger of the unusual situation that existed at Faulkner Manor for himself if he were not so emotionally close to it all. If his displeasure at seeing Jennifer Prescott again had not clouded his powers of deduction…

She gave a rueful smile. 'I doubt it matters either way now.'

His gaze sharpened. 'How so?'

She shrugged slender shoulders. 'If my suspicions are correct, and the lack of further medication succeeds in reviving your mother, then Mrs Prescott must know that we will quickly learn all about your mother's life these past six years.'

His expression was suddenly anguished. 'You seriously believe it is possible my mother has been lied to and deceived all that time? That she may have been kept as a virtual prisoner in her own home these past four months?'

'I think it is a possibility, yes,' Diana answered carefully.

'With what purpose in mind?' Gabriel shifted restlessly. 'What happened four months ago to bring about such a sudden change?'

'That is something only your uncle and his wife can answer…'

'Do you not have some other "theory" about that, too?'

She flinched as she heard the bitterness in his tone. 'I do, yes.'

'I thought that you might,' he sighed heavily.

'Obviously Charles and Jennifer have become accustomed to living here as your mother's guests for six years, a comfortable and privileged existence that I am sure they greatly enjoy. You have also mentioned to me that your uncle is a man who likes to gamble and that he lost his own home because of it.'

'He did, yes.'

'So perhaps the answer lies there? Even larger gambling debts than in the past would mean they needed a tighter control of the estate? I really do not know the reasons why things changed four months ago, Gabriel.' She spread her hands in apology. 'I can only say what I suspect. If I am wrong, then I shall apologise to all concerned.'

'You are not wrong.' He spoke with flat finality, the bleakness of his expression now absolute.

'We cannot be *sure*—'

'Damn it, I can!' His expression was savage. 'And the worst of it is that none of this would have occurred at all if I had persevered in visiting my mother after my father died.'

'Self-recrimination serves no purpose now, Gabriel—'

'It serves the purpose of easing some of my frustration with this situation.' He began to pace the parlour. 'If all of this is true, and I have every reason to believe that it is, then I will strangle the Prescotts with my own bare hands.'

'Having her only son consigned to prison for the murder of his uncle and aunt will not aid in your mother's recovery one little bit,' she murmured.

Gabriel's eyes glittered vengefully. 'It would be worth it.'

She crossed the room to lay her hand gently upon his arm. 'You know it would not.' She smiled up at him gently. 'You love your mother very much, do you not?'

He tensed. 'Always.' His chin rose as if to challenge anyone who might dare him to make such a claim after the heartache his family had suffered on his behalf eight years ago.

But it was a heartache Diana believed had never been of his making. 'I think, when you next speak to Mrs Prescott—'

'I do not intend doing anything so banal as *speaking* to her—'

'When you next speak to her,' she repeated firmly, 'you might also like to ask her who the father of her babe really was.'

Gabriel became very still as he stared down at her, his expression changing from puzzlement, to shock, to total disbelief in the matter of only a few seconds.

'You cannot be suggesting—? You do not suppose it was *Charles*?'

She raised her eyebrows at him. 'It is a thought, is it not? I am aware that it is not unusual for an arranged marriage such as the Prescotts' was to find a measure of success, a mutual respect between them, at least.' As Diana hoped that her own marriage to Gabriel would one day achieve. 'But I believe your uncle's wife talks of her husband with more than just respect; I think that she is deeply in love with him. And she claimed earlier, very convincingly, that their marriage was a happy one.'

'I have every reason to believe that it is,' he said thoughtfully.

She gave a slight inclination of her head. 'My Aunt Humphries—who incidentally met both your mother and your Uncle Charles during her London Season almost thirty years ago—told me that he was then something of a charming rogue. Nowhere near the class of his disreputable nephew, of course,' she teased. 'But a rogue, none the less.'

Gabriel's expression lightened only slightly. 'I can see that it is past time your aunt and I made each other's acquaintance.'

She laughed briefly. 'I doubt that would reassure her in the slightest!'

'Possibly not,' he accepted drily, and just as quickly sobered. 'Do you really think it possible that Charles and Jennifer were intimately involved eight years ago and that the babe she carried was his all the time? Even worse, that they planned my disgrace together, knowing I would refuse to take responsibility for a child that categorically was not mine and so end up being disinherited by my father whilst Charles was paid handsomely to marry Jennifer?'

Diana looked sad. 'I cannot answer those questions with any finality. But I do think all these matters are worth investigating further.'

'I really *will* strangle the pair of them if it should turn out to be the truth of it—'

'Gabriel…? Gabriel, is that you, my dearest boy?'

He froze as if struck at the first sound of that soft and quavery voice calling from the adjoining room, his eyes widening with disbelief and his face becoming even paler as he registered his mother's endearment.

'Go to her, Gabriel,' Diana urged huskily, squeezing his arm briefly in encouragement before she stepped away from him.

'Come with me,' he pleaded.

She shook her head. 'I shall be waiting for you in my bedchamber when you and your mother have had a chance to talk together.' She smiled up at him. 'No matter what time it is.' Diana knew she would be unable to go to bed, let alone sleep, until she had heard whether or not he and his mother had managed to resolve their lengthy and, she suspected, completely unnecessary estrangement. Although the love she had heard in Felicity Faulkner's voice as she spoke her son's name certainly gave Diana hope that this would indeed be the case…

Chapter Fourteen

❦

'I am sure you will not be at all surprised to learn that Jennifer has availed herself of one of the carriages and fled Faulkner Manor as if the devil himself were at her heels!' Gabriel stormed into Diana's bedchamber completely without warning some two hours later, still dressed in only his loosened shirt, pantaloons and boots, his hair in even more disarray, as if he had been running troubled fingers through it for some time.

Diana had tried to occupy herself profitably in Gabriel's absence, as her aunt had taught her to do during moments of idleness. First by reading a book. Then by taking out her embroidery when none of the favourite books she had brought with her succeeded in holding her attention or her interest. After unpicking the untidiness of her stitches for the fourth time, she had laid her embroidery aside too, her thoughts and emotions in too much turmoil for her to be able to settle to any worthwhile occupation.

So she had begun to pace instead. And when she

tired of that she simply sat down in the chair by the fire, staring into the flames. Wondering. Hoping. So very much hoping that Gabriel's relationship with the mother he so dearly loved would once again be the loving one it had been. For his sake. For his widowed mother's sake.

Yet at the same time, she could not help but wonder how that reconciliation with his mother would affect her own betrothal to him. Gabriel had been completely honest with her from the first. He was now the Earl of Westbourne, and as such he felt he was in need of a wife, primarily as mistress of his homes, and eventually to bear his children. Diana was the daughter of the previous earl, therefore she, or one of her sisters, had been an obvious choice for the role of the new earl's wife. But if Gabriel truly had become reconciled with his mother, and the ice about his emotions melted, he might no longer be of the same cynical frame of mind. He could even decide that he no longer required a wife at all at this moment; his widowed mother could run his homes for him and, at only eight and twenty, there was no rush for him to produce his heirs.

Diana stood up slowly, keeping her expression deliberately calm and composed, even though her doubts as to her own future as Gabriel's wife meant she inwardly felt neither of those things. 'No, I cannot claim to be in the least surprised.'

In truth, if his visit with his mother had proven her theories concerning Jennifer Prescott to be true, then she had been able to see no other solution to the other woman's dilemma; Jennifer would need to leave Faulkner Manor immediately, no doubt with the intention of joining her husband in London, or risk facing

Gabriel's considerable wrath on her own. The devil himself, indeed—and Jennifer, whilst defensive and shrill, did not give the appearance of being quite that brave!

'I trust your mother is feeling more herself now?' she enquired.

His expression instantly became less fierce, the lines beside his nose and mouth smoothing out, his eyes a deep and compassionate blue. 'She fell asleep a few minutes ago as we were still talking,' he revealed huskily.

Diana nodded. 'It will take several days for the complete effects of the laudanum to wear off. I—did the two of you manage to untangle some of your differences?'

'We did,' he said.

'I am so glad.'

Gabriel suddenly looked murderous. 'You might also be pleased to know that it would seem most of your theories might well prove to be correct.'

'I'm not exactly *pleased* to hear that, Gabriel,' she protested.

He gave an impatient shake of his head before crossing the bedchamber restlessly to stand beside the fireplace looking down at the flames. 'At Charles's request, my mother apparently put her brother in charge of the estate accounts after my father died. She did it, she says, because at the time she felt quite unable to cope with the intricacies of managing the estate and fortune herself, and in the hopes that the responsibility would sober Charles somewhat.'

'It did not?'

'No.' Gabriel frowned darkly. 'Oh, he was very

clever about his machinations for several years, the amounts that he took for himself apparently quite negligible within the grand scheme of things. Then, four months ago, my mother had to bring him to task when she discovered that a very large sum of money indeed was missing from the estate account.' His face hardened. 'My mother has absolutely no recollection of things since then. She has been kept asleep for so much of that time she was not even aware that Alice Britton had been dismissed.'

Diana drew in a sharp breath. 'That is truly *monstrous*.'

'Nor did she receive my letter following my father's death, when I requested that I might visit her and my father's graveside. And I did not receive any of the letters she wrote to me during the last six years, when she asked if I would visit her. Letters she apparently entrusted to *Charles* for safe delivery.' The loathing in Gabriel's expression promised retribution for that alone, let alone any of the other crimes his uncle might have committed in that time.

'I am sorry—'

'Do not pity me, Diana.' His face was savage in the firelight as he turned to glare at her. 'Pity is for the weak. And I assure you, at this moment my emotions towards my uncle and his wife are very strong indeed!'

She had no doubts that they were. Just as there could no longer be any doubt that Jennifer fleeing into the night was tantamount to an admission of the Prescotts' guilt. 'Then I will reserve my compassion for your mother. For what she has suffered.'

He drew in a steadying breath before making her

a formal bow, a gesture that lost none of its sincerity because of his lack of formal attire. 'I should be down on my knees to you in gratitude, not taking my temper out on you.'

In a similar situation she knew she might feel equally as violent in her emotions. 'What will you do now?'

'Despite Jennifer's flight, I feel it best if I remain at my mother's side for tonight at least.'

It was obvious from this statement that Gabriel did not intend to spend the rest of the night in Diana's own bed—but had she really expected that he might? The horror of the Prescotts' treatment of his mother must be very disturbing for him; although she might still be quivering with remembered pleasure at the depth of their earlier intimacy, it had been far from the first time that he had known such physical satisfaction and it could not possibly have had the same impact upon his own emotions. In fact, it seemed to have had so little effect that he gave no indication of remembering it at all.

She gave a slight smile. 'I was not referring to your immediate plans, Gabriel…'

'As soon as my mother is well enough to travel we will do as you suggested at dinner and travel to London. Once my mother is safely and comfortably settled at Westbourne House I have every intention of seeking out my uncle and his wife, of chasing them down to the ends of the earth if necessary, and ensuring that they pay for what has been done here,' he vowed.

Perhaps it was selfish of Diana, but she could not help but notice that neither she, nor their betrothal, was mentioned in his plans, either with regard to his imme-diate or his long-term future.

* * *

Gabriel had still been reeling, both emotionally and mentally, when he entered Diana's bedchamber a few minutes ago. He could never have imagined the depths to which Charles and his wife had succumbed since moving to Faulkner Manor to live with his newly widowed mother. Beginning, it would seem, with the appropriation of the letters sent between mother and son over the years...

No doubt once Gabriel had chance to check the estate accounts for himself he would find that Charles had been supplementing his gambling habit from those funds for most, if not all, of the past six years. He believed the large sum his mother had brought Charles to task over some four months ago, and which, with his renowned lack of luck at the gaming tables, he would have no hopes of repaying, would indeed prove to be the reason for the dismissal of all the people close to his mother and for the use of heavy doses of laudanum to ensure that she had remained in a haze of sleep for most of the time since.

As for the true events of that supposed scandal eight years ago...

If Gabriel had thought at all about the real identity of the father of Jennifer Lindsay's baby, then he had assumed it must be one of the men from the village. It had never even occurred to him, until Diana had made the suggestion earlier, that it might have been his roguish and disreputable Uncle Charles all the time.

Perhaps it should have done. Even then Charles had been more often than not down on his luck from gambling, and often spent months at a time at Faulkner

Manor, sponging on the generosity of Gabriel's father, as much as avoiding his creditors. And no doubt enjoying the favours of the local women as often as possible, too.

Yes, the more Gabriel considered the possibility of Charles being the father of Jennifer's baby, the more inclined he was to believe that the whole course of events had been contrived in order to disinherit Gabriel, and at the same time provide Charles with a generous amount of money to marry the woman who was already his mistress.

It had taken Diana, with her cool detachment, to stand back and see the possible true course of events. Gabriel felt foolish, even ridiculous, for not having seen those things for himself at the time. Not only that, but through his own pride and arrogance in refusing to visit Faulkner Manor, he had subjected his mother to months of hell.

What must Diana think of him now? For not having seen the happenings here for what they were eight years ago? For allowing his prideful arrogance to leave his mother to suffer for years at the hands of the Prescotts? He knew that Diana, with her no-nonsense attitude, and her very definite views on what was right and what was wrong, would never have allowed that to happen to a member of her own family.

Gabriel looked across at her now between narrowed lids, but was unable to read anything of her thoughts or emotions from the calm composure with which she gazed back at him. Was that deliberate?

No doubt she would need some time in which to digest and accept all they had discovered here. To decide how she felt about those discoveries. And perhaps how, or if, those things affected their betrothal and the regard that had been tentatively growing between the two of them. He would not want her to go through with their marriage if he had given her a disgust of him. Yes, in the circumstances, he accepted that time to think those things over was the least that he could give her.

He drew himself up to his full height, his expression deliberately lacking all emotion. 'Between being with my mother and looking into estate business, I will no doubt find myself very busy during the next few days as we wait for her health to strengthen enough to travel.'

Her eyes were suddenly very blue in the pallor of her face as she steadily returned his gaze. 'Of course.'

'Thank you.' He bowed elegantly. 'You are, as ever, unfailingly generous in your understanding.'

Was she? At this moment she felt an uncharacteristic inclination to scream and wail at the cold remoteness of his expression and manner, when all she wanted to do was throw herself into his strong arms and have him make love to her; she felt in dire need of that evidence of his unchanged desire for her, at least.

She would do none of those things, of course. She had learnt long ago never to ask for, or to expect, the consideration of others in regard to her own emotions, but to keep her own needs to herself and her emotions firmly under her control. Except when she and Gabriel made love…

'I shall endeavour to help in any way that I can to see that your mother's return to full health is a smooth and untroubled one.' Her demeanour was as cool as his own.

He inclined his head. 'I am most appreciative of any kindness you might show her.'

That urge inside her to wail and cry became almost overwhelming as he continued to speak to her with the politeness of a stranger. They had been so wonderfully intimate earlier, which still made her blush to think of it, and yet he was now treating her as if she were nothing more than a kind and considerate friend!

Whereas she now thought of Gabriel as—as what?

Diana frowned, knowing now was not the time to search her own emotions for answers to how she felt towards him. 'Of course. Please do not delay here any longer,' she said. 'Your mother may have reawakened in your absence and wondered if you being there at all was nothing but a dream.'

'Indeed.' Gabriel's jaw was rigidly set as he continued to look down at her for several long seconds. Seconds when he could still read nothing from the calmness of her expression, when he wished for nothing more than to once again take her in his arms and—

'I will wish you a good night, then, my lord,' she added, her tone and demeanour obviously a dismissal.

Gabriel drew himself up proudly. He had felt so close to her when they'd made love earlier, had felt as if they were on the brink of—of what? Feeling real affection for each other, perhaps? An affection that might have deepened over the years, thereby making their marriage of convenience more bearable for them both.

There was no affection in Diana's manner now. None of that earlier warmth and teasing. Instead it seemed as if there was a wall standing between them.

An insurmountable wall?

* * *

'I cannot recall the last time I visited London…' Mrs Felicity Faulkner's expression was rapt as she gazed out of the carriage window at the rush and bustle, the noise, the smells, that was the capital of England; the streets were crowded with other carriages, with children dodging in between the horses, dogs barking, voices raised as women sold flowers on street corners, and men stood behind stands with hot pies and ale for sale.

None of which succeeded in impressing itself upon Diana's inner misery in the slightest.

It had taken two further days at Faulkner Manor for Felicity to recover her wits and to have strength enough to be able to make this slow, three-day journey to London. The two days lingering at the Manor had been excruciating ones for Diana, as she saw little or nothing of Gabriel, and was treated with cool politeness by him whenever they did chance to meet over the breakfast or dinner table. He had been, as he had predicted, excessively busy with estate business, his expression becoming grimmer by the hour, it seemed, as he obviously found further discrepancies in his mother's account books.

Felicity was as delightful as Gabriel had led Diana to believe; a beautiful and vivacious woman who, although sorely tried emotionally for so many years, had quickly recovered her full spirits once she was no longer being plagued with heavy doses of laudanum and could enjoy the return of her son. She was also overjoyed to learn of his inheritance of the title and estates of the Earl of Westbourne.

Forbidden by Gabriel to so much as mention either

of the Prescotts to his mother, Diana often took refuge in discussing Shoreley Park with the older woman as a means of avoiding talking about more personal subjects. Something that had not proved too difficult to do when it emerged that Gabriel, no doubt for reasons of his own, had so far not told Felicity of their betrothal; as far as his mother was concerned, Diana was only the eldest of her son's wards.

Perhaps he had every intention of being asked to be released from that betrothal once they were back in London? She couldn't help wondering miserably. If that were to happen then not one, but two men would have passed her over as their choice for a wife; Malcolm because he had met and wooed a woman who could bring wealth rather than a title to their marriage, and Gabriel because their betrothal had only ever been a matter of convenience to him from the first. A betrothal he obviously no longer found convenient or necessary.

The more Diana's thoughts dwelt on those two rejections the angrier she became. How dare they? How dare those men discard her as if she were no more than a pair of boots that no longer fit them comfortably? Quite when Gabriel intended to ask her officially to release him from their betrothal she had no idea, but the past five days, spent in an agony of emotions, meant that she now had plenty of things she wished to say to him once he did decide to do so. So many, in fact, that she had no idea whether she would be able to stop that flow of words once they had begun.

'You seem pensive, my dear?'

Diana turned from gazing out of the window to look across the carriage at Felicity. 'I am sorry if I am being less than companionable, but there is a slight family… disturbance, which occupies all of my thoughts at present.' Not completely true, when what she wished to say to Gabriel kept her so mentally exhausted, but the nearer they came to London the more her thoughts returned to her missing sister Elizabeth. They had received no news at Faulkner Manor on that subject, from either Caroline or Lord Vaughn, and so Diana could only assume that Elizabeth was still missing. Lost and alone somewhere in this noisy, smelly metropolis…

More than anything she now wished to return to Shoreley Park, if only to lick her wounds in private; something she could not do until they had found and returned Elizabeth to the safety of their family.

Felicity's kind face softened in understanding. 'Gabriel has explained to me the…situation—' she glanced at Diana's maid also seated in the carriage with them, '—concerning your sister.'

Her eyes widened. 'He has?'

'Oh, yes.' The older woman smiled. 'Gabriel takes his role as guardian to you and your sisters very seriously indeed.'

His role as her guardian…

When Diana wanted so much more from him! She wanted a return of the man who had made such beautiful love to her five nights ago and she still wanted to become his wife, in the hopes that he might one day come to truly care for her.

As she truly cared for him…

Her feelings for Gabriel were something she had not questioned too often these past few days. Love, once acknowledged, even to oneself, could no longer be ignored, so she refused to look deeply enough into her feelings to know whether or not it was love she felt for him. Besides, surely if she *were* in love with him, she would not also feel this overwhelming urge to pummel her fists upon his chest whilst calling him a long list of names that would no doubt be more suited to coming from the lips of a fisherman's wife?

'I appreciate his concern,' she replied tightly.

His mother looked wistful. 'I wish you could have known him before any of this unpleasantness occurred. He was so much kinder then, so generous with his affections.' She shook her head sadly.

And in return for that kindness and generosity of affection, he had been disinherited and banished by his family and society. Was it any wonder that he had become the hard and cynical man he was today? she thought. 'He is still kind and generous in his affections towards you,' Diana pointed out.

'Oh, he is.' Deep-blue eyes, so like her son's, became awash with unshed tears. 'I only wish… My husband was not really such a hard or unforgiving man, Diana. It pained him so much to be that way with Gabriel. I am sure, if Neville had lived longer, that he and Gabriel would have eventually made their peace with each other.'

Diana knew that mother and son had visited his father's grave together before they'd departed. Gabriel's expression had been one of such grim emotion on his return to the house that Diana had not dared to so much as speak to him before he'd disappeared into his father's study and had not reappeared again until it was time for dinner two hours later, his demeanour then still so remote that she had felt it best to leave him to his own reflections.

She reached across the carriage now to squeeze the other woman's hand. 'I am sure of it, too.'

Felicity shook off her sadness. 'Now I am come to London and am to become reacquainted with your Aunt Humphries. Dorothea and I were such firm friends in our youth, you know,' she confided warmly.

Diana smiled. 'So she has told me.'

'Not all, I am sure.' Felicity looked far less than her fifty-two years as she smiled mischievously. 'Dorothea was considered something of an Original, you know.'

'Aunt Humphries was?' Diana could not hide her surprise at this disclosure; her aunt had always given the impression of being just a little shy of prudish.

'Oh, yes,' Felicity said. 'In truth, all of the *ton* was surprised when she accepted the offer of Captain Humphries, not only a man so much older than her, but one who could also be very stern on occasion.'

'I believe they were very happy in their marriage.'

'Oh, I do so hope they were!' Felicity's concern for her old friend's happiness was sincere. 'I truly cannot wait to see Dorothea again and catch up on all that has happened in her life these past thirty years.'

And Diana would be just as happy to be relieved of the company; the nearer they had come to London the more difficult it had become for her to hide her true feelings towards Gabriel from his mother. Especially when she did not understand that confusing mix of anger, warmth and despair herself!

Gabriel was tired, stiff and not a little bad-tempered as he stepped down from Maximilian's broad back before handing the reins to one of the grooms who had hurried round from the stables of Westbourne House to greet them.

The first of two discomforts was caused from the many hours he had spent in the saddle, and the latter from an ever-increasing frustration with Diana's recent avoidance of even making polite conversation with him on the few occasions they had been together.

He had hoped—a complete arrogance on his part, no doubt—that with time she might come to feel more warmly towards him again; instead her manner had become cooler with each day that had passed, to the point she now seemed to avoid his company altogether whenever possible.

The stigma of his past so-called scandal had not deterred her from agreeing to marry him—no doubt the kindness of her nature meant she had seen him as a lost soul in need of saving. Learning that the wife of his uncle was the woman from his past had not shaken her composure for too long, either. No, it seemed that discovering Gabriel's pride and arrogance had resulted in his mother's misery and incarceration had finally been too much for the sensitive and kind-hearted Diana to bear. After all, he thought unhappily, it was that very same arrogance that had initially prompted him to propose to whichever of the Copeland sisters would have him.

'You are returned at last, Diana!'

The two ladies barely had time to step down from the carriage before the front door of Westbourne House was thrown open and an excited Caroline ran lightly down the steps to greet her sister with an enthusiasm that attested to their deep affection for each other.

'Mrs Faulkner.' Caroline curtsied politely once Diana had made the introductions. 'My lord.' Caroline's tone cooled slightly as she turned to give him a brief nod of acknowledgement.

No change there, then, Gabriel acknowledged ruefully as he joined the ladies and returned her nod. Even Dominic's championing of Gabriel could not change Caroline's opinion that he was not in the least good enough for her beloved sister.

An opinion Gabriel now shared.

'It is so good to have you back with us in London.' Caroline linked her arm through her sister's as the three ladies preceded Gabriel up the steps to the house. 'And you will never guess who else has come to town?' Her eyes sparkled a deep sea-green as she looked at Diana excitedly.

'I am sure I do not need to guess when you are obviously in such a lather to tell me,' she returned drily.

'Malcolm Castle!' Caroline did exactly that, her face aglow with the enormity of the announcement. 'He called for the first time four days ago, and he has been back every day since in the hopes of learning that you are returned from Cambridgeshire!'

Gabriel's step faltered as he overheard this news, his heart sinking as he realised the significance of this information. Had that young man now realised his mistake and come in search of Diana in the hopes of renewing his courtship?

Chapter Fifteen

'I trust you are not going to be difficult about releasing my sister from your betrothal?'

Gabriel closed his eyes briefly before opening them again, the return to the neat view of the garden outside the study window doing little to soothe the blackness of his mood. How could it, when every time he looked out at this garden he would remember that it was Diana who had instructed the gardeners on how she wanted it to appear? Everything about this house had been lovingly restored to its former glory under her instruction—

'Are you deaf, my lord, or merely choosing to ignore me?'

Just as Caroline would always and for evermore be Diana's champion! That would prove awkward for all of them if—*when* Gabriel's betrothal to Diana came to an end, and Caroline and Dominic were married.

He turned slowly, his expression remaining impassive as he took in the flushed irritation on Caroline's beautiful face as she glared across the room at him.

'I am neither deaf nor ignoring you, Caroline,' he said silkily.

'Well?'

'Well what?

She stepped into the study before closing the door firmly behind her. 'Is it your intention to release Diana from your betrothal without undo fuss?'

Gabriel's mouth compressed. 'To my knowledge, your sister has made no such request of me.'

Those sea-green eyes widened. 'But surely you must know that she will do so?'

'Must I?' he said evasively.

She scowled at him. 'I do not believe you to be either stupid or insensitive.'

'I am gratified to hear it!'

She gave an impatient snort. 'You are being deliberately obtuse—'

'On the contrary, my dear, Caroline, I am trying—and obviously not succeeding—to understand what business it is of yours how or indeed *if* my betrothal to Diana should come to an end.' He looked witheringly at her.

True to character, Caroline did not back down in the slightest. 'It became my business, my lord, the moment my sister, a woman who never cries, only minutes ago began to sob in my arms as if her heart would break!'

Those words were like a sword wound in Gabriel's own chest. He and Diana had parted just over an hour ago, she to go upstairs with her sister, Gabriel to see to his mother's safe delivery to the comfort of her bedchamber where, to his mother's obvious delight, Alice Britton was waiting to welcome her, which Gabriel had arranged whilst still at the Manor. The joy on his mother's face as the two women were reunited was enough to show him in that, at least, he had acted correctly.

Just as he would have to do by releasing Diana from their betrothal?

Diana had assured him when they'd agreed to marry that there was not even the possibility of her ever reuniting with Castle. But it had been a denial she had made in the abstract, in the confidence that it would never happen; her distressed state at learning Castle wished to see her again was evidence of her true feelings in the matter.

Caroline eyed him warily. 'Does it not bother you in the least to learn that Diana is inconsolable?'

He drew his breath in sharply at the mere thought of her in such an agony of emotions. 'Of course it bothers me!' A nerve pulsed in his tightly clenched jaw. 'I am insulted that you might think it would not. I assure you I have no wish to ever cause Diana the slightest discomfort.'

Those sea-green eyes widened in shock. 'I believe you really mean that,' she said wonderingly.

Gabriel scowled. 'I find the disbelief in your tone positively insulting.'

Her expression became quizzical. 'You seem changed since last we spoke, Gabriel.'

His expression became guarded. 'Changed how?'

'Less forceful. Less unyielding. Certainly less arrogant,' she added with a teasing smile.

'Really?' Gabriel rallied drily. 'I am sure your sister will be gratified to hear it!'

'As are we all,' she responded. 'I trust that you *will* speak with her then?'

He nodded. 'You may.'

His expression became grimmer still once she had departed the study, as he contemplated the upcoming— but very necessary—conversation with her elder sister.

'Has that cushion offended you in some way?'

Diana stiffened at the first sound of Gabriel's voice, turning sharply now from where she sat on the *chaise* to see him standing in the open doorway of her bed- chamber, dark brows raised over mocking blue eyes.

He had changed from his dusty travelling clothes and now wore a dark-blue superfine, a lighter-blue waist- coat, beige pantaloons and shiny black Hessians, the darkness of his hair still slightly damp from his ablu- tions.

His very physical presence took her breath away. 'I beg your pardon?'

'You appear to be shredding the tassels on that cush- ion,' he drawled as he stepped into the room. 'I felt sure it must have offended you in some way.'

Diana looked down at the cushion she cradled on her knees, having had no idea it was even there until he'd brought it to her attention. Or that she had pulled so agitatedly on the silk tassels at its corner that the majority of those silks now lay in a tangle beside her on the blue-velvet *chaise*.

She hurriedly placed the cushion down on top of that tangle before standing up. 'What can I do for you, my lord?'

What, alone together in her bedchamber, could she

not do for him? He wondered in despair. The ache he felt becoming a physical discomfort as he hardened with the need to take her in his arms and finally make proper love to her.

A totally ridiculous desire when the evidence of her recent tears was there in the heavy darkness of her eyes and the dampness of her creamy cheeks. When her mouth, those full and kissable lips, seemed to tremble slightly before she set them firmly together and raised her chin to present him once more with that familiar air of cool composure.

Gabriel moved to stand before the window that looked out over the square at the front of the house. 'You must be pleased to find yourself back in London?' he commented.

Must she? Why must she? Diana could think of absolutely no reason, other than continuing the search for Elizabeth—a sister who obviously had no wish to be found!

Nor did she appreciate him seeing her in this way, the evidence of her tears no doubt apparent to him. Although she was firm in her resolve that he should never know the reason for them: because she was so certain that, now that they were back in London, he would waste no time in ending their betrothal.

Her back straightened as if her body was in preparation for a blow. 'It is certainly pleasant to be united with at least one of my sisters.'

Gabriel turned to face her. 'I assure you that Vaughn and I will continue our search for Elizabeth, leaving no stone unturned.'

'I implied no criticism of either you or Lord Vaughn, my lord,' she said quickly.

The sunlight shining in the window behind him gave his hair a blue-black sheen, and threw the grimness of his expression into shadow. 'No?' He quirked one dark brow. 'Then perhaps there should have been. Dominic has obviously been unsuccessful this past week, whilst I have been deeply occupied with other matters.'

She gave an acknowledging inclination of her head. 'I perfectly understood that the continuing welfare of your mother was of greater importance to you at that time.'

A frown creased his brow. 'It is a part of the warmth and caring of your nature to always be so concerned with the happiness of others.'

Was it? She was no longer sure. How could she be, when at this moment it was thoughts of her own unhappiness that consumed her? When the certainty of Gabriel having come here to ask her to release him from their betrothal made her feel as if her heart were shattering into so many pieces she might never be able to put it back together again?

She loved him...

Diana could deny it no longer. Could ignore it no longer. She was irrevocably in love with Lord Gabriel Faulkner, the Earl of Westbourne. The knowledge that Malcolm Castle had reappeared in her life had suddenly crystallised her feelings sharply for her. The only man in the world for her was Gabriel and a huge tidal wave of emotions swept over her every time she so much as looked at him. She wanted to reach out and touch him.

To be gathered into his arms and kissed by him. To be held by him and know that he would never let her go.

When letting her go was no doubt exactly what he had come here to do…

She could see it in the dark regret in his eyes, in the resignation of his expression, in his restlessness of movement as he began to pace her bedchamber. No doubt seeking, searching, for the appropriate words in which to tell her he no longer wished to marry her.

It was a further indignity Diana found she could not even bear to contemplate. She drew herself up proudly, her face pale. 'I believe it is the correct procedure in situations such as ours for the lady to be seen to end the betrothal?'

Gabriel drew in a sharp breath before once again turning to stare sightlessly out of the window, an icy chill filling his chest at finally hearing her ask to be released from her promise to him. At the thought of having to stand back and watch as she gave all of the warmth and caring of her nature into the keeping of someone else. Of having to witness her marrying another man—even to give her away in church!

Gabriel had entered into their engagement without a care as to which of the Copeland sisters should accept his offer of marriage in the erroneous belief that one young woman would do equally as well as another. He now knew just how totally false that was. There was no other woman like Diana. No other woman with her warmth and tenderness of heart. Her loyalty. Her care for duty. As for her courage—he believed she would challenge the devil himself, if she had need to, and never count the cost to herself.

Because it was what Diana did. What she had done unstintingly for the past ten years, for her family and others, regardless of her own happiness. And it was what she would no doubt continue to do if he did not agree to release her from their betrothal…

He could not ask that of her. Would not ask that of her.

How painfully ironic that he, a man who had lived the last few years of his life with almost complete disregard for the feelings of others, could not bear to be the reason that Diana should suffer even another moment of unhappiness.

He turned to give her a stiff nod of agreement, lids lowered guardedly over any emotion in his eyes. 'I will see to placing the announcement in the newspapers tomorrow, or the day after at the very latest, if that will suit?' No doubt he would have to place another announcement in those newspapers a day or so after that, this time announcing Diana's betrothal to that cur Castle!

Her eyes were a deep and shadowed blue in the pallor of her face. 'I would appreciate that, my lord.'

He nodded tersely. 'Is there anything else you wish to discuss with me?'

What else could there possibly be? she wondered numbly. Gabriel no longer wanted her as his wife or anything else—what else could possibly have any meaning? All the things she had longed to say to him this past five days, the anger and hurt that had been steadily building inside her, had all dissolved into sheer numbness at the occurrence of the very thing she had been dreading.

The end of their engagement. There was nothing else—only an unending agony of emotions that threatened to bring Diana to her knees. She needed him to leave so she could break down and cry without him knowing. 'There is nothing else I wish to say, my lord,' she lied woodenly.

'Very well.' He walked to the door.

Suddenly, confusingly, Diana could not bear to see him leave. 'You—it was very kind of you to arrange for Miss Britton to be here to welcome your mother.'

He came to a halt and turned with a humourless smile. 'You did not believe me capable of kindness?'

She looked appalled. 'I—that's not what I meant! I know that you are.'

His mouth twisted. 'Just not where you are concerned?'

She swore she could hear her heart breaking 'I consider it a great kindness to have released me from our betrothal,' she choked.

'So it is.' His nostrils flared as his mouth thinned, the expression in the dark blue of his eyes now unreadable. 'If you will excuse me, Diana, I really am very busy.' He left the room, closing the door firmly behind him.

As firmly as Diana knew that his heart was, and ever would be, closed to her.

'You are going out?'

Diana came to a halt in the cavernous hallway of Westbourne House the following morning, turning away from where Soames stood ready to open the front door for her own and her maid's departure, to instead face Gabriel as he stood framed in the doorway of his study, knowing that the bonnet and burgundy-coloured pelisse she wore over her cream-and-burgundy-coloured sprigged-muslin gown should have been evidence enough of her going out. 'I intended to go to the shops, my lord,' she nevertheless answered him coolly. 'Your mother is perfectly happy in the company of my aunt and Alice, if that is your concern?'

Gabriel was well aware of his mother's preoccupation, both with the return of her companion, and the reunion with her old friend Dorothea Humphries—a woman he had finally been introduced to yesterday and who seemed to view him more kindly now that he had brought her friend home with him.

Even if he had not been aware of his mother's happiness, his immediate concern was not for his mother, but more for the chasm that had only widened between himself and Diana since they had agreed to end to their betrothal last night.

'Perhaps we might talk in private for a few minutes before you go out?' he asked softly.

That was the very last thing she wished to do, especially as he was looking more devastatingly handsome than usual in a fashionable superfine of chocolate brown, a gold-and-cream waistcoat buttoned over the flatness of his stomach, with cream pantaloons and brown Hessians fitting snugly to the muscled length of his legs.

She swallowed before answering. 'Can it not wait until I have returned, my lord?'

He frowned slightly. 'I would rather it be now.'

'Very well.' She turned to request that her maid wait for her here before she preceded Gabriel into his study.

She stood just inside the room as he closed the door behind him and then went to stand behind his mahogany desk. 'I trust it is something important that you feel the need to interrupt a lady who only wishes to shop!' Her attempt at humour sounded flat to her own ears, but she could see by the tightening of his mouth that he did not appreciate even that effort.

And it *was* an effort to try to appear even remotely like her usual composed self after a night of sobbing uncontrollably into her pillow. She had excused herself from having dinner downstairs with the rest of the family on a plea of lingering tiredness from her journey. She had requested breakfast in her room this morning for the same reason. Knowing this avoidance of his company could not continue indefinitely, Diana had finally decided to take herself out of the house completely for a few hours, but even that had been foiled by Gabriel.

'You have news of Elizabeth, perhaps?' She looked hopefully across the imposing desk at him.

'I am afraid not,' Gabriel frowned. 'I had thought, as you have been so involved in the matter, that you might be interested to learn what progress has been made in regard to the Prescotts?'

Her brow cleared. 'You have managed to ascertain their whereabouts?'

'Not yet.' His jaw tightened. 'But with Vaughn's help and resources, I have managed to learn more of my uncle's debts, at least.' He suddenly looked uncomfortable at having revealed that knowledge about Dominic to her.

Diana gave a rueful smile. 'Do not concern yourself,

my lord; I spoke with Caroline earlier this morning and I am now fully conversant with Lord Vaughn's ownership of one of London's better-known gambling establishments!' Caroline had visited her bedchamber after breakfast and confessed all in regard to the weeks she had spent alone in London. Despite her sister having ended up embarking on a brief stint singing in Lord Vaughn's club, which Diana admitted was far from ideal, she had nevertheless realised that Caroline had been fortunate indeed to land in such a safe pair of hands.

Gabriel quirked a dark brow. 'You are?'

'Yes.' Diana gave a rueful smile at the memory of the shocking tale Caroline had to tell. 'I am very grateful to Lord Vaughn for looking after my sister so well.'

'As am I,' he said grimly.

Diana bristled defensively. 'Caroline is very young.'

'She is not much younger than you are,' he pointed out.

'In years, perhaps,' she conceded. 'I trust that upbraiding me for not maintaining more control over my sister's actions was not one of the reasons you asked to speak with me?'

'God, no!' Gabriel exclaimed. 'I defy anyone to maintain control over that particular young lady.'

'Even Lord Vaughn?' Diana teased.

His expression softened into a genuine smile. 'Vaughn seems to relish the challenge.'

Diana felt her cheeks warm at thoughts of the effective tactics Lord Vaughn might use in order to put an end to Caroline's challenges any time it suited him.

'You were about to tell me something of the Prescotts, I believe?'

He nodded. 'With Vaughn's inside knowledge into the gambling world, I have managed to ascertain the exact extent of my uncle's debts.'

'They are considerable?'

'They are enormous,' he admitted.

Diana shook her head. 'But that does not excuse his or his wife's treatment of your mother.'

'No, it most certainly does not!' Having nothing and no one else to turn his frustrations upon, as Gabriel could not bring himself to feel in the least angry towards Diana for ending their betrothal if it meant she secured her own happiness, he was instead concentrating all of his efforts on finding his uncle and his wife.

'Was that all you wished to tell me, my lord?'

It was all that he *could* tell her! Having spent most of the previous night thinking about her, Gabriel knew he was no nearer to accepting the end of their engagement than he was to bearing the thought of her being in love with another man.

Because he wished to have Diana's love for himself.

Oh, he ached to make love to her again, but that was not all that he wanted from her. He also wanted her gentleness. Her warmth. Her courage and her dignity. Nor did he believe for a moment that Castle was deserving of the unique and beautiful woman that was Diana. Any more than Gabriel believed that he was worthy of those things either.

'Is that not enough?' he rasped.

'Of course,' she accepted coolly, any hopes—futile hopes, admittedly—that he might have reconsidered his decision concerning the ending of their betrothal totally dashed. 'If there is nothing else, I should like to be on my way.'

Gabriel returned her gaze wordlessly for several seconds before turning away. 'No, there is nothing else. Except…'

Diana raised golden brows. 'Yes?'

Gabriel clenched his jaw to stop himself from saying words he should not, words that begged her to change her mind about him. 'What would you like me to say to Castle if he should call again this morning?'

'The truth, of course.'

'Which is?'

'That I am out,' she said before quietly leaving the study.

Once again he could not help but admire her pride and dignity; she had obviously decided she did not intend to make it at all easy for Castle to believe he might recapture her affections.

When, as Gabriel knew perfectly well, her affections for the man had remained constant and unchanging…

Diana had absolutely no idea where she went or what she did for at least the first half an hour after she left Westbourne House, the carriage ride passing as if in a haze. Then, once at the shops, she found it an effort just placing one slippered foot in front of the other. So lost in thought was she, so mired down by the inner misery she suffered at the futility of the love she felt for Gabriel, that it took some seconds to recognise the familiar face she saw pressed against the window of a passing carriage…

Chapter Sixteen

'Beg pardon, my lord, but I have an urgent message to deliver from my mistress.'

In the hour since Diana had left the house Gabriel had not so much as looked at any of the work that had accumulated on his desk after almost a week's absence. Instead he had spent that time composing the announcement of his broken betrothal before throwing it to one side and then sitting behind his desk in brooding contemplation of the shiny toes of his boots as he rested his feet on the desktop in front of him.

He turned now to frown at the young maid who stood so hesitant and uncomfortable in the doorway. 'Yes?'

'Lady Diana said I was to tell you—'

'Lady Diana?' Gabriel echoed sharply, his feet falling heavily to the floor as he sat forwards in the chair. 'You are Lady Diana's maid?' Actually, he recognised her now from that night in his mother's bedchamber at the Manor.

'I am, my lord, yes. And—'

'Did you not leave to go shopping with her just an hour ago?'

'I did, sir, yes—'

'Your mistress has returned from shopping and wishes you to relay a message to me?' Had it come to such a sorry state of affairs between the two of them that Diana did not even feel she could come and speak to him herself?

'No, my lord. Yes, my lord. That is—' the young woman looked slightly discomposed '—Lady Diana does wish me to give you a message, but she has not yet returned from shopping.'

'Then why the devil are you not still with her?' Gabriel demanded as he stood up.

That discomposure turned to a look of panic. 'She sent me back to the house, my lord.'

'And you left her alone in the middle of London, without a chaperon? Unless she was not alone,' he added as the thought of Malcolm Castle suddenly occurred to him. He scowled as he envisaged Diana's quiet dignity as she listened to her erstwhile suitor's pleas for understanding, to his declarations of having loved her all along.

'Oh, she was alone, my lord. But—'

'Come in and shut the door, girl,' Gabriel instructed. 'Now, explain, if you please.'

The maid's hands were tightly gripped together in front of her as she eyed him nervously. 'It was the woman in the carriage, my lord. Lady Diana saw her and we followed the carriage until it stopped at an inn and the lady got out, then Lady Diana sent me back to tell you that you must come to her there immediately.'

Gabriel would be more than happy to do as Diana asked and go to her. At any time. To any place. 'What woman in the carriage?' Could it be that Diana had spotted Elizabeth? That she had succeeded where he and Dominic had failed so abysmally?

'It was that Mrs Prescott, my lord.' The maid looked primly disapproving. 'Bold as brass she was, riding along in the carriage as if butter wouldn't melt in her mouth. When all the time—'

'Mrs Prescott!' Gabriel thundered. 'And the two of you were daft enough to *follow* her?' When Diana returned he was going to lock her in her bedchamber and throw away the key for behaving so recklessly!

'It wasn't too difficult to do, my lord.' The girl looked pleased with herself. 'There are so many carriages on the streets at this time of the morning, and—'

'So you followed Mrs Prescott to an inn here in town?' Gabriel cut in, having absolutely no time or patience to deal with this young woman's long-winded explanation.

'Yes, my lord.'

'And Lady Diana is there still?'

'Waiting outside, my lord.'

'Take me there now, please.' Gabriel needed to get to Diana as soon as was possible. He dare not leave her alone anywhere near Jennifer Prescott—that harpy was more dangerous than she looked.

'If you are intending to look inconspicuous in your attempts at window shopping, then you are failing abysmally!'

Diana stiffened at the first sound of that familiar

taunting voice, drawing in a slow and calming breath before slowly turning to face Jennifer Prescott, her gaze coolly dismissive as she looked at the older woman. 'I was attempting to decide which hat I might consider purchasing.'

The other woman looked unconvinced. 'As this is one of the more unfashionable parts of town, I seriously hope you decided on none of them.'

The milliner's was, Diana agreed, a particularly unimpressive establishment, but surely preferable to her simply lurking about on the street corner. 'Perhaps you are right.' She gave a falsely bright smile. 'If you will excuse me?' Diana turned with the intention of walking away, her heart thundering in her chest with the knowledge that she should not have allowed Jennifer to realise that she had seen and followed her back to the inn where she and, possibly, her husband were staying.

'I think not.' Surprisingly strong fingers reached out and took a firm grasp of her arm, preventing her from leaving.

Diana raised haughty brows. 'Release my arm immediately, madam.'

The other woman took absolutely no account of the request. 'Where is Gabriel?'

'How on earth should I know that?'

Jennifer's mouth twisted derisively. 'Because I have learnt that wherever you are, he is sure never to be far behind.'

If only that were true, Diana yearned inwardly, at the same time as she sincerely hoped that her outward show of bravado was convincing—surely May must have reached Westbourne House by now and relayed her message to Gabriel? 'I believe you will find that you are in error on this occasion.'

The other woman looked completely unperturbed. 'You had a maid with you earlier; no doubt she has gone for Gabriel.' She smiled mockingly as Diana gave a start of surprise. 'Oh, yes, my dear sweet Diana, I was fully aware of your inexpert attempt to follow me. Just as you were intended to do when I deliberately showed my face at the carriage window,' she added with satisfaction. 'Charles and I have had someone watching Westbourne House the past few days awaiting your return to town. It was fortuitous indeed that you should venture out alone so soon, thereby making it easy for me to arrange for you to catch sight of me.'

So much for Diana having believed she had followed her stealthily and unobserved!

Jennifer's fingers now dug painfully into her arm and her face twisted into a malicious mask. 'Gabriel?'

Diana knew she could continue to lie, to prevaricate, but what would be the point? Her chin rose challengingly. 'As you say, I have sent my maid back to Westbourne House to inform him of the whereabouts of you and your husband. I have no doubts he will be here directly.'

If she had intended to disconcert the other woman with this announcement then she was disappointed, as Jennifer smiled in satisfaction. 'In that case I must insist that you join myself and my husband at the inn whilst we all await Gabriel's arrival.'

Diana's eyes widened as she realised the implications of this dictate. 'Unfortunately it is an invitation I must decline—'

'Sadly, you will not be allowed to do so,' Jennifer jeered. 'Ah, Charles.' Her gaze shifted behind her quarry. 'Lady Diana has decided to join us at the inn for refreshment whilst we await your nephew's arrival.'

As a ploy to distract Diana's attention it was not very original. If indeed, it was a ploy?

'How pleasant to make your acquaintance, Lady Diana.' The voice that answered Jennifer was lazily charming, and obviously belonged to her husband, Mr Charles Prescott. Obviously not a ploy, then!

Gabriel's frustration and anger, already at a premium after learning of Diana's recklessness in following Jennifer Prescott, only increased when he arrived outside the inaptly named Peacock Inn where Diana's maid had seen her last and failed to find any sign of her.

Where could she have gone? Surely she could not have been idiotic enough to confront the Prescotts on her own?

'Ah, Gabriel, you are come at last…'

He spun round to confront Jennifer, his eyes narrowing as he considered the implications of both the pleasantness of her tone and her complete lack of surprise in seeing him there. 'Where is Diana?' he demanded coldly.

She gave a mocking smile. 'She and Charles are becoming acquainted at the inn. It really is too bad of you, Gabriel, not to have made the introductions yourself, but—'

'Do not play games with me, Jennifer.' The softness of Gabriel's tone was more menacing than any show of anger might have been, even though the thought of

Diana alone with his unscrupulous Uncle Charles was enough to turn the blood cold in his veins.

Jennifer's eyes flashed angrily. 'I suppose Felicity has told you all?'

'You suppose correctly,' he said. 'Now take me to Diana before I give in to the pleasure I would find in wringing your neck.'

She looked unimpressed by the threat. 'How anyone could ever have believed I preferred you over Charles eight years ago is beyond my understanding.'

Gabriel's mouth twisted contemptuously as this statement seemed to confirm Diana's suspicion that Charles was the man Jennifer had been involved with all along. 'Most things are beyond your understanding, Jennifer. Now take me to Diana!'

'Gladly.' She eyed him greedily. 'No doubt, with Diana Copeland as our…guest, you will be only too happy to dismiss any charges you may have thought of bringing against us, as well as paying all of Charles's debts!'

Gabriel did not reveal his reaction to this statement by so much of the blink of an eyelid, his long years of forced exile from his family and home having provided him with the ability to hide his inner feelings. It wasn't that he did not have feelings on the subject, only that they were too strong, ran far too deep, to be allowed out of his rigid control. A control that would undoubtedly snap if he were to learn that this vile couple had harmed one golden hair upon Diana's head.

'—and so you see it was easy for Jennifer to claim that she was with child and that Gabriel was the father.'

Diana eyed Charles with distaste as the two of them sat together in a private parlour of the inn. Oh, he was undoubtedly as handsome and charming as everyone had claimed him to be, with his dark good looks so like his nephew's and his own ease of manner. A charming rogue, in fact.

Except Diana found him far from handsome *or* charming. Not only did she despise him utterly for having just confirmed his involvement with the youthful Jennifer eight years ago, so obviously without any thought or concern for the nephew whose reputation he had so casually destroyed, but the pistol he held in his hand, and pointed directly at her, also gave her reason to fear him.

'For her to *claim* she was with child?' Diana repeated mildly.

'Well, yes, of course; she never actually conceived one—Jennifer has never wanted children, and knows exactly how to go about not having them.' Charles smiled lazily. 'We knew, of course, that none of my family would be so indelicate as to demand Jennifer see a physician to confirm the pregnancy. Not the done thing to mistrust a lady's word, don't you know,' he added. 'It also made it so much easier to say she lost the baby only weeks after our wedding.'

In none of Diana's thinking about the past had she ever considered the possibility that Jennifer had never been with child at all! It was unbelievable. Despicable. And so like the Jennifer Prescott she had come to know that she didn't know why she was at all surprised.

Bright blue eyes narrowed on her admiringly. 'I must say, my nephew seems to have done all right for himself now, inheriting the Westbourne earldom and now becoming betrothed to you. So obviously no harm was done to him in the long run—'

'No harm was done!' Diana was so angry she thought she might actually get up and strike the man, despite the pistol he pointed at her so unwaveringly. 'How can you possibly say that when Gabriel was banished in disgrace for something he had not done and apparently never even existed?'

Charles gave a uninterested shrug. 'The existence of a child made the accusation of Gabriel having seduced Jennifer so much more believable. It was Jennifer's idea, of course, and a damned fine one, too, if I do say so myself.' He grinned unabashedly before sobering. 'Now all we have to do is convince my nephew to hand over a sizeable fortune to us, if he wishes to regain possession of his beloved fiancée, and we can all be on our way.'

He talked just as though Diana were indeed that pair of boots she had so recently likened herself to! 'I am afraid in that you will be disappointed, Mr Prescott.' She glared her contempt and dislike of the man.

'How so?' He raised dark brows so like his nephew's.

She gave a smile of pure satisfaction. 'For the simple reason that Gabriel—'

'Will never negotiate with the likes of you,' Gabriel finished firmly.

Diana was both relieved and frightened to turn and see him silhouetted in the doorway. Relieved because he had come to her, but frightened that he might be injured by having done so. She might no longer be betrothed to him, might never know the joy of having won his love, but she would not be able to bear it if anything should happen to him! 'He has a pistol, Gabriel!' she warned sharply.

He looked at her calmly. 'So I see.'

'With every intention of using it on your beautiful bride-to-be if you do not agree to our demands,' Charles informed him.

Gabriel had entered the parlour in time to hear some of Diana's conversation with his disreputable uncle. 'To that end I intend to remove Diana from your possession.' He crossed the room to take a firm hold of her arm and pull her to her feet beside him. 'Out of respect for my mother's feelings, you both have twenty-four hours in which to remove yourselves from England, never to return.' He looked at each of the Prescotts in turn. 'Failure to do so will lead me to disregard my mother's sensibilities and result in you being arrested and charged with multiples crimes: theft, my mother's enforced incarceration, and now the added charge of kidnapping. All extremely serious allegations.'

'Do something, Charles!' Jennifer prompted her husband fiercely as she moved to his side.

The older man rose slowly to his feet at the same time as he raised the pistol and once again pointed it at Diana. 'You really do not want to do that, old chap.'

'Oh, he really does,' a chilling voice murmured from across the room.

Diana turned to see Lord Dominic Vaughn standing threateningly in the doorway, the pistol in his own hand pointed directly at the waistcoated chest of Charles Prescott.

Diana's knees almost buckled in the relief of knowing Gabriel had not come here alone, that he'd had the forethought to bring his friend with him. As Gabriel had once told her, he had several times trusted Vaughn with his life, and now it seemed he was trusting him with her life too.

'It appears we are at an impasse,' Charles drawled.

'Really?' Dominic said pleasantly, only the icy greyness of his eyes a warning that his mood far from matched that tone. 'I have already shot and killed one villain this past month; I would not hesitate to dispatch another piece of vermin.'

'Do not waste your shot, Dominic.' Gabriel acted so quickly and capably that Diana could barely follow his movements as he used Charles's distraction with Dominic to move forwards and wrest the pistol from his uncle's hand with a mere twist of the wrist.

Charles clutched his arm to his chest, his face turning deathly pale. 'I believe you have broken my wrist, damn you!'

'You cur!' Jennifer turned to glare her dislike of Gabriel even as she tended to her husband.

Gabriel appeared unconcerned as he weighed the weapon he held in his hand before answering. 'No doubt,' he finally said. 'I have no idea what ships are leaving the English docks today and neither do I care, as long as the two of you are on board one of them when it departs.'

Jennifer straightened, her expression one of indignation. 'And how are we to live?'

Hard midnight-blue eyes glittered dangerously. 'Why should I care how, or even where you live, as long as you are both safely out of my sight?'

'News of your own behaviour will cause a scandal—'

'Another one, my dear aunt?' Gabriel eyed her disdainfully. 'I assure you, I am beyond being concerned about any further scandal you might care to create with your lies and deceit.'

'And what of Lady Diana—is she beyond the consequences of a scandal, too?' Jennifer challenged triumphantly.

His jaw tightened. 'She—'

'—will be only too happy to go into a court of law at any time and give evidence against you and your husband for the atrocities you have committed against both Gabriel and his family,' Diana said firmly as she stepped deliberately to Gabriel's side in an unmistakable show of support.

The other woman appeared less confident now as she looked at Gabriel. 'You cannot just dismiss us in this arbitrary way!'

'Oh, I believe you will find that I can and I will,' Gabriel said as he once again took hold of Diana's arm. 'Be on that ship tomorrow or risk finding yourselves arrested and incarcerated on the day following.' The utter coldness of his gaze warned that he meant every word that he said.

Diana gave Dominic a grateful smile as he stepped aside to allow her to leave the oppression of the Prescotts' suite of rooms, keeping his pistol levelled upon the other couple as he and Gabriel then exited the room and shut the door on the indignant faces of the Prescotts.

Diana looked up at Gabriel gratefully. 'I—'

'Don't say another word,' he warned her through

gritted teeth as they began to ascend the stairs of the inn down to the street below.

'But—'

'Best not to speak to him just now, Diana,' her future brother-in-law murmured softly as they stepped out into the sunshine. 'Gabriel is slow to let loose his anger, but when he does it is best to beware.'

Diana looked bewildered. 'But I have done nothing wrong—'

'Nothing wrong?' Gabriel repeated incredulously, his face furious as he turned to hold her up in front of him. 'You followed that woman without thought for your own safety. You allowed yourself to be seen and to be taken to the Prescotts' rooms and held there as their prisoner. Don't you dare interrupt me, Diana!' he said as he gave her a little shake.

'I did attempt to warn you, my dear,' Dominic said sympathetically.

'Stop it, Gabriel!' She pushed against the hardness of his muscled chest—a totally futile gesture as she still suffered the indignity of remaining firmly held in his grasp.

'Perhaps I should take Diana back to Westbourne House, old chap?' Dominic offered pleasantly as two carriages drew up beside them and both grooms jumped down to open the doors. 'It will give you time to walk off some of that temper, perhaps?'

It seemed as if Gabriel had not heard the other man for several long seconds as he continued to glare down at a rather dishevelled Diana for long tense seconds before a sudden stillness came over him. He drew himself up to his full and imposing height and then finally released her. 'That will not be necessary, thank you, Dom.'

Diana turned nervously to Dominic. 'Perhaps it would is best if I go with you, my lord—'

'Dominic will return in his own carriage and you will return to Westbourne House with me.' Gabriel looked down the length of his aristocratic nose at her as he stood waiting for her to step into his carriage. 'And once there you will go immediately to your bedchamber and remain there until I send for you.'

'I most certainly will *not*!' There were two spots of angry colour in her cheeks as she turned to glare up at him. 'How dare you order me about as if I were no more than—?'

'I gave her every opportunity, did I not, Dominic?' Gabriel turned and spoke conversationally to the other man.

Dominic gave a pained wince at whatever else he heard in Gabriel's tone. 'You did, yes. But she is young—'

'Her youth is no excuse for the danger in which she placed herself and others.' He no longer waited for Diana to step up into the carriage, but instead swung her up into his arms and carried her inside himself, the door immediately closing behind them and leaving them locked in the dark confines of the carriage together.

Chapter Seventeen

Diana immediately began to struggle in Gabriel's arms to be released, a move that proved totally unsuccessful as he sat down on the padded bench seat with her still held firmly in his arms and the carriage began to move forwards.

'You will release me this instant!' she demanded.

'No.'

She stilled. 'No?'

'No.' He did not even glance down at her, knowing that if he did so, he could not be held accountable for what happened next. She had deliberately and wilfully placed herself in danger. Had made herself the victim of any action the Prescotts might have decided to take against her. Damn it, she had calmly sat in a room making conversation with Charles whilst the man pointed a pistol at her!

"Gabriel!" she protested, squirming at the sudden instinctive tightening of his arms.

He released her so suddenly she almost tumbled to

the floor, only stopping herself just in time to scramble inelegantly to her knees. And still he did not dare risk looking at her. 'Sit down and do not speak another word until we have arrived back at Westbourne House,' he ordered autocratically.

Diana sat. Not because Gabriel had ordered her to do so, but because a reaction had now begun to set in at the realisation of the danger they had all been in only minutes ago; her legs were now shaking so badly they would no longer support her. The time she had spent with the Prescotts had all seemed so surreal whilst it was happening, but now that she thought back to the unscrupulous Charles Prescott and the way he had so calmly sat and aimed the pistol he held in his hand directly at her...

She clenched her hands tightly together in order to stop Gabriel from seeing their trembling. Although he surely could not have missed the pallor in her cheeks, and the horror in her shadowed blue eyes, if he bothered to look at her. Which he did not. Instead, he sat across from her in complete self-containment as he silently continued to look out of the carriage window at the people milling about on the busy London streets. Almost as if he had forgotten she was even there!

She turned away as her eyes filled with the heat of her tears, blinking rapidly in an effort to stop them from falling down her cheeks. It was humiliating enough that Gabriel had been put to the trouble of rescuing her from the clutches of the Prescotts; she could not bear for him to see her crying at his haughty dismissal of her.

'Diana—'

'Don't touch me!' She turned, her face flushing with

temper as she glared fiercely across at him as he sat forwards on his seat with the obvious intention of doing just that; her humiliation really would be complete if she now broke down in tears at the slightest hint of softening towards her in his manner.

Gabriel drew in a sharp breath before sitting back against the plush upholstery to resume his previous silence, his eyes narrowing briefly on Diana's flushed face before he turned away; she could not have demonstrated any more clearly how abhorrent she now found the prospect of his touch.

Diana was vastly relieved when the carriage came to a halt outside Westbourne House, the groom having barely succeeded in folding down the steps before she moved down them to hurry into the house. Only to come to an abrupt halt in the hallway as Caroline emerged from the drawing room with Malcolm Castle at her side!

'Malcolm insisted on waiting once he knew that you had returned to town yesterday,' Caroline informed her happily.

'Indeed.' Diana turned a frosty gaze on that young man. 'To what do I owe this pleasure?'

'I will tell you everything once we are alone.' Malcolm's face was alight with his own pleasure in seeing her again. He was a little under six feet in height, with fashionably styled golden hair and a handsome evenness of features, his brown eyes first widening and then narrowing on the man who had just stepped into the hallway beside Diana. 'Lord Gabriel Faulkner, I presume.' He bowed formally.

'You presume correctly.' Gabriel's tone was even as

he inclined his head. 'If you wish to talk privately with Mr Castle, Diana, then you may use my study—'

'But I do *not* wish to talk with Mr Castle, privately or otherwise.' She did not even glance at Gabriel as she instead gave Malcolm a sweepingly disdainful glance, at the same time wondering how she could ever have believed she found his insipid good looks in the least attractive! 'Indeed, I have no idea what he is even doing here.'

'Diana!' her sister gasped.

'I believe Malcolm is perfectly capable of speaking for himself, Caroline.' She gave her sister a quelling glance. 'Well?' She eyed the man coldly.

Malcolm flushed uncomfortably. 'I have come to beg your forgiveness, Diana, and to ask you to marry me. I made a mistake when I ended our friendship and have told Vera so,' he continued in a rush as her expression remained distant.

'Then I suggest you return to Hampshire post-haste and beg Miss Douglas's forgiveness instead of mine,' she said in a bored voice, 'for I will not have you.'

His eyes widened. 'But—but—'

'But we are no longer betrothed, Diana,' Gabriel murmured as he stood at her side.

She turned those frosty blue eyes on him. 'And?'

'And so you are now free to marry where you also love,' he explained, scowling at the very thought of her marrying this indecisive young man. Neither was he enjoying being a witness to this conversation in the slightest. Oh, he acknowledged that Diana was perfectly within her rights to want to punish Castle for having ended his friendship with her in favour of a woman with a fortune. But the man had admitted his mistake and was here now pleading for her forgiveness.

Diana gave a humourless smile. 'In saying that, are you presuming I am in love with Mr Castle?'

Gabriel looked surprised. 'Of course.'

'Of course you love me, Diana.' Malcolm crossed the hallway to take both her hands in his. 'You have always loved me—'

'Your conceit really is beyond belief!' Diana said exasperatedly as she extricated her hands from his clinging grasp. 'I am going to say this only once, Malcolm, and so I suggest that you listen carefully. I may have believed I loved you once, but I know now that I did not. I have never loved you. I *will* never love you.'

'But—'

'You don't love him?' Gabriel repeated slowly.

'I have just said that I do not,' she confirmed irritably.

'But you broke off our betrothal because he'd come back to you!' he exclaimed.

She snorted. 'I did not break off our betrothal at all, my lord—you did! It was very clear you no longer wished to be engaged to me.'

'Diana!' Malcolm protested.

'Diana?' Gabriel murmured softly.

'Yes, that is correct, I am Diana!' She crossed the hallway with a flounce of her skirts, her face flushed, eyes glittering. 'A warm, flesh-and-blood woman who is tired of being passed between you two gentlemen as if I have no will or emotions of my own!' She glared from Malcolm to Gabriel.

Gabriel could only gaze back at her with complete

admiration, even though he was still totally bemused by this whole conversation; damn it, he would not have let Diana go at all if he had not thought her to be in love with Castle, would have fought with every measure at his disposal to prove to her he was worthy of her himself.

She turned as she reached the bottom of the staircase. 'You, sir, are conceited and lily-livered!' she told a stunned Malcolm Castle. 'And you—' she turned that blazing glare upon Gabriel '—are so embittered by the past that you cannot see the worth of marrying a woman who loves you when she is standing right beneath your arrogant nose! Now, if you will excuse me, gentlemen. Caroline…' she nodded briefly to her incredulous sister '…I wish to go up to my bedchamber now. And I hope not to be disturbed by any one of you!' She ran swiftly up the staircase.

'Gabriel?'

He dragged his gaze away from Diana as she disappeared round the corner to turn and look enquiringly at the thoroughly dazed Caroline.

'What just happened?' she asked.

Gabriel grinned at her. 'I believe your sister has at last rebelled against subjugating her own needs and desires in order to please everyone else and has decided to please only herself,' he said.

'And she was quite magnificent about it.' Caroline came out of her daze to turn and look pityingly at Malcolm Castle. 'It would seem that you are not the man my sister loves, after all.' She began to smile, that smile turning to a chuckle, then to outright laughter. 'I must say, Gabriel, I much appreciated her comment about your arrogant nose,' she teased.

Gabriel was still trying to decide if that remark had really meant what he hoped it had, or if it were merely wishful thinking on his part. Could Diana, after calling him embittered and arrogant, really have also implied that she was in love with him?

'Is that the same innocent cushion as yesterday that you are destroying, or perhaps another one?'

She should have known that Gabriel would choose not to listen to her wish for privacy—he had never heeded her wishes before, so why should he begin to do so now? She placed the cushion down on the *chaise* and stood up, her profile turned determinedly away from him. 'Has Malcom gone?'

'I am sure he cannot have gone far away if you have changed your mind about marrying him,' he said, testing the water.

'I have not changed my mind in the slightest!' Her eyes sparked furiously as she finally turned to him. 'How he had the audacity to come here at all is beyond me.' She frowned. 'What do you want now, Gabriel? To reprimand me once again for what happened earlier this morning? Or perhaps you wish to upbraid me for refusing what is, after all, an advantageous offer of marriage for someone as without funds as I?'

Gabriel's admiration for her intensified; Caroline had been in the right of it earlier—Diana in this mood was truly magnificent! Her eyes shone as bright as the sapphires they resembled, her creamy cheeks were flushed, her lips red and inviting, and the gentle swell of her breasts was made all the more eye-catching by quickly rising and falling with her agitated breathing. Truly, wondrously magnificent!

'If that is the reason you are here, my lord, then I believe I should tell you now that I do not care!' she carried on before he had the chance to reply. 'Either about the Prescotts or Malcolm Castle.' She began to pace the bedchamber. 'The Prescotts are both too despicable and too beneath contempt to waste my time discussing them any further, and Malcolm can just go to the devil!'

Gabriel was fascinated…no, totally mesmerised by Diana in her present mood of rebellion. 'I totally agree.'

She gave him a startled glance. 'You do?'

'Oh, yes,' he murmured softly. 'Diana, why did you ask to be released from our betrothal?'

Her cheeks flushed. 'I told you, I did not—'

'*Why*, Diana?'

'Because *you* wished to be free of it!'

'I made no such statement—'

'There was no need for you to do so when your every word and action since your mother's return to health has shown that you no longer have need of or require a wife.'

'And *that* was the reason you brought an end to our betrothal?' Gabriel stared at her in disbelief.

She raised her proud little chin. 'You have made it more than obvious recently that you have no further need of my company, let alone wish to take me as your wife.'

'An earl is always in need of a wife, Diana.'

She gave dismissive movement of her shoulders. 'Then no doubt once you are established back amongst the *ton* you will eventually settle for some suitable and accommodating young woman.'

'Suitable and accommodating…' Gabriel murmured consideringly. 'And what if I would prefer that my wife be strong-willed and courageous rather than suitable and accommodating?'

'Then no doubt you will find a woman with those qualities amongst the ton, too.'

'And if I have already found her?' he wanted to know.

She swallowed hard. 'Then I would say that you have acted even more quickly in finding my replacement than I had anticipated.'

'And if *you* are the woman to whom I refer?'

Diana looked at him wordlessly for several long seconds before her back stiffened and her chin once again jutted proudly. 'I do not appreciate your toying with me in this way, my lord.'

'But you will agree with me that you *are* strong-willed and courageous?' he teased.

'You gave me every indication earlier that you considered me reckless and headstrong!' she protested indignantly.

'It takes a certain courage and will to be both of those things, too,' he acknowledged ruefully.

Diana huffed. 'You are talking nonsense, my lord.'

'I am indeed,' he conceded. 'I am discovering love does that to a man.'

She gave a snort. 'Appreciative as I am of Lord Vaughn's assistance earlier, I have no wish to discuss him now, either!'

'Lord Vaughn?' Gabriel repeated in utter confusion. 'But—'

'My lord, I have decided that if I cannot have what I wish in my marriage, then I will not marry at all.' She could see herself years from now, the elderly and spinster aunt to her sisters' children—

'And what is it that you want from marriage, Diana?' Gabriel prompted huskily.

She gave a sad smile. 'Something that is completely beyond your comprehension.' Yes, as time passed she would become an aunt to her many nieces and nephews, and no doubt be considered as slightly eccentric by the rest of her family, and as the long and lonely years passed her by—

'Diana, if I were to get down upon one knee and beg you to marry me, would you at least consider it?' Gabriel suited his actions to his words as he knelt before her and took her hands in his. 'I have been a fool,' he continued urgently. 'A blind, insensitive fool! But I am a blind and insensitive fool who is also deeply, irrevocably in love with the woman who happens to be right beneath my arrogant nose.'

Diana stared down at him as if he had completely lost his senses. 'Get up, do, Gabriel.' She attempted to pull him to his feet and failed miserably as he refused to be moved.

'Marry me, Diana!' he urged passionately. 'Marry me and allow me to love you until the day I die and beyond. Say yes, my darling, and I promise I will worship at your beautiful feet for the rest of my life.'

Perhaps it was she who had lost her senses? Gabriel could not really be kneeling in front of her saying these wonderful things to her! He could not! Could he?

He gave a choked laugh as he obviously saw the

bewilderment in her expression. 'Dominic warned me of how it would be if I ever fell in love; to my shame, I chose to dismiss his warning.' He drew his breath in sharply. 'I do love you, Diana; I realised some days ago just how much. So much, my darling, that my very happiness depends upon your every word and smile. These past days of even thinking of living without you, of some day watching you marrying another man, has been an agony I wish never to be repeated.'

'But you became so cold and distant whilst we were at Faulkner Manor and after we got back,' she said.

He sighed. 'I believed you must think less of me because of my blindness to both the events in the past and my neglect of my mother.'

'I could never think less of you because of those things, Gabriel,' she insisted. 'You and your family were lied to and deceived by your uncle and aunt, and you could have had no idea of their treatment of your mother. Once you did learn of it, you put the matter right immediately. No, Gabriel, I could never think less of you because of those things,' she repeated firmly.

His hands tightened about hers. 'Then will you not consider marrying me? Will you not put me out of this agony of uncertainty and instead make me the happiest man alive?'

Diana could see by the lines of strain that had appeared beside his eyes and mouth that he spoke only the truth. The complete, unvarnished truth. Gabriel loved her! Really loved her. He could no more bear the thought of living without her than she could bear the thought of being parted from him!

She drew in a shaky breath. 'I do not need to consider

marrying you, Gabriel—because I could marry no one else. I love you so very much, my dear darling love!' She placed her hands on either side of his face as he got slowly to his feet and looked up at him with that love shining brightly in her eyes. 'Whatever I once thought I felt for Malcolm is nothing in comparison to what I feel for you. What I know I will *always* feel for you. I love you so very, very much, my darling Gabriel.'

He could barely breathe as he slowly lowered his head and his lips claimed hers in a kiss that showed her just how deep and overwhelming his love for her was—and she returned it whole-heartedly.

'Everyone will be wondering why we did not appear for either luncheon or dinner,' Diana said, scandalised.

'The fact that no one has come in search of us shows that Caroline did not leave them wondering for long!' Gabriel lay back upon the pillows of Diana's bed, his arms about her and her head resting upon his shoulder as she snuggled into his side, the long length of her golden-red curls a warm caress against the bareness of his chest.

The hours since they had confessed their love for one other had been ones of pure bliss for both of them, as they made long and delicious love together, and then talked softly of the misunderstandings of the past few days, before making love again. 'As soon as we have the strength to leave this bed I intend taking you to the best jewellers in town and buying you the biggest sapphire ring we can find,' he announced with satisfaction.

Diana glanced up at him. 'I do not need fine jewels to know that you love me.'

His arms tightened about her. 'Maybe not, my love, but I need to place my ring upon your finger as a warning to other men that you belong to me.'

She laughed softly. 'Can there be any doubts as to that?'

'Hopefully not,' he muttered.

'Definitely not!' she protested.

Gabriel sobered. 'I do think that perhaps we should not delay the wedding for more than a few days or so.' He smiled to himself, knowing that despite his previous intentions, he had been so enthralled by the beauty and pleasure of their lovemaking that he had lost all control and consummated their marriage ahead of the actual ceremony. 'Perhaps a double wedding with your sister Caroline and Dominic?' he suggested.

'Perhaps,' she said quietly.

'Only perhaps?' Gabriel turned to look down into Diana's slightly pensive expression. 'You are not having second thoughts? Now that we have made love, have you decided that—'

'Hush.' Diana placed slender fingers against his beautifully sculptured lips. Lips that had kissed and explored parts of her body that still made her blush to think of. 'I have told you that I love you, Gabriel, and I do.' She gazed deeply into his eyes. 'I love you. All of you. Now and for ever.'

Gabriel's arms tightened about her, only slightly reassured. 'But you will only "perhaps" marry me?'

A slight frown creased her brow. 'I do not believe that either Caroline or I wish to be married without Elizabeth present.'

'Of course.' He finally relaxed, relieved by the obvious explanation. 'Then Vaughn and I must find her as quickly as is possible.'

'I am afraid you must, yes,' she agreed.

'Never be afraid to ask anything of me, Diana.' His eyes glowed lovingly down at her. 'Whatever I have, whatever I am, it all yours, and always will be.'

No woman could possibly ask for more than that from the man that she loved and who loved her in return.

* * * * *

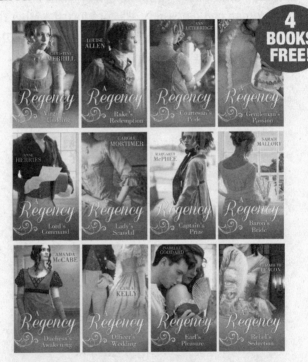

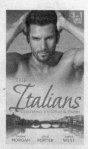

'A fresh new voice in romantic fiction'
—*Marie Claire*

Everyone has one.
That list.
The things you were *supposed* to do before you turn thirty.

Jobless, broke and getting a divorce, Rachel isn't exactly living up to her own expectations. And moving into grumpy single dad Patrick's box room is just the soggy icing on top of her dreaded thirtieth birthday cake.

Eternal list-maker Rachel has a plan—an all-new set of challenges to help her get over her divorce and out into the world again—from tango dancing to sushi making to stand-up comedy.

But, as Patrick helps her cross off each task, Rachel faces something even harder: learning to live—and love—without a checklist.